Some Women

Some Women
by Judith Rossner

TWO NOVELS

To The Precipice

�֍

*Nine Months in the Life
of An Old Maid*

NELSON DOUBLEDAY, Inc.
Garden City, New York

To The Precipice

We run carelessly to the precipice, after we have put something before us to prevent our seeing it.

Pascal's *Pensées*

CHAPTER ONE

I trip every time I pass the house on St. Marks Place. If one heel doesn't catch in a pavement crack, then my ankle turns. It happens much too regularly to be accidental.

"What are you going to do when they tear down this rotten house," I screamed at my father when I left fourteen years ago, "and you have to stumble home to someplace new?"

But they've fooled me. They haven't torn down the house. They've cleaned up the inside and painted the outside and rented the ground floor to people with Japanese lanterns and a very hi-fi set that hawks Ray Charles at the passers-by. The house to the east of it has a ground-floor antique store run by a slim young man who stares out indifferently through a window cluttered with oak schoolroom desks, wrought-iron door hinges, and Tiffany-glass shades. The building on the other side has a tiny clothing store called Stuff. The display window is painted black except for a small hole through which one can view a single pair of purple-velvet knickers one week, a polka-dotted vinyl motorcycle jacket the next.

Walter's daughter, who is only a few years younger than I, bought her house on the next block for twenty thousand dollars in 1952. It is worth more than double that now, between the work that's been put into it and the change in the neighborhood. I used to think that Walter liked to visit her often only because he knew how I hated to go there, and even now I cannot free myself of the notion that each time I go I am paying a penance.

I think of my father as watching with pleasure as I pay that penance. It matters little that he's a thousand miles away and I haven't seen him in years. He might just as well be walking beside me, fondling his thick black mustache, saying with his heavy Yiddish accent, "Look what you got, Ruthie. You couldn't wait till this house should come down. And now look what you got here."

That's how I know what it means, my tripping when we pass the
house. That's why I've finally realized that my stumbling is a mockery
of my life since I left his home.

I remember sitting in my nineteenth-century-literature course at
Hunter that year, listening to old Professor Robinson discuss Trollope
and the importance of money in the nineteenth-century novel. I
glanced at Thea, sitting next to me; her pale serious face had a slight
smile as Robinson condescendingly catalogued the advantages of having been born in this country if one were foolish enough to have been
born poor. Something made me twist in my seat to look at the expressions of the other members of the class; they were the same as Thea's,
and I suddenly realized that I was the only one in the room who failed
to be amused by the dedicated, matter-of-fact quest of Trollope's heroes
and heroines.

After class Thea and I rushed down to gym for the last hour of the
day. She complained about the enforced exercise but I was glad of it,
for I always loved to be moving. (Walter once said I liked golf and tennis because they were rich men's games, but couldn't explain when I
challenged him why I was always the one to run after the ball, or why
I walked to the market when I might easily order groceries by phone,
or why I loved to swim.)

"I should have my head examined," I said to Thea when we were
back in the locker room. "Taking gym the last class of the day. One
hour and twenty minutes to get home, shower, change, eat, and get to
work." I slammed the locker door and snapped the combination lock,
then looked quickly in the mirror. I am pretty. I have big dark-brown
eyes and curly black hair and my coloring, always good, is best when
I'm flushed with exercise. (My father used to call me Beautiful when
he was trying to put me on the defensive. As though I'd stolen my
looks from someone who deserved them more.) I scooped up my books
and shoulder bag without bothering to comb my hair.

"Hurry, hurry, hurry," I said to Thea, who was combing her straight
fine brown hair in front of the mirror.

"I hardly see you since you got that job," she said softly, putting
away the comb and picking up her things.

I laughed. "Everyone else sees too much of me." I grabbed her arm
and hustled her through the rows of rumpled, hot-looking girls still
struggling into their clothes, out of the locker room, up to the main

floor, and out to the bright daylight of Sixty-eighth Street. A solitary veteran, his textbooks looking incongruous with the rest of him, passed by and eyed me.

"I still haven't made up my mind," I said to Thea, "whether Hunter did itself a favor when it started taking those boys."

"They have to have someplace to go."

That was Thea, who sometimes couldn't do her homework for remembering the faces of the old men on the Bowery, and who would get out of bed on a freezing-cold night to let a whining alley cat into the hallway.

"You're walking too quickly," she said breathlessly. "You forget my legs aren't as long as yours."

"I'm sorry." I slowed down with an effort because what I really would have liked to do on that warm exciting spring day was to walk and run all the way home to St. Marks Place instead of taking the El. But I walked sedately with her toward Third Avenue, and only when we reached the shaded corner under the platform did I break loose and run up the long flight of stairs to the El station, then wait contritely while she puffed up after me and in noble silence got her change at the booth.

We sat in our regular place in the first car, talking mostly about school. Occasionally I'd get up to stand at the front window and watch the tracks disappear. It was, and even now is, one of my best childhood memories—trips with my father on the El at times when we might more easily have taken the bus, the noisy delight of standing at that front window, conquering space at the dizzy speed of the 1940 Third Avenue El.

Thea and I walked in silence to St. Marks, where I slowed down more than enough to suit her and then even dawdled for a moment or two in front of her house, reluctant, as always, to leave her and go home.

Thea had a significance beyond herself in my mind. She was the first —and I suppose the only—close friend I ever had. When I was depressed, I was a little less depressed if she was around, living proof that the whole world wasn't rotten. When I was happy, her serenity enhanced my happiness so that I felt doubly blessed. Over the years there were periods when I saw Thea quite often, others when I saw her only occasionally, but always there was the idea of her with me, the knowledge of her goodness and her affection. It isn't the least of what has happened to me this year that the idea of Thea is superfluous to me now.

The hallway was dark. Mrs. Adler on the ground floor swore the landlord took out one dead bulb to replace it with another. I used the key in the event that my mother wasn't in the kitchen to open the door for me.

The kitchen smelled good, as it always did, with one of the stews my mother used to create with bones and water and some wilted greens and perhaps a small tough piece of beef. It was the only way she was canny, food, and it was her special delight to serve a dish that wasn't what it seemed to be but something cheaper—a *gefilte* fish made of chicken, chopped liver made of string beans, cabbage stuffed with chopped meat that was mostly rice cooked in stock. Of course she was also a little ashamed of the deceit; being incapable of badness she turned some of her virtues into vices and then worried over them.

She came into the kitchen when she heard the door open. Small, only a couple of pounds heavier than when I was a child, hair graying although she was eleven years younger than my father, whose mop was still a lustrous black.

"Ruthie, Ruthie, darling," she said, heading for the icebox, "you're late. Sit down, your food is ready."

"No time, Mama," I said, scooping up the peanut butter and jelly sandwich from the plate. "I'll eat while I get dressed." And before she could protest, I dropped my schoolbooks on the table and went into the front room, which I shared with my brother Martin, then eighteen, and with my father's plants. I loved my father then and didn't mind the plants as I might have. Our room, facing on the street, was the only one that got sunlight. The plants, large, lush, overflowing their dirt and water onto the window sill as well as the floor and the table which had been put in front of the window to accommodate the pots the sill couldn't hold, were my father's constant concern. They repaid him by being the envy of the other plant growers in the neighborhood. He was the acknowledged expert on how to fill out the bottom of a stalk which had grown long and skinny with leaves only on the top. He could tell which plants were getting too much water and which too little, which ones loved the sunlight and which luxuriated in cool darkness, which loved care and which thrived on negligence, which needed good drainage and which should be kept always in wet earth. He was a self-acknowledged expert on everything, but when he lectured an admiring neighbor about her plants, it was not simply for the love of hearing himself talk.

Aside from plants there were in the room Martin's bed and mine, both narrow, his nearly covered with a khaki blanket, mine unmade, making the room look even worse than it naturally did. The only thing I'd done was to pile my blanket on top, making sure no end touched the floor. The fine red wool of that blanket (I always liked a wool blanket until summer was actually upon me and even now, during the warmest weather, I cannot sleep unless my entire body is covered, if only with a sheet) represented my entire first week's salary at Arlou Foundations. On the small remaining wall, placed of necessity where someone was always bruising a thigh on one of its corners, was the chest Martin and I shared—four ugly squeaking drawers that jammed every time they were pulled open, two of them for Martin's clothes and two for mine. His two were more than adequate to hold his few shirts, socks, undershorts, and shirts. Mine were just becoming crowded with the things I'd bought since beginning work at Arlou five months before —with the exception of an occasional present from my father in the years when he'd made more money, the first clothing I'd ever owned that was neither secondhand nor homemade.

I undressed quickly and in my bathrobe (a recent innovation) headed back to the shower stall, which was in one corner of the kitchen, the toilet being in the outside hallway and shared with neighbors. If I had to compress my early life into one small ugly symbol, I think it would be that kitchen shower, situated almost directly opposite the kitchen entrance to the apartment, its front shielded by an old sheet from view but not from the blast of cold air that came in the door with each visitor, its cement floor cracked so that as hard as she worked, my mother could not clean it properly, its entire shell a cozy home for roaches and the various other insects that thrived on moisture.

I let the water run for a moment before I went in, to send the bugs to their hiding places. My mother, who understood the violence of my feelings about that shower without sharing them, pretended to be too busy working to notice me as I pulled a chair close to the stall and threw my robe and towel over its back. In spite of its iciness I let the water run hard on me even after I'd finished washing. So I didn't hear the door open or know David had come down until my mother called to me that he was in the kitchen and I shouldn't come out without my robe. I smiled a little but I didn't say anything. I reached past the sheet to get my robe. David grabbed my hand and I knew my mother wasn't looking.

"I can't reach my robe, Mama," I said. His hand was gone before I'd finished.

"May I be of some assistance, madame?" he asked, handing the robe past the sheet. I put it on and stepped down out of the stall, almost walking into him. He grinned at me. A big male mirror of myself. Handsome. Cocksure. I loved to be with him and I loved to be seen with him and I couldn't hide it, and that was where he had me. People meeting the three of us, David, my brother, and me, would look at David and say, "This must be your brother," for my brother's hair was lighter than either of ours and his carriage more awkward, except when he was playing ball.

"You're a mess," David said.

I stuck out my tongue.

"Ruthie," said my mother, who'd turned from the stove in time to see me, "I'm surprised at you."

"She's not kidding," I told David. "She really is." I ran over and put an arm around her. "My mother should never read the newspapers. She's stunned by each new delinquent, every wife beater, every unfaithful wife. Every burglary is a shock to her. How could people do such things?" I was showing off for him and he knew it, but I didn't care as long as he liked watching me. My eye fell on the kitchen clock, bought by me a few months before because I had to keep track of minutes now. "Whoops! Five minutes to get out." I ran into my room and hurriedly put on a navy-blue cotton dress while wolfing down my sandwich. The rule was to dress in the closet while someone was there, but I stood just on the other side of the wall from where David was standing. When I came out he was sitting at the table over a bowl of soup. I gulped down the glass of milk my mother had left on the table for me and kissed her goodbye. Then I opened the door and started down the stairs.

"Hey!" David called. I heard his chair scrape along the floor, then his feet moving quickly across it. "What's the rush?"

"I have a job, you know," I called without looking back.

"Will you wait a second?" he shouted. "I want to ask you something."

I stopped at the landing and looked up at him, trying to maintain my impatient expression. "Well, what is it?"

"I have the pass tonight. Interested?"

His uncle worked for Skouras and each year had a book of passes on which the family had turns.

"What's playing at the Academy of Music?"

"If you're so damn fussy," he said, "I'll get someone else to go."

I took my wallet from my purse and searched for a dime for carfare. "Coming or not?"

"Sure," I said, smiling up at him sweetly. "Unless the boss keeps me late." And I was out of the house before he could tell me to forget it.

That was another good thing about being so rushed. It was the term before David entered law school and he had much more free time than I did. It was the only advantage I had with him. Unless perhaps you could count the way I looked.

From one o'clock until two I relieved Selma at the desk in the reception room, which was not elegant but had, with its linoleum flooring and white walls, a more respectable air than the dark, wooden-floored stockrooms. When Selma came back from lunch, we did invoices together. She read off the names and billings, then computed the totals while I typed. There was no need for it to be done that way, except Selma's need to have someone to talk to in the off season when Lou was out of the office most of the time and her only company was the telephone. And the endless stream of magazines—*Ladies' Home Journal, McCall's, Good Housekeeping, Better Homes & Gardens, Living for Young Homemakers, House Beautiful*—that she pored over each month although her apartment had long since been furnished in a combination of Bronx Modern and French Provincial that would have made any of their editors go pale in the living area.

When we reached the T's, Selma called the luncheonette downstairs and ordered coffee and Danish; it arrived just as we finished, and she paid for it, as she did every day, according to an understanding we had. I could do without coffee and cake, and resented the quarter plus my half of the tip that they would cost me. Selma wanted the coffee, but even more she wanted to sit and relax with someone and talk, mostly about her regular visits to the gynecologist whom her girl friend had sworn would help her to get pregnant. Selma wanted a baby the way I wanted to be rich—with an overwhelming, painful devotion. With a disregard for any of the small things she might have to give up for it. With the conviction that once she had it, nothing could ever make her really unhappy again. Like me, too, she could not help but react to people and things in terms of how they affected her ambition. The gynecologist she held in loving awe—the kindly judge who might rule that the prize was rightly hers. Jerry, her husband, was sweet; why, then, should he be refusing her the one thing she wanted, when the doctor and the doctor before him had said there was no reason he should not give her a baby? Jerry earned a decent salary and his job wasn't bad—or hadn't been, until the month before, when just as the thermometer said her best time was approaching, Jerry had been kept late to do some work and had come home so exhausted he could hardly do anything and Selma hadn't gotten her baby although she'd had a feeling for several weeks that it was a good month for her. So she paid for my coffee and talked about it.

Although maybe there was another reason, too. She'd expected trouble from me and she hadn't gotten it. An infinite number of part-time girls had drifted through the office during her eight years there, most of them college girls, many of them good-looking, many of them smart. Many openly unwilling to take orders from her—even to treat her respectfully—although Lou told them when they were hired that she was their second boss. So Selma had waited for the usual signs from me —the yawning when she talked, the insolent smile that told her how lucky I felt that I didn't spend eight hours a day in a dump like this, the refusal to do her filing, and the eventual suggestion that yes, she *should* speak to Mr. Fine about it if she didn't like it. And she was pathetically grateful to me that the signs had never come. I don't think she ever wondered why I didn't mind filing her letters; she just figured me for a nice girl and about twice a month extended an invitation to come home with her for dinner, an invitation I usually refused on the grounds of too much homework. Maybe I *was* a nice girl, and it didn't matter that I did as she asked without complaints in much the same way as one executes the senseless maneuvers of a dream without questions because questions would only tighten the net of the dream.

Lou Fine came in at around four, as we were separating the invoice originals from the carbons.

"Look at my two girl friends," he said to the elevator operator, who winked at me.

"Hello, Mr. Fine," we said.

Smiling, he came into the reception room, gray-haired, gently handsome, rumpled and perspiring although the worst of the summer was far away, a little apprehensive because he was the type who began worrying about taxes at the moment the sweepstake ticket paid off, and after all these months he still waited for some sign from Selma that I had turned out to be like the others, after all. The elevator doors clattered together behind him. Selma reeled off the messages: Two suppliers with delivery questions; someone who'd gotten a message to call the number but had never heard of the firm; an agent who wanted to know if we needed more space; Lillian. What did Lillian want? She wanted him to pick up a quarter-pound of bologna because the maid was coming tomorrow. Selma's face was impassive and Lou didn't wince, but I couldn't look at either of them. It hadn't been long enough for me to get accustomed to Lillian, who'd been unable to get up from her wheelchair for sixteen years although no specialist had been able to find a reason why she should not walk; who went through maids much more rapidly than Arlou went through extra clerical help, partly because when the current maid looked for her lunch each Friday she found a single bologna sandwich set on a plate in a refrigerator that was otherwise empty, partly because Lillian wheeled around the apartment after her all day, pointing out things she'd missed and loudly despairing to herself over the fact that people didn't take pride in doing a good job as they had when she was a girl.

Selma gave Lou the completed invoices and he disappeared with them into the stockroom. He hadn't returned yet when she was ready to leave at five. I stayed at the desk when she went back to say good night. A few minutes after she'd left the approved invoices with me and gone home, he came out, holding his copy of *Women's Wear*.

"Look here, Ruth," he said, pushing aside the pile of invoices and the box of window envelopes. "Look at that advertisement." He spread out the paper on my desk. The ad covered both pages; the left side was written for the trade and the right showed an ad they would run in consumer magazines. The caption was, "Take inches away, Nature's Way." At my side, Lou stepped back to scrutinize the pages. Without looking, I knew the expression on his face—deep, thoughtful, appraising. He didn't daydream over the stockmarket quotations or the real-estate columns; he just endlessly compared the brand-name advertisements, inspecting the artwork and layouts, asking my opinion, as an English major, on the copy, asking Selma if she liked them so she wouldn't be hurt, cutting out and putting in a folder any that struck him as being particularly clever.

"What do you think?"

"It's okay," I said. "I suppose it's tricky."

"Tricky? What's tricky? You use the same word twice, naturally it rhymes."

"That's true."

"Of course it's true. So what do you do about it?"

"I don't know," I said, going back to stuffing invoices into envelopes. "What would you suggest?"

"It's a hard one. I was thinking of, 'Take inches away and still be gay.'" When I failed to show enthusiasm he added quickly, "I don't say it's perfect. But it's better than this."

I nodded. He picked up the paper and began prowling around the reception room.

"Such ambition," he said to nobody. "She can't stop for a minute with her invoices."

"It's not ambition," I said. "I just want to get out on time."

"And so honest, too."

Not honest, either, I thought—although I don't know why. I always had the sense that if people thought I was nice, or honest, it was because they didn't know me. Not that I think they wanted to; people don't care how you are but only how you are to them. He looked at the ad a while longer before closing the paper.

"So," he said. "Everything's all right."

"Fine."

"Everybody's happy."

"So far."

All of which was code confirmation of the fact that Selma hadn't gotten her period yet. Selma's period was a matter for anxiety to everyone from Lou to the shipping clerk, their concern for her being tempered with their concern over the way she treated them, their nervousness being intensified by the irregularity of her cycle as well as of her behavior during it; she might refuse to talk except when business demanded it, or she might come in deceptively high-spirited and break into tears when someone questioned a bill of lading.

I left promptly at six. I never felt like getting into a bus or subway after my five cramped hours at Arlou. Sometimes I made myself do it, but other times I walked down Fifth Avenue, through the park at Twenty-third, across Twenty-third and down Second Avenue. There were some wonderful stores on Fifth Avenue—an Armenian rug place, and an oriental import house that always displayed richly carved chests and ornate brasses. The stores on Second Avenue weren't interesting to me, though. Food, glass, dry goods. Candy stores. Dry cleaners. Movies. More food. When I read books about the Lower East Side it's like reading about a country I've never seen. The rich fabric of life that writers love to wrap around themselves—if I was aware of it, I was aware in the remote disinterested way that a boss knows his secretary's mother to be ill. I've read more than one loving description of the Second Avenue candy stores with their metal-capped jars of oddly flavored soda syrups and their glass-front cases crammed with penny candies. To me a candy store was a place where the scum of the neighborhood boys collected to tease you as you walked by—loudly or softly, depending on how you looked that day and how great were their numbers, which made them brave.

I stopped off at the grocery for a minute to see my father. He was sitting behind the counter, reading his *Post*. He didn't look up. He never did when people came in—his revenge for being a big handsome man behind a tiny counter (actually, I realized later, I had always seen him as bigger than he was), a clever man using his brains to compute bills in a tiny grocery store owned by a younger brother who didn't have his looks, his intelligence, or his aggressiveness but had somehow managed to save a few thousand dollars during his early unmarried years in this country. I asked for a box of Fig Newtons and he looked up then and came out from behind the counter to kiss me.

"Your mustache is getting too long," I said.

"And my daughter is getting too fresh, maybe," he said.

Back on the street I walked quickly, but slowed up before reaching our block in case David should be looking out of the window. My brother was home, probably because my father wasn't. He was reading a magazine at the kitchen table. One end of the table was set for our dinner (his and mine; he usually waited for me while my mother ate with my father before he left for the store at five). At the other end was a pile of mending, subcontracted to my mother by a so-called friend who had an Invisible Reweaving store uptown and got for each job five times what he paid her. She wasn't around.

"Hi, pal," Martin said, putting down the magazine. He was as tall as David, though slighter, and as handsome as my father. In fact, my mother swore that Martin at eighteen had exactly the face my father had had when she met him, an idea both of them vigorously resisted.

"Hi, yourself." I plopped down at the table, tired for the first time all day. "Where's Mama?"

He looked over my shoulder in the direction of my parents' bedroom. "Another one?"

He nodded.

"What was it this time?"

"Forget it. It's too stupid to talk about."

"I'm sure it is. But tell me anyway."

He pushed his chair away from the table and tilted it back against the wall.

"I had a conference with the guidance idiot at school today. I was

telling Mama about it. He was reading. I didn't even know he was listening or I wouldn't've started in the first place. You know I never—"

"I know, I know. Go on."

"There's hardly anything else. All of a sudden he butted in and
started screaming at me. You know, all the old stuff about—"

He broke off as my mother came in, her eyes dry but still a little red
and swollen, her manner very natural, not at all like the Martyr-in-my-
Own-Time style that Mrs. Landau affected after an argument with
David. She gave us both dinner, the stew and pumpernickel, then sat
down and picked up her mending. She wasn't prying; she just wanted
to be sure someone was there to present my father's side.

"You could go on, Martin," she said to him. "I hear from the bedroom but I feel like an eavesdropper."

He flushed.

"What was the conference about?" I asked him.

"Nothing. Just the regular annual thing. Do you know yet what you
want to major in? Your card says such and such, and is it true? Do you
feel you need assistance in determining your major field of interest?
Garbage?"

"What did you tell him?"

"I told him I didn't know and I wasn't in any great hurry to find
out."

"Oh, that's fine."

"Don't be dense," he said irritably. "You know I didn't say it that
way. I just said I was interested in a lot of things and I didn't want to
confine myself." He attacked his stew as though it were the guidance
idiot.

"Why did you have to come home and talk about it in front of him?
You know how he is about—"

"First of all," he said angrily, "I wasn't talking to him and I didn't
know he was listening."

"You could see he was listening," my mother said quietly.

"Second of all," Martin said, ignoring her, "that wasn't the end of
the conference. The guy went on to tell me how there's no reason why
I should be confined if I feel that way. He said as long as I'm getting
passing grades and taking required courses that'll mostly be good for
any degree, I don't have to know my major for sure. And *that's* what I
wanted to tell her, because they're always so worried that I don't know
what I want to do."

My mother looked up. "You didn't say that."

"He never gave me the *chance!* As soon as he heard what I said to the guy first, he jumped up, slammed down his book, and started shouting at me as if I said I wanted to be a bank robber. Or a gigolo or something."

"How should he know?" my mother asked.

"Damn right, how should he know," Martin said. "He doesn't know anything because he never listens long enough. Not to me, anyway."

"That's not so, Martin," my mother said. But it was, and we all knew it—she with the conviction that although Martin didn't seem to her like a good-for-nothing, my father was smarter than she and must have good reasons for thinking my brother was one; Martin with a futile anger that each day drove him further into his shell and increased the intensity of his eruptions from it; I with the helpless knowledge that my father was almost always wrong and a frequent dissatisfaction that I could not love him the less for it.

"He only wants him," my mother appealed to me, "to know where he's going."

"For God's sake, Mama," I said wearily, "he's eighteen years old."

"David Landau," my brother mimicked bitterly, "knew he wanted to be a lawyer when he was ten years old."

"It's true," my mother said.

"So what?" I asked her patiently. "It takes some people longer than others. Martin's not some bum spending his life in front of a candy store."

"Still," my mother said after a minute, "he shouldn't blame his father for being concerned."

That drove Martin out of the room.

We continued that way for a while, the two of us, almost by rote, never angry with each other, I occasionally exasperated by her slow-witted idolatry of my father but never letting my exasperation show. Two dogged attorneys, both for the defense, arguing gently in a court that couldn't adjourn. I was looking for a way to end it when David knocked and came in, affecting annoyance at my not being ready to go. He dropped it, though, when he saw the two of us sitting at the table as we were. He knew right away what was going on.

We took Martin to the movies with us. David invited him; I paid his admission because the pass was only good for two. Martin never had any money. He'd tried unsuccessfully to get a job after school and my father, having agreed in principle to give him a small allowance, usually forgot it. We saw *Under My Skin* with John Garfield, a household god. The girl was very beautiful and the villain very villainous and we didn't stay for the Dorothy McGuire feature because it was understood among us that Martin had to be home in bed before my father returned from work.

Martin was pathetically grateful when we did this kind of thing for him. He shouldn't have been; we both loved him but we were using him, too. Often one of us would invite him to tease the other—part of a stupid perpetual game whose basic rule was that you scored by denying the other even if in the process you had to deny yourself. So I sat between them in the movies and pretended not to notice David's arm on the back of my seat. Afterward we went into a cafeteria for coffee. Martin was still quiet—the wound-up kind of quiet that didn't let us forget for a moment, whether it was intended that way or not. David tried to jolly him out of it by talking about sports—the only thing that really made my brother come alive. He talked about the swimming team, which Martin had already made, and varsity basketball, which he would probably make the following year. But when Martin's mood did finally improve, it wasn't because of anything David or I said.

A girl named Vivian Mandel, whom he'd loved madly, briefly and typically, stopped by at our table to say hello, introducing her date and then proceeding to ignore him and flirt with Martin. Martin was as cool and remote as only he could be with a girl who no longer interested him. But a minute or two after they'd gone, the three of us left the restaurant, and suddenly Martin's whole manner changed. He told a couple of bad jokes he'd heard at school, laughed at them himself and laughed harder at our failure to be amused, then began whistling and intermittently asking if we couldn't walk a little faster. It was almost eleven when we reached home. David asked if I was tired. I shook my head because that, too, was part of the game, and anyway it was true that I was far less tired than I had been at home a few hours before. Martin said good night and went upstairs, his feet clomping as carelessly as though it were noon. We waited a few minutes on the off-chance that there would be trouble upstairs, then we began walking back up Second Avenue, cutting across Fourteenth Street again, then heading uptown at Herald Square. Both long-legged, both unwilling to admit to tiredness, we kept walking, in silence, sometimes holding hands and sometimes apart, sometimes arms around each other, sometimes not, until we reached Fifty-seventh Street, and then we headed west toward Central Park, staring with paupers' immunity at the occasional midweek sophisticates on their way between cabs and night clubs. In the park we finally sank down, exhausted, under a big dark tree. If there were other people around, we couldn't hear them. The only noises were of cars whipping through the Park Drive and crickets trilling in the grass.

"I don't know why the hell you dragged me here," David said, putting his arm around me, pulling me back so we were leaning against the big rough trunk of the tree.

"Poor David. Always being bullied."

"I don't even have carfare home."

"I do."

He laughed.

"Why do you always make me feel uncomfortable about having a few miserable dollars?"

"Dunno. How much do you have?"

"I don't know," I said, although I did—to a penny. "Three or four dollars."

"Fine. We'll take a cab."

"Why not?" I said, trying to sound very offhand because it was meant to infuriate me and it did. I had already spent too much of the eleven dollars a week I kept out of my salary for clothes and daily expenses. (Out of my net of twenty-one dollars I gave my mother five and put five in the bank.)

"If I promise not to take you up on it," he said lazily, "will you stop shaking?"

I pulled away from him and sat up.

"C'mere," he drawled at my back.

"I don't feel like it."

"I'll make violent love to you. You can pretend I'm John Garfield." As if I had to.

"The bark is too rough against my head."

"You're getting spoiled." He sighed. "All right. You can sit on my lap."

I twisted around and looked at him. He smiled but then when I just sat there he held out his arms, and because all I'd really wanted was to be asked I moved quickly into them and he held me very tightly and kissed me. And instantly I was warm and excited and could only wonder why we had waited so long, teasing and sniping at each other, when this was all we had come for.

I don't know how much later it was that out of tiredness and frustration we fell asleep in each other's arms. David was awake when I opened my eyes. He was smoking a cigarette. The sky was beginning to fade. I stood up and brushed the grass and dried leaves from my clothing and my hair. He watched me and only when I was finished threw away his cigarette and got to his feet. He put his arm around me as we walked out of the park, and a pleasant sensual reminder waved through me. I looked up at him to see if he felt it but his face didn't tell me anything. It never did. I never knew what he was thinking or feeling and maybe if I had things would have been different, although I'm inclined to doubt it. My own thoughts rambled rockily around a circle whose center was David. First I thought how unjust it was that he should excite me so easily when books and movies were full of heroines who succumbed to sexuality only when they were quite ready to—or perhaps when the hero's insistent lips and forceful embrace transformed their ladylike fury into womanly lust. Then I thought of how ironic it was that only outside things should prevent us from making love. Ridiculous things that should have had no importance in human affairs. The time and the place. Long times, that is, in the right place. Not twenty dirty minutes on David's bed while his mother went to the corner for soup meat.

We did end up taking a cab because the first clock we found told us it would soon be five. I fell asleep again during the ride and David had to shake me so I would wake up and pay the driver. (He refused the subterfuge, on occasions when I paid, of letting me slip him the money.) He'd had the driver stop on Second, around the corner from the house. Already there were a few trucks making deliveries. St. Marks itself was dead, and all the uglier for not having an occasional bit of bright clothing to relieve its drabness. We kissed good night in the foyer downstairs and didn't speak again. When we reached my floor David just walked softly by and continued on up. I unlocked the door and tiptoed in, carefully closing and locking it again, not even going to the sink to wash because my father was a light sleeper and I was afraid of awakening him.

Martin was soundly asleep. I got into my nightgown and fell asleep happy with the thought that it was Saturday, and I wouldn't have to get up early.

I was too wrapped up in my own affairs to concern myself with the world the newspapers recorded. But I don't know that it would have mattered if I'd read them; the people who did were no less surprised than I to learn one day that something like a war was going on in a place called Korea. And what a strange war that I should have to remember when it began, or when our knowledge of it began, at any rate, by saying to myself: It was the week before I started working for

Walter, the summer before I turned twenty. 1950. I remember the week itself quite well. Martin decided to enlist.

Thea was going to work in the Catskills and David had a job in an uncle's wholesale house. When I mentioned the possibility of going away with Thea, he refused to display the slightest regret at the thought of not seeing me all summer. This had the effect of making me feel that I had to go and force him to miss me. I began to wonder if there weren't some job that would get me out of the city and still pay a decent salary.

I didn't bother to answer most of the "mother's helper" ads in the *Times*—"Ten dollars a week and all the shit you can eat," David had once said. I answered the Stamms' ad only because it was for a tutor and companion, and it made a point of saying the salary would be good.

The apartment was at Fifth Avenue and Ninety-sixth Street. I was to be there at five-thirty, which meant leaving Arlou early. I had bought my first suit, a tailored black one, not long before, and I wore it to school that day with a white blouse and high-heeled pumps. I suppose I was reaching for the Nanny effect but I didn't make it, of course. The short unruly hair was against me, for one thing. And I didn't own a hat or gloves.

I was surprised at myself—at my growing excitement as I reached school, at my inability to concentrate in any of my classes. It was the last week of the term and Professor Robinson was winding up with Meredith. I'd never been able to get involved with Richard Feverel, anyway; of the two I cared much more for his father, although I succeeded in pitying Richard for a while before all that terribly romantic nonsense at the end turned my pity to boredom; and Thea was disappointed in me, I recall, for not crying when Richard died.

Maybe it was because I'd refused to tell Thea just where I was going that the interview had taken on the proportions of an adventure. Maybe it was just because I'd never been in a Fifth Avenue apartment before. It wouldn't be my first contact with rich people; I'd met a couple of David's relatives who had huge garment houses, and at least a few Arlou clients had more money than they'd ever need, even when they were through planting trees in Israel and having their names engraved on laboratory walls in the Hebrew University of Jerusalem. These people would be different, if only because they lived on Fifth Avenue instead of in Scarsdale or Long Island. If only because they weren't Jews.

The building was simple and elegant with shiny marble floors and newly upholstered sofas in the lobby. I had to pass Doorman's Inspection before being told the floor number, but the old gentleman running the elevator didn't even bother to turn his head when I walked in and asked for fourteen. At the fourteenth floor I stepped out into a small hall; there was only one other door. A girl who looked a few years younger than I opened the door. She was pretty, in an unexceptional way, and dressed more neatly than most of the high-school girls I saw. Her hair was long and brown and pulled back from her face in a pony tail.

"Is this the Stamm home?" I asked.

"Yes," she said in a low, shy voice. "Come in, please."

I followed her into a foyer that could have held most of our apartment. The walls were white; an oriental rug covered most of the floor; several chairs lined the walls, creating the air of a waiting room.

"Please have a seat," the girl said. "My father should be ready soon."

She left the room and I sat down. From behind one of the doors leading off the foyer I could hear a high-pitched female voice. I remembered that I'd meant to comb my hair. After a couple of minutes one of the doors opened. A girl of about my age came out, followed by a slender handsome man who nodded at me as he escorted her to the door. At the door he thanked her for coming and said that the decision would be made within a few days, then he closed the door and turned to me. His face was unlined but his hair was entirely gray, and although his posture was good, something about him suggested fragility, or age. I introduced myself.

"Won't you come in, please, Miss Kossoff," he said. "I'm Walter Stamm."

It was a library. A very proper library, with wood-paneled walls, dark-green carpeting, a huge desk, leather chairs, and floor-to-ceiling bookcases filled with rows and rows of volumes so neatly lined up they could have been the false fronts that stage designers used. The big desk was in one corner of the room; a swivel chair stood behind it and two chairs faced it. He beckoned me to one of them and sat down in the other. A pad with some notations rested on the desk near his arm. He started a new page with my name, address, and number. When I explained that the number was that of neighbors who would give me a message, he was at first unable to understand that I was saying we had no phone, and then he was embarrassed. When he had recovered he asked me to tell him something about myself. I said that I was not quite twenty years old, that I was a junior at Hunter, that I was an English major with a minor in education, and that I intended to teach when I graduated the following year—which was not entirely true, since the education credits had always represented a safeguard rather than a preparation. I told him where I was working, that I had been a camp counselor the summer before, and that during that year I had worked as a tutor to a girl whose parents had moved here from Florida and who was behind her class in most subjects. He asked a lot of questions about the tutoring, then said that if I didn't have another engagement, he would like me to talk to Mrs. Stamm.

Who will not like me, I thought.

"I'll be glad to wait," I said.

He excused himself, saying that I was welcome to browse in the library. I did, not for something to read but because I wanted an excuse to move around. Most of the shelves held bound sets—the *Encyclopaedia Britannica*, law books, atlases. Then there were travel books, art books, hundreds of reference books, and a lot of history, mostly about Russia and Germany. Over in one corner were a few current volumes—*The Wall, The Cocktail Party, American Freedom and Catholic Power*—all with covers slightly frayed. I don't know why I started when the door opened behind me; I suppose because I felt as though I were snooping even if I'd been invited to snoop.

"And what can you tell about us from our reading habits?" a deep woman's voice asked.

I turned around. She wasn't at all what I'd expected. She was short and on the stocky, muscular side. Her features were small and regular yet they created, with their frame of short brown hair, worn in bangs, a weird effect. A middle-aged Buster Brown. Or a circus midget whose face, you felt, ought not to have wrinkles of age. Her smile was bristling, determined, and like everything else about her, down to the tweed suit and incongruous nylon blouse, sexless.

I smiled back. "Only that you have them," I said.

"Safe." Her smile was cunning now, as though she'd cracked a code. "But that's all right. Safety first." From her jacket pocket she took cigarettes and matches and lit one, then held out the pack to me.

"No, thank you."

"You don't smoke?"

"No."

"Don't like it?"

"I can't afford it."

"Good." She nodded. "I like to hire people who need money. They don't quit the first time you look at them sideways." She crossed the room and sat down at the swivel chair behind the big desk, beckoning me to sit across from her. I could feel her little midget's eyes on me as I came over and sat down.

"You dress well for a poor girl."

"I work." I held her gaze steadily and hoped she wouldn't notice my flushed cheeks.

"Spend it all on clothes?"

"Not all. I give some to my mother and put a little in the bank."

"Do you take as much care of your room as you do of your appearance?"

"No."

I'd said it because I thought she would like anything I said if she thought it was honest. I'd been right, too, and I was rewarded with a snorting laugh. She took another cigarette from her pocket and lit it with the first one.

"But I don't let it get filthy, either," I added, caution getting the better of me.

"We have a local woman up at the lake," she said, mashing out the first cigarette in a monstrous marble ashtray. "Comes in once a week to do the cleaning. You'd have to keep it neat. Mr. Stamm and I will be away most of the time. I have a law practice. We both work a good part of the summer, but we might take it into our heads to come up without notice and we wouldn't want to find the place looking like a garbage scow. Mr. Stamm, in particular. He's more fastidious than I am." She looked at me expectantly. I nodded. "You would also be responsible for the laundry; but there's a washer-dryer at the house, so that's no great problem. If there were more ironing than you could handle, we'd bring some of it to the city when we came in. The girl spends half the summer sleeping, anyway, and it doesn't hurt to remind her she's on a salary. Can you cook?"

"Simple things."

"That's all right. I just don't want the kids eating cream-cheese-and-jelly sandwiches three meals a day when I'm not there."

I smiled.

"Lotte's a good cook, as a matter of fact. I'm an excellent one, myself, and I've taught her. But like most people she'd rather cram a piece of rotten store bread into her mouth than cook a meal when there's no company." She paused to trim her cigarette ash on the tray rim.

"Is Lotte your daughter?"

"Oh, for heaven's sake," she began, "didn't Walter—? Never mind.

Yes. Lotte's my daughter. She's sixteen. Boris is eleven. And that brings us to the important part of the job. Mr. Stamm didn't tell you anything about it, I gather."

"No."

She opened the desk drawer and took out a pack of little brown cigarillos, lighting one and mashing out the cigarette although there was a good part of it left. "Boris is in the fifth grade. He is a nice boy and a likable one, but he is not particularly intelligent." My face must have betrayed surprise because she flashed her belligerent, small-toothed smile and said, "If you're shocked, it might help to bear in mind that your shock is only due to the fact that parents so rarely assess their children with any degree of objectivity. At any rate, in a public school Boris's intelligence would be adequate to carry him through and get him into one of the mediocre colleges the country abounds in. But for a boy with a background like his, an education of that sort would be the kiss of death when he began looking for a niche in the world after graduation. Any fairly intelligent personnel director, say, who looked at his résumé would immediately see the discrepancy between his address and his schooling—might even know the family, and the schools Boris should have attended—and would at best offer him one of those awful little pseudorespectable clerkships that many men these days find preferable to the honest manual labor for which they're suited."

She went on that way for a while. Boris attended an excellent private school where he managed to keep his head above water by virtue of having private tutors who helped him with his work both in advance of and during the school year. The tutoring was not exactly a state secret but obviously he was not particularly encouraged to discuss it at school or with his friends. The most important single facet of my job during the summer would be to anticipate his curriculum for the coming year, with review, where necessary, of the previous year's work. Emphasis would be on English and social studies, since Boris held his own in arithmetic, but if I should be competent to help with arithmetic as well, that would be all the better. She was pleasantly surprised to learn that I was good in math, since usually English and language majors were not. She loathed women who were horrified by figures, yet she had to admit that she herself had no aptitude for them. Lotte, who was so much more intelligent than her brother, had to struggle much harder than he did with math courses.

I listened only enough to let the words lodge in my brain where they could be picked over later for sense. The rest of me was thinking of her ugliness, of her wealth, of her fake-academic brutality. And of how little I wanted to work for her. She finished finally and sat looking vaguely expectant, as though I should keel over with her brilliance.

"Any questions?"

"Can you tell me, please, what the salary is?"

She laughed, then looked at me speculatively. "What did you have in mind?"

"I wasn't thinking of a specific figure," I told her, irritated.

"Were you thinking of a general one?"

"I can make sixty dollars a week in the city," I lied.

"Not including room and board."

"I don't pay for those at home."

"Carfare. Lunches."

"That doesn't come to much."

"You can hardly compare a summer in the country to one in the city."

I hated her more as I saw how much she was enjoying the game of bargaining.

"I'm not working for the sake of the scenery."

"True." She lit a new cigarette. "How does forty a week sound? It's more than I'd expected to pay."

"I'm sorry." I stood up. "I can't afford to work for that."

She stood up with me. "What is the minimum you would consider?"

"I'm not sure. Fifty or fifty-five a week."

The smile again. "You drive a hard bargain, Miss Kossoff."

I shrugged. "Not for the fun of it."

"Well," she said, motioning to me to walk with her to the library door, "let's say this. Mr. Stamm has your references. If they're as good as your manner suggests they'll be, and if we can't find someone as good who's a trifle less hungry—" she paused to watch my reaction but anger simply made me more rigid—"then you will have yourself a rather good job. I expect to get the whole business settled this week so that the girl we hire will have adequate time for preparation." She opened the library door and we walked into the foyer. "If you're hired, I'll want you to come back next week to meet the children and get the syllabus material. Fair enough?"

I nodded.

"Fine."

She extended her hand and instinctively I grasped it harder than I normally would, which was good because it would otherwise have been crushed in her fleshy vise.

The elevator man nodded at me this time, apparently in recognition of the lengthy period I'd spent at the Stamms'. I didn't nod back.

My anger was out of proportion to the incident and fed, I think, by my knowledge that I could not touch, change, make a dent in, these people whose foolishness and cruelty were so well buttressed by their wealth. The whole thing would have been perfectly at home in a Trollope novel. I'd done my final paper for Professor Robinson on Trollope—an attempt to show how false was the attitude that he was writing about another world. I'd gotten the paper back with an A scrawled on the cover page but next to it, in a small and genteel script, the words "My goodness!" which served to negate everything I'd said and leave credit only for the way I'd said it.

I walked across Fifth Avenue and sat on one of the park benches, but I was too restless and upset to stay there for long, and I began walking downtown, trying to blot out the interview but being reminded of it by every chauffeured limousine, French poodle, and colored cleaning woman waiting for a bus. Finally I gave up and headed toward Third Avenue to take the El. Instead of going directly home when I got off, I walked to the store to see my father. There was a woman at the counter, but he stopped waiting on her when he saw me and walked around to kiss me.

"Wait in the back, Ruthie."

From the back I could hear him say to the woman, "Excuse me. My daughter."

"A good-looking girl," the woman said.

"The looks have no importance," he told her solemnly. "It's what's inside the head that counts."

And in the storeroom's darkness I grinned, remembering how a few years before I had split my lip in a fall and he'd come into my room twice during that night, having awakened from a dream that my looks were ruined.

"No light?" he asked when he came in a minute later. He pulled the chain on the ceiling bulb. "You're saving money for Daniel?"

"God forbid," I said, because saving money for Daniel was one of the most serious crimes in my father's book. He was constantly looking, in the lists my mother gave him of things to bring home from his brother's store, for evidence that she had skimped for fear of taking advantage of Daniel.

"A quarter-pound of American cheese," he would say, scrutinizing the list. "That adds twelve cents to my salary this week. Are you sure

Daniel can afford it?" And it was a source of irritation to him that his brother should have bought a grocery instead of a market with proper meat and produce departments where all our food needs could have been satisfied.

"You're all dressed up," he said.

"I had a job interview." My depression, momentarily forgotten, returned. "Some people named Stamm."

"You didn't get it?"

"It's not that." I waved a hand to dismiss the whole thing, but of course I could not. So I got up and began roaming around the storeroom, looking at the stacked cartons—Sacramento tomato juice, Chicken of the Sea, matzos, cookies, toilet paper, kosher soap—and telling him about the interview. I could indulge in more rhetoric with him than with my mother, who would be sympathetic but would say I was upset for nothing, or would, if Mrs. Stamm's exact words were forced upon her, assure me that people said things they didn't mean. I described everything—the house, the elevator man, the Stamms. Twice customers came in and I had to assure him the story would hold before he would go out to wait on them. When he came back he repeated exactly the words at which I'd broken off. Occasionally he would interrupt to comment on the basic injustice of a world where it was such people who had the money, or to ask for some detail I'd overlooked— Mr. Stamm's exact first words to me, or whether Mrs. Stamm had offered me a cigarette when she took out the first one for herself. He hated my being in the position of having to ask for anything, and long before I'd gotten to Mrs. Stamm's final dig at me he was running his hands through his thick black hair in exasperation, starting to interrupt, then realizing he had nothing to say, circling furiously around the chair where I'd been sitting, so that, catching sight of him, I stopped pacing for fear someone would walk in unheard and find two lunatic figures doing an angry dance in a dimly lighted storeroom.

"That's all?" he asked when I'd finished.

I laughed. "What else did you expect?"

"I expect you should have some pride. To say nothing to them! To let them spit on you like that! Germans!"

"Really, Papa," I said, becoming calmed by his anger. "It wasn't all that bad. I mean, it wasn't just what she said that got me. It was everything about her. The whole place. And the whole business."

"So?"

"So nothing, love," I said. "All this is silly because I'll probably never see any of them again."

"So they *didn't* want you."

"I think they did. But they won't pay me enough."

"If they paid you a million dollars," he said, "I wouldn't let you work for them."

"Time enough to worry about that," I said, laughing at him, "when they hold out the million dollars."

Helen Stamm called four days later and offered me the job. I asked her what salary she would pay me. She said fifty dollars a week, and I said I was sorry, it wasn't enough. She said fifty-five, and I said I would consider and call her back. She said that if I would give her a definite answer then and there, she would make it sixty. She reminded me that aside from having virtually no expenses in the country, I would need fewer clothes, and said that as a matter of fact, teenagers being what they were, Lotte cast off many things which were still in perfect condition and which I would be welcome to if I wanted them. What I wanted was to tell her to go to hell. Instead, I accepted the job.

I went up to their apartment one evening the following week to get the tutoring material, as well as to meet the children. Boris was very much a boyish version of his father, with light hair and a shy, serious manner. Lotte was quiet, too, but whether out of shyness or indifference I couldn't tell. For all that I talked with either of them, I need not have come; Helen Stamm chose to acquaint me with her children by talking about them, first while they sat with us, then later, when they'd been excused, while we sat together over coffee and cake in the living room. Toward the end of the evening she gave me all the material and mentioned that I had succeeded in pulling off my "little highway robbery" only because my references had been superb. She offered to have someone pick up my luggage the day before we left for the lake. I thanked her and said it would not be necessary. She looked amused—I don't think that even she had any idea of how little luggage there would be—and said that in that case I should be at the apartment at nine in the morning. I took a cab home and told myself that my extravagance had nothing to do with Helen Stamm, I was simply eager to see David.

I knew something was wrong before I opened the apartment door. I could hear angry voices from the hallway downstairs. They stopped briefly when I reached the landing, but then I opened the door and saw that my father was standing in one corner of the kitchen when he should have been at the store. My mother, her expression a combination of misery at what was happening and relief at seeing me, stood

near him, one hand clutching the rim of the shower stall. I walked in
and closed the door behind me. Martin was framed in the entrance to
our bedroom, his face sulkily defiant. He didn't look at me.

"Ruthie," my mother said, "make them stop."

As though it had been a signal, my father resumed his shouting
while pretending to talk to me.

"A bloodsucker!" he said. "That's what you got for a brother!"

I put my bag and the folder on the table.

"Ruthie," my mother said.

"Never mind," my father said. "We're not concerned with Ruthie.
We're concerned with this . . . this bloodsucker."

"If you're going through the whole thing again for her benefit," my
brother said, "I'll leave. I heard it already."

My father moved toward him, a hand raised, but my mother and I
grabbed his arms to stop him.

"What happened?" I asked her.

"Your father is upset," she explained helpfully. "Martin—"

"Martin is a bum," he said, struggling free of us but not advancing
on Martin. "A bum. He doesn't work, he doesn't help in the house, all
he does is go to school a few rotten hours and then he doesn't pass his
courses."

I looked at Martin. He was staring at my father in astonishment.

"What—?"

"Here's what," my father shouted, taking some postcards from his
pants pocket. "Here's what. Mr. Martin Kossoff, the genius. C in English, F in history."

It knocked the defiance out of Martin and left him wilted. I wanted
to run and put my arms around him but I knew that would make my
father worse.

"For God's sake," Martin said. He leaned against the doorjamb, his
eyes closed, his face drawn. "If that's what it was about, why didn't
you just tell me?"

"So I told you," my father said. "So what are you going to do now?
Go out and change the mark?"

"Come on, Papa," I said. "Have a seat. Calm down a little. I could
hear you downstairs."

"So what?" he demanded. "I got nothing to be ashamed of."

"Abe," my mother said. "Sit. You'll make yourself sick."

Martin sank into one of the kitchen chairs, his elbows on the table,
his head in his hands.

"Worry about your son," my father said, thickly sarcastic. "He's tired from bumming around all day."

I sat down at the table near my brother. He looked up.

"I told you about the history exam," he said to me softly. "The stupid bastard spent the whole term on the Greeks, then gave a final on the Romans."

I nodded.

"Who're you calling a stupid bastard?" my father asked behind me. Martin stiffened.

"Abe," my mother said.

"A responsible man," my father intoned. "With an education. And a steady job."

He had expressed quite different opinions about teachers who failed to appreciate *me*.

"*Who's* a stupid bastard? *Who* bums around the city and comes home two hours late for dinner, his mother doesn't have enough to worry about?"

"I don't mind, Abe," my mother said. "Ruthie was going to be late anyhow."

"You don't mind. He could put you in front of the door to wipe his feet, you wouldn't mind."

"Is that how it started?" I asked Martin.

He nodded helplessly.

"That's right," my father said. "Ask your sister what to do. The big man!" I could feel him moving closer in back of me.

Martin stood up, his back against the wall. I turned to my father.

"Papa, please come for a walk with me. Please. I want to talk to you." I could see Martin, like a cornered animal, sidling toward the entrance to our room.

"Look at him," my father taunted. "What's the matter, your sister can't help you? Such a big man, with the swimming, and the basketball, and the-this ball and the-that ball?"

Martin backed through the doorway. My father followed and I tried to hold him back but could only slow him down. The room was dark except for the light from the kitchen.

"Ruth," my brother said, his voice trembling, "don't let him come in here."

"What are you saying?" my father yelled. "Whose house is this?"

"Ruth," Martin said, standing silhouetted against the window, leaning against the table, his body framed by the tall plants on the table and sill, "Ruth, you better stop him."

"Ruth," my father mimicked in savage falsetto, "please save me, Ruth."

I held my father's arm, but I felt as though I were the one being held. Not just held but torn at. Torn in two by the two of them. And before I'd even realized the meaning of Martin's plea, he had whirled around, picked up one of the flower pots, and hurled it at my father so that I heard first a loud oath as the pot grazed my father's shoulder and then a crash as it split wildly against the doorframe and its pieces thudded to the floor in their own dirt.

"Abe!" my mother screamed, running to him.

He stood motionless. My brother didn't move.

"Martin," my mother said, weeping, "what did you do?"

"Papa," I said, "are you all right?"

"Abe," my mother said, "come under the light where I could see."

Dazed, he permitted himself to be turned and led into the kitchen. Neither Martin nor I moved as my mother fussed over him, insisted that he drink a little water, led him into their bedroom. Then Martin moved limply to his bed and collapsed on it, face down. A moment later my mother came out to the kitchen again, put up some water to boil, took out the can of tea. I stood in the doorway but we avoided looking at each other. While the water was heating she got the broom and dustpan. I took them from her and pushed the dirt and pottery fragments onto the pan and dumped them into the garbage bag near the sink. My mother poured the boiling water into the teapot and took the pot and a glass and a strainer into the bedroom with her. I put away the broom and pan. In a minute she was back for a spoon and a piece of lemon. When she went into the bedroom this time, she closed the door behind her.

I went to turn off the kitchen light and noticed on the floor, half under a chair, the postcards. I picked them up. There were four, not just two. One was addressed to me; I'd gotten my A from Professor Robinson. Then there were the two for Martin and a third my father hadn't mentioned, a B-plus in economics. I turned off the light and groped my way back to the bedroom, dropping the cards in my dresser drawer, then finding Martin's bed and sitting down on its edge. I could feel his whole body shaking. I put my arms around him and let my head rest on his back, my cheek against his poor damp shirt. It took a long time for the shaking to end. Finally he turned on his side. I put out my hand to stroke his forehead; it was wet, as were his cheeks, his ears, the pillow.

"Baby, baby, baby," I whispered.

"I went up to school with a couple of guys," he said, his voice damp, too, and muffled, "to see if any of the marks were posted yet. My eco prof—I got a B-plus in eco but *he* didn't see *that* card—anyhow, he was just posting the marks and one of the guys started talking to him, then he asked if he could give anyone a lift to Brooklyn. Turned out he has a boat he docks in Gravesend Bay. He took us out with him, four of us. He had a couple of rods and he used one of them and we took turns with the other one. Sammy Meyer got sick and he stretched out on the back seat and we were throwing the porgies right over him. It was great. We didn't feel like coming in when it started to get dark, so we just put away the rods and talked. I don't even know what we talked about. It was great. I never wanted to come home."

I could feel him beginning to tremble again, so I held him more tightly and after a while it went away. A little later his breathing became regular, and when I was sure that he was asleep, I undressed and got into my bed.

I'd forgotten to set the alarm and my mother got me up the next morning. Selma was taking two weeks of her month's vacation in June, before I left, and I was working full time those last two weeks. Martin's bed was made. I looked up at my mother questioningly when she came into the kitchen. She said she'd heard him leave quite early in the morning.

In the next few days I saw very little of him. He seemed to be avoiding me, as well as my parents. My father, too, was invisible most of the time. He had his late snack in his room these nights instead of at the kitchen table. We moved around each other like shy ghosts in a haunted house. I spent the night after the fight at Thea's. The next night I went up to the Landaus' before going to our apartment and asked Mrs. Landau to ask David if he could come down. Mrs. Landau, tight-lipped, self-righteous, informed me that: (1) her son was not home; (2) it was getting so no one could stand to stay home, with all the terrible noises some people in the house were making. I went down the steps and stood outside her door for a few minutes, trying to control my anger so that I would not have to explain it to my mother. But my mother sat over her mending with swollen red eyes and it turned out that Mrs. Landau, after refusing to speak to her for two days, had informed her when they met while putting out the garbage that we were lowering the tone of the building.

"That's very funny," I assured her. "Lowering the tone of the building. Maybe the roaches'll get mad and move out."

"Ruthie," my mother said reprovingly. But she smiled slightly.

"Mrs. Bertha Landau, Elegant Wife of the Sour Pickle Salesman—"

"Shah, Ruthie. Someone could hear."

"—expressed concern today that the lofty moral tone of the palatial domain where she held court was being—"

There was a knock at the door. My mother looked at me, stricken.

"Who is it?" I barked out.

"David."

"Come in," I called; then, as the door opened, "if you're still permitted to associate with us."

"Don't mind her, David," my mother said. "She's upset from work." She shouldn't have bothered. I didn't trouble him at all.

"My mother said you came upstairs."

"That was my mistake," I said. "I forgot what a sensitive creature she is. How the slightest noise disturbs her delicate ears."

"You'll have to admit," he said, grinning, "it was quite a blockbuster."

"And you'll have to admit," I shouted to get the words through my aching throat, "that if that little spring pickle you call a father ever answered *her* back you'd have quite a blockbuster up there, too."

He stopped smiling and stared at me curiously for a moment while I held my breath for fear that if I let it out, tears would come, too. Then he turned around and walked out, closing the door carefully behind him. I moved only when I'd heard the downstairs door close, too. Then I sat down at the kitchen table, rested my head on my arms, and cried for the first time in years.

I went through the rest of the week in a kind of daze. At the office, Lou and I continued to convalesce after Market Week. He told me that my job would be waiting for me in the fall if I wanted it. I said I probably would. On my way home from work Friday I met a boy who'd been in my history class. He asked me if I wanted to go to the movies. I thought of all my half-formed plans to happen to run into David, and said I'd like to go. We ate at the Automat and I told him I didn't know his name. He said he'd been trying to talk to me for weeks but I always had my girl friend with me. I suggested that we should go to the movies, if we were going, because I couldn't be home too late. I was jumpy and abstracted in the theater, but I managed to sit still until the first picture was almost finished and he put his arm around me. Then a wave of revulsion, not so much toward him as toward the whole situation, washed over me, and I told him I had to go to the ladies' room and walked through the lobby, out of the theater, and all the way home. I spent the rest of the night feeling guilty about it and wondering how to find out where he lived so I could drop him a note of apology. By the next day I had convinced myself that such a note could serve no purpose, and by the day after that I'd forgotten his name, anyway.

I spent Sunday with Thea. She would be leaving for the Catskills during the week (as would Martin), so this was to be my last full day with her. We went to Coney Island and in the afternoon, walking along the boardwalk, we ran into Jerry Glickman and a bunch of other neighborhood boys, Martin not among them as he would normally have been. For once I wished that David were the type to travel in that silly pack so that in all the noise and self-conscious hilarity I could have found myself next to him and things would have gone back to normal without uneasiness and without the apology I could not frame.

It was a warm, humid day and Thea and I were tired. We tried to shake the boys; when that didn't work, we let them buy us hot dogs and escort us back to the beach. Bob Cross had a portable radio and he turned on some band music. We stretched out on the sand and ate the hot dogs, and against the music heard the boys relating for our benefit tales of their prowess on the basketball courts, their delinquencies in the classrooms, and their conquests among the coeds. There were groans when the music gave way to a news broadcast, but then someone suddenly said, "Ssshh."

"Huh?"

"Communist radio," the announcer was saying, "broadcast the hostilities, saying the war was declared effective at eleven A.M."

"Where?" Jerry whispered. "Where?"

"I dunno," someone said. "Korea."

"Never heard of it," Jerry said.

"That's because your head is full of rocks," Bob Cross said.

"All right, wise guy," Jerry said. "So where is it?"

"Shut up. I'm listening."

"China," someone said. "Japan. Around there someplace."

". . . President Truman, from his home in Kansas City, earlier today assured the nation that we are not at war."

"So who said we are?" someone asked.

Bob whistled a few bars of "We're in the Army now," and someone told him not to be such a jackass. A short while later Thea and I let them talk us into stripping to our bathing suits and going back into the water. By the time we came out, the sun had gone down and there were few people left on the beach. We tossed a handball around for a while, then turned on the radio; setbacks for the North Korean invaders were being reported. Not long after that Thea and I became too chilly to stay any longer, and ignoring various loud unfunny suggestions on how we could keep warm, we got up to go.

My parents weren't home. Martin was in bed although it was just past eight o'clock. If he wasn't asleep, he wanted me to think he was. I turned on the light and for the first time made a mental inventory of my clothes, trying to figure out if there was anything I absolutely had to buy for the summer. The answer was almost everything; I decided to coast by on a minimum until I saw whether Helen Stamm remembered about her daughter's castoffs. Then I went to sleep and had a dream I couldn't remember the next morning except that it had to do with David, and broken glass on the beach at Coney Island.

Korea didn't enter my head again until I saw the headlines of the elevator boy's *News* when I went to work the next morning.

"Listen," he told me when I asked what was in the headlines, "I got troubles of my own."

When I came home from work Tuesday night I found my brother lying on his cot, a bunch of leaflets scattered around him.

"Hi, Butch," I said.

"Hi." Super-blasé.

I went into the closet and groped for my jeans and sweat shirt.

"What're you reading?" I called.

"Nothing."

"Sounds like a waste of time."

There was no answer. I peeked past the closet door and met his eyes. He looked away. I dropped the jeans and sweat shirt on the closet floor, ran out and dived for his bed, reaching under his pillow and pulling out the pamphlets before he could stop me. I'd done it more for the sake of breaking the tension between us than because I was curious, and I was amazed at the fury with which he grabbed them back—a second too late to prevent my seeing the title of the top one, "What the Army Can Do for You." I don't think I understood right away, although any idiot should have. It must have been Martin's defiant expression, as he suddenly abandoned any attempt to hide them, that made me realize he was serious.

"You must be kidding," I said foolishly.

He didn't answer me.

"Martin, are you angry with me?"

"Don't be stupid."

"You've been avoiding me all week."

"I haven't been avoiding you." He picked up one of the pamphlets and leafed through it without reading. "I've been busy."

"Busy avoiding me."

He turned on his side so that his back was to me.

"Did I do something? Martin?"

"No."

"Then why am I getting the silent treatment? Why are you reading all that stupid stuff and not even talking to me about it?"

"There's nothing to talk about," he said.

"You mean you're not really considering it?"

"I didn't say that."

"Then why won't you talk to me about it?"

Silence. Then, the dead voice taking on a bitter edge, "Little Ruthie Kossoff. Convinced she can change anything if she puts her mind to it."

I felt as though I'd been hit by a weapon I couldn't see.

"I don't understand," I said.

"Forget it."

"How'm I supposed to forget it? Am I supposed to stop being your sister, or what?"

"No," he said. "Don't stop being my sister. Just stop being my sister and my mother and my father and a couple of dozen other things thrown in."

"When," I asked, trying to keep my voice low and steady, "have I done that?"

He sat up and turned around.

"Always," he said. "You always do it. You do the same thing as Papa, only in a different way. You think things can be different just because you want them to be. You don't want him to hate me, so you keep telling him I'm really a nice boy and then you're surprised he doesn't believe it. You don't want us to fight, so you put yourself in front of him and start explaining things as if he was a reasonable human being. Then when it's all over and you don't want me to be upset, you sing me to sleep and you're shocked when I remember it all the next day."

He stopped so suddenly that I sat there for a while waiting for more. Then I said I was sorry, although I didn't know exactly what I was sorry for, and walked out of the apartment. I heard him call my name as I closed the door, but he didn't come after me and I let the door click shut. Then I walked up the stairs to the Landaus' and knocked on the door. Mrs. Landau opened it. Covered with flour and stuffed with piety.

"Is David home?" I asked.

"Yes."

"I have to talk to him."

"He's resting," she said, brushing some of the flour off her arms so that it powdered the air between us. "Some boys work hard, you know, miss."

"I know," I said, speaking loudly as I realized she was almost whispering so he wouldn't hear from his room, "but I have to talk to him."

"Mom?" he called. "Who is it?"

She didn't answer.

"It's Ruth," I called past her. "I have to talk to you."

I heard him come into the kitchen and only then tried to think of what I would say to him.

"If you're tired," his mother said, turning from the door, "you should rest."

"Oh, stop it," I heard him say.

She moved from the door and he appeared on the threshold. I hesitated. I hadn't been in that apartment since I was fourteen years old.

"We can talk in my room," he said. David, the king in his household, had the bedroom with the door. He led me through the kitchen, his mother eyeing me with floury hostility over the table where she was rolling out her egg-noodle dough, and into his room. I sat on the bed, which was rumpled where he'd been lying on it; David pulled the desk chair over and sat down, waiting. I rubbed my hands together like an idiot, and suddenly found myself trying to remember what I was wearing but not wanting to look down to see.

"Too bad I don't smoke," I said finally.

He smiled encouragingly.

I'd had vague ideas that I must find a way to apologize to him. Instead I blurted out, "Martin's going to enlist." And was relieved to see his stunned expression, having been afraid he would take it lightly.

"You're kidding."

"No. I mean I'm not certain, but I came home from work and he was—"

"Hey, hey," he said softly, "relax. You're going a mile a minute." He took my hands and held them between his. When I tried to begin again he shushed me and said I should wait. I took a few deep breaths and then began again.

"I guess you haven't talked to him all week."

"I haven't even seen him around."

"He hasn't *been* around," I said, and remembering that David hadn't seen me around, either, I looked away from him. "He's been avoiding everyone. Since the fight."

"What started it? The usual business?"

"More or less." I told him about the postcards. "The only thing was, it was worse than usual. I guess you know that. My father just kept goading him and finally he—Martin—threw a flower pot at him." I could see David suppressing a smile; he had no particular love for my father.

"Did he hit him?"

"No. Or just barely, anyway. But he stunned him. I don't think they've talked to each other since. For that matter, no one's been talking to anyone, except my mother and me. The only time I saw Martin until today he pretended to be asleep. Then today he was reading those damn pamphlets when I came in, and he tried to hide them from me."

"Army pamphlets?"

I nodded.

"Crazy kid," David said. "He must've started reading the papers all of a sudden."

"You mean Korea? There aren't even Americans fighting there, are there?" I asked.

"As of today there are. That doesn't mean Martin's automatically going to get shipped to the front lines."

"Oh, my God," I moaned, pulling my hands out of his in my agitation. "What's that nut going to do? He'll probably beg them to send him there, the nut."

"Oh, I don't know," David said. "Did you try to talk him out of it?"

"I couldn't." I stood up, slipped between the bed and the chair, and walked over to the window. It was still light out and the early summer warmth had brought many people out to the streets. "He's mad at me, too. He . . ."

"I'm listening."

But I'm not talking, David. Don't you realize how difficult it is for me to speak with you like this? Haven't you ever noticed that I don't come to you with my problems? I've always been afraid that if you pitied me you wouldn't love me.

"He thinks I'm trying to run his life."

David snorted. "He needs someone to run it."

"That's not the point."

"I know, I know." I heard his chair scrape against the floor as he moved it back. Then he came over and stood next to me at the window, looking down at the street.

"What was it that made him say it? Do you know if it was something special?"

I could hear his mother moving around noisily in the area near the door, wanting to hear but afraid to actually put her ear to the keyhole.

"I tried to stop them from fighting," I said in a very low voice, almost sick with shame. "He said I should've left them alone. And afterward I . . . I sort of babied him so he'd fall asleep."

He was silent for a long time. Then he asked me what I wanted him to do.

"I don't know," I whispered. "Hold me a little."

I turned and he put his arms around me. Limp with relief, I let my head rest against his chest.

"David," Mrs. Landau's voice came, thick and obvious, through the door, "are you hungry?"

"No," he called.

"You hardly ate any supper."

"I'm busy."

As her feet tracked dispiritedly away from the door, he kissed me.

"I'll go downstairs with you," he said. "We'll try to talk to him."

Martin was sitting at the kitchen table, drinking milk from the wax container. I thought he was about to say something, but when he saw David in back of me he changed his mind. My mother still wasn't around.

"Where's Mama?" I asked.

"She went to the Hartmanns'. She said she'd be late."

"I'm starved." I went to the refrigerator where I found two plates set up for our dinner and covered with two other plates. (That summer it would come as a revelation to me that there were people who used waxed paper and aluminum foil all the time to cover food and threw them away when they'd been used once.) I set places for both of us. David had sat down opposite Martin and I sat between them. Martin took another long swig of milk from the container.

"So," he said to David, "come down to help with the problem child?"

I started pecking at the sardines and potato salad on my plate.

"Will you just tell me one thing?" David asked.

Martin nodded cautiously.

"All right. Your father has no use for you. Your mother may not feel the same way, but she won't interfere."

I held my breath and kept my eyes on my plate.

"That leaves Ruth," he went on, "and maybe me. Are you saying you want us to leave you alone?"

"Ruthie brought her lawyer," my brother said softly. When I looked up, he was smiling; the smile vanished quickly, but the sullenness was gone, too. "No," he said, "that's not what I'm saying. I don't want you to leave me alone."

"Okay," David said. "What's with the Army pamphlets?"

"It's not such a bad deal. When I came out I'd have the G.I. Bill. I could go to night school and work full time and have a place of my own."

"It's a beautiful deal," David said. "The Army's all honey and roses."

"*This* is honey and roses?"

"But Martin," I put in, "you're going away this week. For two months. Why should you do it *now?*"

"Great," he said. "Two months in the Catskills. Two months of clearing greasy dishes and getting propositioned by fat old ladies."

"And playing basketball."

"And playing basketball. If I'm not too shot when I finish all the crap."

"You know perfectly well you're never too tired for basketball."

"And what about making the team in September?" David put in. "How long is it that you've been waiting to make it?"

Martin ignored him because it was unanswerable. Ever since any of us could remember Martin had looked forward to playing varsity basketball at City.

"All right," he said to me. "Two months of grease and basketball. And then, when I get back in September, everything's the same. Anyhow," he added as an afterthought, "there's a war on, in case you haven't been reading the papers. Bet you haven't." He smirked at me. "I don't know why *you* didn't fail history. Teacher's a man, I bet."

"I know enough about it," I said, "to know it's not the kind of war you enlist in."

"What do you mean, the *kind* of war you enlist in?" he demanded.

"I think she means," David said, "like the Second World War, where you knew what was being done to the Jews."

"That's pretty stupid. You don't enlist because it's not the Jews, it's just the whole world."

"Korea?" I said. "Since when is that the whole world?"

"It's not Korea," he said with exaggerated patience. "It's Russia and the United States. Why don't you read past the headlines?"

"They're fighting for Korea, anyhow. Some stupid little place nobody ever heard of. Could you even show it to me on the map?"

"Get the map."

"All right. So you looked it up. A week ago you couldn't have showed me. No one could. And now you're ready to go and get killed there."

"Don't be so dramatic," he said. "And can't you get it through your skull that Korea isn't the issue?"

"As far as I'm concerned it is. If you're going to—"

"Look, Ruth," David cut in, "he's right in that respect. It's not going to do any good to argue that."

"Clarence Darrow to the rescue," Martin murmured.

"But it seems to me," David went on, "that that's a very good argument against enlisting."

"Do tell," Martin said, and I prayed David would continue to ignore the sarcasm and not simply get up and walk out.

"Okay," he said after a moment. "Korea's a testing ground. Russia's trying to see how much shoving around the West will take. Agreed?"

"Agreed."

"Well, who the hell wants to die on a testing ground?" He waited, then when Martin didn't reply, he went on. "Especially when the test is only a test of strength? A guy who found himself going in the Second World War could tell himself some jazz about making the world safe for democracy. If it helped. Or the Spanish Civil War, where they really believed they were dying for freedom. Anyway, this isn't a conflict of ideas, even on the surface. If we win this one, it's not going to prove that democracy's stronger than tyranny. It's only going to prove that we called a bluff and won. Not only that," he went on as Martin seemed about to interrupt, "but there are plenty of political scientists around who say this is what the next few decades are going to be like. No big countries dropping bombs on each other. Just a bunch of little wars in places people'll be scurrying to the *Times* to find a map of. I'm not saying they aren't necessary. I'm not even saying if you get called you should go down to the draft board and pull out your eyelashes or say you're queer. I'm just saying it's the kind of thing where you let the poor bastards who're in it anyway, or who're too stupid for anything else, get theirs. It doesn't pay to screw up your life and risk your neck. Not for something like this."

"The two of you," Martin said irritably, "you talk as though everyone who goes into the Army dies."

"In wartime," David said, "they have a much higher percentage than civilians of the same age."

Martin shoved away his plate, the food untouched.

"All right," he said. "So what if I do?"

"Oh, come off it."

"It's easy for you to tell me to come off it. You've got a couple of slaves upstairs. And a room with a door on it."

"A barracks doesn't have doors."

"It doesn't have my father, either. And when I come out I can finish school and get a place of my own."

"Martin," I said, "I'll be finished next year. Maybe I'll get a place, and if things are still bad here you can stay with me."

"You know how long it takes to finish college at night?" David asked. "There're plenty of guys still in who started in 'forty-five. Even when they can manage to keep their eyes open after a day of work, they don't learn much."

"I'm not learning much now. Maybe in a couple of years at least I'll know what I want to do."

"Maybe you'll know in a few months but it'll be too late."

"Oh, Christ," Martin said. "Why'd we have to start all this, anyway?"

"Martin," I said, "listen to me. Please. At least wait until the fall. The Catskills'll be bearable. If they're not, I'll look around up where I am. Or we'll do *something*. Please wait. Maybe it'll be better in the fall. At least give it a chance. Please."

"You're leaning on your sardines."

I moved back from the table. He stood up and stretched.

"All right," he said, yawning. "All right. I'll wait."

"Promise?"

"What should I do? Cross my heart and spit? If I said I'd wait, I'll wait."

I sank back in my chair, my eyes closed.

"Who can lend me a buck?" he asked. "I feel like a movie." I opened my eyes. He was grinning idiotically. It was the grin I'd seen the night we ran into his old girl friend in the cafeteria. "Now, please," he said, "don't anyone tell me I don't *look* like a movie."

"Ouch," David said dutifully.

I got my bag from the bedroom and took two dollars from my wallet.

"Thank you so much, madame," he said with a deep bow when I handed them to him. "Please let me know the next time I can be of service." And with an airy wave of his hand, he was out of the front door.

David and I sat at the table in silence for a while. I tried to eat, but the only thing that would go down was some milk. I scraped Martin's dish and mine into the garbage, rather than let my mother know we hadn't eaten. Then I washed the dishes and dried them.

"Hey," David said suddenly. "Where'd Martin say your mother was?"

"At the Hartmanns'. In Queens." I looked up at the clock and had to look again to make myself believe it was just past seven-thirty. "She told Martin she'd be late."

"Hmmm," he said. "This evening begins to have possibilities."

"I'm going to change," I said. "I started to change before, and then everything happened. I'll be right out." I went into the bedroom and standing near the closet, unzipped my dress. I could hear the bolt sliding across the front door and as I pulled the dress over my head, I heard him come into the room. When the dress was off and I opened my eyes, he was stretched out on my bed, on top of the red blanket.

"Make yourself at home," I said.

"My mother," he said, "says that women who wear black underwear do it so they won't have to wash as often."

"The next time I go upstairs in my underwear," I told him, "I'll make sure it's white."

He nodded gravely. I stood in the middle of the room, a little too far away for him to reach out for me, holding my dress but not wanting to go back with it to the closet.

"What are you being coy for?" he asked finally. "You heard me lock the door."

"One nice thing about this room," I remember saying a little later, "it gets dark early."

He made love to me twice that night. The first time was very painful but good, too; the second time was better and barely painful. I don't know just what time it was when he got up, pulled the blanket from under me, covered me, and left. I didn't feel very different than usual the next morning, but while I was in the lavatory at Arlou I discovered I had my period, and for the rest of the day I was unaccountably depressed.

CHAPTER TWO

My mind refuses to be tantalized by the problem of good and evil. What is much more interesting to me is the question of seeing things and not seeing them. If I was evil to marry Walter, why didn't he perceive that I was so before he married me? I never said I loved him. If the omission didn't bother him before our marriage, why should it have begun to torture him later on? Why should he have brooded increasingly on the fact that I wouldn't have married him if he were poor?

I'm no less guilty than he of this failure to use my intelligence where it matters. I once reminded Walter that in accepting his proposal I'd said nothing about love. He came back at me (so quickly I had the feeling his part had been rehearsed) with the words of my marriage vow. The fact of the words, or perhaps only his fake religiosity in uttering them, must have aroused some guilty anger, for I very quietly said one of the most deadly things I've ever said to him—"All right, Walter, I promised to obey you, too. Give me an order and I'll obey you."

God knows, I had a better opportunity than most women to observe the men they will marry. That whole first summer I observed Walter Stamm and his family. And learned nothing from my vigil but to perpetuate my hatred for Helen. On the occasional weekend when her husband came up without her, we were like kids on a holiday—doing things as the inclination moved us, eating whenever we happened to be hungry, acting generally like carefree children until perhaps some chance remark would make Lotte stiffen with loyalty to her mother, and her stiffness would sober the rest of us. I could think only of how pleasant it would be to be free of Helen Stamm's domination, how wonderful the summer would be if I never again had to hear her suggest I get in some extra work with Boris in view of the poor weather; tell Lotte to get her father in from the garden before the food got cold; tell him, once he came in, that he would get overheated if he didn't take off his sweater. I must have assumed she would veto any of his ideas; I may be wrong now in thinking she would have welcomed them. I may have come to feel between that sad ugly woman and myself a bond that doesn't exist.

But how could I have failed to be struck, then, by the fact that on

the rare occasions when Helen Stamm issued no directions, her hus-
band asked for them?

Mr. Stamm did not drive. When he and his wife used the car together, she drove. On other occasions—if he had, for example, to look at
a piece of property—one of the young brokers at his real estate office
was pressed into service. Mr. and Mrs. Stamm sat together in the front
seat during the trip to the lake. Sitting between Boris and Lotte in the
back, I remembered with pleasure how their imperious old elevator
man had flinched as he drew back the door and saw Mrs. Stamm, sore-
thumb resplendent in a red-plaid shirt and tight fly-front jeans.

The previous night David and I had prowled the streets until it was
late, then spent the time until morning investigating the various grassy
knolls of Tompkins Square Park and Washington Square. I was
exhausted now, and glad of a reason to close my eyes, for I felt ill at
ease. Lotte had responded politely to my attempts at conversation: Yes,
it was a nice day for the drive; no, she wasn't sorry to be finished with
school for the year; yes, there were girls of her own age at the lake. But
when I'd run out of meaningless questions she had been quite content
to sit next to me in silence, and for some reason that poised silence of
hers disturbed me. I opened my eyes. Leaning back against the seat I
could see her without moving my head. Pony tail. Serene, unstrikingly
pretty face. Pink blouse and neat blue jeans. Hands loosely clasped in
her lap. Anyone's idea of the wholesome American girl. Then why
didn't she bubble a little, or say jeepers, or act sullen—do something, in
short, that would let my mind settle her in a teen-agers' world, if not
the comical vaudeville-complex world of *Henry Aldrich* and *A Date
with Judy,* then at least the morbid, inward world of my own adolescence? It couldn't be just that she was rich; I'd gone to Hunter with
girls of seventeen who were far from poor, and they might have been
happier than I but no one of them had ever possessed this degree of
remote tranquillity. I closed my eyes, assuring myself that it was foolish
to be unnerved.

I awakened with a start when the car swerved off the highway and
onto the rutted dirt road that led to the house. I looked around. The
area was heavily wooded, and the few homes along the road were set
well back from it. In a few minutes we made another turn.

The house was very beautiful. The road sloped up through the
woods approaching it and suddenly there was a large rolling lawn that
ran down to the lake's edge. There were two buildings, both white
frame trimmed in green. The large one stood at the hill's crest, a

screened porch spanning two of its sides; the small one, looking like little more than a one-room cottage, was set about twenty yards back from the other, close to the line where the lawn ended and the woods began. A gravel driveway led from the road to the back of the little house and a small gravel parking lot.

Mrs. Stamm pulled into the lot, walked around the car, and opened the trunk. Mr. Stamm, immaculate in a gray suit, white shirt, and foulard tie, then Boris, Lotte, and I, followed her.

"We may as well take in as much as we can now." She handed me my three-dollar cardboard valise and took a satchel herself. "Lotte, you and Boris can take the food hamper between you. Then if your father takes one of the big suitcases, there won't be too much later."

I followed her along the flagstone path to the side entrance, the others coming up behind me. She opened the side door and stepped up. I walked into the kitchen after her. I'd been taken once to a French restaurant where you walked through the kitchen to reach the dining room; until now I had never seen anything like that room. It was huge, tile-floored, with yards of raw-wood counter space, and high racks and hooks holding gleaming pots and pans. I felt a physical pleasure in the place and I was really glad, for the first time, that I had taken the job. Boris and Lotte put the straw hamper on the table and vanished through the kitchen entrance. Mr. Stamm, still carrying a suitcase, went after them, and I could hear them all going up the stairs.

"There's probably six months' worth of dust under the beds," Helen Stamm said, "but my pots are polished because Mrs. Bannion likes to polish pots. Well, come upstairs, Ruth, and I'll show you your room."

As she led me through the main hallway I caught quick glimpses of the dining and living rooms. The apartment had been all townish austerity; here the motif was determinedly rustic. Chintzy upholstery, cobbler's-bench end tables, and braided rugs suited each other with a slick self-consciousness, a quality I would later recognize as the hallmark of a bad decorator. (At the time I would never have assumed any home to be professionally decorated. I was aware of the existence of such professionals—about half of my high-school class had listed Interior Decorator as its career aim in the yearbook—but it would never have occurred to me that someone of Helen Stamm's overwhelming assurance would hire such a person to decorate her home. I seem to have easily absorbed the contradiction between her blatant bad taste in dress and her dull good taste in decoration. I needed years to find credible the fact that she could have been afraid to choose her own furniture.) I followed her upstairs and through the wide central hallway, past the open

doors of her bedroom (oranges and browns, twin beds with brass head-
boards) where Mr. Stamm stood motionless at the window; of Boris's
room (greens and browns, double-decker bunk bed); and the closed
door she pointed out as Lotte's. My room was at the far end of the hallway. The wallpaper was floral; the headboard was brass; the rug, also
braided, was a solid bright-blue.

"That's a closet," she said, pointing to one of the two doors. "And
that's your bathroom. There's a bedroom on the other side opening onto
it, but that room will be empty except for an occasional guest."

To stop myself from running to look at the bathroom, I walked over
to the window, staring out at the forest and a curving patch of the lake.

"You don't seem overwhelmed," she said, thickly ironic.

"I'm sorry," I said. "It's very lovely. I—" But of course I couldn't tell
her.

"There's just a shower stall in this one," she said. "If you prefer
baths, you can use the master bath across the hall."

*We don't have a tub at home, either, Mrs. Stamm. As a matter of
fact, we don't have a bathroom. We have a shower in the kitchen and a
toilet in the outside hall. We share the toilet with a very old man we
never see, and it might amuse you to know that before I leave work, or
anyplace I happen to be, I use the toilet there so that I won't have to
go, any more often than necessary, into that damp, rusty, foul-smelling
little cubicle which my mother cannot with all her efforts make fit for
human beings.*

"Thank you," I said. "That's very kind of you."

She said that she was going down to take care of lunch and I should
come down when I heard the bell, or sooner, of course, if I wished. She
left, and I closed the door behind her. It had a lock, which I turned. I
looked all around the room again—at the chintz-covered armchair, the
maple table in one corner. It was larger than the room Martin and I
shared at home. I opened the closet; there were many more wooden
hangers than I had dresses. In the bathroom, fluffy towels were hung
on racks against sparkling yellow tile. I came back to the room and sat
down in my armchair. When I heard the cowbell jangle a little while
later, it didn't immediately strike me that I was being summoned. I
wanted to stay in that room for a long time. Then I realized it was the
lunch bell, and went in to wash. A moment afterward there was a
knock at the door.

"Who is it?" I called.

"Boris." His soft voice, still boyishly high, barely reached me through
the door.

I turned the lock and opened the door for him.

"My mother asked me to tell you lunch is ready."

"I heard the bell. I was just washing."

He stood on the threshold, trying to decide whether to wait for me or run ahead.

"Before that, I was just sitting and looking around," I said. "I suppose I'm being silly."

He smiled uncertainly.

"I've never had my own room," I said.

He looked at me uncomprehendingly.

"I share a room with my brother."

"How come?" The ignorance of the foreigner.

"We have a very small apartment," I said.

He was quite fascinated.

"That's why I like it so much here."

He nodded.

"I guess we'd better get down to the kitchen," I said.

He nodded again. I followed him into the hallway, closing the door behind me.

"Can you play tennis?" he asked, suddenly turning to me.

"I've never had time," I told him seriously. "But I'd like to learn."

"I can teach you," he said. "Mr. Barnet who owns the Somerset, across the lake, he's a friend of my dad's. We use the courts all the time."

"That sounds fine," I said.

For lunch there was an excellent cold buffet, the first of many meals that would have spoiled me for my mother's improvisations had I not come to dislike them on principle long since. Helen Stamm made most of the conversation, focusing her attention on each of us in turn. With her husband she discussed things to be done at the house; with Lotte and Boris, which families were already at the lake. Then she turned her attention to me.

"Tell me, Ruth, did you have any specific plans for working with Boris? Or was it your considered opinion that he should have a little vacation?"

"I'm looking over the material you gave me," I said. "But of course I won't really know what to do until we begin working."

"That sounds reasonable."

I'm so glad.

"I sort of assumed," I said, "that we'd wait until Monday to begin."

"Until I'm out of the way."

"Partly that. But more because I imagine everyone needs time to settle down. I doubt that Boris could concentrate on schoolwork during his first two days up here."

"You have a good line, Ruth," she said.

"I didn't know I had a line," I told her.

"But no sense of humor," she said.

"Maybe," I said, feeling my face flush hotly, "we don't have the same idea of what's funny."

"That's what I mean," she said. *"I think you're funny."*

My embarrassment was overwhelming, far too overwhelming for me to consider anything outside of it. Such as the taut, almost sexual nature of the little verbal duels in which she was fond of engaging me. Or the truth of what she said.

It was at a somewhat later time than that summer that I became capable of viewing myself with occasional humor; certainly she was right in suggesting that I could not then. My ironic sense was acute, but as far removed from genuine humor as the housewife's complaint that it *would* rain on her only night out. I was sure I was at war with fate; I had no sense of personal absurdity in the waging of such a war. Perhaps one cannot view victory with sophistication while it still seems possible to win.

I saw very little of Walter Stamm that first weekend. At meals he was polite and remote; between them, he read on the large screened porch facing the lake (and beyond the lake, Mount Mantinoc); or disappeared in one of the three boats that was tied to his dock; or walked off into the woods, alone or with Boris. Lotte, too, was away most of the time, usually with a friend who lived down the road. Mrs. Stamm was always busy. If she wasn't in the kitchen she was bustling around the house with papers and books and folders. I talked with Boris a few times; he seemed to like me and sometimes came up to my room when there was no one around. After breakfast on Sunday morning I finally unpacked the carton of Lotte's clothes that Helen Stamm had given me. It was easy to see that most of them would fit. There were dresses, slacks, and blouses that looked as though they'd been worn once or twice, if at all, as well as a bathing suit that was considerably newer than the faded black one I'd brought with me. A couple of the things were slightly shabby and out of a pride that few people before Helen Stamm had managed to arouse to such a fevered pitch, I put them aside for Mrs. Bannion's grandchildren. ("The Irish, Ruth, run out of money and brains, but never out of grandchildren.")

The Stamms left Sunday night when Boris had already gone to sleep and Lotte was in her room, reading. I'd been given an alarm clock and as Helen Stamm had "suggested," I'd set it for seven so I could make breakfast for Boris and Lotte. It took me a long time to fall asleep, but I didn't mind. It was a luxurious insomnia on a soft bed in a pretty room cooled by a fresh country breeze. And I had never felt percale sheets before. It is a petty but inescapable fact that no amount of ironing will turn muslin into percale.

I awakened without the alarm the next morning—at about six, when the sun came streaming through the window because it hadn't occurred to me to shut the venetian blinds. Now, lying in the brightly cold room, warm under three blankets, more truly alone than I had ever been in my life, I felt steeped in an almost unbelievable luxury.

I would not even want David here with me now.

It popped into my head, half-connected to my previous thought, and left just as quickly as I looked across the room at the maple dresser, an ordinary piece of furniture made momentarily beautiful by the sun's warm light.

I couldn't stand to have anyone in the whole world here with me now.

It occurred to me that Lotte and Boris might still be sleeping and that if I dressed quickly I could nose around the house for a while. If I wanted to.

Later on I'll miss David and it will be wonderful if he can come up. But not yet.

At seven I turned off the alarm and forced myself to get out of bed although the sun was just beginning to really warm the room and I was naked, having slept without pajamas for the first time since I was five and Martin, four, and my father had decreed we were now too old to see each other bare.

That first week was the best one of all. The newness of the privacy I enjoyed, as well as of the country's beauty, the simple nature of the life I was leading, all these contributed to a steady serenity unlike anything I'd felt in my life. Some lucky instinct made me begin my work with Boris by reviewing his best subject, arithmetic. I started with a few simple questions: Did 7 x 6 equal 6 x 7; which was larger, a quarter or an eighth; how many ounces in a pound, quarters in a dollar, inches in a foot, feet in a yard, nickels in a quarter? His answers came slowly but they were invariably correct, and from there we went on to more difficult problems. I stayed away from English during the first few days and made only brief forays into history and geography, the result being that when we did begin some reading work, he didn't start off with the idea that I thought him stupid.

I'd been a little concerned that my lack of professional training would prevent me from helping Boris with his reading problem—whatever it was—for Helen Stamm had only specified lack of intelligence. When we did get to reading work, though, it was obvious that the problem was less one of intelligence than of concentration. Without the specific symbols of a math problem or a science experiment to moor itself to, his mind strayed from the passage before him and wandered abstractly down a variety of paths. Sometimes I would bring him back with a question about what he was reading; he would be able to answer easily once he'd gone back and reread the passage. Yet often, after missing a question and having me skip the passage instead of going back, he would reveal, in discussing some other point, that he could have answered the original query.

Whatever success I had with Boris was a result of the way I was with him rather than of anything I did. Because I actually did nothing. We would read and talk. He liked to read when we were sitting around together, particularly if I'd been able to get two copies of a book and we were reading at the same time. We would sit curled up at opposite ends of the sofa, half-facing each other, and when I finished a page I wouldn't turn it, but would pretend to still be reading until I saw that he was finished, too. Sometimes, my head tilted down toward the book, I would secretly watch his nice serious little face as he read. I remember watching him a great deal when we read *Tom Sawyer*. He never smiled. Yet he laughed often when we talked about the book's episodes, and I don't think it was just out of a desire to please me.

The weather was generally good, and we would often take a swim before lunch. Occasionally Lotte was down at the dock, but more frequently she was at the Loebs' dock with her friend Nina. I had met Nina (Nicky to her friends and any adults who would play the game) and her parents over the weekend and hadn't been charmed by any of them. Manny Loeb had the kind of forceful geniality that prevented you from realizing, until it was too late, that he had no business asking the questions he did. His wife Penny was about ten years younger than he and wore her dyed black hair in a pony tail in the apparent conviction that this made her look twenty years younger. They had a son who was a couple of years older than Boris. A likable boy with many friends at the lake, Arthur sometimes let Boris hang around with him out of generosity. I couldn't understand why Lotte should choose Nina as a friend; there were many nicer girls around the lake. The other girl was a few months younger than Lotte but could have passed for my age with her dyed-red hair and aggressive sexiness. A juicy little suburban plum that would rot before it fully ripened and already seemed too ripe for its season. In the meantime, it was Nina who became acquainted with the counselors at the boys' camp on the other side of the lake; it was Nina who was sure to be Lotte's companion when she disappeared for a day at a time without telling me in advance; it was Nina's casual insolence, more than Lotte's remote calm or her mother's sweeping authority, that caused me to panic at being out of my depth.

Not that I let it stop me. A list of the things I learned to do that summer reads like a beginner's guide to the good life. In school I'd played basketball and volleyball; now, with Boris and then with his father, I began tennis. Then golf, with Helen Stamm, who would sometimes take me to the club. Martin and I had learned to swim in the rough dirty water at Brighton; now, in the cool calm of Lake Quanthog, I discovered how much more fun rich people could have in the water. I learned to water-ski and to run a motorboat, in addition to tackling the rudiments of sailing. Indoors I learned: To mix a passable cocktail; to be an adequate fourth at bridge; to adopt the correct tone of amused condescension with Mrs. Bannion. I began to smoke. Helen Stamm left cartons of cigarettes in the pantry and by my second week there I could no longer resist the impulse to take a pack. I stole them frequently after that, but although she'd occasionally tell me that if I wanted to smoke I should feel free to take cigarettes from the pantry, my smoking remained a secret vice. A stronger sense of the ludicrous might have prevented me from stealing up to my room each time I wanted a cigarette—like an eight-year-old finding his first live butt and stealing behind a bush to try it.

And I ate. More than I'd ever eaten in my life or have eaten since. I ate well at meals and frequently between them. I would take fruit and cheese from the overstuffed refrigerator, dried fruits and nuts from the huge pantry, cookies from one of the large ceramic jars on the counter. I ate so much that by the end of the summer I had put on eight pounds in spite of almost constant physical activity, and I had to starve myself for two weeks to get into my school clothes again.

Martin came up on his day off the second week I was there. He brought woeful tales of starvation and overwork but he looked wonderful and he admitted, when pressed, that he was on the staff basketball team, got in a few hours a day at the pool, and was frequently fed on the sly by solicitous female guests. Boris and I were finishing up our morning's work when he arrived. We all put on our suits and went out to the dock. Boris had been shy of Martin in the house, but he became excited when Martin did a beautiful racing dive from the dock, then swam, without surfacing, to the float that was twenty or more yards away. After that he begged Martin to teach him to dive, and Martin immediately began instructions. I watched the two of them standing at the dock's edge and became aware that over at the Loebs' float, Nina and Lotte were craning their necks to see who was with us. After a while, of course, Nina could bear it no longer. The two of them swam in from the float, disappeared behind the Loeb dock, and a few minutes later, sauntered onto ours. Or rather Nina sauntered onto ours, with Lotte in tow. I introduced them to Martin, who was in the water with Boris. He was polite but didn't come out of the water.

They hung around us all day so that Martin and I never got a chance to talk. It was funny but irritating to see the change in Nina's manner toward me. Casual insolence was replaced by easy camaraderie as she made certain that Martin looked good from close up, too. By afternoon, when she invited all of us for a speedboat ride, I could almost have believed she wanted me along. Even Lotte was different—a little less remote, a little more aware of me as a human being—now that I was found to have a handsome brother who could swim and dive and not keel over when a couple of rich sixteen-year-olds flirted with him.

"Come again," I said when he left after dinner. "You're doing wonders for my popularity." But he wasn't alone the next time he came.

It was a cold rainy Tuesday. Instead of turning on the heat we had built a fire in the living-room fireplace and settled, with our books, on the rug in front of it. It was a lazy day, we were reviewing dull material, and I had to fight to stay awake in the fire's warmth but was far too contented to move from it.

"English claims to territory in North America were based on the explorations of . . . The great English sea captain who failed in three attempts to establish colonies in the New World was . . . The trading company that was permitted by King James to found an English colony in the New World was called the . . ." I struggled to make my mind check each answer before going on to a new question. Finally my eyes did close but I doubt that Boris had been enjoying the joke for more than a couple of minutes when the doorbell rang. It only half-awakened me and I let Boris go to the door, drifting back into a light sleep.

"—hears about this, young lady," a stern voice was saying. I sat up before I was even awake. David was standing above me, laughing; a smiling Martin and a good-looking girl I didn't know were standing near him.

"You don't look overjoyed to see us," Martin said.

"You scared me out of my wits," I told him.

"Well, unscare yourself, girl," he said with a joyously abandoned wave of his arm. "You're giving Rhoda a bad impression of my family."

That reminded me of Boris and I scrambled to my feet to look for him. He was leaning against the archway, watching us all through the dim rainy-day fireplace light. I held out my hand and he came over shyly.

"You know my brother," I said, taking his hand. "This is a friend of ours, David Landau, and this is Rhoda . . ." I turned to smile at her politely and realized for the first time that she was colored. Part colored. Part Negro, as I always had to say if I didn't want to incur Martin's wrath. At any rate, it is a matter of simple fact that at the moment I realized this, the slight tension I'd felt upon seeing a good-looking stranger with David and Martin disappeared.

"Rhoda Watkins," my brother said happily, "Ruthie. Ruthie, meet Rhoda. The sole ray of sunlight in my shitty summer."

I told Rhoda I was glad to meet her and mentally tried to calculate whether the number of weeks left before my brother was to go home would be adequate for him to get over her.

"I hope you don't mind my dragging along," Rhoda said easily. "Martin swore you wouldn't."

"We're delighted," I said. "We were just sort of moping around, being lazy. There's nobody else here, except for Lotte, and she's out with her friends. Please sit down. Be comfortable, everyone."

I felt David's amused eyes upon me and became self-conscious. Without looking at him, I said I'd put up coffee. Boris tagged into the kitchen after me, helping to set up a tray with sandwiches and cookies then carrying it into the living room for me. When I came in again with the coffee, he was telling everyone that his father had said I was a natural tennis player. I'd known exactly what amused David before— my Mistress-of-the-Manor air, the ease with which I'd welcomed them, the way I'd said *we* were delighted they'd come. The tennis talk only increased my self-consciousness and I managed to spill coffee twice while filling the mugs. Rhoda, Boris, and I each had a sandwich. Martin and David between them knocked off the rest of the sandwiches and all the cookies.

"Are you working at Kressler's, too?" I asked Rhoda when everyone was served.

"Uh-huh."

"As a chambermaid!" said Martin with ready indignation. "They wouldn't give her a waitress job. Isn't that fantastic? As though their waitress jobs were some kind of goddamn privilege!"

Rhoda shrugged, obviously a little embarrassed by his outburst. "One's as bad as the other," she said. "My hours are longer but at least I work straight through and then my whole evening's free."

"It's not pleasant work, though," I said, feeling David's eyes upon me again, wanting to turn and ask him if he had any better idea of how I should conduct myself.

"Neither is waiting table," she said.

"But couldn't you have done better in New York?"

"I don't know," she said. "Every college kid in the city is looking for a job in June. I've never worked before, so I didn't have experience or references. Anyhow, this work doesn't bother me so much. Making beds and dusting, mostly. I think I prefer it to being cooped up in some office in the city all summer."

I nodded. Into my mind flashed the memory of Mrs. Landau, the year before, indignantly telling my mother how the *schvartze* she'd hired for a day during recent back trouble had refused to get down on her knees to scrub the kitchen floor. My mother, who at no time in her life had been preoccupied with the question of her own dignity, was baffled by this refusal to do a job the only way it could properly be done. Mrs. Landau, inflated with false pride, perpetually concerned with the maintenance of what she conceived to be dignity, understood the refusal perfectly. And was infuriated by it. My own reaction— delight—was not to the initial situation but to Mrs. Landau's fury. Now I tried to imagine Mrs. Landau's reaction if she were to meet Rhoda, much younger than the stubborn *schvartze*, probably a great deal smarter, and so unconcerned with the possibility that being colored detracted from her dignity that she could prefer making beds in the country to doing office work in the city.

David said something about money and Rhoda said, with a smile, that money hadn't actually been the major problem; her parents had insisted she take a job because they knew otherwise she'd just sleep all summer.

She offered to help clear the dishes but I told her not to bother, and

Boris and I brought them into the kitchen together. A moment later
Martin appeared at the door to ask if they could stoke the fire. I sent
Boris back with him to show him the wall door that led to the wood-
shed. I did the dishes right away because in the back of my mind, since
everyone's arrival, had been the question of how Nina and Lotte would
react if they came home and found my friends—specifically, Rhoda—
settled comfortably in the house. I was determined not to be put on the
defensive. I was also determined that if they (I always thought of Nina
and Lotte together as one person possessing Nina's malignance and
Lotte's influence with the Stamms) were going to relate horror tales to
my employers, they should be deprived of small embellishments like a
sink full of dirty dishes. When I got back to the living room, Boris had
vanished and the three of them were lying on the rug, staring contentedly into the fireplace.

"Can't these people afford steam heat?" David asked when I
stretched out beside him. And I knew right away that the fireplace had
saved me from a lot of ribbing. Because they could tease me from then
to doomsday and it would still be there, a splendid, substantial monu-
ment to money. Mute testimony that I might be ambitious but I was
not mad.

"Steam heat is for poor people," I said.

"Right," Rhoda murmured drowsily. "Rich people have fireplaces
. . . and big copper pots . . . and clay pottery . . . and grass to cook
out on . . . and horses to ride instead of time-payment Caddies . . ."

"Listen to her," Martin said admiringly. "She's compiling a goddamn
catalogue."

I'd been listening carefully, anyway, impressed with her knowledge
of specifics.

"Go on," I said to her. "I like your list."

"Hmm," she murmured. "Embroidered skirts, coarse handwoven
shirts. Leather sandals . . . fresh flowers and dried mushrooms and
wild rice . . . horses to ride instead—"

"You said that already."

"Don't make no never-mind," she drawled, her eyes still closed.
"Only thing on whole list I give a damn for. Horses."

"You like riding?"

"My mother tells me to ride my bike," she said sleepily. "It doesn't
cost five dollars an hour. Have to laugh. Nothing in the world like
being on top of a horse."

"How about under?" David asked. "I understand Catherine the
Great—"

Martin snickered.

"Even Central Park," she murmured, ignoring them, her words becoming less and less distinct. "D'you ever see the white trash in cops' clothing on top of those horses? Feel like kings. Better'n buying themselves monogram underwear at Saks Fifth Avenue." She said more, but I couldn't understand her. Then the sounds lapsed into a steady, heavy breathing.

"Look at that girl sleep," Martin said. "I never saw anyone who could sleep like that."

I became aware of the sound of a motor outside just as Boris called to me from upstairs.

"Good grief!" I pulled away from David and scrambled to my feet. "Roo-ooth, guess what! My parents are here!"

"Thanks, dear," I called back. "Come on down." I turned to David and Martin. "Surprise, surprise," I said in a low voice. "Look, suppose you both make believe you're asleep, too. Give us all time to collect ourselves. Try to listen, though, when I explain. In case I tell a lie you won't say anything wrong."

"What a nice surprise," I said to Boris when he came downstairs. "It's a shame we're not having good weather." I took his hand and we went into the kitchen, opening the outside door as Mrs. Stamm reached it.

"Hello, Ruth," she said. "Hello, Boris. It looks as though the chamber of commerce is paying off the weather-forecast people again."

"I'm sorry it isn't better out. Hello, Mr. Stamm."

"Hello, Ruth. Hello, son." He bent over to hug Boris affectionately. "Having a good week?"

"Great," Boris said. "This is the first bad day."

"It's true," I said. "We've had perfect swimming weather."

"If not studying weather," Helen Stamm said, with her half-amused, all-ugly smile.

"Ruth is developing a great serve," Boris told his father proudly.

"Wonderful," his mother said. "That's what she's here for."

"I gather," his father said to me, genuinely smiling, "that everything is great, great, great."

"Oh," Boris said suddenly, "and guess what!"

"I guess," said his mother, "we're tired of standing near the kitchen door holding our suitcases."

"Sorry, dear." Mr. Stamm took her valise and we walked through the kitchen. Boris, disconcerted, didn't speak again.

"I think," I said when we reached the hallway, "that what Boris was going to tell you was that some friends of mine are here."

"Oh?" Mrs. Stamm said. "Where?"

"In the living room. Sleeping. I hope you don't mind. I'd have checked with you in advance if I'd known they were coming."

"I'm sure it's quite all right, Ruth," Mr. Stamm said, looking at his wife.

I smiled at him gratefully.

"Of course, of course," she said with an abrupt wave of the hand. "But tell me, how many are there? *They* has an ominous sound. Two, five, ten?"

"Three," I said. "My brother, and a friend from our building . . . and a girl my brother's working with in the Catskills."

"Brother? That's funny. I'm sure I'd have remembered if you'd told me you had a brother."

I smiled spitefully. "I'm sure I would have told you if you'd asked."

Mr. Stamm cleared his throat. Boris smiled up at me, impervious, as usual, to the barbs being exchanged.

"Fair enough," Mrs. Stamm said briskly. "Now, tell me, where are these sleeping beauties of yours? In the living room, you said?" Without waiting for a reply she walked into the living room and over to the fireplace rug, looking at each of them in turn.

"I must say, Ruth," she murmured, looking down at David, "your parents produce good-looking offspring."

I thanked her, not bothering to tell her she wasn't looking at my brother.

"I don't suppose," she said, still looking down at David, "you can tell me where my daughter is."

"With Nina and Mrs. Loeb. They were going to shop in town, and then maybe go to a matinee if the weather stayed bad."

"Fine." She walked back to the arch where Boris and Mr. Stamm, still holding the suitcases, stood waiting. "We'll have lunch at two. You can tell your friends they're more than welcome to stay."

"That's very kind of you," I said. "Actually, I don't know if they'll be hungry. I made some coffee and sandwiches when they came."

"Young people can usually find more room," she said. "Anyway, I doubt that you'll have to tell them anything at all. One of them does a fairly good imitation of regular breathing but if the other two haven't heard every word I said, I'll eat the front lawn, mud and all." She walked quickly up the steps, her husband behind her. Boris stood uncertainly at the bottom step. "You come too, Boris. I want to find out how much information has been fed to that complex brain of yours lately."

I waited until their bedroom door had closed, then walked back into the living room. Rhoda was still asleep. David was sitting up, laughing silently, but Martin, also sitting, was not amused.

"Jesus," he whispered, "how can you stand it?"

I shrugged. "Come on. I'll show you the lake, David."

They got to their feet, following me through the kitchen to the lawn. The rain was falling lightly now.

"Is she like that all the time?" Martin asked.

I would have continued to fake indifference but David said, "The trouble with you, kid, is you've got no sense of humor."

"Oh?" I said coolly. "I'm afraid I don't get the joke, either."

He spread his hands in an exaggerated gesture of resignation. "No joke. I just think she's cute."

"You know I must loathe her," I said, "so you decide she's cute."

"The lake is gorgeous," he said. "Now all it has to do is stop raining."

"Cute like a steamroller," Martin said.

"I always knew I could depend on you," I told him.

"You're jealous," David said gleefully, "because she thinks I'm good-looking."

"You're being ridiculous," I said, taking him up as heatedly as though he'd been serious. "She just happened to be standing on your side of the rug when she said it."

He sighed. "United they stand. What can a slob of an only child do against you two? I guess I should grab Rhoda and beat it."

"Why don't you?" I said quickly. "You can buy a zoot suit and do the town."

It was out before I realized how it would affect Martin. The stupid spiteful words hung in the air around me, making my face hot with shame. David whistled softly.

"What the hell's wrong with you, Ruthie?" he asked angrily. "You know better than that."

"I'm sorry, Martin."

"Jesus," Martin said, staring out at the lake, "you don't even know what you're talking about."

"I wasn't talking about anyone, Martin. I was just being rotten."

"Her father's a sociologist and her mother's a teacher," he went on, still not looking at me. "She could've had a scholarship to Radcliffe, only she wanted to stay in New York with her friends. She's been at City all year, only I never knew her there. I can't believe I never knew her. She's the most intelligent female I've ever met."

"And a good sleeper, too," David said, thereby drawing Martin's anger toward himself.

"Now you, too," Martin said. "Jesus Christ, what's the use of having brains if you're gonna act as stupid as—"

"Thanks," I said to David. "I need someone to compound my errors."

"Ah," David said, "together again. That's the way you two look your best. When you're both bawling me out for something one of you did. Now that we're back to normal, has anyone happened to notice that it's not raining any more?"

It was true. The clouds were moving away from the lake, leaving large patches of blue sky.

"No sun, though," I said.

"Well, I don't know about anyone else, but I'm going for a swim. Now."

We followed him into the house. I went up to get into my suit, leaving them to change in the downstairs bathroom. The Stamms' bedroom door was still closed. When I came down, Rhoda still hadn't moved and the boys were already outside. An hour later, the three of us returned from a race across the lake. Martin had won, and David and I had reached shore together, minutes later. Cold and shivering we traipsed into the kitchen. Rhoda was sitting at the table, being talked at by Mrs. Stamm, who was preparing food.

"Ah," she interrupted herself when we came in, "it's our athletic contingent. How's the water?"

"Fine," I said. "Mrs. Stamm, I'd like you to meet my brother, Martin, and our friend, David Landau."

"You barely need an introduction, Martin," she said, smiling at David. "I think I could pick you out of a crowd as Ruth's brother."

"But *this* is my brother, Mrs. Stamm," I said, putting an arm around Martin, who stood, wet and frozen, on the other side of me. It stopped her cold for about two seconds. Then she uttered an uncertain little laugh. And *blushed*. It was almost unbelievable to me, seeing this terrifying bulldozer of a woman so completely thrown by a petty, reasonable error.

"You're not the first person to make the mistake," David said, shortening my malicious moment of triumph.

"Nor is it the first time I've made it, David," she said, glancing at me sideways with a little smile so I could see that she was quite herself again.

"I gather you've met Rhoda," I said. "Will you excuse us if we change? The water wasn't bad, but the air is freezing now."

"Of course, of course." She waved us toward the staircase. "Rhoda and I are having a fascinating conversation."

I looked uneasily at Rhoda; she smiled tranquilly back at me. So nothing had happened to upset her equilibrium.

"We'll be right down."

"I have been trying," Mrs. Stamm said, as we headed for the stairs, "in my perennial quest for knowledge, to acquire some information about the Negro middle class." The three of us stopped in our tracks, just as she must have meant us to. "But Rhoda," she went on as I turned and stared at her incredulously, "claims no awareness of such an organized group, and insists that if I know of its existence I know more than she does on the subject."

Beside me, Martin quivered with rage. I looked at Rhoda. She winked. The three of us went upstairs to change.

At lunch, having failed to disturb Rhoda, Mrs. Stamm looked for a new target. Which school did David attend? And Martin? Oh, this had been a bad week for CCNY, hadn't it? Martin's face remained blank.

"I'm talking particularly about the Rosenberg story, of course," she said, "although I imagine Henry Wallace's defection from Russia left the City faculty drowning in its own tears."

"Now, Helen," Mr. Stamm said slowly—startling her, I think, as well as the rest of us, by coming out of the private retreat of his body—"I imagine you do the school an injustice, generalizing that way. It's doubtful that the entire—"

"Yes, I know, I know," she cut him off impatiently. "Generalizations are unjust. But the fact of the matter is that in order to think on any but the most primitive levels, it's necessary to generalize sometimes. And in any event—" She turned back to Martin without giving her husband a chance to reply; his withdrawal from the group was almost physically visible. I looked at Martin and then David; Martin looked about to choke, but David was absorbed in his food. "—if you haven't seen today's paper, I'll read it. It's too beautiful to be missed. Where did I leave the paper now? In the car? Upstairs? Walter?"

"Mmm?"

"Do you know what I did with the *Times?*"

"In the canvas bag. Upstairs in the bedroom."

"Lotte, please go up and bring down the *Times*. It's in the canvas
ag in our bedroom."

As though her husband were so ineffectual that his words couldn't
ave reached his daughter.

"Of course," she said, "the paper is generally full of good things. A
Democratic investigating committee has come up with the fascinating
onclusion that Senator McCarthy is serving the interests of the Communists by exposing Communists in this country. By 'arousing baseless
uspicions among the people,' I think they called it. Which doesn't ex-
lain why they also recommended an investigation of our loyalty proce-
ures."

"I imagine they're just covering themselves," David said.

"Aha!" she said. "There's a young man with a head on his shoulders.
What school did you say you went to? Never mind, I remember. Of
ourse that's what they're doing. They can't deny the evidence or guar-
ntee that another nest of redbreasts won't turn up in the State Department day after tomorrow, so they try to destroy the man but they cover
hemselves with an investigation." She looked around the table expect-
ntly. Who would provide her with the next take-off point? Nobody
poke. "Do I gather, David, that you have managed to avoid contract-
ng that widespread adolescent disease, the Red Plague?"

David smiled. "No."

"No, what?"

"No, I doubt that by your standards I've failed to contract it."

Lotte came back with the newspaper, giving her mother an easy out.
was torn between sympathy for Martin and pride over David, the
nly one of the three of us who was unbothered by Helen Stamm, the
nly one of the three of us who could shut her up.

"Ah, here we are," she said enthusiastically. "'The FBI today
rrested Julius Rosenberg, 32 years old, of New York, on charges of
pying for Russia. He was the fourth American held this month in con-
ection with the passing of U.S. atomic secrets to the Soviet
Inion. . . . Mr. Hoover described Mr. Rosenberg as another impor-
nt link in the Soviet espionage apparatus that included Dr. Klaus
uchs, British atomic scientist, Harry Gold, Philadelphia biochemist,
lfred Dean Slack, Syracuse scientist, David Greenglass, former U.S.
Army Sergeant . . .' Let's see, now, where's that beautiful line? Here it
. Listen to this. Rosenberg made himself available to Soviet espionage
gents so he quote could do the work he was fated for unquote and so

quote he might do something to help Russia, end of quote. Now, here's
the part you'll love. 'The FBI director said that the gravity of Rosenberg's offense was accentuated by the fact that he, as an American-born
citizen, aggressively sought means to secretly conspire with the Soviet
government to the detriment of his own country. . . . Rosenberg was
born in New York on May 18th, 1918, *and took his Bachelor of Science degree in electrical engineering from the City College in February, 1939.*'" She looked up triumphantly. "How did I guess?" she
asked us all.

"From his age," David said calmly. "And his name. And the fact that
he's a New Yorker. There weren't many New York Jews at Harvard in
1939, not to speak of any other time."

"I think I'd have suspected it, anyway," she said, "although your
point is well taken. At any rate, you're sidestepping the fundamental
issue. What is there about the whole free-education syndrome that nur-
tures the traitor mentality? I see you smiling, Rhoda, David, Ruth, but
the fact of the matter is that my taxes helped send this idiot through
college and now, twenty years later, or whatever, he announces that he
was doing the work he was fated for, he had to do something for Russia. Russia never sent him to school; his parents left it because they
couldn't survive there, presumably. Why doesn't he feel a debt to
America? I'll tell you why. Because people are occasionally grateful to
individuals, but never to government. Government they resent or take
for granted. And that is why governments should spend the smallest
possible amount of time and money on its citizens' education and wel-
fare. It educates them only to be ungrateful and improves their lot only
to the point where they can blame it for not being even better off." She
took a deep breath and again looked around. Finally her eyes rested on
David. David smiled his Deceptively Innocent smile.

"All right," she said sharply, although she couldn't resist smiling
back, "let's have it. I'd hate to miss anything."

"I was just wondering," David said, "if Klaus Fuchs went to City
College."

I don't know if she was really amused but she had the good grace to
bow her head in acknowledgment of temporary defeat. For the rest of
the day she followed David and me around, engaging him in arguments on any subject she could think of. Sometimes she came out the
winner, but even then I think she usually found she'd lost her teeth
during the battle.

I assumed then that she was arguing to win. I may be again imprint-
ing my daydreams upon her when I say I think now that she enjoyed

the sensation of losing, that David, in conquering her, might have made her feel—briefly, pathetically—like a woman.

The rest of the summer passed quickly. I was seldom alone with Walter Stamm, although often, during the day, the two of us were alone with Boris. (Lotte rarely chose to join any activity in which I was participating—although I fancied for a while that her manner was becoming a little more friendly.) I remember the best weekend we had. Walter Stamm had come up alone. We played tennis Saturday morning and went sailing in the afternoon. Lotte had spent the day with Nina and on Saturday night she had a date with a counselor from the camp. We had cocktails (Boris being permitted a glass of wine) and then dinner in front of the fireplace. After Boris had gone up to bed, his father made huge mugs of hot buttered rum and the two of us sat on the hearthrug for hours. He got a little drunk and talked more than he had in the whole time I'd known him. He'd wanted to be an architect and had actually completed his studies. But then his father had convinced him that there was a need for his kind of talent in his real estate firm, which was gradually going into suburban shopping centers. The field being quite new, there was room for imagination. Yet having been sucked into the office routine, he'd discovered that there was actually very little need of architectural planning at his end of the business. It had taken him years to make up his mind that at the risk of angering his father he must get out of the firm and go into the creative work that interested him. And by that time the war had come along and he'd felt obliged to let himself be drafted, although he might have been able to get out of it. Lotte was seven when he'd entered the service, and Boris was born several months later. By the time he'd come out he had a child of eleven and one of five and had simply lost his sense of adventure. He'd had a wife, too, of course. He'd married the year before he graduated from Harvard. His mother had died that year and a few months later, his father had married a woman who, Walter had realized much later, must have been his mistress for years before.

The rum had made him soggy, but not actually disloyal. There was an occasional sad smile. ("And a wife, too, of course.") I saw his sadness then as having a romantic quality, a touch of Byronic tragedy. Later I saw it as having more than a touch of self-pity and no romantic undertones at all. I *liked* him so much then. His reticence seemed admirable—the only graceful course open to someone having made the initial terrible error of marrying a Helen Stamm and being unwilling to correct the error at the expense of his children. His quietness had a soothing quality, serving, as it did, as a counterpoint to Helen's verbal barrages. He seemed gentle. Patiently he instructed me in sailing, or taught Boris some new sailor's knot. And when, that evening in August, he finally did talk to me with a degree of frankness, I never wondered at his need to do so, but only felt flattered that he should want to. Flattered and perhaps a little excited, too. He made no advances to me—nor did I want him to. Yet neither of us could have been oblivious to the intimacy of our situation. Even without such effective props as a fireplace and mugs of rum and a thick rug, we were together in the country, on a cold night, with a child upstairs sleeping, and he was telling me about his life. Even had I not hated Helen Stamm as I did, I might have enjoyed his attention; as it was I exulted in my advantage. We had between us the bond of being in some sense her victims; had I known how fully he felt his victim status, I might have liked him the less for it.

CHAPTER THREE

The year following that first summer at the lake was the most terrible one in my life. For weeks after my return I couldn't bear to be in the apartment for more than an hour at a time and would take the slightest excuse to run out—for a walk, for a bus ride, to do an errand for my mother or some imaginary one for myself. The Stamms had asked me to continue tutoring Boris on Saturdays. I came home each week to feel that my surroundings mocked me. I'd gone back to work for Lou Fine. Selma was pregnant and her happy absorption in babies helped to relieve the drudgery of Arlou. But there was nothing to soften the ugliness of home. I attributed malignance not only to the roaches and water beetles that paraded boldly from the kitchen to our bedroom, but to each grimy shabby piece of furniture in the apartment, to the rusty toilet in the hall, to the rickety stairs that creaked under my weight as I ran down them and out of the house in escape.

David didn't help any. I carefully contrived not to mention my revulsion and renewed discontent, but he knew anyway and teased me constantly about what he was pleased to call my lowered station in life, my fallen status, or my riches-to-rags story. During the first few weeks of this Martin would tell him to lay off, and although it never worked I felt comfort in having an ally. But then Martin began having troubles of his own. First he failed to make the basketball team because there were so many good players that boys who would normally have made first string were relegated to second, and promising sophomores like Martin, who in other years might have made second, had to be content to be eagerly involved from the sidelines. Then he began having a bad time with Rhoda, and because he could not cope with her at all he joined forces with David in torturing me.

Not that Rhoda wasn't nice to him; it was simply that he was in love and she was not. Martin, who'd become quickly sick of any girl who really liked him, was totally, painfully in love with this girl who kept asking him why he had to take life so seriously, why he couldn't just relax and have a good time. He asked if she was ashamed of him, that she never invited him to her home; she invited him and he came back to tell me how her mother, a Polish Jew, and her father, a Negro sociologist, were more in love than any two married people he'd ever seen. He asked her to come home to meet his parents and she was always busy. He told her she was afraid and shouldn't be; she laughed and said he was a silly boy and she couldn't help it if she was busy. Desperate to be more involved than he was, he told my father the girl he was seeing was colored. My father, seeing how eager Martin was that he grasp the bait, instead chose to laugh and say it was a good idea for Martin to grab what he could get. Martin, in lofty rage, informed him that if he had his choice of any girl in the world he would take Rhoda because he loved her and was proud of her. My father smiled cunningly and said yes, Martin must be very proud, so proud he wouldn't bring her home with him. Martin shouted that if my father were so damn smart he might be interested to learn that Rhoda had no interest in coming home to meet them.

"Hah!" my father said. "No interest in the parents means no interest in the son!"

And seeing the color go from Martin's face he knew he'd touched the right spot, and from that time through the next couple of months, whenever there was an argument about whether Martin was doing his schoolwork, or whether Martin had tried hard enough to get a job, or whether Martin was spending too much time watching the basketball team practice, or whether Martin was this, that, or the other thing, my father would end it with, "If it's not good enough for your *schvartze* princess, why should it be good enough for me?"

On the one or two occasions when I tried to reason with him on Martin's behalf, he used my interference as proof of my brother's weakness, so that their quarrels were just one more reason for me to run from the house.

My father was generally less reasonable, more belligerent than he had ever been, although his belligerence ranged from his brother Daniel to the neighbors to Martin and my mother, stopping short of me. The grocery was doing well and he had been given a small raise, but the only change this seemed to bring to our lives was that he was home less often and when he did come home, more often brought with him a gallon jug of California sherry or a bottle of some cheap rye. Once, when I was particularly depressed and he was trying to comfort me, I asked why we couldn't look for another apartment. I was prepared for anger, but instead I got sudden drunken agreement. He took me down to the candy store and bought a *Times*. Together we sat down at the inside counter, where he ordered coffee for both of us and asked to borrow a pencil. Then he went through the rental ads, solemnly circling anything that looked like a possibility. He was so serious and determined that I found myself believing we might really move, and when he circled a couple of Bronx ads I even panicked at the thought that if I lived that far away I would never see David.

"That's too far from the store, Papa," I said. "It'll take you hours to get to work."

"So?" He shrugged. "So I'll get a job out there, once we're settled."

I laughed. "Just like that, huh?"

"Sure, just like that," he said, injured. "You think I couldn't get a job anyplace? You think your uncle Daniel's doing me a favor, giving me a job out of the kindness of his heart?"

And he promptly circled several Bronx ads, muttering that he would check those first as they looked the most promising. It was a Saturday afternoon and I had a tutoring session with Boris, so I couldn't go with him; but when I returned that evening he had already obtained the Sunday Classified and was poring over it at the kitchen table. My mother, darning socks, looked worried.

"Listen to this, Ruthie," my father said as soon as I sat down. "Central Park West. Seven large light rooms in fine building. Two and a half baths."

"My God," my mother said. "Two and a half baths. How could you have half a bath?"

"The half's just a toilet and sink," I explained. "Two regular bathrooms and then the half."

"Think," she said, "to clean them all."

"How much?" I asked him.

"Doesn't say. It just says Rent Control. Must be cheap if it's Rent Control."

"Cheap for who?" asked my mother.

"She's right, Dad," I said gently. "Central Park West couldn't be very cheap."

"So, how much will it cost to settle the question? There's a phone number right here."

"Phone calls cost money, too," my mother said in a low voice.

"What's the matter with you?" he exploded, standing up so abruptly that he knocked down his chair. "You talk like I wanted to throw my money away gambling! I'm talking about a better place to live. You want to live in this garbage dump forever? *I* don't want it, *Ruthie* don't want it!"

"Garbage dump," my mother repeated. Her expression was all pain and bewilderment, and as I sat there, watching her, it was borne upon me that the attitude I'd always admired as peaceful resignation was not resignation at all, but acceptance. My mother didn't fail to read advertisements for homes, clothes, cars, travel, because of the futility of daydreams, but because she didn't want to own a home, to travel, to. . . . An almost forgotten day flashed into my mind. I was ten or eleven. 1941, 1942—not long after America's entry into the war. My father had gotten a defense-plant job the week before and on the day he'd received his first check, he had come home with two packages from Bonwit Teller. I'd trembled with excitement as I opened my package, then cried with pleasure as I pulled out the beautiful red-plaid woolen dress he'd bought me.

My father and I must have become aware, at the same moment, that my mother hadn't opened her package. Only when she saw us watching did she begin to pull the tape—with an expression that could only be described as fearful. She took out a lovely, simple black-crepe dress (my father always had superb taste—much better than hers, even discounting her reluctance to spend money) and held it in her hands for a moment before looking up at my father.

"Well?" my father had prompted, smiling benevolently.

"Where," she'd asked slowly, "would I wear it?"

The next morning she had taken the dress back to Bonwit's, but by that time my father had disappeared for the weekend. Not for the first time. During those war years, when he was making good money for the first time in his life, he often failed to come home for one, two, even three nights in a row. After the war ended and he went to work for

Daniel, making much less money and working nights and many week-end hours, he'd disappeared less frequently.

Now, as I watched him clutching the Sunday *Times* real estate section, I wondered why, during all those years when he'd been making good money and apartments had been plentiful, I had never heard any talk of moving.

"Our friends are here," my mother was saying.

"Friends? What friends?" he asked venomously. "The fat ugly whore upstairs?"

"Abe!"

"You can't stand to live like a human being!" he shouted. "That's what it is. You—"

He continued, but I had turned him off. With my memory of the war days had come the realization that if we had stayed here until this time, we would not move now; that my father's rage was caused less by my mother's words than by his own knowledge that in the long run they would both choose to stay where they were, deeply rooted in familiarity and pain.

I spent about four hours with Boris each Saturday, usually breaking for an hour or so in the middle of the afternoon. If the weather was good, we would walk during that time—through the park, or down Fifth Avenue to the Metropolitan, or even, on occasion, across Ninety-sixth Street and north on Madison, over the invisible boundary line separating the Haves from the Have-Nots. I was amused to find Boris oblivious to the neighborhood change; above or below the money border he stopped to look in hardware-store windows and at photographic-equipment displays. Any ironic remark about the change in scenery left him looking blank and unperturbed. I remember asking him once, when we'd walked over to Park Avenue, why he thought there were trees below Ninety-sixth Street and railroad tracks above it; he said he supposed that was just where the trains had to come out.

We stayed in when the weather was bad, sometimes playing checkers in the library—or even chess, which he'd taught me during the summer —sometimes just chatting. At some point during the fall Boris finally got permission to set up darkroom equipment in his bathroom, and after that we were always taking pictures, or he was teaching me how to develop film or illustrating a new enlargement process. If he made an error in showing me some new achievement, he would mutter savagely and kick the side of the bathtub. I would laugh and tell him that no matter how hard he tried to fool me, I knew he could really do it. He reminded me so much of Martin and my father; any small failure was never simply that, but a reflection on his entire manhood. Once assured that he was still manly in my eyes, Boris would easily do the job.

One evening at the beginning of December, Helen Stamm called me into the library as I was on my way out.

"Tell me, Ruth," she said, puffing on one of the Nat Sherman cigarillos she was now smoking exclusively, "do you have any plans for the Christmas holiday?"

I said I hadn't.

"I assume you're aware by now," she said, "that my son is hopelessly, passionately in love with you."

I laughed uncomfortably. "I know he likes me."

"Likes!" She raised her eyes to the ceiling as though to invoke some deity—Freud, I suppose. "The inside of the closet door is lined with photographs of you. Each Saturday after you leave he's conspicuously mopey and depressed; and when we ask him if something's wrong, he doesn't answer but a while later comes out with some question about David's age, or where we think the two of you are going that night. Any suggestion that his schoolwork has improved so greatly that he might not always require tutoring is met with test failures during the week. We now go out of our way to assure him that we consider you totally responsible for his improvement, and, therefore, an essential and permanent member of the household."

"Well, that's very nice to hear, naturally," I said. "Although I'm sure you're exaggerating."

"On the contrary," she said, mashing out her cigarillo in the huge ashtray, "I've confined myself to straight undramatic reportage. I've omitted any kind of speculation or interpretation for fear of embarrassing you. I could, for example, make out a case for your being a substitute object of Boris's oedipal worship. I might dispute his wisdom in selecting you as a mother figure," she paused briefly to light another cigarillo, "but I readily concede your greater worthiness as a pin-up subject."

I could feel myself blushing. I was as numb and helpless as I had been during that first interview with her.

"I mention all this," she went on briskly, "because we're going to spend most of Christmas week at the lake and Boris feels he will languish and die unless you accompany us. There aren't many people around at this time of year, and generally each of the children brings a friend. The two girls Lotte was interested in having up are going away with their parents this year. We assumed, although we obviously shouldn't have, that Boris would ask a boy in his class. His preference for you, he says, is based on the fact that most of the boys in his class know how to ski, while he can *teach* you."

"I'm afraid skiing doesn't appeal to me," I said, smiling stiffly.

"Oh?" She pounced on it, a starving rat on a piece of cheese. "Odd. You're such a sportswoman, I assumed it would. What is it? Heights bother you?"

Damn you, damn you, damn you. How can you be so blind yet always find my sorest spot to rub?

"Well," she shrugged impatiently, "it's irrelevant, anyway, since skiing is only an excuse. Do you want to come or not? I should tell you in advance that I have no intention of paying for your presence. I will go so far and no further to indulge my son's neuroses. You'll be our guest, and I won't make any demands of you, but I won't pay you, either."

"If I say I won't go now, you'll think it's because of that."

"Why should you care what I think?"

"I don't know."

She squinted at me speculatively.

"Of course," I said slowly, "it's very appealing to me in some ways. Even people who live nicely like to get away. I've had a hard year, anyway, between work, and school and . . . a few other things. If I don't accept—" I hesitated, then took a deep breath to push out the words, "it will be because your attitude toward me is so insulting that I can hardly bear it. I know you think I'm a little ridiculous," I went on before she could interrupt, "with my surplus deposit of pride, but when poor people deal with rich people the only thing they have is their pride. You can be amused by it as much as you like, but if I didn't have it, you'd despise me. You talk as though you despise me, anyway, even when you're asking me to be a guest in your house." The words were coming out in a torrent now; its flow gave me immense relief. I couldn't have stopped if I'd wanted to; I wasn't even embarrassed by the tears she must see welling in my eyes. "You'll go so far and no further to indulge your son's neuroses. As though you were opening your house to some disease and warning it at the same time that you'd be wearing a mask. Why should you take so much trouble to insult me? You could have just invited me and said Boris was eager for me to come. Aside from everything else, it makes me ill, the way you talk about what's going on in his mind. Maybe it's just lack of sophistication. I hate to hear children talked about as though they were sick, complex adults. I'm the dumb little servant girl who's to be taken in briefly to satisfy the perverted drives of an eleven-year-old boy. How can I accept your invitation—however much I want to go to the country for a week, however fond I am of Boris?" I was ready to go on and on; it took me a moment to realize that no more words were coming. Slowly I let out my breath into the quiet room. She wasn't smiling, anyway. That was an achievement of sorts. She held out the box of cigarillos, and I took one and lit it. It was the first time I'd let her see me smoke. She walked over to the window and looked out. I reached up a hand to wipe the tears from my eyes and discovered that they were no longer there. She turned from the window and faced me.

"All right, Ruth. My manners have always left something to be desired. Like my looks. Otherwise, part of what you say is true, but part isn't. Now, when all is said and done, you are an employee of mine and I've extended you an invitation to be my guest. If you can forget my manner of extending it and simply remember that it's been extended and that such invitations aren't common, you'll realize that I couldn't possibly despise you. After all, Boris may have wanted you along, but he gets what he wants only when his parents approve of it. Not only do I approve of you, but on the whole I rather like you. Which is more than you can truthfully say to me. I like your looks, I like your style, I like your nerve, I like your brains, and I like what you've done for Boris. You were hired to teach him; nobody said you had to like him or have confidence in him. His feeling that you do both has been a great help to him. One of the reasons I'm not an ideal mother is that I can't have much feeling for anyone I think stupid. Boris's mentality has struck me, since he was very young, as unexceptional. You might bear in mind that I was thinking partly of that when I said you were a substitute mother to him. Blind faith is not my specialty."

She paused to give me a chance to speak, but my mind was in complete turmoil and I couldn't have thought of anything to say at that moment if my life depended on it. She sat down at the big desk, mashed out her cigarillo, reached for the box, changed her mind, and instead picked up the tortoise-shell letter opener, running the fingers of one hand slowly along its edge.

"Now, to get back to the matter at hand. I assume I've made it clear that we would like to have you accompany us. I gather you find the vacation idea appealing. I hope some of your reservations about accepting have been removed. Let's say, therefore, that you've accepted the invitation and we need only mention it again if you find yourself unable to go. Is that satisfactory?"

I nodded.

"Fine." She put down the letter opener. "We leave the day after

Christmas and come back on January first. You need have no concern about clothing, except that it be warm. It wouldn't be a bad idea to buy yourself some long woolen underwear. I can't think of anything else I ought to tell you, but I'll be seeing you before then, anyway."

"All right," I said, feeling drugged. "Thank you. I guess I'd better go now."

"Good night."

"Good night." I turned and walked to the door.

"Ruth?"

I turned. A small tremor ran through me because for the first time since my outburst, that cunning animal smile was back.

"Yes?"

"Every young child, Ruth, goes through a series of painful mental contortions before approaching anything that resembles a sane concept of himself and the world. Until some point in Lotte's third year, for example, she would watch highway signs as we rode past them and ask, when they disappeared, where the signs had gone to. I tried to explain that it was we who'd moved, not the signs, but she held onto the idea that we were the fixed constellation until the day when she could finally bear to realize it wasn't so."

"I don't understand," I said. "I'm sorry. I'm tired."

"If you examine reality a little more objectively than you have been," she said, "you'll stop flattering yourself that I go out of my way to insult you. I am quite the same with you as with any other person I know. If anything, it is *you* who alter in *my* presence."

You couldn't just let me go, could you?

She waited a while to see if I would reply. Then she lit a cigarillo and swung her feet up onto the desk's sideboard.

"Well," she said abruptly, "it doesn't matter. It's just that if it weren't for some of this silly nonsense, I suspect we could be fairly good friends."

I stood in the outside hallway for a while, trying to regain my equilibrium. I took out my purse mirror and examined my face for signs of the misery and confusion within me. I put on some lipstick, put away the mirror, and rang for the elevator. Downstairs, I headed automatically for the El. I was sitting on my train before I realized that if I stayed with the Stamms through January first, I wouldn't be with David on New Year's Eve. Not that we ever did anything grand, but we'd been together for every one since I was twelve or thirteen. There was never any formality; he never actually asked me in advance to go out with him that night. It was like the other times we went out, except that instead of mentioning that he had the movie pass, he would list the various parties that would be given.

"Art Lubow's throwing a party," he'd say, "but that means bringing a bottle. We *should* bring one to Mickey's, but we won't get kicked out if we don't."

And so on, until by a process of elimination he had selected the place where we could have the most fun at the least expense.

Maybe I could go up with the Stamms and take the bus home a day early.

Suddenly it struck me as funny that I was planning this way. Helen Stamm had said, "We'll assume," and I'd nodded and assumed. I closed my eyes. It was a relief, though, to be spared the necessity of picking over and sorting the things she'd said. She wanted me to come and would assume that I was coming. Fine. I was too tired to think about it, much less to arrive at a decision. I couldn't remember, as a matter of fact, ever having been more tired. My eyes would not stay open, and my body generally felt as though it had been put through the mangle of a washing machine.

"I might dispute his wisdom in choosing you for a mother figure, but I readily concede your worthiness as a pin-up subject. . . . What is it? Heights bother you? . . . You flatter yourself. It's you who move, not the sign . . ."

The conductor shook me awake at the last stop. I walked up several cars and stood during the ride back. I had a bad headache which I thought might be from hunger. But it hadn't gone away by the time I finished dinner. Martin was at Madison Square Garden, watching City play Missouri; my father was at the store. My mother, who'd seen very little of me since my return in August, was in the mood for conversation. My father was angry with her because he'd found out she had given Martin the money to take Rhoda to the game. She had tried to explain how important it was to Martin, and my father had stormed out of the house. She would like to discuss that with me, although if there were something else on my mind, she would love to hear about that, too. But I had a very strong desire not to talk about Helen Stamm, who had pushed everything else out of my head.

David came down while I was in my room after dinner, changing into slacks and a sweater.

"Hey," he called, "picture goes on in a few minutes." I put on makeup most scrupulously, feeling that at last my face showed signs of age and exhaustion.

"Jesus," he said, the moment I walked into the kitchen, "who put *you* through a meat grinder?"

My mother looked from him to me, then back to him. "What's the matter?" she asked. "Ruthie doesn't look good?"

"Oh," he said quickly, "she looks fine. Just different. Must be the haircut."

"Haircut? She didn't have—" and then she realized he was kidding and gave him a playful push.

I got my coat and we went downstairs. The night was so clear and beautiful that it seemed a crime to go into a movie. But the park would be cold, and I was too tired to walk for long.

"What's playing?" I asked as we walked up Second Avenue.

"I dunno," he said, putting an arm around me.

"But you know when it goes on."

"I don't, actually. As a matter of fact, I don't even have the pass."

"David. I'm too tired to be teased. Tell me what we're doing."

"Well," he said slowly, "there are several choices. If you're tired we don't want to walk much. Let's see. What doesn't take much walking? We could do something desperate, like going to a pay movie. We could even pay to go into the Academy of Music, strange as it would feel." He paused so I could interrupt but I was determined to wait out the punch line. "On the other hand, you probably wouldn't want to do that because we might run into my parents there and then we'd have to be polite and sit with them and we wouldn't be able to—"

I stopped walking as the words hit me.

"Did I say something?"

I snorted. "Oh, no. Nothing at all. Only I thought they gave up movies when Roosevelt died."

"You exaggerate. They went once last summer. I remember distinctly because it was a hot night and—"

"Oh, cut it out," I said, not permitting myself a laugh. "Tell me what happened."

"Well," he said, his manner terribly serious as we began walking again, "as you know, my mother is reluctant to leave me alone in the apartment at night. Weak and undernourished as I am, she fears that in her absence any sinister creature could break in, overpower me and— uh—make off with the—uh—family jewels."

I had to laugh this time. "All right, but what happened?"

"Hard to say. Apparently she wanted to get out, anyway, after having been sick in bed for a couple of weeks. The conflict between maternal love and self-interest was causing her a great deal of anguish. I tell you, Ruth, it would have wrung your heart to see her—"

"All right, all right. But *what happened?*"

"Nothing actually happened. She just somehow seemed to get the impression that we were going to the Garden with Martin and to a team party afterward."

"My goodness," I murmured, "where do parents come up with their funny ideas?"

"Ours not to reason why," he said. "Ours but to kill ten or fifteen minutes." He steered me off Second at the next corner, and we walked up Tenth Street, past St. Mark's-in-the-Bouwerie.

"It's cold."

"We could try your old hideout," he teased.

"They wouldn't let you in. You look too Jewish."

"Can't I just say I'm with you?"

"Oh, you're so funny," I said, walking a little more quickly.

St. Mark's had once been a frequent temporary refuge of mine. When my father was yelling at Martin for playing hookey; or when he'd returned, morosely drunk, from one of his weekends, and was berating my mother for not asking where he'd been; or when it turned out that graduation or no graduation, there was no money for a white dress, I would run out of the house and up to St. Mark's, slowing to a walk before I reached it lest some church authority see me running and recognize me as a hasty disreputable child who didn't belong there. Not that I'd ever been questioned. Often I was alone during the whole time I was there; sometimes a minister would glide quietly down the aisle past where I sat on one of the long hard benches, waiting out my trouble.

It wasn't a godly place to me; I don't think I'd ever seriously considered the possibility of a God. There wasn't even a mystical feeling; it was too austere and clean for mysticism. Mysticism was for the synagogue, where I'd gone once or twice with my uncle Daniel and his wife and my mother, before my father put a stop to what he called my mother's hypocrisy. A gloomy place where old women with crow's-nest hair, or else hair so fine that their heads were half bald, and old men in yamilkes who smelled as though they had yet to discover running water in the New World, rocked with bowed heads and invoked God, not even hoping to achieve peace, but only to achieve virtue by sanctifying their discontent. The plaintive monotony of their prayers differing from the plaintive monotony of their everyday conversation only in that they spoke Hebrew instead of Yiddish or Yiddish-carved-and-basted English.

This place, St. Mark's, was peaceful, with its angel pointing up to heaven, his gentle stone words asking, *Why seek ye the living among the dead? He is not here, but is risen. . . . Suffer little children to come unto me* . . . Many of the engravings I read each time I came. I liked best the ones about people. *Jacob S. Herrick. He died, having the testimony of a good conscience; in the communion of the Catholic Church; in the confidence of a certain faith; in the comfort of a reasonable religious and high hope; in favor with God and in perfect charity with the world.* It never occurred to me that, not believing in God, I should doubt those words. Nor did I doubt that *Charles Henry Baldwin, Rear Admiral, United States Navy, Born September 3rd, 1822, Died November 17th, 1888* was *Safe in Port.* Why should I? No demand had been made upon my belief.

I'd been fourteen the last time I went into St. Mark's. Mrs. Landau had seen me coming out. She'd been in the kitchen with my mother when I reached home.

So, Rose, so? Ask her if it isn't true. Ask your little shiksa.

Ruthie, (my mother, not looking at me) *it's true?*

For God's sake, Mama, you act as if she caught me in a whorehouse!

Aaiii! (Mrs. Landau, clutching her great breasts as though I'd tried to take a slice from them) *You should excuse me, Rose. I pity you, but I couldn't stay in this house.*

You don't belong in this house, you fat ugly pig! (screaming at the top of my lungs)

Ruthie! (my mother, near tears, as Mrs. Landau stands rooted to the floor in shock)

What are you waiting for? (still screaming, my body shaking with rage) *Why don't you get out of here? Go on back up to your pickle factory!*

Ruthie-darling-stop-I-can't-stand-such-talk! (as Mrs. Landau jerks to life and walks out) *Where did you get such talk?*

From David! (screaming it as the door slams shut so she will hear me) *I got it all from David!*

My mother had wept. My father had chortled and made me repeat the story. And clever David. He'd acted in such an ordinary way that I couldn't be sure he knew. Until months later, when I'd asked him to take me to some girl's party.

My mother (fresh sixteen-year-old grin) *doesn't want me to go out with gentile girls.*

You think you're so funny. And of course you always do what your mother wants you to do.

Not always. But my mother says I'll get warts from going out with gentile girls.

I looked up at him and smiled. We were at Third Avenue and he steered me around the corner and back downtown.

"What's so funny?"

"I don't know. I was thinking of the St. Mark's business."

"Since when did anything as funny as that make you laugh?"

"Since now, I suppose."

We passed a liquor store and he stopped and dug into his pockets.

"This calls for a celebration," he said, triumphantly pulling out a single crumpled dollar bill. He dashed into the store and came out two minutes later with an unwrapped bottle of white wine, which he put into his coat pocket. Happily we hurried down Third Avenue, turning onto St. Marks Place with caution and walking close to the buildings so we could spot people before they saw us. But we ran into no one.

The lights were out in the Landau apartment. We tiptoed up the steps past my apartment with extraordinary care and giggled like children as we walked up the second flight to his place.

"Won't you come into my parlor?" He opened the second lock and pushed open the door.

"All right," I said, sweeping past him into the dark kitchen. "But I can't stay more than a few days. I have a reputation to maintain."

He unlocked the door and switched on the kitchen light, then immediately switched it off. "What the hell," he said softly. "Why tempt fate?"

We took off our coats in the darkness; I heard the bottle being set down someplace before we dropped the coats on the floor in an excess of bravado.

"Where are you?" I whispered—then giggled at having whispered.

"Just a second. I'm looking for a candle."

I heard clattering noises at the cupboard, then a small match flame flickered and I saw him melting the wax on a sabbath candle to make it stick to a saucer. He took two empty *yartzheit*-candle glasses from the cupboard and at his instruction, I picked up the bottle of wine. I started to follow him into his room but then, on impulse, turned and moved away from him, banging a thigh on the edge of the kitchen table, then moving through the arch into his parents' bedroom.

"What the hell are you doing?" he called.

"I've gone wild with power!" I shouted back, groping for the light cord and pulling it. "Do you realize how long it is since I've seen this room? Since I've been in this house, for that matter, except for . . ." I trailed off because I didn't know how to say "except for the night I came up begging for help."

"If you like the house so damn much, you shouldn't have arranged to get banished from it." He disappeared into his room. I turned to look at the room I was in; there had been no appreciable change since I was fourteen years old. Mustard-color walls; the big high bed that nearly filled the room, magnificent false testimony to the sexuality of its occupants; the pictures hanging on the wall above the bed, subtly giving the lie to that testimony. Bertha Landau's Bedroom Hall of Fame. Newspaper photographs, mostly, with one or two mail-this-coupon-and-ten-cents glossy photos: Franklin Roosevelt, Paul Muni, Eddie Cantor, Albert Einstein, Bernard Baruch, Irving Berlin, Louis Brandeis, David Ben-Gurion, Samuel Goldwyn. They were arranged in a pyramid whose top had once been formed by the full-color photo of Roosevelt; Roosevelt's picture now shared that elevated station with a large tinted photo-portrait of David Marcus in full regalia as General of the Israeli Army. I moved closer to read the portrait's caption, printed in Hebraic-style letters between an American and an Israeli flag: *David "Mickey" Marcus, 1902–1948. He traversed continents to die for the Jewish People.*

Clutching the wine, I whirled around and plopped down happily on the bed. David was watching me from the doorway.

"I hope your backside is clean."

"My soul is, anyhow." But I felt like a child caught doing something naughty. I stretched out luxuriously to disprove my guilt. He came over and took the wine.

"Come on. The glasses are in my bedroom." He pulled the cord.

"Hey! I can't see!"

His hand grabbed mine and pulled.

"This is more comfortable than your bed," I said petulantly.

"You've never tried my bed."

"You've never tried this one. Come here for just a second, okay?" I pulled away and moved to the other side of the bed. "Hey, this side's even better. It's *softer*. How come?"

"There's a board under half of it," he said irritably. "She has a bad back, and you know it."

Suddenly I was afraid of ruining the night.

"Don't be mad at me, David. I'll be good." I got up quickly and followed him into his room, groping in the darkness. On his desk, the candle burned with a gentle steady light. He opened the bottle and filled our glasses. I sat on the bed, my back against the wall. He handed me a glass and stretched out next to me, leaning on his elbow. The wine wasn't cold enough, but it seemed to me unbelievably good. I sipped it very slowly and each time was reluctant to swallow. He didn't refill the glasses right away; we were both afraid the wine would go too quickly.

"My God," I said, "what a crazy day this has been."

"What happened?"

"Oh, something stupid. I don't even want to talk about it."

"You looked like hell."

"Do I still? Because if I do, I'll blow out the candle so you won't have to look at me. I don't want you to suffer."

"Move down where I can see you. I'll let you know."

I slid down so that I was lying beside him, my head on his pillow.

"Better," he said, examining my face critically. "Maybe it's the dim light."

"Thanks."

"What am I supposed to say?"

"Oh, something nice. Something that'll make me feel good. I was put in my place so beautifully today that it'll be weeks before you have to worry about giving me a swelled head."

"Okay." Very matter of fact. He reached past me to get the wine from his night table, drank a little from the bottle, put it back. "I love to look at you. Before I ever knew what hot pants were I used to love to look at you."

I watched him in wonder, trying to find some trace of irony in his expression. There was none.

"When I was twelve years old you and Martin ganged up on me one day and we had a pretty bad brawl. I came upstairs raging against the two of you. My mother said you were a cheap ugly little brat and I should stay away from you. That calmed me down, for some reason. I said maybe you were mean but you weren't ugly; she said anyone who was mean was ugly. I got terribly logical and tried to explain to her in a rational manner why that wasn't true. She didn't talk to me for two days." He slipped a hand under my sweater and absently caressed the skin just above the waistband of my slacks. "I don't know what the hell it is about your face, Ruth. I don't know why the imperfections work. I don't know why a small bump in the nose should improve anyone's looks."

I touched his nose and ran a finger along it, as though I were testing something he'd said about himself. Then I touched his lips, his chin, his neck. Then he moved on top of me, almost his full weight resting on my body, one of his legs strong between mine. And kissed me.

It may not have been chance that that terrible year should have held within it that night, when I was more happy than I had ever been. We made love, we talked, we drank the wine. I found myself telling him about Helen Stamm, although an hour or two before I'd been sure I would rather die than have him know a word of our talk. He rewarded me by kidding me about some parts of it and being sympathetic about others, instead of teasing me unmercifully about the whole business. I told him that at the moment I didn't much feel like going to the lake. He said he'd be working, there wasn't much fun around home, and my boss would probably be glad to give me the week off. So I should go but be home by New Year's Eve. I'd been afraid he wouldn't ask me to do that but would just say I should do as I pleased.

"I have a confession to make," I said. "I never thought I could tell you—"

"Hey, hey," he stopped me, laughing. "What, do I look like your friendly neighborhood priest or something?"

"I can't see you."

"Do I sound like him? Do I feel like him?" He rubbed my belly, caressed my breasts. I drew his head to me to kiss him. He let me kiss him but then sat up on the bed. "Jesus, I'd better check the time."

"If I had a time machine," I said, "this is where I'd jam it."

"If you jammed your time machine," he said, "you'd go out of your head with boredom."

I didn't answer, but I wasn't at all sure that he was right. He got out of bed and made his way around to the desk, where he lit the candle again. He went into the kitchen to check the clock and came back to say it was late. But we'd both known that it must be. If the time had seemed short, that would be because each second had been crammed with pleasure, and fearful anticipation of pleasure's end. We got dressed and straightened up the room. He held the candle while I washed and dried out glasses and put them back in the cupboard. He stuck the empty wine bottle back in his coat pocket and just before we left, went back into his parents' room, turned on the light and looked around. I could hear the soft sounds of the spread and pillows being whacked into shape. I smiled to myself. Outside the door, he blew out the candle, separated it from the saucer, scraped the remaining wax off the saucer, and put both behind the garbage can outside the door.

"I'll wash it off later."

I nodded. He put his arm around me and we pressed together to get down the narrow staircase without separating. At the landing we walked quickly on our toes, then started down the second flight, stopping abruptly because Martin was sitting on the bottom step, doubled over as though he were in pain. He didn't turn around as we continued down. Single-file, we edged past him to the landing. He didn't look up.

"Hey," I said softly.

He looked up. His face was dead.

"What's doing?"

He shrugged.

"Where's Rhoda?"

"At the party."

"How come *you're* not?"

"Because we lost," he said bitterly. "And it seems to me it's a god-damn stupid thing to have a celebration for losing."

"Lost?" David and I repeated. It had been the year when City College was never again going to lose a basketball game.

"Lost. You heard me. Fifty-four to thirty-seven."

David whistled.

"What happened?" I asked.

"What difference does it make what happened?"

"We should get out of here," David murmured to me, and I suddenly remembered his parents.

"Come," I said, tugging at Martin's coat. "Walk with us a little." He let me pull him to his feet. We left the house and began walking downtown on Second.

"Now," I said to Martin, "if someone's having a party anyway, and if Rhoda wanted to go, why shouldn't you go?"

"Because it's stupid," he said savagely. "Do you do things you know are stupid?"

"What's stupid about trying to have a good time?"

"Have a good time, have a good time. I'm sick of that line. You and Rhoda must be reading the same book."

We'd reached Sixth Street, where we couldn't be seen from our own block. David and I stood there indecisively. I knew I should tell my brother to come along with us, but the night had been too good to end that way.

"Where're you going?" he asked.

"I don't know," I said. "No place in particular."

He waited. But I couldn't ask. Even if I didn't mind having him along, David would. It would almost be a signal to renew hostilities.

"Wait for me upstairs," I said, my eyes appealing to him to understand. "I won't be long." He looked down at the sidewalk. I leaned forward and kissed his cheek. "I'm sorry," I whispered. "Wait for me. We can talk."

He wheeled abruptly and walked away from us.

"Hey, kiddo?" David called. Martin turned. "If you should happen to run into my folks, we were at the Garden with you and we're still at the party."

Martin looked at him blankly for a moment, then shrugged and turned back up Second Avenue.

We did take a long time, and I was full of guilt when I finally came into the house. But Martin wasn't there. I left on the bedroom light, hoping it would keep me up, but it didn't work. I awakened the next morning with the light still on. Martin's bed hadn't been touched. I spent the day doing homework. My father was sleeping. Periodically my mother asked where Martin could be and I replied that he could take care of himself, he was a man now, not a boy. I didn't believe myself on either count. In the afternoon I took a walk up Second, detouring several times to go past Jerry Glickman's house and a few other places where I thought Martin might be. I finally found him sitting on the top landing of the stoop of Vivian Mandel's house. He was holding his hands upright in front of him; Vivian was earnestly playing cat's cradle with the complex of string that wound around his fingers. She giggled when she saw me.

"Hey, Ruthie," Martin called. "How's tricks?"

"Tricky."

"Oh-ho." He turned to Vivian. "Wit runs amok in our family."

Vivian giggled. He leaned forward and loudly kissed her nose.

"Martin, should I tell Mama I saw you? She's worried."

"Sure, sure. Tell them you saw me, tell them I'm just—how does that song go? I forgot."

Vivian giggled.

I looked at her for the first time. A cheap little *curva* of the sort that Mrs. Landau swore could be found only in the Catholic schools, she had a vacantly pretty face, slim legs, and breasts that were a neighborhood legend by virtue of their disproportionate size, their unbelievable tilt, and the inordinate pride which their owner took in them. I'd never thought twice about Vivian, much less troubled to dislike her, and it was a surprise to me now to see a series of intense feelings distorting her face as she looked at me—fear, defiance, hatred—all made ludicrous by that silly nervous giggle.

"Can I talk to you down here for a minute?" I asked Martin.

"Big sister," he said, an imitation of her giggle escaping him, "anything you wanna say you can say in front of my friend here, big sister."

"I'd just like to know if you'll be home tonight."

"Well, I'd like to, big sister, but you see, I'm—uh—" he held up his string-cradled hands, "—being kept prisoner here by a kindly widow and her charming daughter."

Vivian giggled.

"It's not that I don't want to escape," he ran his hands wildly through the tangled string, "but when I struggle with my bonds, they get tighter."

I stood silently for a moment, trying to make up my mind to walk away.

"Don't worry," Vivian said, suddenly brave. "We won't eat him up."

"Oh," he said to her in mock indignation, "but you promised!"

She was torn between real amusement and false pride. In an attempt to serve both, she laughed and told him he was terrible. The result was so coyly sluttish that even Martin looked repelled.

"Look, Ruth," he said, "just tell them I'll be there sooner or later, huh? Tell them I'm alive, not that they really worry, and I'm getting tender loving care."

"Better than home, prob'ly," Vivian stuck in.

"If you can't keep quiet," I said, "why don't you go upstairs and polish your tits?"

"Well!" Outrage jolted her to her feet. Martin was choking back a laugh, but she wasn't looking at him. "I never heard such language in my whole life!"

"I'm sure."

"Especially from someone thinks she's the fanciest goddamn piece of business in the neighborhood!"

"All right, honey." Martin got to his feet and pulled the string from his fingers. "Let's call it a day."

"You don't care!" she screeched at him. "She could say any filthy thing she wants and just because she's your fancy sister it sounds like the Gettigsburg *Add*ress or something!"

"She's jealous, Vivian. Vivvie." He dropped the string on the stoop. "She's flat-chested." He put his arms around her and pressed the back of her head so that her face was against his coat. "Besides," he went on, winking broadly at me, "when I'm not home there's nobody to keep her feet warm."

She pulled away and looked up at him, trying to decide if he was kidding her.

"Didn't you know me and Ruthie sleep in the same bed?" he asked. "Jeez, I thought everyone knew. As a matter of fact, every once in a while I'm walking down the street, I get this funny feeling people're saying, 'There goes that guy sleeps in the same bed with his sister!'"

I began walking away from them.

"They don't realize that it's all perfectly okay," he shouted after me, "because she sleeps with her head at the head of the bed and I sleep with my head at the foot!"

I didn't tell my parents I'd seen him. My father was up and eating his early dinner with my mother. She wanted to stop to prepare a plate for me but I wasn't hungry. My father was having sherry with his meal; I brought over a glass and asked for some.

"All of a sudden she's a *shikker*?" my father asked the bottle.

I laughed. "Why so flattering, Papa? Not just a *shikker*, a hopeless lush. How could you not have noticed, all these years I've been swilling the lousy stuff?"

"I don't like your language, Ruthie."

"Sorry." I slumped deeply in the chair and closed my eyes. "I meant to say the Gettisburg Address." I finished the glass of sherry and went into the bedroom to do homework, but I fell asleep over Vergil and my Latin dictionary, and didn't wake up until nine o'clock. My mother had turned off the light. I brought my books into the kitchen, where she was darning her good black dress, also known as her good dress, her black dress, or simply the dress.

"My God, Mama," I said, "I bet you don't have a square inch of plain material left on that thing."

She fondled the material. "It holds up, this dress."

"Listen," I said in a burst of enthusiasm, "let me buy you a new one."

"Don't be foolish."

"I'm not being foolish. I'm making plenty of money. I'm rich. You don't know how much I have in the bank. We'll go to Klein's next week and get a new one. Not expensive, just nice."

"Please," she said. "Don't upset me with such talk."

So there it was again. Don't upset me with talk of a nice apartment, a new dress. Why had I bothered trying?

"I'm getting hungry," I said. "Can I have some dinner now?"

She brought my food and I forced my attention back to the *Aeneid*. Martin burst in exuberantly at about ten-thirty, kissed us each on the cheek, hummed as he went into his room, undressed and came back into the kitchen, a towel around him, to shower.

"Where were you, Martin?" my mother asked when he came out.

He looked at me quickly then grinned. "Vivian Mandel's."

"Oh? You're not seeing the other one any more?"

"Rhoda? Sure I'm seeing Rhoda. As a matter of fact, I have to see Rhoda tomorrow and straighten out a couple of things." His face had clouded but then suddenly he was exuberant again. "You know, I've been very stupid? Just because she's different than the girls I've known —more intelligent and everything—I've been treating her differently, like she was some kind of princess or something. How could I be so dumb? Women love to be pushed around, no matter how smart they are. No woman loves a man she can bully."

He went on like that for a while, spouting in bright artificial tones his revised ideas on life and love. He never waited for corroboration of his statements or answers to his questions. My mother and I glanced at each other once and then, by common consent, kept our eyes on our work. I had an almost unbearable sense of disaster. I kept telling myself that if Martin provoked Rhoda to a complete break, it would be more good than bad. I reminded myself of his youth and the fact that people in general, not just young ones, recover from wounds they think will never heal. Still, I could not make myself feel better. The thing was, Martin wasn't changing as he grew older, changing or modifying. With each year his angry times became more violent, his happy times more feverish, his withdrawals more complete, until it sometimes seemed he would burn himself up before he reached the point of diminishing intensity.

"Oh, what's the use?" he said suddenly. "Nobody's listening. I'm trying to give you the benefit of my extensive experience with women, and you can't concentrate long enough to hear one full sentence." He went into his room. We could hear him undressing and getting into bed. "Good night, you two addle-pated females."

"Good night."

I closed my books and pushed them away from me.

"He never has any homework," my mother whispered to me.

I shrugged.

"You tell me not to worry but how could I not worry? Could he get through school with no homework? What's going to happen, Ruthie? How will he get through school?"

"I don't know, Mama," I said. "Maybe he'll straighten out soon."

"You think so?" She was pathetically eager to believe me.

"Why not? Everyone grows up sooner or later." I stood up and collected my books. She stood up and motioned that I should bend down so she could whisper in my ear.

"Ruthie," she whispered, "talk to him, he shouldn't make her pregnant, Vivian or the other one."

I was so surprised at this bit of realism from her that I wasn't sure I'd heard correctly and I made her repeat it.

"I can't tell him that, Mama."

"Ssshh. Whisper."

"I can't say it to him any more than you can," I whispered.

"Sure you could." She became very agitated, shaking her hands in frustration at having to whisper. "You're the only one he listens to."

"Not that much, any more."

"Listen to me, Ruthie." She grabbed my arms. "He's a good boy. You and your father think I only know from food or a thread and a needle, but I see people, too." Her fingernails were digging into my arms and hurting me. "She'll come to him pregnant, he won't say to go prove it, he'll marry her."

"Mama," I said, trying unsuccessfully to free myself from her grasp, "you're getting so excited and for all you know, there's nothing to worry about. You have no reason to think there *is* anything to worry about."

"She'll have tears in her eyes and he'll marry her," said my mother, her eyes brimming with tears, "and he'll hate her for the rest of her life." The tears came in full force now. Slowly her hands unclenched until my arms were free. I looked down at one arm. Four deep-red crescents were etched in it. My mother sank onto one of the wooden chairs, folded her arms on the table, and let her head rest upon them. I stood looking down at her for a while, still clutching my Latin books. Then I kissed the top of her head and went to my room.

When I came home from Arlou the next night my mother told me that Martin had come home and gone directly into the bedroom to study, without eating dinner and without saying a word to anyone. I found him lying on his bed, his head propped against both our pillows, a textbook propped up by his legs. He pretended to be so deeply immersed that he didn't notice me, but I was sure he wasn't reading. He was unnaturally still and never turned a page, even when I spied on him while changing in the closet.

He was home more than usual during the next few days but never spoke to any of us unless he was asked a question. Then his answers were polite and perfunctory. At the end of the week I ran into Jerry Glickman, who asked what was wrong with Martin.

"He hasn't been in school?"

"Whoops." He was embarrassed. "Look, he might have been. I just haven't seen him."

"Do you always see him when he's there?"

"Look, Ruth, I—"

"Please, Jerry. It's important."

He sighed. "Yeah, just about."

"Thanks." I walked away.

"Hey, Ruth?" he called. "Leave me out of it, huh?"

I assured him I would, and said goodbye. I racked my brain for something to say to Martin and ended up by realizing I could say nothing. It hadn't occurred to me that trouble with Rhoda would keep him from school. What could I say? If he said nothing to me, how could I talk to him at all?

Then again, why couldn't I? I'd talked to him through his shell before. There'd been a time when I was the only one who could.

There goes that guy who sleeps in the bed with his sister.

Why couldn't I talk to him now?

It's okay because she sleeps with her head at the head of the bed and I sleep with my head at the foot.

That was it. He had blown up at me in past times but this one was something different. Vicious mockery in front of a cheap little slut we both despised. This was something new. And unbelievable. So unbelievable that I'd managed not to think about it since Sunday. Except that it had made me afraid of him.

Not me, Martin. That was what I would say. *Hate anyone else you want to hate.*

Yet when I reached home it seemed absurd to have thought in terms of hatred. He was lying in bed again with a textbook. There was no air of defiance about him, or even sulkiness. There was only the emptiness of a puppet between shows.

He even had my father puzzled with his refusal to respond to goading.

"Ah!" my father said upon hearing where Martin had been until Sunday, "Vivian Mandel. You finally found a girl smart enough to keep up with you."

Martin looked at him as though the sound track had never been turned on.

It all had the ironic effect of making my father feel for Martin for the first time in nineteen years.

"Look, Martin," he said during the second week (when I was washing dishes and he thought I couldn't hear him), "you gotta talk to someone. A man. A woman's no good to talk to." Pause. "I'll make a bargain with you, Martin. Tell me what's on your mind. If I could help, I'll help. If not, I'll leave you alone. And when you're feeling better, you could be free to hate my guts again."

"Abe!" said my mother. But Martin had no visible reaction.

On Friday before the last week of school in December, I called Rhoda. I'd fought the idea, knowing Martin would be furious if he found out, but finally I had to know. Her father answered and told me she wasn't home. He asked for my name and reluctantly I gave it to him.

"Oh, yes. Hello, Ruth. Was it about your brother?"

"Yes. Do you know when she'll be in?"

"Not exactly. But maybe I can help."

"I doubt it," I said, becoming irritated.

"Well, let me put it this way, Ruth," he said, his tone no less pleasant, "I'd rather you didn't talk to Rhoda. Breaking completely with Martin wasn't an easy thing for her to do. She did it partly on our advice. I don't think that reopening the whole question would do anybody—"

"I did not call," I interrupted angrily, "to beg her to see him. I just wanted to know what happened. He's been very . . . upset," I ended lamely, for want of a better word.

"Of course," the smooth voice said. "I understand that. Martin is a very unhappy boy. The point is, he was an unhappy boy long before he met Rhoda. This idea of his—getting married and starting a new life in Canada—he thinks he would be happy if she consented to do that. But it's an adolescent fantasy. Certainly not worthy of a young man who's ready for the responsibility of marriage."

I stared dully at the mouthpiece, unable to think of anything I could say to stop that calm easy flow of words.

"Ruth, are you still with me?"

"I'm here."

"May I offer some advice? Rhoda gave Martin the same advice, but he chose to—anyway, perhaps you could react a little more objectively."

"Go ahead."

"All right. We feel that your brother needs professional help. Now, we realize that the cost of this sort of thing is—"

"What do you mean by professional help? A psychiatrist?"

"Something of the sort."

"You think he's some kind of nut? You do. I can tell by the way you talk about him."

"Nut is a very poor word to use. It's meaningless. Plenty of people—"

"I know," I interrupted furiously. "Plenty of people are nuts. Well, did it ever occur to you that Martin's troubles aren't just in his head? He's got plenty to be unhappy about. You don't know anything about him or his life."

He didn't answer me.

"Rhoda gave him that advice, you say? Well, I'll tell you, if I asked a girl to marry me and she told me to see a psychiatrist, I'd be pretty unhappy. I think I'd be nuts to be *happy*, don't you?"

"I'm sorry," he said after a moment. "I don't think we understand each other."

"Oh, we understand each other, all right," I said bitterly. And hung up. And walked out of the phone booth. And remembered only at that moment that in spite of the way he sounded, Rhoda's father was the one who was colored.

The next day I told Mrs. Stamm I couldn't go up to the lake. I said I wouldn't like her to think it had anything to do with our talk. When she said she hoped nothing was wrong, I said that my brother had been brooding about a girl and was so depressed that I was afraid to leave him. She said that if I would like to bring him along, I was welcome to do so. In astonishment, I thanked her and said that if I could get him to go, it might be just what he needed.

"Martin," I said that night, "would you like to get away from here for a week?"

He put down his textbook and looked up at the ceiling.

"The Stamms have invited us both up for Christmas vacation. I know you're not crazy about her, but it'll be good to get away and there's plenty to do up there. Skiing, ice-skating, sledding, all that stuff. It should be great. Evenings around the fire."

No response.

I took a deep breath. "I don't want to nag you, Martin. But I have to be able to tell the Stamms soon. Do you think you'll want to go?"

"Sure," he said, still looking at the ceiling. "Why not?"

I kissed his forehead. He brushed me away as though I were a fly, but he was a little better during the following week. He wasn't exactly a member of the family, but he was more like a human being than the husk of one that he had been. My mother was delighted when I told her. The fresh air and exercise, she said, would restore Martin to his old self. My father was less enthusiastic. He didn't actually say we should not go; he simply made it clear, by one or two waspish observations about the charity of rich people, that he couldn't understand why we wanted to. I vaguely felt it was the fact of our both going that bothered him. This was no longer a little adventure for me; it was a conspiracy to desert him.

But as we drove up to Lake Quanthog the following week, I began to feel the vacation would be well worth my father's displeasure. If I'd been the least bit uneasy about Martin's behavior, I needn't have been. He'd been polite and friendly from the time we'd met the Stamms in front of their house. It was all right if he hadn't come entirely out of his shell; neither was he keyed up in the brightly frightening way that I'd often seen. He was quiet, but his quietness seemed to pass, in Lotte's eyes, for rugged masculinity, and she was a great deal more friendly and at ease with him than she had ever been with me. The three of us sat in the back, while Boris sat between his parents in the front. The talk got around to skiing, eventually, and was still there when I fell asleep.

As a matter of fact, we—or rather, they—talked about little else during the next few days. In the morning there was talk about the weather for skiing; later there were the preparations; and much later, the talk of how each one had done that day. After the first time I didn't even go along. Boris was disappointed at my refusal to even try skis, but I gave him a great deal of attention when he was around, and after a while he seemed to rather like the idea of returning with the other triumphant warriors to find me waiting by the fire, eager for their tales of glory.

They left at ten or eleven each morning, and were home between four and five, having had lunch at The Lodge at Mount Mantinoc. Meanwhile, I had the house to myself. I spent at least two hours each day cramming the schoolwork I'd missed because of my job. Then I would give myself over to a walk through the beautiful snow-covered woods, or to ice-skating practice (using the skates Lotte had outgrown the year before) at the edge of the lake, which was frozen clear through. Or to just rambling around the house, having pleasant day-dreams in which it had been bequeathed to David and me, and I was showing him around the various rooms, being softly witty. I was half-pleased, half-resentful when Martin and the others trooped in, late in the afternoon, chattering excitedly about the day.

On the first day at the slope, when I'd accompanied them, Martin's natural ability on skis had been the talk of everyone around.

"I have never in all my years," said the handsome blond instructor, "seen such an affinity for the sport."

"Anything my brother does, he does well," I said proudly.

On the second day they came home to tell me that the instructor had refused to take money for Martin's time, saying it was a privilege to teach him.

On the third afternoon they burst in with the news that Martin had gone down the intermediate trail, which it took most people weeks or months to try.

"He's a little reckless," Helen Stamm said. "But he's good."

"For heaven's sake, be careful," I said, rumpling his hair. "I'll be held personally responsible if you get so much as one small bruise on your precious body."

"Yes," Lotte said softly. "You really should make him be more careful, Ruth."

The appeal startled me, not only by its earnestness but because it was the first time she'd ever asked the smallest thing of me.

"Martin?"

"Oh, no," he groaned, looking from me to Lotte. "See what you've done, *Latke*? You pressed the Mother Button. It's open-school night at P.S. Naught, and Mother Ruth has been called in for a conference."

"I think," Walter Stamm said, "that your sister is only trying to—"

"D'y'know, Boris," Martin said, cutting him off, "from the time I started school my mother always sent Ruthie to my teachers on open-school days to get a message about me? She was ashamed of her clothes. Or her English. Or something. What do you think of that? How'd you like to have *Latke*, here, go in and talk to your teachers on open-school day?"

Boris was open-mouthed at the idea. Walter Stamm and I were embarrassed. Helen Stamm was amused. Lotte was still staring at Martin as though he were the first piece of male flesh she'd ever seen.

That night she and Martin walked the three miles into town to see a movie, although her mother had offered to give them a lift. The rest of us watched television.

On the fifth afternoon Helen Stamm came in first, alone, to tell me that Martin was dead.

I didn't cry. I was frozen in time, frozen at the moment Helen Stamm told me I'd better sit down and something inside of me had said, *Martin is dead.* I sat down.

"Martin has had a very bad accident, Ruth. Look, I would drag this out and circle around it if I thought it would do a damn bit of good, but I don't."

I nodded. My mouth was very dry.

"He's dead."

"You're sure?"

"Yes."

"Sometimes," I said, "they think people are dead and it turns out they're badly hurt but not really dead, they've got some pulse left."

"I'm sorry," she said. "There's no chance of that."

"I see."

"Should I leave you alone for a bit?"

"I don't know. Where's Martin?"

"At the lodge. Walter stayed there."

"Should I go see him?"

"I don't think so." She paused. "He looks pretty bad."

"What do you mean?" I was startled for the first time.

"It was a very ugly accident. He went into a tree."

"A tree?"

She nodded. "Would you like a cigarette?"

"Yes. Please."

She lit two and handed one to me.

"It was a crazy business, Ruth. It never should have happened. Everything about it was wrong. He'd been pleading with Randy to try the advanced trail, and Randy said it was ridiculous since he'd done the mid-slope for the first time just two days before. He was doing beautifully on it, of course. But still, the top of the slope is another matter." She shook her head. "Martin couldn't stand it. Each time he came up he'd try to change Randy's mind. Finally Randy asked me to talk to him. He told me there was every chance Martin could make the slope but he simply couldn't take the responsibility of permitting it. I said I thought he was absolutely right. The next time Martin came up, I said that if he didn't make the advanced this week, he was welcome to come along any weekend that we drive up, and try it then."

"That was very kind," I said.

"I'm not telling you about it," she said quickly, "in order to ingratiate myself with you. I'm telling you because it's part of what you have to know to see the insanity of the whole thing."

I was vaguely aware that Boris and Lotte were walking through the hallway and then up the stairs, to the accompaniment of loud snuffling.

I smiled absently. "Why is it so important that I see it?"

She shrugged. "I don't know. It's always been a passion with me that people see as much of the truth as they can."

"Oh, yes," I said. "Of course. Now I understand."

"Would you rather I didn't go on?"

"Yes, I would. I mean, no, I wouldn't. I would rather you *did* go on. There isn't much more, is there?"

"No." She looked at me speculatively.

"I'm all right," I said, even forcing a little smile to reassure her. "Honestly, I'm all right. You can tell me. I'm quite—"

"He did it when we weren't looking," she said abruptly. "Walter and Boris had quit for the day. I was just getting off the lift when I heard a terrible scream and realized it was Lotte. I ran over; everyone else on the top did, too, those that hadn't been watching already. By the time I got there, it was over. Randy had already started down after him. He'd gone off at the first real bend and smashed right into a tree with his whole body. Except his arms and legs. They were tangled around it."

I shuddered. "It's a very dangerous sport, skiing. I'm surprised more people aren't killed."

"I don't think you understand what I've just told you, Ruth," she said quietly.

My temples began to throb painfully. She wanted something of me but I was far too dazed to understand what it was that she wanted. It was like the first time I'd gone to a French movie, after studying French in high school for a couple of years; I'd been able to pick out the words but I needed the titles to comprehend them. The titles, in turn, defeated me in my attempt to concentrate on the spoken words. While now my mind did not slip away to focus on something concrete, but only to rest in undistinguishable gray places.

"What is there to understand?"

"It's not that easy to kill yourself, skiing," she said. "Trees don't

grow on top of each other. There was space to the right of the tree and
space to the left, but he didn't steer in either direction. He went
straight toward it—with his legs spread wide apart, from what we're
told."

"I can't see why he would do that," I said, pressing my fingers to my
temples to relieve the throbbing.

"Nobody can." She began pacing back and forth in front of me.
"We thought he might have lost his goggles and been blinded, but the
goggles were—he was wearing the goggles."

"Were they prescription goggles?" I asked, and then, because I
thought it was a rather funny joke, I giggled. From a distance, I heard
myself; I sounded as though I were under water.

She stopped pacing and looked at me.

"Sit there for a moment, will you, Ruth? I'm going into the kitchen
to get you something to drink."

I nodded numbly.

"You promise you won't move until I get back?"

"I promise I won't move until you get back." *I can't move until you
get back. I can't move at all.*

She left and returned no time later with a glass and some aspirin. I
drank the whiskey, gagged on the aspirin but finally got it down, and
handed her back the glass.

"Is there someone you want to call?" she asked. "Or do you just
want to go right home? I imagine you want to tell your parents in person, not on the phone."

Oh, my God, my parents. I hadn't thought about my parents.

"Do I have to tell them?"

She sighed. "Look, Ruth, why don't you lie down on the sofa for a
while. There's no point in our talking any more now." I let her help me
out of the chair and over to the sofa, where I willingly lay down. "I'm
going to pack your clothes. As a matter of fact, I'll pack *all* the clothes.
The kids can't stay," she went on, half to herself. "I'll send the car back
for Walter when he's finished making arrangements. Or he can take
the bus."

"I'm sorry," I mumbled to her as she walked out of the room, "to put
you to all this trouble."

She turned around and started to say something. But then she
changed her mind and just left.

I don't know what happened after that. The next time I was awake
and aware of being awake, I was sitting in the back seat of the
Stamms' car, looking out of the window. At St. Marks Place.

"*No,*" I said.

The three heads in the front swiveled. Boris's face was terribly white, but Lotte's was red and swollen and ugly.

"I'm afraid it's true, Ruth," Helen Stamm said.

My difficulty, Mrs. Stamm, is not that I awakened with no memory of it and then, upon remembering, tried to deny it. My difficulty is that I awakened knowing it as though it were a fact I'd had to live with for years.

I looked with jealousy at Lotte's tear-swollen face.

If I could be surprised, even for one moment, then I would be able to cry.

"I meant," I said, "no, I can't go upstairs."

"You'll have to sooner or later."

"In an emergency, everyone resorts to clichés."

"Emergencies aren't subtle."

"All right, all right." I leaned back against the seat and closed my eyes.

"Ruth?"

I opened my eyes.

"Do you want me to go up with you?"

"Would you?"

She got out of the car and came around to my side. I pushed open the door and she helped me out, then she went back to the trunk and got my cardboard valise. I looked into the car and was suddenly enraged by the sight of Lotte, sitting shriveled up in the front seat, crying again.

"You don't have to cry so much," I said. "He wasn't *your* brother."

Mrs. Stamm was waiting near the steps, holding my valise. I led her into the house and up the inside stairs. Halfway up, I realized that I was tiptoeing.

"Oh, my God," I whispered at the top. "My father. What time is it?"

"Four-thirty."

"Oh. It's all right. He'll still be home."

She nodded.

"He'll help me," I explained. "With my mother. I don't know what this will do to my mother."

I used my key to get in. I didn't see my mother around. My father was sitting at the kitchen table, tinkering with the radio.

"Hah!" he said. "A day early. You were bored!"

I shook my head, moving into the room so Mrs. Stamm could come in.

"Papa," I said, "this is Mrs. Stamm."

He stood up and came over to us, saying, "How do you do? I'm pleased to meet you," obviously undismayed by the possibility that he'd just offended her.

"I'm glad to meet you, too," she said, extending her hand to meet his. "I'm sorry that the circumstance is a very unhappy one."

"Circumstance?" He looked at me. "What circumstance?"

I tried to talk but I couldn't. If it was this way with him, how would it be with my mother?

"Where's your brother?"

"Mr. Kossoff," Helen Stamm said, "please sit down."

"Where's Martin?" he asked me, ignoring her.

"Papa, please sit down."

"Never mind!" he barked at me angrily. "I don't like what's going on here. Strangers walking into my house and telling me to sit. I ask you where your brother is and *you* tell me to sit. I don't want to sit. I want to know where your brother is."

"He's dead."

So I'd been able to tell him, after all. But too flatly. Too quickly. I should have said something about an accident to prepare him, but I'd been thrown off by the way he'd shouted at me. My father didn't shout at me. In the solitude of our home he shouted at the teacher who didn't like me; the shopkeeper who had let me buy his junk; my friend who had been, intuition told him, the instigator of the trouble we'd gotten into the day before. But not at me. Until now. And now before he'd even known.

The room was dead, as if in echo. My father stared at me. Numb. Uncomprehending.

"He went skiing, Papa. It was a crazy accident. It never should have happened. He was doing very well, but he wasn't satisfied—you know Martin—and he kept wanting to go from the highest slope. They told him not to do it, everyone told him, the instructor, everyone, the instructor said he absolutely couldn't permit him to do it, but he did it anyway, when nobody was watching him."

Nothing.

"Papa?"

Still nothing. I took a step and reached out to put my hand on his arm. He shoved me away so violently that I fell back several steps, striking my head and back against the concrete edge of the shower stall. I stared at him unbelievingly.

"Mr. Kossoff—"

"Shut up," he said, without taking his eyes off me.

"I understand the way you feel, Mr. Kossoff, but—"

"Get out."

"Shall I go, Ruth?"

"When Ruth pays the rent, Ruth decides who goes."

"I'll be outside, Ruth. If your family wants to know what arrangements—"

"*Out!*"

She walked out. The sound of her footsteps banged through the apartment wall. My head hurt where it had slammed into the stall, but the link that would have made me mind the pain was missing. The downstairs door creaked open and slammed shut but still his eyes wouldn't let me go.

Papa, Papa, given the way Martin was, there was a logic to the way he—to what happened to him. But there's nothing between us that makes sense of the way you're looking at me now!

"Where's Mama?"

Hoarse words in a dead room.

"What do you care, where's Mama?"

"I—"

"You don't care, that's the answer. For her, for Martin, for any of us. You care for nothing but your own rotten self!"

"Daddy—Papa, no. Please, no. Don't do it. You don't know what you're doing."

"*I* don't know what I'm doing, ah?"

"Papa, let me go. I'll go out of the house and come back later. Please let me—"

He spat on the floor. I reacted as though he had spat poison in my face. My throat constricted and then the tightness spread through my whole body so that I couldn't move.

"What did you do?" I whispered.

"What did *I* do?" he shouted. "You kill your brother and ask me what did *I* do?"

I had a sense of total unreality, of almost physical removal from the room.

"You're crazy," I said after a moment. "I don't know what's going on in your head, but it's crazy."

"Oh?" He lowered his voice a little now that I no longer spoke in whispers. "I'm crazy, am I? Who took him to that place? Who sent him down a mountain when he was never on skis?"

"I wasn't even there, for God's sake. The Stamms were with him, and the instructor. And he *had* been on skis and he was doing very well, but the instructor still told him not to go and he went anyway." My throat ached as though I were going to cry yet I knew that I would not.

"And you let him go."

"I told you, I *wasn't there*."

"You should of been there," he said. "He was your responsibility. You take your younger brother someplace, he's your responsibility."

"My younger brother. Eleven months younger than me."

"So? It never stopped you before. For nineteen years you pushed him around—"

"I *what*?"

"You heard me." He was shouting again. "For nineteen years you told him what to do and he did it if he wanted to or not. Now all of a sudden you can't lift a finger to stop him from getting killed. Why, hah? Why?"

"All right." My voice trembling but not breaking. "Why?"

"Because you don't give a damn, that's why! Because—because maybe you wouldn't even want to stop him. Maybe you don't like the way he acts lately. He's growing up a little. He doesn't listen so fast when big sister tells him what to do. And you don't have to share a room this way. More money to go around at home, too, hah? You care more for money than people, Ruthie, that's the trouble with you."

"You . . ." very slow, very deliberate, "you . . . filthy . . . dirty . . . disgusting . . . old man."

He rushed at me to choke me.

"You filthy-dirty-disgusting-old-man!" I screamed, my voice breaking loose from me as I brought up a foot and with all my force kicked him in the groin. He reeled back against the table then fell to the floor.

"Slut!" he groaned out through clenched teeth, his arms around his hunched body.

"You made his life such hell he couldn't stand to walk into this house!" I screamed. "He couldn't stand to come home! Don't you know he killed himself on purpose, you stupid old fool? I shouldn't have taken him away at all. You were right. I should've known better. I should've known he wouldn't be able to stand the sight of you again once he'd been away enjoying himself for a few days. *He could not stand the sight of you, so he killed himself!*"

"Liar! You're lying!" He struggled to get up, but he couldn't. The kitchen chair he was holding onto crashed past him to the floor between us. "Liar, liar, liar, liar, liar!"

"He killed himself. He smashed himself into the middle of a tree when there was so much space around the tree he needed perfect aim to hit it. He went into the middle of it. His face was such a bloody pulp they wouldn't let me see him.

"I wasn't even there. I only heard about it. Everyone who saw it'll tell you the same lies. Mrs. Stamm couldn't get over it, such a crazy thing, someone committing suicide on skis, smashing into a tree headfirst with his arms around the tree as if he couldn't smash hard enough."

He sagged back against the table leg.

"Get out of my house." His voice was cracked and spent.

"Your house!" I shrieked. "Why don't you say your shithouse? I'll be glad to get out of it. You don't think that's a punishment, do you? Don't you wish you had the guts to get out? What are you going to do when they finally tear down this shithouse and you have to stumble home to someplace new?"

I bent over to pick up my valise. He reached out and grabbed the wrist of my free hand. I brought the valise around and slammed it into the side of his head. He went limp and slumped sideways down to the floor. I walked out of the apartment and down the steps, holding onto the banister with a sweaty trembling hand that wouldn't save me if I were to stumble. I reached the bottom without mishap, though, and stood there for a couple of minutes, waiting for my breathing to slow down, for some small trace of composure to return.

After a while, I left the house, carefully closing the door behind me. I turned and looked up at the building in order to ensure a last fixed memory of its ugliness. Then I walked down the outside steps and toward the car parked at the curb. When I was halfway there I tripped over some invisible object on the sidewalk and fell, my shoulder striking the pavement, my head cushioned from real harm by the cardboard valise that fell between it and the concrete.

CHAPTER FOUR

I remember the hollow aching thud as my head banged into the valise, and I remember too the feeling of the textured cardboard when I turned on my side to let my head rest upon it. I think I lost consciousness for a moment after that. And then there was Helen Stamm's voice, asking me if I could hear her.

I opened my eyes and pushed myself up to a sitting position. The throbbing in my head sharpened to a pain that made me squint my eyes to focus clearly. A woman walked past us; I saw the hem of her black dress, her ugly lisle stockings, her black oxfords with the leather broken over one corn-swollen toe. I didn't look up to see her face, even when she stopped a few feet away and I knew that she was staring back at me. It didn't occur to me that I might know her; I was in a strange place.

Awkwardly, with Helen Stamm's hands under my elbows, I got to my feet. I started to bend over for my suitcase but she stopped me and picked it up herself. She opened the car door for me and as I turned to enter the back, my eyes met those of the staring woman. Her eyes remained fixed on mine—not so much as an eyelid's blink to suggest embarrassment at having been caught watching. Pauper's immunity. I slid into the back seat and Helen Stamm slammed the door. Boris had fallen asleep, his head resting on Lotte's shoulder. Lotte was frozen in position; her head never moved as her mother got in and started the car. We drove past Thea's house and automatically my eyes scanned the block for sight of Thea.

I'll have to call Thea as soon as I'm . . .

As soon as I was what? I pressed my temples; the pressure diminished the ache but didn't enable me to finish the sentence. My brain groped for some word that would give me an idea of what I had to do before I called Thea. I turned to look back at her house; it told me nothing.

I would have to settle somewhere—settle, that was it. But how was I to know where to settle? I didn't even know where the car was taking me. I almost asked that the car be stopped so I could run back to Thea's, but then it occurred to me that if she weren't home I would be completely lost.

We turned the corner and went up Third Avenue. Where were we going, aside from away?

David!

Panic flashed through me for the first time since I had unbelievingly seen the hatred in my father's face and tried to leave the house before it was too late. I jerked forward in the car seat as though I had to fight someone who was trying to push me back.

How will I reach David?

You can call him.

What if he's not home? Or SHE answers?
So, you'll hang up and call again, idiot.
Phone calls cost money, too.

I almost laughed out loud. That ridiculous line. Why had it popped into my head?

My mother! How will I reach my mother?

The panic washed through me more thoroughly. For the first time I had the sensation of having been unwillingly cut off from something—I didn't know what. Surely not the place. The people? I could see those that I cared about. Except, possibly, my mother, who might not be permitted to see me. That was sad, but not terrifying. I loved her, but it was years since I'd gone to her for advice or comfort. For advice she consulted her mental anthology of Ladies' Home Martyrdom clichés. For comfort she offered her conviction that we could do anything we really wanted to; her inability to view us for a moment with our enemies' eyes; approval of us even when our actions weren't easily approved. Applause from a blind audience.

"Blind faith is not my specialty."

I looked at the back of Helen Stamm's head and shuddered. I moved back into the corner of the seat, curling up my body as tightly as I could, then wrapping my arms around myself. I had begun to shiver with the cold.

Step right out, folks. Five hundred degrees colder outside.

A wave of heat passed lightly over me, leaving my cheeks and forehead burning and my mouth dry, but failing to dissolve the deathly cold that had invaded my body. I pulled my suitcase toward me on the seat. My trembling hands fumbled at the catch-locks until they snapped open. My purse was on top of the clothes inside. I took out my cigarettes and matches and put a cigarette in my mouth, but I couldn't pull a match out of the book. After a few tries I realized I didn't really want a cigarette, anyway, and I dropped it on the floor. I picked up my purse and turned it upside down, emptying its contents on the seat between me and the valise. Wallet, makeup, hairbrush, toothbrush case. No bankbook! Where was my bankbook? My terror increased until I remembered that I always kept it in the zipper compartment. The zipper wouldn't come undone, though, and I finally tugged at it so hard that the cloth around it ripped as it opened. I pulled out the book and opened it to the final entry: $1,270.27. I leafed back through the pages, my stiffly awkward hands creasing each one in turn. $1,033.42 in September, right after my summer with the Stamms; $868.12 on June 26, just before I'd gone away with them; beyond that time, numbers growing smaller at a creeping, laborious five-dollars-at-a-time pace until the first entry, July 15, 1946—a five-dollar deposit made within half an hour of receipt of my first week's salary as a summer salesgirl at Kresge's, lay naked and shivering for my examination. I felt dizzy as I looked at it; and between my dizziness and my headache and the shaking of the page in my hands, the numbers and dates became confused in my mind so that I was suddenly convinced that I was looking not at the first entry, but at the last.

"There's been a mistake," I croaked out in a voice I didn't know. "Please take me to the bank."

But the car didn't move. I looked up. The engine wasn't even running. Helen Stamm was staring at me instead of driving.

"Please," I begged, feeling tears well in my eyes, "please get me to the bank before it closes. There's been a mistake in my account."

"It's rather late already, Ruth," she said—so calmly I could tell she had no idea of how serious the error was. "We'll call them first thing in the morning."

"It'll be too late," I said, pressing the bankbook against my stomach. "They may give my money to someone else by then." I began crying. "They may have done it already."

"Let me see the book, Ruth." She held out a hand and I reluctantly gave it to her.

"I don't see any mistakes," she said. "It looks to me as though it's in very good order."

"Oh, God! Look at this. Will you please look at it? They say I've only got five dollars."

"No," she said, "that's not so. They say that you've got $1,270.27 as of December 22, 1950. The last entry is $1,270.27."

I grabbed the open book from her and looked at it. There it was. She was right. I laughed.

"You were right," I said. "I don't know what's wrong with me." I laughed again.

"Grief and exhaustion," she said. "That's what's wrong with you."

That seemed even funnier—her using a word like grief about a bankbook. I laughed so much that my stomach became painfully cramped and the tears of my laughter blinded me completely. Then, before I knew it, I was crying and shivering again. I put my head down on the pile of clothing in my suitcase.

"Ruth, do you think you could possibly make it upstairs?"

I tried to answer, but my body, racked with sobs, wouldn't let me.

Doors slammed and then her voice was close to my ear, her hand on my arm.

"Come, Ruth. Try to get up. I'll help you."

"Noohhhhh," I moaned, trying to free my arm.

The hand let go. Something tugged at the suitcase beneath my head and pulled out the purse from beneath me, then my face was against the cool upholstery of the seat. Beyond the sound of my crying I could hear words. I couldn't tell if they were meant for me. Something heavy was wrapped around me but even so, it took a long time for the shivering to end.

When I awakened I was lying on a bed in what had to be a guest room in the Stamm apartment. It was a lovely room. About the same size as the one I'd had in the country, with pale yellow walls, gray carpeting and gray velvet drapes that were drawn across the window wall. After a few minutes I got up and stretched. I ached, I felt dirty, I was extremely hungry, and I had to go to the bathroom. Somewhat shakily I walked out of the room and through the hallways. No one was around—or at least no one was visible. I found my way to the library, knocked at the door, and walked in. Helen Stamm was sitting on the leather couch, her head resting on the back cushion. She was holding a cigarillo; the air around her was thick with smoke. A book rested on the seat beside her, pages down. Her head came up when she saw me.

"Hello, Ruth. I didn't hear you come in."

"Hello." I felt shy. My knees were weak and I leaned against the doorway to keep them from buckling under me. She walked over to me. She'd been chain-smoking the cigarillos; her whole body reeked of them and the smell was sickening to my empty stomach.

"You may have noticed your things in the guest room," she said. "I'd recommend a hot bath, clean clothes, and food, in that order."

"I'm afraid I've caused you too—"

"Nonsense." She steered me out to the foyer, back down the main hallway, then into the left wing. My suitcase was resting on an olive-green leather armchair near the window; over its arm was a pink-wool robe that must have been Lotte's. I sat down on the edge of the chair. Mrs. Stamm went into the bathroom and after a moment I could hear water running in the tub.

"I couldn't recall your having a robe with you," she said when she came out. "The one on the chair was Lotte's. I had it aside with some other things, anyway, to ask you if you wanted it. Don't bother getting dressed in street clothes when you're finished; it's not at all necessary.

You must be famished. If I thought you could enjoy eating in your present condition, I'd say you should get some food first. I'll be in the dining room or the library." She left without giving me a chance to thank her.

I let my clothes fall to the floor as I took them off. I felt as though I'd been wearing them for years; there was nothing in their appearance to suggest that I hadn't. The bath water was too hot, but I got into the tub anyway and slowly sat down, holding my breath until I could bear the heat more easily. When I stretched out, the water covered me up to my neck. I turned off the faucets, leaned against the back of the tub, and closed my eyes. But after a couple of minutes I felt myself drifting back into sleep, so I sat up and washed myself thoroughly, even kneeling to give my hair a fast shampoo under the spout. When I'd dried myself and put on Lotte's robe, I opened my suitcase to look for my hairbrush. I found it, along with my purse and several things, including my bankbook, that should have been in the purse. I couldn't understand the crumpled condition of the bankbook until I leafed through it to the final entry—December 22, 1950—$1,270.27—and remembered. I put the book back and closed the suitcase, then quickly brushed my wet hair. And fighting a momentary impulse to grab my belongings and run out of the Stamm apartment forever, I went into the dining room.

She was reading the paper and having coffee at the big table. I sat down and took one of the cigarettes she offered me. She poured coffee for me and more for herself, and a couple of minutes later Fernette came in with ham and eggs and a basket of rolls. I ate rapidly, ravenously, grateful that Helen Stamm had gone back to her paper instead of trying to engage me in conversation. I didn't stop eating until every roll in the basket was gone. And then I was surprised to find myself yawning. She put aside the paper, smiling at me.

"Ready for sleep again?"

"I guess so. I shouldn't be."

She shrugged. "Should, shouldn't. There are no ground rules for times like this." We sat in silence while Fernette came in, cleared the dishes from the table, and vanished back into the kitchen. I yawned again.

"Why don't you go to bed, Ruth? You don't have to sit around for the sake of being polite."

"I feel as though I—" I hesitated. I had to say something about being there, about the room. Yet I could not with any honesty say that I would get out of their way soon, because I had no idea as yet of what I could do. "I don't want to overstay my welcome."

"That would be impossible," she said. "You need a place to stay and you cause us absolutely no inconvenience by being here. I don't know if you'll be able to go home eventually, or if you'll want to—"

"No," I said quickly. "Definitely not. Never."

"Well, in any event, you're welcome to stay here for as long as you find it convenient. Indefinitely, in other words. As a matter of fact, as far as I'm concerned, you can live with us until you finish school."

I was overwhelmed. She was showing me an almost smothering kindness—yet it wasn't really the kindness that affected me so much as it was guilt at the way I'd felt about her. And at the fact that while I could no longer hate or dislike her, I could not bring myself to really like her, feel comfortable with her. I felt my cheeks flush and I looked down at the white tablecloth, toying with crumbs.

"I don't—"

I don't what? Don't know what to say? That, but not just that. I don't understand.

"I don't—I find it hard to understand your—that you can be so extremely kind to me when I've—" But I gave it up at that point.

"Oh, it's probably very simple," she said, and I looked up to see her smiling faintly at some point behind me. "Aside from normal human compassion after what's happened—there's the fact that in the long run, we do things for people because of the way we feel about them, not because of the way they feel about us. Mmm?"

My eyes, unable to meet hers, went back to the table crumbs. I felt as though I'd been up for days.

"If you don't get to bed," she said, "you're going to fall asleep at the table."

I stood up. "I wish that there were some way I could—"

"Don't worry about it," she said, waving an arm impatiently. And then, when I still hesitated, "I'll tell you what, Ruth. If you find my hospitality too great a burden to bear, try telling yourself that I'm only doing it because if your parents decide to sue us over Martin's death, I don't want you to be a hostile witness."

I stared at her in total bewilderment. It seemed improbable that she would joke about such a thing, but impossible that she could be serious. It couldn't be serious, that was the answer; it had to be a joke.

"You're not serious, are you?"

"Oh—" she waved both arms in the air this time, "what difference does it make, Ruth? Really, what difference does it make?" She walked quickly through the archway and disappeared from my sight. I went back to my room, padding soundlessly along the green-carpeted hallway floor. By the time I'd taken off the pink robe and slipped beneath the bedcovers, I couldn't remember what question had been in my mind.

When I awakened I was hungry again. I washed and returned to the dining room, prepared to find Helen Stamm there, but finding her husband instead. He was eating a sandwich and drinking. A bottle of Scotch stood near his plate on the table. He rose when I walked in and came up to me, taking my hands between his and pressing them gently together. He was still wearing his skiing clothes from the day before. He had a slight beard; the hair in it, unlike that on his head, was still blond. His eyes were sunken and bloodshot, and like everything about him, suggested exhaustion. Tears came to my eyes and I felt my lips tremble. My hands were cold between his.

"Ruth," he said finally, "I wish I could say something to comfort you."

I nodded.

Fernette came in with more sandwiches. A little embarrassed, we broke apart and sat down at the table. He asked her to get another glass and some cubes, and when she returned with them, he poured me a drink. I took a sandwich. He finished the one he'd been eating and had another.

He said, "Strange, I've been hungry all day."

I said, "Me, too."

We finished eating and sat back in our seats, sipping at our drinks.

He said, "Mar——your brother's body is at the funeral home."

I thanked him.

"The arrangements have been tentatively made," he said. "With the proviso that the home contact your parents, who will be permitted to make any changes they wish."

"I'm very grateful for all you've done," I said, wondering why I could accept his kindness so much more easily than his wife's, even though I knew she was generally the initiator.

He cleared his throat. "There was a phone call for you," he said. "Your friend—Thea? I think that's her name. She asked me to tell you that she would go to your parents' or the Landaus' tonight, since David is coming up to see you. She said she would be up tomorrow, after the funeral."

"Why does she assume I won't go?" I asked, half of myself, although the truth was that I hadn't thought about the funeral.

"Maybe she assumes you won't be permitted to."

"Oh, no," I said, startled.

"I'm sorry," he said. "I didn't mean to be presumptuous. Helen told me about—"

"But he wouldn't do that," I said. "He wouldn't dare."

Walter Stamm said nothing.

"It's my brother's funeral," I said urgently.

He nodded. He was obviously uncomfortable.

"They don't have to talk to me if they don't want to, but they can't keep me from going."

"Helen said—" he began, then paused. "Helen seemed to think that your father was in a somewhat—unbalanced state of mind. At the time, I mean. It's hard to say . . . exactly what . . ."

"You don't understand," I said, without any particular logic. "You don't know how close we are—were—my father and me. We were like— Everything good, practically everything good that I can remember from my childhood had to do with my father. He took me places, he bought me things. He loved me much more than he loved Martin and I always knew it and I felt guilty about it, but there was nothing I could do because that was just the way it was. That's why all this is so crazy."

It was a crazy thing. It never should have happened.

"Much crazier than Martin's death, in a way. Do you know what I mean?"

"I think I do."

"I wanted to tell him that, but he wouldn't listen. You can't imagine how close we were."

"I think I can," Walter Stamm said. "He raised a very fine young woman." He was still uncomfortable but he was sympathetic, and I felt a little guilty at burdening him further with my difficulties.

"He doesn't think so," I said. "He thinks I—" But I couldn't say it. I couldn't tell him that my father had accused me of causing Martin's death. I think I was afraid that if he knew half the violence I had come from, he would be repelled by me. I'm not sure now that I was wrong.

When we had finished our drinks, he went in to shower and change, and I went back to sleep. I was awakened by Fernette, who told me that David had called and would be up in half an hour.

I waited for him in the library, still wearing the pink robe because I hadn't had the energy to change. Lotte and Boris came into the apartment while I was waiting, and Lotte walked past the open library door, glancing at me then walking quickly on, but Boris came in and ran over to me and kissed me.

"How come you're in here alone?" he asked.

"David's coming," I said.

Without a word he got up and started out of the room.

"Boris, please don't go," I called. "Don't think you have to go."

"I'm sorry about your brother," he said without looking back.

"Won't you stay and keep me company?" I asked.

"I better not," he said. "I better get to bed." And he disappeared from my sight.

When the bell rang I went to get it before Fernette could. It was a boy I'd never seen before, Lotte's date for the evening, apparently. His name was Brook Carpenter, or some such exotic thing. Fernette came to the foyer, herself dressed to go out, and I told her to tell Lotte her friend was here, and as I walked back into the library, I realized that Lotte's friend was there because it was New Year's Eve. New Year's Eve, generally spent in a frantic effort not to be weighed down by reality. While here I was, grasping only for a bearable anchor to it.

David came a few minutes later, carrying two large cartons by the wood-and-brass handles attached to the ropes around them. I led him into the library where he put down the cartons and closed the door behind him. I sat down on the sofa and he sat beside me, putting an arm around me. I rested my head on his shoulder. We stayed that way, without talking, for a long time. Finally I raised my head.

"Thea left a message she would see me tomorrow after the funeral."

He nodded.

"Why *after*? Does she think I won't go? I can go and not talk to them."

"Are you sure you want to?"

"No." I looked away from him and my eyes came to rest on the cartons.

"What's in those?" I asked, saying to myself, *You know what's in those, Ruth. What are you hoping to hear instead of the truth?*

"Your stuff. Clothing. Books. All that."

I nodded. "Bag and baggage, as they say. . . . Who gave it to you, David? Who packed it, I mean? I can't see my mother being capable of doing it so soon. *Was* it my mother? Did she say anything—give you a message for me?"

He shook his head. I stood up, exasperated as he remained silent.

"Why are you being so mysterious?"

"I found the stuff on the landing when I came home," he said. "I think your father must've thrown it out as soon as you left. Your mother wasn't even home yet. I took the stuff upstairs. My mother'd heard a little of it, and she saw what went on outside, from the window."

Naturally.

"My father won't let me go to the funeral. Will he?"

"No."

Tears welled in my eyes.

"David, if someone just told you about all this, I mean, if you didn't know it was true, you wouldn't believe it, would you? I mean, it's crazy, isn't it?"

He nodded.

"It's hard for me to believe it's all happening. The last thing I believed . . ." *No. I can't tell you I knew. You'll think there's something wrong with me.* "What if I came, anyway? To the funeral? He has no right to keep me out."

"It might be pretty awful. He's not particularly rational."

"You don't go to a funeral to have a good time."

"You said you weren't sure you wanted to, anyway."

"I didn't mean about the funeral. I meant about seeing *him*."

He nodded.

"I don't suppose," I said bitterly, "that anyone's tried to argue the subject with him."

"There'd be no point to it, Ruth," David said quietly. "He's like a wild man. He has a fit when anyone mentions your name."

"Good," I burst out, "I'm glad. I hope one of his fits kills him."

He said nothing.

"You're not going to tell me I'm a louse?"

"I don't even know what happened, Ruth."

"I thought you did. I thought your mother heard."

"Not really. Not all of it. She heard you telling him Martin had done it on purpose. To avoid coming home."

"But not what came before that. She didn't hear what he said to me first."

"I don't think so. She didn't repeat it, anyway."

"He said I . . . he accused me . . ." But I couldn't tell him that, either. What if he were to think my father was right, that I was responsible for Martin's death? I wouldn't be able to bear that. I could bear the rest of it, if I had to. But I couldn't bear to have David hold me responsible.

"Do you want a drink?" I asked.

"Uh-huh."

"Come," I said. "The stuff's inside."

He picked up the cartons on the way out, and I led him into the guest room with them.

"Nice," he said, looking around. "Are you going to stay here for a while?"

"I don't know. I guess so. She said I can stay as long as I like—even until I finish school, if I want to." I think I wanted him to see that there was someone who wanted me, that I was not a complete orphan.

"That's great."

I shrugged. "Financially, it is. And physically, of course, it's much better than anything I could rent."

But you'd still have to sneak out at night like a thief, David. We wouldn't have to be sneaks if I rented a room.

"So, what's wrong with it?"

"Oh, nothing," I said. "I'll probably take her up on it. Come. Let's see if we can get a drink."

I led him into the living room. The Stamms were there, playing chess. He had a drink, she had a cup of coffee. It was the first time I'd ever had the sensation of intruding upon them. We started to walk out, but Helen Stamm looked up and called to us.

"Come in, kids, have a seat," she said.

"We don't want to interrupt you," I told her.

"You're not interrupting anything except my lousy end game," she said. "As a matter of fact—David, you must be a chess player—" She waited for his nod. "Fine. Why don't you take over for me and I'll make you drinks." She bounced up from her seat and David obediently took it. She went into the kitchen for ice cubes and made drinks for the three of us at the bar that was part of the dining-room buffet. She and I sat on the big sofa while David and Walter Stamm finished the game. We talked about school, about how we could arrange matters satisfactorily if I were to live with them, about Boris and Lotte. Boris, who'd gone down briefly to visit a friend in the building, came up and was permitted a glass of wine before going to bed. Lotte and her friend Brook came in a short while after midnight, when the four of us were sitting around playing some silly word game. She looked wan but pretty; her hair had been pinned up in back and she wore a black velvet dress with a full skirt. They took off their coats and Lotte went to hang them up, without having looked at me once.

"How was the party, Brook?" Walter Stamm asked.

"It was all right, sir," Brook said. "But you know, Lotte wasn't much in a party mood."

"Of course."

He seemed a little embarrassed, as though his question had been improper under the circumstances. Yet the circumstances themselves were
so improper that I could not think of anything within them as strange.
I could remember deaths; this was not like them. Two of my grandparents had died in this country and within my memory; my mother's
brother had been killed in the war; a girl in my high-school senior class
had died of a brain tumor. They were talked about, all of them. For
days after their deaths that was all we talked about—as though to discuss ordinary matters would have been an affront to their memories, a
suggestion that not only could life go on without them but it pressed
with such gay urgency that there was no time for mourning. Yet here
no one talked of Martin. One talked of rooms and school and clothes.
Aside from the almost incidental mention of Martin in my talk with
David, the only time I could remember his name's having come up during the day was when Helen Stamm had mentioned the funeral arrangements to me earlier in the day. I wondered if they were talking
about him back home. Probably there, I was the one who had never
existed, and Martin was getting his due.

Lotte came back into the room, and Helen Stamm gave her and
Brook some wine. They joined us in the word game for a while but
nobody was really interested in it. My own eyes were again growing
heavy with sleep, so that I withdrew from the game a few minutes before they all stopped playing. I don't remember what the conversation
was about when Helen Stamm happened to mention to Lotte that I
might be staying with them for a while—she rather hoped for a long
while. I could not forget, though, the way Lotte's hands went to her
chest as though she had been stabbed, or the way she stood up and ran
out of the room.

"Good heavens!" Helen Stamm exclaimed into the embarrassed silence. "Does anyone know what that was all about? Ruth?"

I shook my head. A half-lie.

"She's been strange today," Helen Stamm said. "But that seemed
natural enough, under the circumstances. Is she angry with you about
something?"

"I don't know," I said. "She might be." I glanced at David; he was
staring into his drink. "Maybe I should talk to her."

She nodded. I got up, shaking my head to clear away the sleepiness.
Before going in to Lotte, I washed my face with cold water at the
kitchen sink. Then, feeling slightly revived, I walked down the hall-

way, knocked at the door, and asked if I could talk to her. After a moment she said that I should come in.

Lotte's room, like Lotte, surrendered few easy clues to what went on inside. Pleasant floral wallpaper, frilly white-organdy curtains and bedspread, a neat desk, a comfortable chair, soft blue rug, a few shelves of books over the desk. The books were all covered, as though their owner feared the titles would reveal too much about her to the casual eye. But covered prettily, with bright oilcloth and printed papers, so that no one could be certain it hadn't been done for purely decorative reasons. Lotte was standing in front of the mirror, hairbrush in her hand; I had the feeling she'd picked it up a second before, for the sake of seeming occupied.

"Can I talk to you for a couple of minutes?"

"All right." She began brushing her hair, still looking into the mirror. I closed the door behind me and waited for her to finish. Finally she put down the brush and turned to me. Her face had as much expression as the blue quilted bathrobe she had put on. I'd mentally prepared a little of what I could say, but now, confronted with that bland, poised face of Lotte's, I lost it.

"Do you mind if I sit down?"

She shrugged. I leaned back against the door.

"Lotte . . . Lotte, you're not the first person I ever knew who didn't like me. But usually, when someone doesn't like you, it's someone you dislike yourself. Or at least you know *why* they feel that way."

A trace of a smile.

"It's not Martin," I said quickly. "It has nothing to do with Martin."

The smile, if it had been one, was gone now.

"If you think it's because of what I said to you the other day—" I broke off because her eyes had narrowed, in speculation or in surprise. I smiled this time. "Did you think I'd pretend to forget it? Plead temporary insanity or something?"

"Yes."

"Well, I'm not. I'm not even pleading that I can't imagine what made me say it. Because I can. I'll tell you if you're interested."

Again a shrug. I took a deep breath.

"That's what I mean, Lotte. It didn't really matter. You disliked me before you ever knew I had a brother."

She said nothing.

"That's true, isn't it?"

"Yes."

"Why?"

Her chin came up slightly. "It's a free country."

"Oh, for God's sake," I said irritably. "Do you think I had to come in here to find that out?"

"I didn't ask you to come."

"All right," I said, my voice rising in anger. "You didn't ask me to come. You didn't want me to come. You didn't offer me a room here and you don't want me to accept it. I *won't* accept it. How's that? If I promise not to live here will you try and talk to me for a couple of minutes as if I were a human being?"

"I'm not sure," she said calmly, "that I'd believe you."

"What would you like me to do, Lotte? Put it in writing? Cross my heart and hope to die? What kind of crazy ideas do you have about me, anyway? Do you think I could live here with things like this between you and me? If I could, I wouldn't have bothered coming in to talk to you."

"All right, then," she said after a moment. "Go ahead."

I laughed shortly. "You'll die with your boots on."

No response.

I sighed. "All right, Lotte. All I wanted—I just want to know what there is about me that you dislike so much."

"Everything."

I stared at her blankly, startled in spite of myself. I repeated it. "Everything?"

She nodded.

This time I laughed in embarrassment. I'd been prepared for accusations of having insinuated myself into her parents' good graces; of dominating my own brother; of attempting to steal the affection of hers. But this!

"Right away," I said. "From the first time you met me, you knew you disliked me."

"I was pretty sure."

"When did you become absolutely certain?"

"I guess when we'd been at the lake a few days."

"Did I do something that made you certain?"

"Everything."

She left me at a loss. But then she always had. I racked my brain for specific memories of those first few days, but I couldn't remember the smallest unpleasantness between us.

"Everything," I said. "That word again. It's meaningless. You couldn't possibly dislike everything I do."

"Why did you ask me if you were only going to say it wasn't true?" A tiny tremor broke through the surface calm of her voice.

"I don't say that what you *mean* to tell me isn't true. But you're making it sound ridiculous. You dislike everything I do. Do you dislike the way I brush my teeth? The way I hold my knife and fork?"

"Everything!" Her voice broke away from her this time, in passionate hatred. "I hate the way you do everything! The first time you ever came here, I didn't like the way you walked in. As if you owned the house. Not the least bit scared or nervous or anything. For a minute I thought you must be a friend of my mother's, something like that."

I stared at her for a minute, wondering why I had a sense of familiarity with her words when it wasn't possible that I'd heard them before.

"Oh. I'm not sufficiently humble. Is that it?" Deliberately prodding so she wouldn't stop, so she would keep talking. As though an invisible detective were tracing the connection for me.

"Make me sound stupid," she said vehemently. "I don't care. I don't care about anything you say. Even when you tell the truth you sound as if you're lying."

It tempted me to laugh and made me want to cry at the same time. Serene little Lotte, so remote, so poised. It was nearly a year since I'd met her, and I hadn't even been sure she disliked me. How often had I wondered what part of her manner was a natural reticence, what part a specific withdrawal from me? It was unbelievable that the frenzied adolescent standing in front of me should be the same Lotte, only a few years younger than I, a girl I'd thought might be, in spite of our age difference, nice to have for a friend. While all the time, somewhere in Lotte, a child's demonic imagination had been conjuring monstrous images of me. What had I done to her? Nothing, apparently. She didn't even claim injury—except through my very presence—and certainly I would have remembered any trouble, however small, between us.

Except why, then, should I have this sense of familiarity, this sensation that overruled my surprise at each new thing she said, the sensation of walking a new treadmill past old scenery? I was surprised by her hatred but not fully convinced by my surprise. Her attitude was unjust, her manner almost consciously cruel. Why, then, was I not angry with her, did I not feel the warmth of righteous indignation? Her view of me was so grotesquely distorted as to provide no real view at all. Why, then, could I understand without effort exactly what she was talking about?

"I'm sorry," I said. "I don't . . . I can't . . ." I turned from her and opened the door.

"Ruth?"

I turned back.

"You won't forget, will you?" Her expression was startlingly different —as though she were caviling to someone she feared.

"Forget what?"

"You promised not to move in if I talked to you."

I smiled. Wearily. The smile I smile now at my five-year-old when she cannot understand why I won't read one more story just because my throat is sore. I shook my head. She relaxed visibly. I closed the door and went into my room. I turned on the light and looked around and wondered briefly what my next room would look like. I took off my robe, folding it over the chair's back. I went into the bathroom and, when I'd washed and was drying my face, caught sight of my reflection in the mirror. It seemed not to stand out from the things in the room but to have a flat outlined quality—as though I had been painted on the wall in back of me. I put the towel back on the rack and looked again, but I couldn't dispel the illusion. Perhaps I was going mad. I could think of no other explanation for the sense of unreality that still gripped me. Something had happened to me—or to everyone else, and the latter seemed unlikely. My father and me. Helen Stamm and me. Lotte. And me. Me. Me. Me.

The last thing I'd really believed was Martin's death, and I'd believed that too soon.

I went back into the bedroom and got into bed, but I was reluctant to turn off the light and leave myself without even the assurance of visible objects. I lay down but deliberately kept my eyes open, looking around the room suspiciously as though it were trying to lull me into an unhappy sleep. There was a knock at the door and David's voice called my name. I'd forgotten. How could I be so dumb? I called to him to come in. He opened the door. His coat and hat were on already.

"I'm sorry, David. I forgot. I was upset."

"Don't worry about it."

"Lotte's a funny kid. I don't understand her."

"What happened?" He closed the door and came over to the bed.

"I'm not sure. Anyway, I don't think I'll stay. I don't want to stay if it's going to be complicated, you know?"

He nodded. I held out my arms and he sat down on the edge of the bed.

"Lotte's friend's going to give me a lift," he said.

"How come?"

"It's not far from his place." He grinned. "Eleventh Street—and Fifth Avenue. . . . The old lady went to bed and Stamm disappeared, too. The kid and I've been sitting around wondering what the hell was going on with you two." He paused to see if I was going to tell him, but I didn't want to. "He's not a bad kid."

"I'm not either," I said, a little petulant.

"You're a champ." He smoothed the hair back from my forehead as I loved him to.

"Champ? That's a funny thing for me to be. What does it mean?"

"It means you're holding up pretty damn well under—under all of this."

"I'm not so sure," I said slowly. "I've been lying here wondering if I'm losing my mind."

"That's funny," he said, with the old teasing smile. "I was thinking you seemed a little saner than usual."

"Very funny."

He leaned forward and kissed my cheek lightly. "I'm sorry I don't amuse you any more."

"Try something else."

"No good. I'll lose my lift."

"Well, now I know what's important in your life, anyway."

He stood up. "I'll call you tomorrow, Ruth."

"Lotte is angry with me," I said to keep him from leaving me alone, "because I told her to stop crying."

"I don't get it."

"About Martin."

"You told her to stop crying about Martin?" He looked as if he didn't believe me.

"It wasn't the way it sounds, David. I was half out of my mind. I couldn't cry. I was numb. From the minute they told me. And there she was. Carrying on. Crying like crazy." I was getting more and more agitated in the attempt to explain. I sat up in bed. "Do you understand what I mean?"

"I guess so."

"I knew before they told me, David. That's what I wanted to talk to you about all night, but I couldn't. They came in to tell me—she came in—Mrs. Stamm—and she said there was an accident and I knew right away he was dead. Before she said it. It froze me. You don't know what it was like . . ."

He came back and sat down on the bed.

"Lie down, Ruth."

"I can't. I have to talk."

"You can talk. But lie down."

I let my head fall back on the pillow. I reached out for his hands; he took mine between them.

"Why did I have to know? It was horrible. I didn't want to know like that. I wanted to be shocked and to scream and cry and say it wasn't true and cry again, the way Lotte was. And I couldn't cry at all. It was as if I was frozen into a piece of ice. I couldn't cry until we got home. Here, I mean. I couldn't cry, and there she was crying for him as if her heart was going to break because she had a crush on him for five rotten days."

"Wait a minute, Ruth. I'll be right back." He let go of my hand and stood up.

"Where're you going?"

"I'll tell the kid not to wait for me."

I started to sit up.

"Lie down," he ordered. I stretched out again. "I'll be right back. Just stay there."

"All right."

He took so long that I was half-afraid he'd gone, but then he came back, with a glass of warm milk and honey, and two sleeping pills. I sat up and took the milk.

"I don't need the pills."

"Take them, anyway."

"I don't want to go to sleep. I'll only have nightmares."

"I'll stay here. I won't leave until I see you sleeping peacefully."

I took the pills and swallowed them with the sweet milk, closing my mouth tightly to keep from gagging. Then I lay down again.

"You must think I'm a nut."

"Don't be silly."

I giggled nervously. "Don't be a nut, you mean."

"Look, Ruth, you've got to stop talking now. It's not doing any good. We can talk some other time."

"Don't go."

"I won't go if you'll just stop talking." He drew the quilt up over my shoulders. "Just close your eyes and try not to think about anything." I turned on my side and closed my eyes. "You'll be all right," he said softly. "Just try not to think about anything for now." He turned off the light.

He went on like that, speaking in a low voice, not saying anything that meant something and might keep me awake. After a while I stopped trying to force open my eyes to make sure he was still there. Still later, I fell asleep. I dreamed that I had to get up a steep snow-covered mountain, but when I got into the chair lift it turned into a treadmill. I pedaled furiously, trying to reach the top, but I didn't know if I was getting anywhere because the seasons kept changing and I couldn't tell if the golden-leaved tree I was passing was the same as the lush green tree of summer, the naked barren one of spring, or the snowy giant of the winter before. When I tried to look behind me to see how far I'd come, the treadmill wobbled so that I nearly fell off the mountain. Stupid old treadmill, I kept thinking. Stupid old treadmill. And then, finally, just as I became convinced that the scenery had really changed, I lost my balance on the treadmill and fell off the mountain with the sound of harsh laughter in my ears as I fell farther down down down and awakened in darkness. *It wasn't the scenery,* said a voice in the part of me that was still with my dream. *It was the treadmill that changed.* I switched on the light and looked around the room. It was the same, but David was gone. A twinge of ironic self-pity touched my groggy, sleep-filled mind as I remembered his promise not to go until he saw me sleeping peacefully. I put my head down on the pillow.

It isn't the room, it's the David that's changed.

I curled up tightly under the quilt.

It isn't the David, it's the dreams.

It isn't the dreams, it's the bed.

Rockaby, baby, your cradle is hard.
Your pa picked it up in the junkman's backyard.

In the quiet room, my eyes already closed, I smiled. Why had I thought of it? It was years since I'd jumped rope to it, or bounced a Spaldeen to it, or whatever that particular one had been for. I hadn't thought of any of those crazy things. Nonsense for all occasions. No jump rope or Spaldeen providing itself, words to be spouted at little girls passing the drugstore on their way home from school:

She likes herself she thinks she's grand,
She goes to the movies to hold her hand.
She puts her arm around her waist,
When she gets fresh she smacks her face.

Or perhaps stage-whispered at your younger brother as he hurried down a school staircase he thought was deserted because he couldn't see you hiding underneath:

> *I had a little brother no bigger than a thumb*
> *I put him in the coffee pot, he rattled like a drum.*

I knew it was late because Fernette took pains to inform me that the others had long since had breakfast and vanished. I avoided clocks. I didn't want to know whether the funeral was just beginning, or in process, or over. I think that if my father had called me any time up to the time when it was over, I would have forgiven him. Not so much out of generosity as out of need, for I had awakened without losing that frightening sense that I was not where I seemed to be, that my eyes were frames through which I viewed moving pictures in which I only seemed to be taking part.

I read the newspaper. Mrs. Stamm had left the *Times* at the dining table, so I read the paper and convinced myself that the world existed, even though I was not in my assigned place on it. I reached the classified ads and went through the real estate section, trying to figure out where I could afford a room. I began with the idea of finding something close to either Hunter or Arlou (thus saving me time and carfare) that would also be reasonably easy for David to reach. The more often he could visit, the more bearable the next few months would be. One run-through of rentals shattered my original idea but substituted a consoling possibility; most of the reasonable rooms listed were in the Columbia area, where David could reach me easily and often. I listed a few of the ads and took the list back to my room with me.

I put the room in order, then opened one of the cartons and took out a skirt and sweater. I had Fernette bring in the ironing board and steam iron, and I was pressing the skirt when Boris knocked at the door. I was so happy to see him that I put down the iron and ran over to hug him. He blushed happily.

"It's so good to see you," I said. "I was lonely."

"I didn't know. My father said he'd take me ice-skating, and you were still sleeping, and he said maybe you wouldn't feel like talking and anyhow—"

"Hey," I said softly, "don't get all upset about it. I just wanted you to know I was glad you were back."

He sat on the edge of the bed, watching me iron. "Ruth, I'm sorry about—you know—that you can't go and everything."

It was the second time he'd said something about Martin. Both times so grave. So pained for me. So undramatic. I wanted to hold him in my arms and rock him back and forth as though he were my baby.

"You know," I said, "that you're very dear to me?"

His face flushed. "If I was David," he said, his voice trembling but determined, "I'd have *made* your father let you go. He has no right to stop you from going."

"I don't know. I don't know if he has a right. Anyway, it's not just a question of rights. What if I went and he tried to keep me out? Or I went in and we had a fight? That would be terrible. Much worse than not going."

He pondered that for a moment, then said with vehemence, "I would hate your father if I ever met him!"

It made me smile. (And see myself smiling. And wonder that I could stand watching myself smile. An endless chain whose links were artificial but broke only at their own will.)

"Well," I said, "that's all right. That's fine, as a matter of fact."

"Do *you* hate him?"

"I don't know. I think so."

"I hope I don't meet him until I'm much bigger, because then if he says something to you I'll—"

"Boris," I cut him off, "let's not talk about it any more, okay?" Then, because he looked hurt, "It's not you, sweetheart. It's me. It's hard for me to talk about it now."

"I'm sorry."

"Don't be sorry. You didn't do anything."

He looked unconvinced.

"Tell me," I said, "do you and your dad have plans for the afternoon?"

"Uh-uh."

"Want to go to the movies with me?"

His face lit up. "Sure. Which one?"

"You pick it. I'll finish up here and you go look in the paper, all right?"

As it turned out, the three of us went together, Boris, his father, and I. After the movies we had ice-cream sodas at Addie Vallins and then, in spite of the biting cold, we walked across Eighty-sixth Street and back up Fifth Avenue to the house. Most of the time we were silent, but I remember that at one point, looking at the bare trees in Central Park and the frosty now-gray sky behind them, I suddenly told Walter

Stamm that I was having trouble regaining some sort of equilibrium, that everything around me seemed strange. Artificial. He murmured something vaguely sympathetic, and we walked the rest of the way without speaking.

Thea was waiting in the library, wearing black and looking very beautiful because black set off her features. She was sitting in the red leather chair. Walter Stamm had gone directly to the back rooms. Boris began walking away from me, too, toward his room, but I called him back and brought him into the library with me to meet Thea. They shook hands shyly. I noticed that her eyes were still slightly swollen. She seemed to be waiting for Boris to leave, but I didn't particularly want him to.

"I guess I should do some homework," Boris said.

"No," I said. "Stay with me. You don't mind, do you, Thea?"

"No, of course not," she said softly. "Not if you don't." She seemed on the verge of more tears.

Boris sat down on the sofa, facing her, and I was about to sit next to him but then changed my mind. The sofa wasn't far enough from those swollen eyes. I walked around to the back of the sofa and lit a cigarette. Boris turned sideways on the sofa; I could feel them both watching me.

"All right," I said to Thea. "Tell me all about it. Make me cry. I dare you."

"Oh, Ruth." A tearful whisper.

I threw up my hands and walked away from them. Around the big desk, toward the window.

"All right. Don't tell me about my own brother's funeral. See if—" But then I stopped my fake raving because it had a frightening, familiar sound.

You sound like Martin on one of his crazy days.

I mashed out my cigarette in the desk ashtray and lit another one. I couldn't look at Thea. I leaned against the desk and stared at the molding between the ceiling and the wall opposite me.

"Thea? The casket was closed, wasn't it?"

"Yes."

"Was the eulogy decent? Or did they give some horrible spiel about how he loved mankind and got good marks in school?"

"They—it wasn't horrible, Ruth. It was actually quite nice."

"Nice?"

"Well, I mean, moving. It was really quite beautiful, Ruth. They—the rabbi—goes on what you tell him about the person, you know. He didn't pretend he knew Martin. He said he wished he *had* known Martin and he wished Martin had known *him*, because he would have liked to be the one to show Martin that—oh, dear, I'm trying to remember it exactly but it's hard—that he, Martin, I mean, had been closer than he realized to both his future and his past."

"What does that mean?"

"Well . . ." She pulled at her upper lip as she usually did when she was concentrating. "He was talking about, you know, about being Jewish, and being religious, and all that. He said that not all good Jews were found in the temples."

"That doesn't sound like any rabbi I've ever heard of."

She nodded. "I know. He's Reform. He's a very intelligent man."

"Where'd they find him?"

She hesitated. "Mrs. Landau. Her brother who lives in Rockville Center. It was a personal favor, he doesn't usually come to New York."

A surge of helpless anger at the sudden dominance of David's mother in our household.

"He said that Martin was a boy who loved his family and his friends and would have come to love Judaism, too, if this tragedy hadn't cut off his life."

"Do you believe that, Thea?"

"Which?"

"Any of that stuff?"

"Well, the family and friends part, naturally. The part about Judaism . . ." Furrowed brow. "Maybe he meant Judaism in a more general way. You know, loving God. A feeling for the past, all that." Momentary embarrassment as she remembers: Ruthie says she doesn't believe in God, and while Ruthie couldn't possibly mean it way down deep, there it is and you mustn't hurt her feelings.

Boris was kneeling on the sofa now, his chin resting on the back. Without looking at him, I knew that his large serious eyes were riveted to my face.

"What about my mother?"

Thea's face brightened. "She's been wonderful, Ruth. You'd be proud of her. You can see what it's done to her when you look at her face, but she's been carrying on so beautifully. She's been so dignified, not hysterical or anything like that. Of course—" Hesitation again, but over what this time? "Of course, Mrs. Landau has been a tremendous comfort to them." The words in a rush now lest Ruthie cut off the fair praise. "I know you've never gotten along with her too well, Ruth, but honestly, you'd feel different if you could see her now. She's been marvelous. She's taken care of everything."

"I don't doubt it."

"She got the rabbi, of course, and she called everyone who had to be called, and she put one of those little announcements in the paper, and—"

"It's a shame she never graduated from public school. She would have been the perfect funeral director."

"Not just the funeral." Too intent or too Thea to notice even this heavy-handed irony. "People have brought food, naturally, but anything else they need, she makes or she buys. They're sitting *shivah* up at her house, she said it would be easier on your mother; this way, even if people were around, she could go down and rest if she wanted to. Your father keeps saying he can't understand how he failed to appreciate all these years what a good person Mrs. Landau really was."

"He never knew how much they had in common."

She nodded. She went on with the details for a while, sitting there, earnest, ingenuous, eager that I should see the good in all of them. If I'd interrupted to assure her that my father's attitudes could hardly be of interest to me since I would never see him again, she would have told me that time heals all wounds.

"Have you talked to my mother?"

"A little. I went up this afternoon."

"Did she say anything about me? Do you know if she tried to get an idea of what really happened?"

"I don't think so. But there really wasn't much chance. You know, with so many people around."

I forced a smile. She stood up, and I was afraid for a moment that she was going to come over and pat me on the shoulder. I walked over to the window, then stood looking down at Fifth Avenue through the haze of the streetlamps.

"Tell me something, Thea." I turned back to her. "It's not important, but I'm curious. Did anyone say anything, at any time, I mean during the funeral, or before, or after, did anyone say anything during the whole time that would give people the idea that Martin ever had a sister?"

Blank look. Then, finally, comprehension. Poor Thea. She really hadn't thought of it that way.

"Oh, Ruth." A quiver in a vacuum. "How can you think that, Ruth?"

"I didn't say I thought anything, Thea. I just asked a question. Have you heard my name mentioned in the past two days?"

"I can't remember, but I'm sure it was. I'm sure I'd have noticed if they—if they purposely—"

"Don't get all upset about it. Honestly, I didn't mean to upset you. *I'm* not upset." Not so honestly.

She sat down again. I sat on the window sill.

"The Stamms have offered to let me live here with them."

"How lovely."

"Mmm. But I'm not going to accept."

Boris, who had disappeared behind the sofa back, popped up again. I'd forgotten his presence, and the fact that he didn't know yet. I pretended that I still didn't notice him.

"I feel as though I have to get out on my own. You know, struggle a little. It's too comfortable here. The longer I stay, the harder it'll be to leave."

She nodded, understanding. Why are lies so much easier to grasp than the truth?

"I'll probably rent a room around Columbia someplace. There seem to be cheap ones available up there. And it'll be easy for David. You'll visit me, won't you? You won't forget me just because I'm up there in the wilds of the West?"

"Of course not."

I walked over to the sofa and put my hands on Boris's head. "And this character. If he doesn't visit me, you'll have to drag him up there for me. No, never mind. I'll come here and drag him myself." I looked down and was rewarded with a brave eleven-year-old smile. I let my fingers drum a little tune on his head.

"I guess I'd better get back," Thea said after a moment.

"Why so soon? Can't I give you a cup of tea or something?"

"I promised my mother I'd be home for dinner."

"Ah, of course, Princess Thea must be back by six or the ghetto gates will slam in her face."

"Oh, Ruth." Giggling a little, this time, with relief that I was back to the old kind of teasing. The kind she could be sure was in fun. She put on her coat. No, it wasn't her coat, but her mother's black one—a little too wide, and too short. I walked with her to the front door, after holding out my hand to Boris so he would walk with me.

"Ruth, I . . ." She looked from me to Boris, hesitating.

"What is it, Thea?"

"Ruth, I know how you feel right now. But—" I watched her curiously, trying to understand her difficulty. "Don't—but don't be too— They've had a very bad time, Ruth. Don't be too hard on them."

I stared at her, thinking how I would have hated anyone else who dared to make that earnest plea for my clemency.

"Thea," I said, "I didn't run away from home. I was kicked out."

"Oh, but he didn't mean it."

"Has he told you that?"

"No, but he doesn't have to, Ruth. I know he couldn't have meant it."

"Do you think it was a joke? That's quite a joke, to accuse me of murdering my brother" (out of the corner of my eye I could see Boris's head swivel sharply up to me), "and then order me out of his house."

Pause to consider, if not digest, this information. Then, hopefully, "But, Ruth, you have to make allowances for his state of mind."

"I do? Why? Did he make allowances for mine?"

She looked at me sadly for a moment. This was so much more complicated than a starving kitten or a bum freezing to death in the doorway. She sighed.

"I just don't want you to hate him."

"You'd better get home, sweet, I'll see you at school."

She hugged me quickly and walked a few steps to the front door. Boris's hand slipped into mine as we followed her. It was very cold, although he was still wearing his sweater. I glanced at his face; he was staring at Thea with an intensity quite unusual for him.

"You're wrong," he burst out fiercely as she opened the door. "You're wrong! He shouldn't of done those things. He shouldn't of said that, about what he said. Him, too, Martin. He shouldn't of said things. Sometimes he said such mean things to her I wanted to hit him!"

Not looking at Thea, foolish tears in my eyes, I knelt on the floor and hugged him, my arms around his waist, my face against his slender sweatered chest. He put his hands on my shoulders and patted them comfortingly. My eleven-year-old Lancelot. Behind me, the door closed.

In the long run, though, it was not Boris but Lou Fine and Selma who restored my sense of reality. Lou, and Selma, and the shabby sameness of Arlou when I went there Tuesday afternoon. Selma stared at me as though I were a ghost when I walked in.

She knows.

I must have assumed that I would have to tell them both, but I hadn't thought at all about what I would say. And now I was thrown off by the knowledge that I could not, after all, tell them in my own time and way.

"Ruth!" She stood up and came over to me. "Whaddya doing here, honey, for God's sake?" It was less a question than an exclamation of distress. She took my arm and led me to her chair, making me sit down, as though I were the pregnant one and I had just done some crazy foolhardy thing.

"I'm all right, Selma," I said. "Please don't fuss over me."

But she took my books and pocketbook, and insisted upon helping me off with my coat, all the time muttering to herself about crazy young girls who saw too many moving pictures and thought you had to carry on like nothing had happened no matter what happened.

I laughed. "You sound like some old crow."

"Never mind," she said severely, wagging a finger at me. "Never mind this business. You think I don't know how you're feeling, Miss Smarty, you gotta put on a laugh?" She turned from me in maternal anger, picked up the telephone, and gave our room number to the luncheonette downstairs. "Two teas, one with lemon, one with milk, and two poundcake." Her prescription, apparently, for the grief-stricken and those sorrowing with them, for I never drank tea and she had had it only occasionally during the first months of her pregnancy. "Hold it a second." She put a hand over the speaker. "I bet you didn't have lunch," she said accusingly. I shook my head. "One grilled cheese and one burger, medium well. And a pack of Pawl Mawls and a Clark Bar. And a pack of Life Savers. Butter rum." She put down the phone and turned back to me, easing her now mammoth backside onto the edge of the desk. She was wearing an incredibly frilly white maternity smock, the sort of thing she'd never have dreamed of buying before she was pregnant, when she'd stuck to inexpensive tailored clothes in the dark colors that were best for her size-eighteen shape. She must have weighed over two hundred pounds by this time, her sixth month, and her frilly white contentedness seemed to fill up the whole office.

I smiled at her. "Have you seen Dr. Zwicker yet this month? He'll have a fit when he weighs you. Clark Bars!"

She stared at me, all majestic seriousness. "I don't know, Ruth," she finally said. "I never figured you for such a big joker. What's going on?"

I suppose she was the first one to really call my bluff. The others had been inclined, at best, to let me drift whichever way I pleased, sympathetic in turn to my self-pity and my self-delusion.

"I don't know," I said. "I mean, I do know, but it's a long story."

"I don't mean to pry," she said quickly.

"You're not prying," I assured her. "You're being very sweet."

"Sweet," she said. "What's sweet?"

The phone rang; she answered it and wrote down a message.

"Is he out to lunch?" I asked.

"Sort of. He was gonna drop down to your house. We figured you'd be sitting *shivah*."

I closed my eyes in dismay. "When did he leave?"

"Around eleven."

I looked at the wall clock. It was almost twelve-forty.

"He called me yesterday," she said, "after he saw it in the paper. We were gonna go to the funeral. Then Lillian pulled something, you know, one of her fits or something, so he called me back. He had to take her to the doctor. I felt funny, to go by myself. I'm sorry. I—I'm sorry about your brother."

The lunch was delivered. She paid the boy, refusing to take any money from me. Then she doled out the food in businesslike fashion.

"Which one you like—cheese, or burger medium well? It's all the same to me. How'd you like your tea—milk or lemon? I could take milk and sugar, or lemon and sugar, so it's the same to me."

"I never saw you drink tea, except in your first months," I told her.

"I drink it all the time," she said, "at night. All I have to do is smell a cup of coffee at night, I don't sleep a wink."

We finished our sandwiches in the embarrassed atmosphere of an almost established intimacy. She took the wrappings before I could throw them away myself, then neatly spread the poundcake on napkins on the desk. I watched her fussing around me like a mother hen, thinking how strange it was that in the past few days most of the people within the circle of my life had moved to its perimeter or beyond, while people like Boris and Selma had become very important to me. Lou Fine came back while we were still eating. He stopped short when he saw me, but then nodded slightly, as though it were not really surprising to find me there. He came over to me, unsmiling, and put a gentle hand on my shoulder.

"You didn't come because you thought you had to come."

"No, Mr. Fine."

He went to hang his hat and coat on the rack near the door, then he looked back and forth between Selma and me as though trying to puzzle out what had been said.

"It's all right to speak?" he finally asked me.

I nodded.

"I talked with your poor mother."

I hadn't had a cigarette since coming in, but now I instinctively groped in my bag, found one, lit it.

"She sends you her love."

I dragged deeply on the cigarette and waited. But he seemed to want some acknowledgment from me. I thanked him.

"I don't know why I knocked," he mused. "There was a sign on the door saying the family was sitting *shivah* upstairs, but I knocked anyhow. Thinking maybe to find you without all the people."

Let's talk about girdles. I was suddenly frightened of what he might tell me.

"Maybe I knocked from Selma's instinct." He smiled vaguely. "Selma asked me why don't they say in the *Times* 'beloved brother of Ruth,' am I sure it's the same one? I tell her I'm sure, it's not such a common name, and the neighborhood of the parlor, and the wording, and it must be just a mistake. She tells me no, they don't make mistakes like that."

I hadn't thought to find out whether I'd been abolished from the public record.

"With no instincts of my own, I have to trust to women's more, ah, Ruth?" But he didn't look to me for assent this time. "I don't think I woke her up. I don't know if she sleeps, yet. We talked for a while, then someone came down. The woman from upstairs, I think. A big woman, gray hair. Bertha?"

I nodded.

"She—"

"Just don't talk about her," I said quickly. "Please, Mr. Fine," I added more gently, seeing how I had startled him, "I want to hear the rest of it but I can't . . ." I could feel Selma's curiosity pulling at me. I put out my cigarette and lit a new one; then I waited, feeling for him as he tried to adjust his train of thought to a track that would not run through my nerve center.

"What did my mother say to you?"

"I don't know that I could tell you exactly all the words," he said, providing me with a hedge against disappointment. "I remember she said over and over again, 'My own son, Mr. Fine. My own daughter.' I don't know what else." He glanced at Selma. "She's all mixed up, you know. She told me a little, but she—she's confused. She doesn't understand. Your father told her what happened, but she doesn't understand." He waited, demanding nothing.

"My brother was acting—my brother was very depressed and I was

afraid to go away and leave him home," I said quietly. "He and my father were always at each other's throats, and I was worried. The people
who were taking me to the country offered to take Martin too. Naturally, I accepted. It would have been crazy not to accept when all he'd
have done at home would be to hang around the house and go out with
his crazy friends and fight with my father and—"

"Yes, yes," he said gently, making me hear the sudden intensity in
my voice. "Of course."

"It's near Mount Mantinoc," I said, calm again. "They all ski. They
said they'd teach us, and I didn't want to learn, but Martin was dying
to go—" *No! No! That's not what I wanted to say!* "Martin was—"
Selma's whiteness loomed terrifyingly over me, blocking out the words
I needed. I pushed my chair back away from her and the desk, and
dragged deeply on my cigarette. "Martin was terribly excited about it."
The words made the whiteness retreat farther; she was Selma again.
"They said he was the best natural skier they ever saw. Five days. Five
crazy days. Every day a little more than he was supposed to. He loved
it. It was as if he'd been born on skis. He was wild for it. They said he
couldn't go from the top, but he did it on the fifth day anyhow, before
anyone could stop him." I moved my chair back to the desk and put out
the cigarette. "I don't like high places. I never liked them. In fifth
grade my class took a trip to the Empire State Building and I got my father to write a note so I wouldn't have to go."

Selma took out her package of Life Savers and held it out to me. I
took one and rubbed it between my fingers as though it were beach
glass.

"It's a terrible thing," Lou Fine said, "that they should hold you responsible for this."

"No!" Selma said, so forcefully that the Life Saver popped out of her
mouth and onto the desk. "No. They don't!"

"*She* does, too?" I said to Lou Fine.

He saw that he had made a mistake, and pondered. "No, Ruth," he
finally said. "I wouldn't say she does. I would say your mother is very
confused. She knows you are a good girl, and yet your father . . . her
attitude toward your father I must admire."

I thought of Lillian, who over the phone whined at Selma and me
such instructions as, "And make sure he gets the train schedule right,
will you?"—although as far as we could see, Lou's head never jumbled
any figure.

"He does not simply hold me responsible," I told Selma. "He con-
siders me a murderer."

"Oh, my God!" Selma moaned. "How crazy can people be?"

"This I didn't know," Lou said, running his fingers through his gray hair. "Are you sure, Ruth, that from being hurt you're not letting your mind make it worse than it is?"

"He said that I murdered Martin. That I deliberately let him go where I knew he'd kill himself. Because I wanted a room of my own."

"The pig!" Selma said. "The rotten pig!"

"Now, Selma," Lou said slowly, "say nothing you'll be sorry for when this is over."

"Over!" she exploded.

"Now, now." He raised a hand to stop the flow of her wrath. "Please. I don't say it will be over, but you don't know for sure. People forget things you don't dream they would forget."

"You do not forget," Selma pronounced with angry authority, the creased and frilly white mountain of her a comfort to me now, "that your own father calls you a murderer. Of your brother, yet!"

I had told only the truth, yet I vaguely felt that I was exploiting their innocence. I hadn't indulged in gory histrionics, or even made the slightest attempt to convey the obscenity and violence of my father's attack on me. Why, then, the tiny nagging guilt at the measure of their sympathy—as though I had omitted some fact the telling of which would have made them less sympathetic to me?

"Try to have patience with your mother, Ruth. She must be afraid to do anything now. For her it's an impossible situation now, to do anything."

"I know," I said. "I know you're right."

And if I don't feel that you're right, besides knowing it, well, maybe that's more than she can ask.

The Life Saver was sticky between my fingers. I threw it in the wastebasket and rinsed off my fingers at the water cooler.

Then they got down to the practical matters of my life, as though it obviously fell to them to provide for my well-being. I explained about looking for a room, and it was agreed between them that as soon as Selma had gotten one or two important letters out, she was to go uptown with me to help me find one. The idea had surprising appeal, but I felt obliged to remind them that it was January, and with market week coming up, they had to take advantage of the few slow days after the holiday.

"Thank you," said Lou, "for reminding me that in January comes market week. It's good you came in today to remind me."

As far as my hours at Arlou were concerned, they worked out a perfect arrangement under which I would, for the balance of the school year, work as much or as little as I desired. Selma professed herself to be at a point in her pregnancy where she would rather not work every day, anyway. So that if I should be able to work out a three- or four-day school program for the spring term (I had only eleven credits to go), she would gladly let me put in the other days in her place at Arlou—if it was all right with Mr. Fine, which it most certainly was. During intersession, I could take over full time if I wanted to, and she would come in part time then; and, if it should be necessary, we could both work full time. Otherwise, she would be glad of a total vacation—not that it would really be a vacation, she assured me. There were a million things she hadn't had a chance to do, like ordering the crib. When I asked Lou whether he wouldn't have a more difficult time, then, when Selma really left in April, he assured me that he'd learned years ago that with office personnel, unlike merchandise, it did not pay to think ahead.

"Selma," he said, "Mrs. Weinstock, here, is the first girl I ever hired I didn't try to ascertain she would be here a year or more. The others I tried to make sure there was no boyfriend, no school to go back to in the fall, no baby already in the belly that months later they would claim astonishment to find there. My anxiety weighed heavily upon them; they did not share my feeling against change. After the Depression, I couldn't hold on to girls. With the war, you know, so many found new things open to them. It was like asking a butterfly to light on one flower only, a flower whose beauty maybe is the kind the butterfly doesn't see." He smiled at us. Thank you, his smile said, for your patience with this foolish old man who cannot tell between his girdle business and a flower. "So along comes Mrs. Weinstock, then Miss Gertner. I note that she has a large diamond ring on her finger but I do not ask if she will get married soon and leave me. This is a nice girl, I tell myself, with good penmanship and a clear speaking voice, people will understand her on the telephone. I will hire her, even if in a few months she will be taken from me by a husband, or by a munitions factory that will pay her double what I can pay so she can stand on a line all day putting something into something." He paused. "So?" He looked at her fondly. There were tears in his eyes. "So, when was it?"

She lumbered over to him and stretched past her monstrous belly to give him a loud kiss on the cheek.

"Ai, yai, yai," he said, happily overwhelmed. "If I knew what was there all these years just for the asking."

"June, 1943," Selma said to me, her eyes also full of tears. "Nearly eight years. My first job. I was a dopey kid right outa high school."

The tears, in their gentle contagion, reached me.

A short while later Selma and I took the IRT subway up to 116th Street to investigate the various rooming houses on the side streets between Broadway and Riverside Drive.

Without meaning to, I kept looking for David as we walked quickly along the cold windy streets, and every once in a while I would see a back that looked something like his and quicken my pace until I became aware that Selma was puffing frantically to keep up with me, by which time I would realize that the boy wasn't David, anyway. I had no idea of where he would be at this hour, of all the possible buildings, or even whether he would be up at school, and I kept telling myself not to be absurd, there wasn't one chance in a million that I'd run into him. But it had nothing to do with the likelihood, only with the desire, and I looked for him as often during the years when he was in San Francisco as I did when I knew him to be in New York.

We must have tried a dozen buildings. Selma was indignant at the condition of most of them, but I hadn't managed to wipe my home out of my mind so completely as to be anguished by the falling plaster and rusty pipes of an apartment building that was only twenty or thirty years old.

The Mattracorne was on 112th and had not yet sunk into total indifference to its past glories. The lobby's marble floor wasn't clean, but it wasn't littered with used Kleenex and candy wrappers, either, and the elevator was fairly new and not nearly so frightening as some of the gasping, heaving monsters we'd ridden in during the afternoon.

The strange skinny man who took us upstairs explained that it was a bad time to find rooms, what with final exams at the school only a couple of weeks away, but he just happened to have a single available by virtue of the fact that the young lady who had inhabited 3A-3, a major in literatchoor who had spent part of her Christmas vacation in Havana getting an abortion, had become ill upon her return and not a week before had been taken on a stretcher to St. Luke's, which was, I would be glad to hear, conveniently close. Behind us in the elevator, Selma made a faint noise of disgust but I pretended not to hear. I had too many reality factors to consider; I couldn't afford to be affected by previous occupants.

"How much is it?"

"It's on special," he said. "Nine-fifty."

"Why is it on special?" I asked.

"Well, uh, you know," he said, grinning conspiratorially, "you have to take things into consideration. There's lots of people don't want a room, you know—superstitious. Soon as they hear what happened they don't even want to look at it."

"Did you ever consider not telling them?" I asked as the elevator doors opened and we walked out into the hall. Injured, he refused to answer me. At 3A he knocked on the door.

"Fussy ones," he said with a shrug. "They're not allowed to lock the outside door so I have to knock first to see if someone's home."

One for their side.

"Tell me," I said, "what was the rental before all this happened?"

He turned to me, his equanimity restored. "Nine dollars and fifty cents," he said, as a tall girl in jeans and a plaid shirt opened the door for us.

"Good afternoon, Miss Baum. I would like to show 3A-3 to this young lady, if you do not mind."

"Sure," she said, looking at me. "But would you mind taking off your shoes? I'm waxing the hall floor and the stuff's just dry enough to polish but heels'll scrape it off."

"Not at all," I said. As I slipped off my pumps I glanced at Selma to see if she was registering approval of this good omen. But she was bent over her stomach, grunting as she tugged off her own shoes.

"I believe I will wait here," the man said. "I'm not sure my socks are of a cleanliness that would warrant walking on your floors."

"I'm not sure you're wrong," she said calmly, opening the door further so that Selma and I could slip past her.

"Now don't say anything to discourage these nice young ladies, Miss Baum," he told her.

"Don't make me laugh," she said coolly, and closed the door.

It was like being in a different world. The pleasant smell of the wax as we walked cautiously through the central foyer; the cheerful yellow walls; the generally immaculate look of the place; and the prints on the walls—nothing interesting, the standard dull Utrillo street scenes, a Rivera child, the Toulouse-Lautrec poster of Aristide Bruant. But they contributed to the impression I had of having left the seedy squalor of boarding houses for a place where the Girl Scout virtues prevailed. A hand-painted sign, bordered with flowers, testified to someone's awareness of the effect:

WELCOME
to an Isle of Sanity
in the Sea of Distress

I laughed. "That's just what I was thinking."

It was as though I'd said the magic word. Her manner changed from casual politeness to warm friendliness as she gave me various details about the apartment and led me toward the vacant room, with Selma trailing behind us.

The room was small and might have been dark, as its windows fronted on the stone wall of the adjacent house. But the walls were a clean new-looking white, the furniture had been painted blue and decorated with Pennsylvania Dutch designs, a bright-red corduroy spread covered the bed, and most of the floor was covered with a gold cotton-pile rug.

"Where do I pay the rent?"

She laughed. "Don't you want to look around?"

I shook my head.

"Well, are there any questions I can answer?"

I turned to Selma and realized for the first time that she had remained in the hallway, just outside the door.

"Tell the truth," I said, pulling her into the room. "Have you seen anything like this?"

"It's very attractive," she said politely, and I wondered if she was a little offended. I'd virtually forgotten her existence since we'd come into this apartment.

"Without Selma," I said, "I wouldn't have survived long enough to reach this place."

Rita nodded. "Let's see, did I tell you about the bathrooms? There are two. You have to go through my room to get to this one, then there's the master bathroom on the other side of the hall. The girls over there share it, but they're used to having us drop over now and then."

Quick vision: a rusty toilet in a dark outside hall.

"If you don't mind me asking," Selma said suddenly, "who did all this? I mean, does all this stuff belong to someone?"

"Oh, no," Rita said quickly. "The rug and curtains used to be mine, but I gave the curtains to the girl who used to be in this room when I got new ones. I helped her paint the furniture. And then, the rug, well I wanted a new one, anyhow, and after she moved out I put this in here."

"Why?" Selma asked.

Rita sighed. "I gather the ghoul has told you. I thought maybe just this once he'd kept his fool mouth shut."

Selma was unmoved by her candor.

"Look," Rita said, talking only to me, "I don't see any sense in talking about it. Lu——the girl was a nice girl, or at least I thought she was, then it turned out she was leading this whole crazy double life I didn't know anything about. She only told me when she needed some help to arrange for her—her trip. I'm trying very hard to wipe it out of my mind. I did want to get rid of the rug, but it's also true that there was a little blood left on the floor—she started hemorrhaging in here—and I couldn't scrub it out, and I wanted to cover it. I've always tried to make the place look attractive, though, for the three years I've lived here. After all, it's to my own interest to get desirable tenants. I can't see that I'm trying to put anything over on you."

"Of course not," I said. We left the room and in embarrassed silence walked through the outside foyer. She gave me the number of the hallway telephone and asked when I expected to move in. I hadn't actually thought about it, but I automatically said that I would be back later in the evening. The man had vanished from the hallway.

"He must have gotten restless," Rita said. "Or thirsty. Do you want me to go down to the office with you?"

"Thanks," I said, slipping waxily into my shoes. "We'll find him."

"Just ignore everything he says," she called down the hallway. "And make him give you a cash receipt."

Selma and I had hamburgers in a place on Broadway after she'd made sure her husband was working late and I'd called the Stamms and told Fernette I wouldn't be home for dinner. Selma was clearly unenthused about my new room. I might have shrugged off her attitude had I not felt a little guilty that having leaned on her so heavily a few hours before, I needed her so little now. So I said more than once that I valued her opinion and only wished that I could understand just what her objection to the place was. What her answer amounted to was that she did not object to the room, she was just suspicious. There was something about the whole thing that was phony. Something about that girl that wasn't quite right. And when I jokingly asked if she thought the whole thing had been staged for our benefit, she said no, not really, but . . . and trailed off as though she did mean something like that but had realized she couldn't express it in a way I would understand. We went on to easier matters, like making lists of the things I would have to do, the people I would have to call. We skirted around specific matters involving the room, embarrassed by our failure to understand each other on the subject.

Weeks, or months later, of course, I did come to understand what had bothered Selma about Rita Baum and her Isle of Sanity. Not that I regretted moving in; the room, the setup, Rita's habits, were no less virtuous than she had proclaimed them to be. What Selma had reacted to instinctively but I came to see only when realization was forced upon me, was that suite 3A was not so much an island of sanity as a shrine to it, and Rita, the self-appointed embodying spirit, the High Priestess of Normalcy, perpetually redecorating the chintzy temple of her domain. Pennsylvania Dutch in the bedroom, Ivory Flakes in the bathroom and Girl Scout cookies in the kitchen. And above them all, a Peggy Ann Garner kind of voice saying, "Gee whiz, folks, step right up and see the Most Super-Normal Girl in the World." Rita talked about meeting a nice normal guy the way girls I'd known in high school talked about meeting a doctor, and about the state of normalcy as though she were the sole human being with an indisputable right to dwell there. Eventually, I came to understand why.

In the meantime, I found in her a friend who was even more eager than I to nullify the sordid facts of life by denying them both mind and voice. If I sound either snide or nostalgic, then I am investing myself with a sophistication I don't possess. I'm not at all certain that our silent method was a bad one. I have heard one too many cocktail-party drunk loudly enunciate the gruesome facts of a ghastly childhood or the promiscuous adventures of a tortured adolescence—only to collapse on the floor afterward in a drink-dampened coma of self-pity. Confession may sometimes pave the way to virtue, but it seems more often to provide an excuse for the soul to wallow pleasurably in its own guilt. If I need now to record and examine the facts of my life, my need stems not from the hope that I shall feel cleansed when I have done so, but from the fear that I shall go mad if I do not.

CHAPTER FIVE

Breakfast at school cafeteria—one or two coffees and Danish (thirty or forty cents); lunch at desk at Arlou—coffee and grilled cheese or cream-cheese-and-olive sandwich (forty-five cents plus ten-cent tip); dinner at the apartment—eggs, or a can of hash, or chili, or occasionally a chop with baked potato and salad. If I came home in time to eat with Rita, I ate relatively well, but she sat down promptly at six-thirty each night and I didn't like to ask her to prepare food for me unless I was sure I'd be home on time and wouldn't have to rush through the meal. It was important to Rita that the kitchen not be simply a cafeteria for transients, and I could understand her feelings on the subject too well to violate them. So generally, even when I could leave Arlou early if I chose, I would study there for an hour or so before going home. I kept a small stock of canned goods at the apartment, as well as a supply of apples and oranges, but there were days when the thought of opening one more can made me feel ill. Then, if I had too much work for a leisurely dinner with Rita, I would buy a quarter of a pound of chopped beef, and a fresh bakery roll, and a bag of fresh peas or string beans. At home, I would spread the raw beef on the roll, heavily salt and pepper it, and eat it with the raw vegetables while doing homework. After my two-thirds-of-the-day cheese and starch diet, I invariably had a craving for fresh fruits and vegetables, and although Thea (worriedly) and David (teasingly) kept telling me that I was getting too thin, I could not force myself to eat Thea's chocolate bars or the marble cake my mother would give David to bring up to me.

Nor could I give up the walking, in spite of the knowledge that it must be contributing to my loss of weight. I walked from school to Arlou almost every day, and occasionally I walked part of the way home from Arlou, too. Not often, though, because evening time was too precious to be wasted, particularly when it was a struggle to keep my eyes open after ten or eleven at night. Then, too, in the back of my mind I always entertained the dim hope that I would find David waiting for me when I reached home. I'd had an extra room key made up for him, but he hadn't been able to use it as often as I'd have liked. He had a couple of particularly rough courses that term and he was, in addition, serving as a research assistant to a professor at the school who was writing a book on international law.

Still, every once in a while I would walk in and find him reading in my room, or chatting with Rita in the kitchen. Rita let me know very quickly how much she approved of David, how "solid" he seemed. She expressed neither curiosity nor disapproval of our intimacy, primarily, I think, because of her conviction that what we did was all right since we were nice normal people. (I'd said, after all, that I'd known David since I was a child, and there was something very nice and normal about childhood sweethearts.) Rita gave nice normal people a leeway in their actions which could not safely be granted the less stable.

I did see David every Saturday night. Sometimes we met downtown, but if he'd spent the day at the school library, he would be waiting for me at the room when I came home from my afternoon with Boris. We might take a nap together, then go out and get something to eat, and return to the apartment—to talk, to make love, to sleep and make love again.

There was a strange quality to our evenings together. We were both matter-of-fact and ill at ease. There was so much that we didn't want to talk about; yet our awareness of those things, coupled with our consciousness of how little time we could spend together, prevented us from being comfortable in silence, either. The result being that David, who had always been a voracious newspaper reader, became my courier, not from the Lower East Side but from the outside world. The second Hiss trial was on. We'd briefly discussed Alger Hiss the year before in my history class; I'd been left with the vague impression that Hiss was an innocent martyr of the McCarthy era. Now, with calm perspective, David told me not only about Hiss and Chambers, but about Judith Coplon, William Remington, Elizabeth Bentley, and about the era of the Thirties.

So we sat around and chatted about Communists and civics and international law, as though we'd been married for twenty years. Yet always with a slight strain in our conversation—as though we'd been separated for a while during those years, and neither knew what the other had been doing during that period.

And then, in the middle of February, the City College basketball scandal broke and bridged the gap between the world we could share and the world we couldn't discuss.

Funny, about arguments. I could count on the fingers of one hand the ones I had with Walter that ended on the subject that set them off. Almost always there was some anger just beneath the subject's surface, only obliquely related to it, but waiting to break through at some convenient point to distort the original question beyond recognition, and make it clear that the original question wasn't the problem at all. Some deliberate hypocrisy of his would irritate me more than usual; some willful honesty of mine would not be permitted to pass. And we were at each other. Deadly, deadening rites in which the truth was soiled along with the participants.

Walter would talk about underprivileged minorities and would really be telling me he was deceived when he asked me to marry him. I would explain to Walter how I felt about Negroes and I'd be saying that at least I wasn't a hypocrite. We talked about the world and we were talking about our marriage. We knew at once so much more and so much less about ourselves than about the rest of the world, I suppose it was natural that we should have imprinted upon it what we did know of ourselves, while hoping that through resolving its issues we would solve the unhappy riddle of our own personalities.

Walter, suddenly involved in politics, world problems, racial issues, would make some stupid remark about the liberal Jewish community and the Jews' readiness to fight for the Negro cause.

"Oh, Walter," I'd say, "the biggest bigots I know are Jews. They only love the Negroes when the Negroes are being persecuted by someone else. The persecution makes them half-Jewish or something."

"What makes you think your attitude is so unusual, Ruth?" Pained. "Why do you have to be the only Jewish person in the world who's not a bigot?"

"Jewish person. Jewish person. You make it sound so genteel. Not like being a Jew."

"You change the subject at rather convenient times."

"What's the subject? Who's not a bigot? Whoever said I wasn't a bigot?"

"You'll say anything for an effect, won't you?"

"But I'm not saying it for effect," I told him quickly, although this was only partly true; I was telling the approximate truth for the perverse pleasure I took in its effect.

He searched my face for indications of trickery.

"I'm not kidding, Walter. I'm full of prejudices. I would have told you before, if you'd asked me."

"Apparently there are a lot of questions I should have asked you."

"You should have drawn up a questionnaire, Walter. Ruth: Are you a greasy Jewey kind of Jew or are you a nice nigger-loving Jewish person?"

He cringed as though I'd struck him. How Walter hated strong words, profane words, dirty words. His specialty was genteel cruelty. The art of suggesting he'd been betrayed without actually pointing at his betrayer. The battle fought in the guise of withdrawal so that the enemy's victory was dimmed by qualms at having shot while the opposition was in retreat.

"What . . ." quietly, with a dangerous smugness, "what about your friend—that girl who came up to the lake the first summer you were with us?"

"Rhoda Watkins." I noted, but let pass, that he had phrased the question so it somehow suggested that my basic status hadn't changed since then. "What about her? For one thing, she wasn't my friend. She was Martin's—she was just some girl my brother was screwing."

"You pretended to like her," he said, quickly, to cover the cold-water shock of my crudeness.

"I did like her."

"You respected her?"

"She was a very smart girl. Very hip. Good background. Much better than mine. As a matter of fact, you should have considered marrying *her*. She'd have been a much better wife for you than I am. Much more genteel. Her mother's a white-collar Jewish person and her father's something very respectable. A big black respec—"

"That's enough!" he shouted. And having broken that loathsome glacial façade I could ease back a little, even feel contrite. Half-willing victim to the illusion of a one-sided battle.

"I'm sorry, Walter. I was being melodramatic. It's very frustrating when you're being truthful and someone doesn't believe you."

"Well, I believe you now." Prim words, voice strung like a high wire.

"Maybe you believe the wrong thing. What I was saying just now isn't really the way I feel."

"Isn't it?" Remote.

"No, Walter. It isn't. I don't go along the street and see one of them and think to myself, *There goes a big black nigger*."

"What *do* you think?"

"Most of the time I don't think anything. I just know they're colored."

"Well, then, why all this hysteria?" Cool proclamation of my insanity. "After all, Ruth, no one expects you not to see what's in front of your eyes."

"But it's not that simple." Why couldn't I let it go? "If someone's a blond, I see that, too, but it's not always there in the same way. When Martin was having a hard time with Rhoda, I'd say to myself, *That black bitch, who does she think she is?* You see? It was always there. Something against her when I wanted it."

"Maybe I was wrong, Ruth. Maybe your attitude is more unusual than I thought."

"Oh, I don't know, Walter. I don't know if it's so unusual."

Our manners now fake-casual. Our sides apparently reversed. And the argument—whatever it was—just as bitter as before.

"It's my understanding that Jewish people have been traditionally more prepared to accept—"

"Ohh—" I interrupted, impatient of his pseudoacademic style, "half the time it's just the reverse side of the coin. All those girls who're just dying to go out with colored boys. Not that I can't understand it. There is something exciting about them. I remember going to a couple of basketball games at City and watching one or two of the colored players and thinking how gorgeous they were, how sexy."

Walter was startled but silent.

"This whole business of Negroes' being more sexy, the natural sense of rhythm business. You can say it however you want to, to make it sound all ethnic and respectable, but it comes down to meaning the same thing—that they're not so contaminated by intelligence as the rest of us."

Walter squinted at an artificial horizon on the wall in back of me, not so much considering my words as maintaining the appearance of considering them.

"That's quite a generalization," he finally said.

And generalizations are unjust, but anyone who attempts to think on any but the most primitive levels . . .

Why did Helen Stamm's words so often return to dog me? While being deluged by a stream of her violent rhetoric I barely separated one line from the next. Then weeks, months, even years later, at some moment when I least needed to feel the masculine assurance of her torrential oratory, when what I really needed was to be blind to Walter's self-induced stupidity, coyly unaware that his words rolled like oil beads off the sides of the place where his mind had once been, then some apt and pointed line of hers would be reborn fully coiled in my mind, eager to strike, a weapon not to be used lest I hurt him far more than I could hurt him by myself.

"I know it's a generalization, Walter. I wouldn't even swear it's a good one." A peace offering that time, perhaps out of uneasiness at having thought of Helen, perhaps because with my memory of the basketball games had come the memory of the scandal, and with that had come thoughts of David.

Walter said nothing. Unwilling to accept or openly reject my peace offer.

"What's that strange smile for?" he asked.

"I didn't realize I was smiling."

"Well, you were." His tone was petulant.

"I guess I was remembering the basketball scandal at City College. Before we were married. Do you remember anything about it?"

"None of the details," said Walter, at whose memory for details I had once marveled.

"Oh. Well . . . at first they arrested just three boys, two Jewish and one colored. There were really four big stars on the team, the fourth one was also colored. I remember Thea talking about it when I saw her at school. It was a couple of months after—you know—after I moved out. Anyway, all the parents were a little indignant that the score was two-to-one against the Jews. They were sure something was fishy. But for the kids, it was the only thing that cushioned the shock, that it was a capital-N Negro who'd saved their honor." I smiled. "I don't know if that was color prejudice or anti-Semitism, wanting the other guy to be better than they were."

Walter wasn't amused, but he smiled politely because we had somehow returned to a more civilized plane.

"There was a game the following week and of course the three boys who'd been arrested didn't play, but the fourth one did, and the whole school turned out to cheer for him, and the next day the D.A.'s office picked him up, too. That really did it. They'd made a kind of a black Jesus out of him and when he turned out to be a mortal it was worse than everything else combined, they felt horribly betrayed. I remember I had an impulse to write him a letter and tell him who he was or what he was didn't make a damn bit of difference, what happened was what would have happened to anyone and he shouldn't let himself believe he had any more responsibility to his race, or to anyone, than any Jew or anybody else on the team."

"Well," Walter said thoughtfully, "it's probably just as well you didn't. You wouldn't have wanted him to think that you condoned what he'd done."

He was waiting for me to say no, of course I wouldn't want the boy to think that. At what point would I finally hesitate to reveal my terrible self to him? He would have liked to trick me into a lie, and I was tempted. On the other hand, his eagerness repelled me.

"I wouldn't have wanted him to think I condemned him, either," I said.

So I was back at it—half-reluctant straight man to my particular version of the Real Honest Truth.

"*Condemn*, of course, is a strong word." His own words he clipped out carefully.

I was silent. *Can't we drop it now, Walter? You won't argue nearly so well as David, nor come so close to forcing an admission from me.*

"I hope . . . Ruth . . . that you aren't telling me that you approved of what he'd done."

"What difference does it make, Walter?" I was tired, and I sighed. "You know we don't feel the same way about these things. What good does it do to talk about them?"

Nothing will come of it. We'll only hate each other a little more.

"I would like to know," clip, clip, clip, clip, clip, "whether you approved of what he'd done. Of what they'd all done."

Mail in your coupon. Get yours by return mail in a plain brown wrapper.

"I can't honestly say that I disapproved."

The news of the first arrests broke on Sunday; I heard it on Rita's radio. She asked if I knew any of the people on the team, and I said only from parties. I wondered briefly whether Martin had known. I had recently had the desire to talk about Martin, but the one or two times I'd mentioned him, David had gone on to another subject. I couldn't tell whether this was deliberate, or understand why he should want to avoid talking about my brother. I wasn't even sure why I now had the need to discuss him.

I suppose what I wanted was reassurance that I had been guiltless in Martin's death. Yet no one had said I was guilty of it except my father, who was mad, and who himself had in a sense murdered Martin over the years. I didn't think at the time in terms of proving my innocence. It was more an "Emperor's New Clothes" kind of feeling; it was one thing not to discuss the unknown previous occupant of my room with Rita, but another to avoid speaking of my brother, who had been important to me, and whom I'd never understood. I wanted David to tell me whatever he knew about Martin. I wanted to know if he'd meant what he was saying, all those times he'd called Martin a crazy kid, and if he thought that Martin, in turn, had believed the things he'd said to us. I wanted to know what David's very first reaction had been to the news of Martin's death. Most of all I wanted to know what there was in my brother, or in me, or in both of us, that had made me believe his death before I knew of it. And I couldn't understand why David should shy away each time I tried to talk about my brother—as though he were embarrassed by Martin's nakedness. Or my own.

So I almost welcomed the news of the scandal as an excuse to bring up Martin when I saw David that week. At least, I thought, I'll be able to talk to David now.

He was waiting for me in my room when I got home on Saturday. He was lying on the bed and I thought he was asleep. I sat on the edge of the bed and looked at him for a while, then leaned over to kiss him—lightly, so that I wouldn't wake him up. But when I sat up again, his eyes were open and he was looking at me.

"I knew you were faking," I lied quickly.

"Of course," he said. "You know everything."

I got up and walked away from him, kicking off my shoes, then taking off my blouse and skirt, and my stockings.

"I gather," he said, "that you're not hungry. Not hungry enough to go out for food, anyway."

"Are you?"

"I'm starved."

"I can get dressed again."

But he ended up going out for sandwich makings. While he was gone I took off the rest of my clothes and put on the pink-wool bathrobe. David had remarked on how much he liked that bathrobe, although I couldn't see why; the wool was soft and pleasant, but the style was ordinary and the color pink had always struck me as dull, and somehow a little vulgar.

"Mm," he said, when he returned. "Why don't you wear that more often?"

I laughed. "Like to school?"

"Not the robe. The color."

I shrugged.

"Pink," he said judiciously, "is your color."

"No," I said, "red is. Anyhow, since when are you so interested in women's clothes?"

"Darling, clothes juth fathinate me," he said, and began emptying the food onto the dresser. A few minutes later we were sitting on the bed with ham-and-cheese sandwiches and navel oranges.

"I gather," I said, "that the basketball thing has caused at least as much of a furor as anyone would expect."

He nodded, smiling.

"Do you think Martin knew?" I asked, remembering his bitterness the night they'd lost to Missouri, trying not to remember the way David and I had walked down Second Avenue, leaving him staring after us.

He shrugged. "Hard to say. I imagine he had some idea. Most of the guys on the team did, apparently."

"Do you remember the night we—the night he didn't go to that party with what's-her-name?"

"Uh-huh."

"I've been thinking. Maybe that's why he was so furious. Because he knew, and he thought it was terrible having a party."

"Maybe."

I would obviously have to try another tack. I asked how my parents were. My mother, he reported, had sent her love, which by this time I could accept without irony. That is, I could acknowledge that it existed, even if it wasn't strong enough to make her see me in defiance of my father. I asked how she was and David said she seemed very tired but otherwise all right. My father had been given a small interest in the grocery and was claiming that Daniel had done it for fear of losing him. Which for some reason reminded David, he said, smiling, that Mrs. Glickman had been overheard, while discussing the basketball business with someone, to ask if it was for *this* that Mr. Glickman worked and she slaved to let a son go to college. And Normie Cohen's mother—Normie was on the fencing team—had come up to the Landau apartment Monday morning, weeping and asking why this had to happen to *us*.

"Six million Jews in Europe," David said, "and now this. She wants to know why."

"She's not the only one," I said. "I spent half one morning trying to explain why to Thea. Or, I should say, trying to explain why the question was ridiculous." I wiped off my fingers, sticky with orange juice, gathered the supper remnants together and put them on the floor, then moved back on the bed so I was leaning against the wall. "I tried to explain to her that all she was asking was why poor boys want money. It isn't even as though they had to do something really awful to get it. Some gangsters came along and offered a bunch of poor boys more money than they'd ever seen to throw away a few points in a game. Thea said I knew it wasn't that simple, but I don't know it at all."

"Well," David said, moving back so that he was resting against the pillows at the head of the bed, "you should."

Startled, I said nothing.

"I don't say that I'd expect you to, but you should."

"Just what," I asked coolly, "does that mean?"

But how could I not have known? I must have known.

"It's doubtful," David said casually, "that Thea is totally oblivious to the charms of money. As a matter of fact, there's a certain simplicity involved in your interpreting the question that way—although I can't tell if the simplicity is calculated or not."

"Thanks."

"I could actually make out a case for the people who're asking why as being amateur philosophers."

"I'm sure you could."

"They're asking about the nature of things, Ruth," he said, obviously enjoying himself. "The social order. Stuff like that. Why do some people have money? And given that only some do, why is it so often the wrong ones? Given that often it's the wrong ones, is it inevitable that they corrupt others? And why are some of the others more prone to corruption, and some less?"

"That's easy," I said. "Some of them are more prone to poverty than others."

"It doesn't hold up."

"Why not?"

"The guy who started the investigation by reporting a bribe offer isn't rich."

"Well, he's the exception that proves the rule."

"If there're enough exceptions, it's not a rule."

"Ohh . . . you can always outtalk me. What'm I supposed to say to that?"

"Try saying, 'David, you're right.' "

"You'd love that, wouldn't you?" I muttered stubbornly.

"For the entertainment value," he said. "You know, the novelty of it all."

I slid off the bed and walked across the room, putting away some of the things I'd left around.

"Well, I won't. I won't admit that being poor has nothing to do with being dishonest. I don't believe it, and I won't say it just to salve your ego."

Why is my heart thumping with such violence? As though I were about to learn whether I'd passed an important exam?

"I don't mind your putting words in my mouth, Ruth." Slow and lazy. "But I resent your suggestion that my mind works on the same simple distorted level as yours."

I stared at him, my mouth a little open in surprise. As though he'd slapped me. There was no hint of humor in his expression to soften the effect of the words.

Say you're sorry, Ruth. You'd better say it. He's not kidding around now. Say you don't think that simply either, but that with him, especially, and especially about money, you always feel on the defensive. You have to simplify things, or they become too difficult to talk about, even think about.

I took my hairbrush from the dresser and began brushing my hair.

"I'm sorry, David. I know that I'm not so terribly brilliant and complicated as you are. It's hard for a simple soul like me to grasp the—"

"Damnit," he shouted, springing up from the bed in a sudden fury, "you're doing it again!" Walking toward me. Waving his hand angrily through the air as though to dismiss devils. "When are you going to cut out that shit? It's much more infuriating than it would be if you were really stupid."

"Is that supposed to be a compliment?" My calmness a façade for the fear-edged excitement I felt welling within me. I'd stopped brushing my hair, but now I began again. "Because if it is—"

"No, damnit, no!" He slapped the brush out of my hand and sent it flying across the room to bang into the wall and clatter loudly to the floor. "It's not a compliment. It's an insult. *You're* an insult. To your own intelligence. I've never seen anyone so ready to throw her brains in the garbage as soon as the thinking gets rough. You go along like a normal intelligent human being until something endangers one of your crazy lopsided ideas, and then all of a sudden you're a wide-eyed idiot. No. A simple little country girl who just can't understand what all the fucking noise is about. It makes me ill, goddamnit. I'm sick of it."

I have never seen him so angry. The whole room is alive with his anger. I am alive inside of it. I am afraid of David, and I am excited by his anger and by my fear. I want to kiss him, to bite him, to hurt him, but I am afraid that if I reach out to him he will throw me off. I cannot bear to stand looking at his beautiful raging face without touching him.

I walked around him, picked up the brush, sat on the bed. He turned to face me but I didn't look at him. My senses required no reassurance of his rage. I slid back so that now I was leaning against the pillows, my legs stretched out in front of me.

Come, David. Don't be paralyzed by your rage.

I was warm. I opened wider the collar of my pink-wool robe and rubbed my neck. I bowed my head and blew at the exposed skin. I looked at David.

I love to look at you. I don't know what the hell it is about your face, Ruth. Before I ever knew what hot pants were, I loved to look at you.

"I'm sorry that I make you ill, David."

He hates me. His lips curl in disgust at my coy shabby art. I'm scared. I only wanted to talk to you about my brother, David. Why couldn't we talk about Martin?

I raised the brush to my head but before I had taken two strokes he was on top of me, pinning back my brush hand against the pillows, squeezing my wrist so tightly that the hand opened and the brush lay lightly across my palm; his other arm around my neck and my back, fingers digging mercilessly into my shoulder blade, the first of the bones that he would grind to dust inside of me; his teeth in my neck until I screamed voicelessly in pain, and then the teeth unfastening themselves from the cut flesh, pulling my robe away from my breasts and sinking their knife-sharp wet-mouth-rimmed edges into my breast; hand freeing my unfeeling wrist to knead my breast while he sucked and gnawed and tore at my nipple, a dog at a bone; hand then traveling down the center of my body, under his suffocating heaviness pulling open my robe; fingers thrusting blindly into me until they realized they couldn't hurt me and withdrawing to free his penis, bruising-hard against my thighs; penis huge and fiercely hot thrust into me, filling my whole body with deathly pleasure. His mouth found mine and entered it; his tongue filled it. He was everywhere in me; there was no escape.

God help me, I cannot wait to die!
David.

It is not possible for me to detail the afternoon that I finally saw my mother and she told me that she was pregnant. I can't even remember the way she looked; my memory presents me with a frightening faceless being when I try. She could not have looked well, for it was a question from me about her health that made her confess that she had become pregnant in January. Even were I less ashamed of the rest of it, I could not be proud of the way I reacted when she told me.

It was April. At bad points during the winter and the beginning of spring I had comforted myself with the thought that my life had reached its lowest possible point during the brutal battle with my father. Toward him I'd felt the fury of betrayal, the wrath of accused innocence. I had wanted to shame him, but I'd no sense of humiliation, myself. The battle was between the two of us, and the rage too great to allow for humiliation.

This act now, this attempt to replace a child they'd never properly loved with one they didn't need and couldn't properly care for, this was between them, yet it filled me with shame. I could not look at her. I tried to find out if she could get an abortion. And learned that the child wasn't a moment's ghastly error but a deliberate design of my father's, and she was willing to have it for his sake.

"How could he?" I started to ask, and she began to apologize for him and tell me about the terrible headaches he'd been having since Martin's death, and I saw that I could only agitate her further by questions and arguments. How could I argue, anyway, when I could not meet her eyes?

By the time I achieved a semblance of composure, it was too late, for she was already in the position of comforting me.

She told me what a nice young doctor she had at the clinic; how wonderful Mrs. Landau had been (no, David didn't know, only Mrs. Landau and one or two friends); whose daughter-in-law was going to give her which of the things she would need. She was not visibly disturbed by the fact that it would not be her friends, but her friends' daughters who would be passing along hand-me-downs, with whom she would be sitting in Tompkins Square Park, gently rocking a carriage, talking about . . . but my mind balked at considering their conversation. I wasn't even sure that she would have friends to talk to among the mothers at the park. How would the others, some of them younger than I, react to her talk of diapers and formula and her arrangements with the super to keep the carriage in the downstairs hallway, when I, who loved her, was disturbed by such talk from a woman with lines of age in her face?

She took to calling me sometimes in the evening, while my father was at the store and she was up visiting the Landaus. I told her that she should have a phone put in, in case she needed someone in a hurry. She said that if they'd gotten along all this time without one, she could continue without one now; that she would never have such an emergency that she couldn't go to the outside hall and call up to the Landaus' apartment. Bertha Landau now kept the front door open at night for just such an emergency, closing the door when she went to sleep at around eleven. It wasn't much after that when my father came home from the store.

I began to dread the calls, which came two or three times a week. Her present condition repelled me, and her future frightened me, and since all her talk was of one or the other, and all of it was determinedly cheerful, I was under a constant strain to make sure none of my feelings was coming through. She would talk of how wonderful things were going to be after the baby, how we would all be together again, with everything in the past forgiven and forgotten, and I would want to scream into the mouthpiece or throw the receiver against the wall. I once found, upon hanging up, that I was clutching in my fist several strands of hair pulled out of my head during our conversation. It became a standing joke of Rita's that if she were in the mood to take a walk and I was busy, she would sit around and hope I would get one of my phone calls. After them, I couldn't work and generally couldn't even bear to stay in the apartment.

Rita never questioned the calls, but one night, after a particularly bad one, we went out for a cup of coffee and she said hesitantly that if I needed to confide in someone, she was there.

"Thanks," I said. "But I don't think I can."

"You probably think I shock easily," she said suddenly.

I smiled. "Maybe I do."

She stared down into her coffee. "My father," she said, "has spent most of his life since the time I was born in mental hospitals. My mother walks a thin line, but she's managed to stay out of them most of the time, if only because my father needs someone to visit him on Sundays. My older sister's a high-priced whore in Chicago, and I have a seventeen-year-old brother who's a cinch to follow in my father's footsteps."

I stared at her in wonder.

"I'm only telling you," she said, "so you'll know you can talk to me if you want to."

"I wish I could," I said after a while. "I wish I could, Rita. But I can't."

Still, I needed to talk to someone, and there was no one else around. I didn't even want to tell Thea, much less to have her greet the news with a set of cheerful homilies about home and the family. There was nobody else at school I really talked to. Lou Fine was too harassed, with Selma leaving shortly, to be bothered with my problems, and it didn't seem appropriate for me to raise such an issue with Selma, a short time before she herself was to give birth. Then there was David. To whom I could no longer talk at all.

He'd been gone when I awakened the morning after that savage night, although I was quite certain he'd slept with me. I stayed in bed for most of Sunday, bruised and exhausted. And not quite certain that I would ever see him again. I could not see why he should come back to me, when he hated me so much.

Wanting David to make love to me had been part of being in love with him. I had made the mistake of thinking that he would not want to make love to my body were I not inside it. A particular person.

Smart enough so that he could feel proud of defeating me in every argument, keen enough so that he could enjoy my blindness to his faults. Sex without communion was for stupid people—or perhaps for intelligent men and dumb women.

Now I was bitter at my own naïveté. For in the weeks that followed he came to see me as often as before; he just didn't talk with me. We made love or we went to the movies, or we went to the movies and came home and made love. We greeted each other; he asked what I would like to do; he ignored or followed my wishes, as he pleased. He teased me less, was more attentive in matters of my physical comfort. Yet I found his attentions insulting rather than flattering. Each time he helped me on with my coat, or carried a package for me, or made sure the window wasn't open too far, or I had enough of the covers, I had the fleeting sense that he'd decided that my soul being irretrievably lost, particular care must be taken of my body.

I remember his coming up one night when I was reading Nietzsche for a comparative lit course in the nineteenth-century Germans. It was a weekday night and I was pleasantly surprised to see him. I was sitting on my bed, wearing a slip, leaning back against the pillows, reading and making notes. He knocked once, then opened the door with his key.

"Hi," he said, putting down his books on the dresser.

"Hi."

He took off his jacket and came over to the bed. He looked tired, although the Easter vacation was just past. Seeing him so tired renewed the sense I'd had often lately of knowing nothing of his life, of what he was doing. Of which things were making him tired. He sat facing me. His eyes moved down to the book on my lap.

"I'm having an exam," I explained.

"Mm?" he said, and I realized he hadn't been looking at the book, at all, but had been looking me over.

"You look tired," I said. "Want some coffee?"

"Just had some. Thanks."

He didn't seem to think it strange that he'd had coffee right before coming to see me; maybe it wasn't.

"Are you having a bad week?" I asked.

"I don't know. I guess so." His hand rested on my thigh, caressing it through the white nylon of my slip.

"Well, anyway," I said, "I'm glad you're here. You can talk to me about Nietzsche."

"Just what I came for," he said—as though I'd known all along exactly what he *had* come for. But it was not, in fact, until that moment that I really let myself know.

He can't wait to get into me.

I felt his strong eager hand on my thigh, and saw the sardonic intelligence of his face.

He doesn't care if we never talk again. He only wants to get into me.

"It must be nice," I said, "having a place so near school to get laid."

"Isn't that why you took it?"

His hand moved insolently up my body. As though nothing we said could have any effect upon what we would do. Resentfully I found my body responding to him.

"Partly," I said, feeling my face flush. "But it wasn't the way you make it sound."

"I won't talk any more," he said. He leaned over me and kissed my neck, my ear.

"You weren't planning to, anyway," I said, annoyed as my voice caught in my throat and my arms, without instruction, pulled his body down against mine.

Later, when he was gone, I lay awake in bed and wondered where it would end, this deliberate exclusion of everything between us that was not sexual. For a while it had seemed like a natural, almost inevitable, result of our battle that night. A mixture of anger and embarrassment left sex as the only way we could be open with one another. But at some point our lovemaking had become as much a source of frustration for me as a relief from it. For as my awareness of what was happening between us increased, my concern often kept me from fulfilling my pleasure. And when it did not, my pleasure intensified my concern. If I had been wary always of the responses that David aroused in me, now I was frightened by my helplessness in resisting them. I felt cheapened by my inability to refuse him. I was certain that if I could hold him through this period, then things would go back to where they had been, or perhaps on to a new, better stage. But I couldn't deceive myself that I would break with him if they did not. I could no more have arbitrarily broken with David than I could have suddenly stopped wanting to be rich. Both meant too much to me. I had wanted both for too long.

Meanwhile my mother's phone calls continued to come, although I didn't see her again until a Friday in May. She had called the night before to ask if I could possibly go to the clinic with her the next day. She didn't like to go alone and Bertha Landau, who usually accompanied her, was laid up with her back trouble. My first impulse was to search desperately for a way out. To ask why my father couldn't accompany her, or one of her friends. I am thankful now, of course, that I simply consented to go, although God knows, I wasn't much of a help to her.

I met her on Second Avenue, in front of the clinic, and went in with her, and sat in the decrepit old waiting room while she chatted with women she'd apparently come to know during the months of her pregnancy. Most of them were very young, but I remember being surprised to see a couple of others who looked as though they might be grandmothers. They were Puerto Rican and spoke to each other in rapid Spanish, showing no more interest in my mother than in any of the other waiting women.

We had to wait well over an hour. The room was close and I hadn't had lunch that day. I had a bad headache and felt somewhat nauseated. Smoking a cigarette didn't help, and I was about to excuse myself on the grounds of needing a little fresh air, when the nurse called my mother's name. The doctor was young, casual, and somehow less like a professional than like a backyard *yente*, asking my mother, with gossipy interest, questions whose significance I didn't at the time understand—about staining, urinating, and whether she'd felt life as yet. (She hadn't.) He patted her backside when we were about to leave, but as she went through the door, he detained me for a moment.

"You're her daughter?"

I nodded, forcing myself to meet his eyes steadily. I felt that he was looking at me as though I were a specimen, but I may have been attributing to him my own distaste for our situation.

"Do you give her any help at home?"

"I don't live at home."

He seemed to be trying to make up his mind about something.

"What is it?" I asked.

"She shouldn't do any physical labor. *Any*. I've told her every time I've seen her, but these women . . ." He trailed off.

"Is something wrong?"

He laughed shortly. "There's something wrong, all right. She's not in very good shape. She stands a good chance to lose that baby, if she's not careful, that's what's wrong. As it is, I don't think she'll go full term."

I must have looked at him incredulously, and he must have thought I was play-acting.

"Why so surprised?" he asked, not bothering to conceal his disdain. "You were sitting right here. You heard us talking, didn't you?"

"Not really," I said, stammering slightly in my confusion. "I mean, I did but I didn't—I mean, I don't know much about—" I waved a hand at the examining room "—about these things," I finished lamely, hating him for putting me in this position, yet feeling too guilty to object.

"Go to night school," he said sarcastically. "Take a course in biology."

And you go to hell.

But I didn't say it. I walked out of his office, through the waiting room, to the front door, where my mother was standing. We walked together down the outside steps.

"What'd he say, Ruthie?" she asked. "What was he telling you, a lot of nonsense?"

"He said you work too hard."

"He's a sweet boy. What does he know from work? He's a baby."

"He's a doctor," I said. "And he knows what he's talking about. Come. I'll take you to Ratner's. We'll get some cake and coffee."

"I got to watch my weight, you know."

I looked at her. She was wearing a brown skirt and a black topper that was at least one size too large for her. She looked thinner than I'd ever seen her, except in the middle, where her stomach bulged ever so slightly against the coat.

"I bet the doctor didn't tell you that."

"He doesn't have to," she said. "It's a rule, not to gain too much weight when you're pregnant."

"Don't worry about it," I said, steering her down Second Avenue. "I'll be responsible."

So we had cake and coffee together, and she told me how wonderful Bertha Landau was, and how hard my father worked, and how she felt like a schoolgirl, having such a treat in the afternoon. With difficulty, I got her to talk about housework. She tried to deny that she did anything strenuous but couldn't lie well enough to convince me. I made her promise to hire a girl to come in one half-day a week to do the heavy cleaning. I told her that I would pay for it, and when she said I couldn't afford it, I told her that I was making more money, and that if she wouldn't hire a girl, I would come down and do it myself, although I could spare the money more easily than the time. She consented, finally, but I had no real illusions that it would help. She had always been one of that breed of housewives that couldn't see a crumb on the floor without stooping to pick it up, and I could tell from the way she spoke that the realities of her condition hadn't changed that. When I said goodbye I made her promise that she would call me by Monday to let me know that she had hired a girl.

I will *have* to talk with David about her now, I thought that night. I will have to find out if he knows, and what's happening in general. He'll have to talk to his mother about it and tell me. He'll have to do that for me.

I couldn't concentrate on my work, and ended up going to some terrible movie with Rita. Over breakfast Sunday morning she made fun of the plot, but by that time I remembered so little of it that I barely knew what she was laughing about. I was tempted to ask her questions about pregnancy, to clear up some of the confusion in my mind, but I stopped myself in time, realizing how she would take such questions.

On my way to the Stamms' later that day it occurred to me that perhaps I could talk to Boris's father. Mrs. Stamm might have been able to offer more substantial and hard-headed advice, but I still found it difficult to talk with her, and besides, I hadn't seen her around the house at all in recent weeks. Her husband, however, had seemed to find an increasing pleasure in time spent with Boris and me, often now sitting quietly in the room while we worked together, and almost invariably joining us in our walks. I made up my mind that I would ask for a few minutes alone with him when the afternoon was over, but as it turned out this was unnecessary, for Boris wasn't in the apartment at all when I arrived. Walter Stamm opened the door for me himself and invited me into the library, where he sat down behind the big desk and explained to me that he and his wife had separated and would shortly be divorced. That in accordance with his wife's wishes she and her daughter had taken another apartment. That he hoped this change would not affect my arrangement with Boris, which was very important to the boy.

"Of course not," I murmured. Thinking, *What does it have to do with me? Does the divorce have anything to do with me?*

"This is going to be a difficult time for Boris," his father said.

I nodded.

"I'll be grateful for any additional time you find it possible to spend with him."

"Of course. I'll do whatever I can." Wondering exactly what keeping such a pledge would involve.

"I must say," he was a little embarrassed but still determined, "that I think the fact of your attention for him is making this business a little bit easier for him to bear than it would have been otherwise."

"I'm glad," I said. "I suppose you know how I feel about him."

CHAPTER SIX

If I never thought I loved Walter, I was at least guilty of that danger-ous adolescent fantasy: I *could* love him. Certainly I enjoyed being with him in the months following his separation. He seemed, if not a different person than the one who'd been married to Helen, a much happier, a more youthful version of the same man. He had been reti-cent; free of the weight of Helen's personality he seemed to open up, to be eager to express himself. I remember being astonished during those months at the volume and range of his conversation. Astonished and pleased, for his talk was good, and came at a time when I felt cut off from most other communication. Memories, observations, ironic little jokes, random bits of knowledge—from that Saturday in May when he told me of the coming divorce, they gushed from him in a torrential flow that never ebbed, until we were married and it died.

As the weeks passed I found myself arriving earlier and earlier each Saturday, and staying later, so that I often had to rush to make my Sat-urday night dates with David. When the days got warmer, Boris and I spent more and more time outdoors, and almost always, Walter was with us. (In late spring he surprised us both with a driver's license, and began taking us for short rides in the car, which had been stored in a garage until then.) I discovered that he was one of those people who absorbed huge quantities of random information and rarely let any of it go. He told us about the various statues in Central Park, about which churches were modeled on which European cathedrals. He showed us the brownstones where various well-known families had lived, and told us which ones would be, sad to say, demolished before long. I had al-ways thought of New York as having pretty sections and ugly ones, failing to distinguish between rich-pretty and rich-ugly, dull-pretty, poor-ugly, ugly-interesting, etc. He got me to look at the city, not be-cause he made an effort to do so, but because he talked about it con-stantly and naturally during our walks. In museums he talked about

he paintings, the sculpture, the craftwork, the dioramas. I was over-
/helmed by a fund of information that I conveniently mistook for
visdom. I remember that every once in a while he would mirror my
urprise at his knowledge on some new subject.

"My goodness," he would say. "I'd forgotten I knew that. My mem-
ry's coming back to me, Ruth."

His talk was not just fodder for my brain, but distraction from the
umerous problems that troubled me. It was after our marriage that I
egan to see it in another light, that I began to think of it as a protec-
ive device against feeling, that I wondered why Walter could not look
t a statue and let its beauty wash over him, instead of pushing it away
vith his erudition. Like his rotten, "I love you, Ruth," it came to repre-
ent in my mind a substitution for the real thing. In the months of that
pring and summer, though, talk seemed the most wonderful gift he
ould give me.

At the beginning of June, Helen Stamm went to Reno to establish
ix weeks' residence for her divorce. Lotte finished school and left with
wo friends for a summer in Europe. And Walter asked if I would go to
he lake with him and Boris that summer. I couldn't decide. I was
ware of his interest in me, and of the possibility that he would ask me
o marry him. I didn't expect that I would consent, and I was con-
erned with the possibility that it was wrong to become more involved
vith him if I were going to refuse. Yet there was a tremendous tempta-
ion in the idea of escaping the city, and my mother's pregnancy, and
Arlou's confinement. In the fall, perhaps earlier, my mother would
ave her baby. In the fall, barring miracles, I would take an emergency
xam to qualify for a teaching license (I had the minimum number of
ducation credits allowable). But the thought of working at Arlou all
ummer, then heading straight into some junior-high-school jungle in
he fall, filled me with dread. It would be like mailing myself to purga-
ory.

Then there was David.

"David," I said, "I told you the Stamms are getting divorced."

"Mmm." He was lying on my bed, reading the newspaper.

"He and Boris—Walter Stamm and Boris—are using the house at the
ake again. He asked me if I'd do the same thing as last summer, only
vith just Boris this time, instead of Boris and Lotte."

He looked up and grinned.

"What's the dirty smile for?"

"You know damn well what it's for."

"You always expect the best of me, don't you."

He shrugged.

"He's a gentleman, David. I don't have to get involved with him. He doesn't expect it of me."

"So, when are you leaving?"

I'm only looking for an excuse not to leave, David. If I thought this awful nonsense between us might end, I wouldn't leave. If I thought you might ask me to marry you, I couldn't be persuaded to leave.

"I don't know," I said. "I can't make up my mind."

Nor could I during the week or two that followed. I tried to figure out whether my being away for two months would heighten the barrier between us, or cause him, à la the ancient treatises on the subject, to grow fond of me again. I had just about decided that the latter was more likely when he came to my room quite early one weekday morning.

I was lying in bed, resisting the idea of beginning the day. There was a knock at the door, and assuming that it was Rita, I got out of bed, dragging along the blanket, which I wrapped around myself as a cover. I opened the door and David was there. It must have been because I was so happy to see him that I failed to notice his expression.

I won't have to go now.

It was the first thought I had. That I wouldn't have to go to the lake, that he'd come because he really wanted to see me, perhaps ask me not to go, that something had transformed me back from David's steady lay to David's girl, and things would be all right now. I didn't care what it was that had happened, whether he'd been touched by spring, or he'd suddenly realized the insanity of what was going on between us. I only cared that it had happened.

Except that it hadn't. It was not spring, nor love, nor any such romantic notion that had brought him to me that morning, but the necessity of telling me that my mother was dead.

My father had found her in bed when he came home from work; she had lived for only an hour or so after they got her to the hospital. She had miscarried the baby in bed and then continued to hemorrhage; she must have been afraid to leave the bed for help once she felt the baby dropping.

"She never wanted a telephone," I said to David, before I began to cry.

Her death filled me with guilt as her pregnancy had filled me with shame—senselessly, uselessly. I fought against the unreason of my feelings, reminding myself of how little I could have done. It helped not at all.

I went home. I asked David if I should, and he said I would have to decide. My sense of guilt was fed by his new gentleness, for it had taken my mother's death to make him gentle to me.

"Has my father mentioned me?" I asked.

David shook his head.

"Do you think seeing me would make him angry?" I asked.

"He doesn't seem," David said, "like a man who'll ever be angry again."

That should have prepared me, but of course it didn't.

When I had cried for long enough, I got dressed in my black suit and a white blouse, and we went home. We took the subway down and then walked across town because I wanted the time walking would give me. I felt nothing as we walked through the neighborhood—or even when I first saw the house. But when we were in the downstairs hall, I looked up the narrow flight of steps ahead of us and thought of my poor mother, stomach heavy, sick, tired, walking up them once, perhaps twice or three times a day, and cried again. I cried so bitterly that I felt drained of even the strength to walk up the stairs, and when we finally went up, David was almost carrying me. At the apartment he knocked and waited. There was no answer. We walked slowly up the second flight, to the Landau apartment. Bertha Landau opened the door. Her swollen eyes looked first at David, then at me. It was the first time in my memory that there was no hatred in them. She moved aside.

What little sunlight there was in the kitchen fell on the white-enameled table near the window. Two old men sat silently warming their hands around glasses of tea. I blinked as though a bright light had been switched on in a pitch-black room. One of the old men was David's father. The other was mine. Both nodded, but my father's head continued to nod. I stared at him without moving, even when I felt David's hand on my arm, trying to draw me into the room.

It was not my father's age that shocked me, so much as it was his size. Even now I cannot say how much of the change was in him and how much in my own view, but he had shrunk into himself so much that at first realization of who he was I almost screamed. The scream of a child in a horror movie, intended to ward off the unknown terror that will follow. For the change was so great that it seemed almost as though he might shrink further before my eyes. I had always known he wasn't a big man, perhaps not even quite my own height. And yet he had never seemed small to me, with his solid build and erect carriage and the violence of his personality. Now he seemed not just small but dwarflike. Shrunken. A pathetic little man, dwarfed by his surroundings. Fit company, after all these years, for Bertha Landau's beaten little pickle salesman.

I had expected that I would need forbearance. That I would have to briefly set aside what had happened with my father if I were to be permitted to mourn for my mother. But there was nothing to set aside. The old man at the table, wrinkled, concave, nodding abstractedly as though he had recognized death and was beyond caring, was not the man with whom I'd quarreled.

I said, "Hello, Papa."

The nodding ended. I came farther into the room. David came in just behind me and closed the door. I heard the click as though it were a key being turned in a lock outside. My father looked at the half-empty glass of tea in front of him and gently pushed it away. I looked at David's father. His eyes met mine and then slid back to the kitchen table and safety.

"A terrible thing," he said.

I had a momentary sense of watching a dream. Two old men, concentrating and abstracted. Two old park-bench chess players, working out a problem that wasn't there. I shook my head.

"Come into my room," David said. I followed him gratefully. In his room, I took off my jacket and sat on the bed. It was not a triumph for me to be there now, but a defeat, a defeat less connected to my mother's death than to mine and my father's, to my sense that things between us were forever fixed. Not at a point of indifference to each other, of hatred many times through time removed, but at the height of our mutual fury. It was as though we had died while we were fighting, and were unrecognizable to each other in our new lives, anger being our only record of the old.

And there was something else. Every detail of the house—the street, the stoop, the creaking steps, the starched curtains and polished linoleum of the Landau kitchen—all were as natural and familiar to me as though they were part of each day of my life. I think it was the first time I ever had the sense of being inescapably burdened by the past. Or, rather, by the knowledge that the past was not simply that, but a part of the present, as well. And that no matter how successful I might be from day to day for endless months in forgetting its reality, it would always be hovering in wait for me, as welcome as an outgrown lover, as visible as a homely girl in a crowd, but no less present for all of that.

"Want some *schnapps?*" David asked.

I nodded. He went into the kitchen and came back a moment later with the shot glass of whiskey. I drank it quickly; it was smooth whiskey. People who don't drink can afford the best.

"Has he been drinking?" I asked.

"Not that I know of."

"He will," I said.

"Probably."

The doorbell rang. David's mother went to the door. Mrs. Adler from the ground floor came in. Crying, she walked to my father. I couldn't see them, but I could hear him cry with her. David got cake and coffee for the two of us. A little while later my uncle Daniel came in with Rose. More crying, chairs scraping against the kitchen floor. David brought out his desk chair because there was a shortage of seats. He returned and sat beside me on the bed. Daniel and Rose came in to see me. They were sweet to me, as they always had been. I remembered with guilt how my father and I had laughed at them, how I had let my father bitterly denounce Daniel's superior ways, although I had seen for years that what Daniel gave my father he offered in almost pathetic humility, as though he, too, felt that his success in life, however measured, however hard he had worked for it, had been robbed from his more deserving brother. Rose, from years of resenting this, had grown remote toward our family, but she wasn't a bad woman. If there was something of Bertha Landau in her, it was probably no more than she needed to get along, and there was also in her something of the gentleness of my mother. She whispered to me her grief that it was my mother's death that had brought me home. I kissed her cheek.

I stayed there all day. The funeral was held the next morning. I stood near my father to receive people. We were like two strangers whose children had died in the same automobile accident; only a twist of fate had made us privy to each other's grief. Everyone cried and told me, in case I hadn't known, how lucky I was to have had such a mother, and told my father, who had not known, how lucky he was to have had such a wife. David stayed near me, as did Thea, who wept quietly the whole time. I myself did not cry until my father and I, the others having filed past the coffin and taken their seats in the chapel, walked in and stood looking down at her. She was wearing a black dress that I had never seen before. Her brown hair, lightly streaked with gray, was brushed neatly away from her forehead and temples. There was more makeup on her face than she had ever worn. The shock to me was that the face under that makeup was quite free of lines.

I cannot say whether it was mortician's art, or the ease of death, or whether it is memory's exaggeration that makes me now see her dead face as the face of a young woman. If it was art, I should congratulate the mortician. If it was death's ease, I must again pity my mother her life. If my vision was clouded then by my tears, or my memory is confused now with the passing of time, then there is a certain justice to the fact that my mother's death should have been made more bitter for me by the sight of her dead youth. For just as I had always seen my father as a bigger man than he really was, I had always seen my mother as an older woman.

She was forty-three years old when she died.

A few days later I told Walter that I would go to the country with him. David afterward accused me of using my mother's death as an excuse for that decision. I think it more likely that I used David's indifference, although I am not sure that I "used" anything at all, in the sense that he meant the word. David's mind, which normally took pleasure in illuminating subtle errors in the obvious, always presented him in my case with a melodramatic burlesque of it.

In any event, we had a wonderful summer at the lake, Walter and Boris and I. It is the time I have to remind myself of when I am accusing myself of madness in having married Walter. I later occasionally thought of my going there as some sort of self-imposed punishment for my mother's death, but even then the idea seemed ridiculous, and certainly it was anything but a punishment at the time.

If I was cowardly in seeking escape, I was a successful coward. In the weeks following my mother's death, I had thought of nothing else; but once we got to the lake, the physical activities alone forced her out of my mind for hours each day, and the good exhaustion that followed was a help as well.

Walter usually spent a three- or four-day weekend with us. On the days when he wasn't there, we swam, played tennis, badminton, and Ping-Pong on the basement table. It was a hot summer. The worst weekends we spent boating on the lake, swimming, having picnic lunches at the lake's edge. On cool or rainy weekends, though, Walter would take us for long drives through the country, and we would return home quite late on Sunday nights, or even sleep one or two nights in an inn. He knew every beautiful old house in New England and thought nothing of driving half a day to show us one of them. We went through almost every town on the coast between Gloucester and New Bedford, then inland to Marlboro and Sturbridge and Williamstown. Most of them were blended together in my mind by the end of the summer. One lovely town with quaint Main Street shopping, stately white houses, elm-lined streets. We attended the Marblehead regatta with Walter's friends, Carl and Emily Simpson, who had a home right on the water there. He explained to me briefly that he had seen little of the Simpsons in recent years because Helen hadn't gotten on too well with them. This made me eager to like them, but I was only partly successful. Carl repelled me from the beginning, although I didn't come to truly hate him until Walter made it his mission to teach me to appreciate his friend, and failing to teach me, blamed the student instead of the lesson.

The truth is, Walter proclaimed, that this has nothing to do with Carl. . . . The truth is that it's your own guilty feelings. . . . The truth. . . .

I wonder what determines our individual appetites for the truth. I would like to adjust my vision to take in (conveniently) less or (helpfully) more of the truth than it does now. I would like to understand why innocence is virtue. The equation bothers me, yet I remain a victim of its final illusion. Walter maintained that I despised Carl Simpson for qualities that I should only have despised in myself. He couldn't admit the gross injustice that statement did me; I couldn't deny its truth.

But we are alike only in our most contemptible parts. We are both cowards and we are both opportunists. We are both without honor but Carl is not without pretensions; the most nauseating fiction he has created is that he *earned* his wealth by marrying Emily. He is his own favorite Alger hero—a lower-middle-class boy whose father owned a haberdashery in Boston, who through his own great industry in high school, and his parents' working belief in higher education, was able to attend Harvard, where his roommate (Walter) introduced him to a Radcliffe girl named Emily Story. With stupid drunken arrogance he has related to me the story of their meeting.

"Emily Story," he said to her, troubling to be charming although she was only an ordinarily pleasant-looking girl and nothing about her excited him. "Emily Story. What a nice name. Where did you dig it up?"

"Oh," she said, smiling shyly, self-deprecatingly, "I didn't really have to dig it up. It's been around Salem for hundreds of years."

That excited him.

Two years later they were graduated, and married, and Carl went into Alden Story's Boston brokerage in the kind of fake-lowly position from which the birth of his first son quickly rescued him, and otherwise settled into a richly pleasant life of tradition, not his own. Yet Carl's eyes, set in a rugged-vapid cigarette-advertisement kind of face, were hungry and dissatisfied, his smile was more a gauge than a reaction. Increasingly through that weekend I was discomfited by his attentions to me, by his servile flattery of Walter, by his willful schoolboy-style provocation of Emily, a pleasant, sexless sort of woman whose tolerance of his antics seemed unlimited, in spite of her knowledge that her hair was no straighter, her legs no more muscular, her wit no less acute than it had been when he asked her to marry him. I remember being surprised by Walter's failure to react to some of the things Carl said to Emily, and realizing, only as we drove back to the lake and he asked whether they weren't lovely people, that he didn't react because he thought it was all in good clean fun. One year later, the smallest provocative comment of mine would be considered a piece of major villainy.

Evenings at the lake, after Boris had gone to bed, we talked. Once he asked me about David.

He said, "Whatever became of that interesting young man who used to come up with your brother?"

I said, "David? He's working in the city, I think."

He said, "Have you two been friends for very long?"

I said, "Oh, my mother and his mother knew each other before we were even born."

He was interested in anything that I cared to tell him about my life, my family, the neighborhood where I'd lived. Later he would read Jacob Riis and Oscar Handlin and I would laugh and ask him if he was trying to rearouse his feelings for me. Still later I would resent the fact that my background had become a social-political asset to him, a cocktail-party gambit to be dropped at meetings of Filthy-Rich Liberals for Stevenson. That summer, though, I was gratified by his interest, grateful to have an ear less critical than David's to hear me verbalize my self-pity. To Walter, my mother was not just one more dull member of the Good Jewish Mama Club, the tragic aspect to be filed in some mental recess of matters too important to be entirely forgotten. My mother was an exotic to him, whose memories of his own mother were ornamented by silver tea sets (How beautiful mother looked at teatime —red taffeta and gleaming silver!); nannies, stiff and unattractive by comparison, bringing one in to be kissed before bed. (There was an er-mine neckpiece on one of her dresses. He loved to touch it and once was severely punished for grabbing hold of the fur and refusing to let go when nanny was ready to take him upstairs.) Beautiful mystic rites at the Catholic church on Third Street, where he was sometimes permitted the luxury of a Sunday service with his mother (his mother's mother had been Jewish but no one thought to mention this to Walter until he was seventeen years old; his father was that not-so-puzzling paradox known as a freethinking Methodist). He talked about his parents always as part of the past, and I remember being surprised to discover, a good way through the summer, that his father was alive and living in Carmel, California.

They were not really very different, Walter's father and mine, although I had to meet his father years later to realize it. The differences in the two men might have amounted simply to the differences in what they had when they began. It would be easy to assume that Walter's father, having made a fortune in millions, began life with a greater ambition. But Walter's father, unlike mine, did not have to make his own ocean crossing to begin life in America. Walter's grandfather had made the voyage in 1856, and by the time Walter's father had been born, the last of eight children, in 1876, had owned the shoe-repair business on the ground floor of the brownstone off First Avenue where the family lived. By the time of Walter's birth, his father owned the entire brownstone, as well as the adjacent one, with its prospering ground-floor grocery, and two beer halls that faced each other across Houston Street. By then, however, Walter's parents didn't live in either brownstone. They had left Kleindeutschland for uptown, a brownstone again but this time on Eighty-sixth Street, in the neighborhood that would later become known as Yorkville, the neighborhood which we who grew up in what had once been Kleindeutschland were trained to stay out of for fear of the Nazi hordes, the neighborhood in which, if we had to pass through, we were not to order an eggcream for fear of our lives. Walter's father still drank beer with his dinner, but his mother, over her glass of dinner wine, would shyly admit to visitors that she couldn't bear the taste of Lagerbier. She still went to church on Third Street, but she no longer took out books from the German lending library downtown. (She had come to this country when she was an infant but had spoken no English until she began public school.) And although she had prevailed upon her husband to buy season tickets to the opera, she had been heard to say that she found Wagner a bit heavy and rather leaned toward the Italians. With all her new interests and pleasures, she was not really a happy woman, and Walter could not remem-

ber precisely how she looked when she smiled. His strongest visual
memory of her was as she sat in a high-backed, needle-point-seated
chair near their main-floor parlor window, her eyes averted from him
and yet not quite looking out of the window.

He was their only child, born when his mother was thirty-four. He
was never aware of their having wanted other children; as a matter of
fact, he was not at all certain that they'd wanted him. Not, he hastened
to assure me, that they didn't love him. Among other things, his father
by this time had become aware of the necessity of having an heir. But
they hadn't seemed to *need* children the way most couples did. His
mother worshiped his father so completely, was so eager to fulfill his
needs (she competed with the servants, afraid that they would become
more useful to him than she was herself), that she didn't really have
the need to care for children, as many women did. Not that his father
needed special care. He was a marvelously healthy, vital man. At
seventy-five the old man had walked every morning from his home (by
this time an apartment on Park Avenue, just off Eighty-sixth Street) to
his real estate office on Forty-second, and claimed that he rode home in
the evening only because the crowded sidewalks forced too slow a
pace. At seventy-eight he retired and built a beautiful home in Carmel
facing the ocean, where he lived with the woman he had married less
than a year after the death of Walter's mother. Walter hadn't seen the
house yet, but he supposed that one of these days he would get out
there. Lotte and Boris had been devoted to their grandfather, and perhaps some summer . . .

He never touched me, except perhaps to lightly hold my elbow while
we were crossing a street, or briefly take my hand as I jumped across a
narrow brook in the woods. At the beginning, still bruised and tender
from my mother's death and raw with the memory of David's savage
lovemaking, I was grateful for what I took to be a self-imposed ab-
stinence, a conscious respect. Later there were moments, as we sat together in front of the fireplace, or I stretched out on the hearthrug
while he sat nearby, his back against the upholstered front frame of the
sofa, when I wanted very much for him to touch me—to put his arm
around me, to comb my hair with his fingers, to kiss me, even to make
love to me. I admired his gentlemanly self-control but began to resent
my poor-girl status with him, which, I assumed, made him feel that he
must be extraordinarily cautious to treat me with respect.

A respect, strangely enough, which I did not require of him. I had
never felt my pride in danger in dealing with Walter, as I had with his
wife, or with David. As a matter of fact, it strikes me now that this has

always been true, even through the worst years of our marriage. Walter
would attack my villainy and I would defend myself, only indirectly attacking him. Yet Walter respected me while I was at best indifferent to
him and at worst, despised him. Could it be something as obvious as
the superficial gentleness of his personality? Or could it simply be that
I have never loved him? Love contains in itself a willingness to be vio-
lated, and to the extent that I fear that violation, Walter is a refuge for
me and always has been.

Certainly it didn't occur to me then that the reason Walter never
laid a hand on me was that it never occurred to Walter to lay a hand
on me, that Walter was not moved by the desire to lay a hand on me.
Should I have realized then, or in the month or two between my accepting his proposal and our wedding, when he would lightly put his
arm around me as we sat on the sofa discussing our plans, or kiss my
cheek or forehead as we said good night, that there was no conscious re-
straint involved in his behavior? That the idea of sex between us was
premature since my being pregnant would have been undesirable?

Because that was it. For Walter, the idea of sex was for a long time
inextricably bound up with the desire for children, whom he adored,
particularly in their unborn condition. We got married, and he was ap-
propriately lustful until he discovered that I possessed and used a diaphragm, whereupon he did not make love to me for a month. Nor did
he explain what it was that was bothering him. He simply hid in himself and left me to assume that he had been shocked and disturbed by
his discovery—egads—of my unvirginal condition, or repelled by some
facet of me beyond my own knowledge.

"Walter," I said finally one night, "what is it? What is it that's
bothering you, that you never make love to me?"

Startled, he looked at me for a moment, then looked away.

"Is it something about me?"

Hesitating. "No, Ruth. Of course not. It's the—" Vainly he searched,
some reply being requisite, for an abstract way to phrase it. Failing an
abstraction, he found safety in a generality.

"It's . . . the whole question of birth control is . . ."

I was bewildered. The virgin business was absurd but compre-
hensible.

"Is what, Walter?"

"Well, I was a bit surprised. That you should find it necessary."

"Well of course it's necessary." Still not understanding. "I mean, I'm
not sterile, or anything. Not that I know of, anyway. If I don't want to
have a baby . . ."

"Why *don't* you?" Looking directly at me now.

The question floored me. I laughed uncertainly.

"It isn't even that I don't want one, Walter. I haven't even thought about it. It never occurred to me that I *should* think about it. I just automatically . . ."

He looked relieved, even hopeful.

"I love children, Ruth." With what I would later think of as Sunday-school piety. "Helen and I didn't . . . I've always wanted a large family."

My cue.

Well, now that I know, old pal, let's hop into the sack.

I was frightened. My mind telescoped time so that I was very old and fat and had hordes of children pulling at my skirt, tugging at me, following me around the house, crying. I reminded myself that I was rich and having children wasn't the same for rich people, but the reminder did not diminish my fear.

"I think large families are wonderful, Walter." A lie. Where I come from, large families were for the Puerto Ricans down the block who were Catholic and didn't know any better. They were noisy and grubby and they started on credit at the grocery three or four days after last payday, instead of a day before next payday, like everyone else. "It's not that I don't like large families. It's just that I hadn't thought about having children so soon."

"Why not?"

"Oh, I don't know. I'm pretty young, you know."

"I'm not."

I smiled. "You don't exactly have a foot in the grave."

"I'm not young for a father."

I paused. "Well . . . I guess maybe I need time . . . you know, to get used to things. Being married. Living differently."

"I thought,"—a little stiffly—"that you were adjusting with remarkable ease."

The first tiny hint of his dissatisfaction with my adaptability.

"Look, Walter," I finally said, "I'll try. I'll try to want a baby soon. But you'll have to give me a little time. We've been married a little over a month. You wouldn't want me to be a mother before I was ready, would you?"

"Of course not."

And that was *his* lie for the day. For I think Walter did want me to bear children I didn't want, and care inadequately for children I did not love. It was part of some sly martyrdom that he wanted to perpetu-

ally act out. He was quite different with Boris when he and Helen
were married than he has been since our marriage. He cared much
more for Boris when he was his son's sole champion and defender than
he has cared since there was someone else in the house who loved
Boris. He didn't really care very much about Lotte, or pay very much
attention to her, until his dissatisfaction with me made him feel close to
her for the first time. That second summer at the lake, the three of us,
Walter, Boris, and I, were in marvelous harmony, and it didn't matter
to Walter that Lotte had refused to come up, even for a week, after her
return from Europe, once he told her that I would be there. He was
puzzled. He asked if I could understand the source of our misun-
derstanding, and I said that she seemed to have strongly disliked me
from the time we met. He smiled and said something mild about adolescent girls. I don't know if he thought about her again for the rest of
the summer. Certainly there was no suggestion then, as there would be
later, that I had committed some crime against Lotte which I was covering up and which Lotte nobly chose to conceal from him.

He waited until the last weekend in August to propose to me. Boris
had gone to bed and we were both reading in the living room. I looked
up from my book and found him watching me. He smiled, not minding
having been caught.

"It's been very pleasant having you here, Ruth."

"Thank you," I said, sensing what was to come. "It's pleasant to be
here."

"My wife and I—Helen and I didn't have the sort of—well, you
know Helen. She's not a very placid person."

I smiled. "I'm not sure that I am, either."

"Oh, but you know what I mean. Helen was never able to just sit
around like this . . . reading, or whatever. There were always all her
. . . activities."

"There's so much to do here during the day," I murmured, aware of
a maidenly modesty in my tone which was not contrived and yet wasn't
natural to me, either. It was as though I were without conscious con-
trivance playing a role that had been assigned to me. Until then, if
Walter had seen only the best in me it was because the best in me was
all he had brought out. In this moment our relation had become more
complex. He was arousing a mixture of emotions, and I was only letting one of them show.

He was telling me how much he had always enjoyed my enjoyment
of the lake. "I remember the very first weekend you were here last year.

It was a delight to see you reveling in it all, Ruth. Swimming. Running around with Boris. Just enjoying yourself. It was like seeing a young animal, if you don't mind my saying so. A colt, perhaps, that's been kept in a corral too long and then suddenly been given the freedom of the field. It made me feel . . . well . . ." My eyes were averted. His words trailed off.

"I do love it here," I said finally.

He said, "I'd like to give it to you, Ruth."

In spite of my expectations, I was startled by the words.

"What I mean," he went on, his difficulty in expressing himself making it apparent that he thought his proposal would come as a surprise to me, "is that I'd like to marry you, and to share what I have with you. Because I love you."

I looked at him and wondered what David was doing at that exact moment. Then I wondered if Boris was asleep yet. Then I thought of David again, wishing that I could talk with him. Then I thought, if only Martin hadn't died we would never have had that crazy argument. Then I told myself David was irrelevant at the moment and then I asked myself whom I thought I was kidding, David was about as irrelevant as I myself was.

"I realize," Walter said, "that it's a very big decision to make. I don't really expect you to answer me right away."

"You're very kind," I said, and then I added, because in spite of himself he looked crestfallen, "It's just that . . . I'm very . . . I'm very flattered, Walter. I just have to think for a while. I didn't expect . . ."

"Of course." Relieved by my little lie, eager to embroider it and make it truly worthy of the occasion. "I understand perfectly. There are all sorts of things to be considered. I'm not unaware of the difference in our ages . . . and our religious backgrounds."

I'd have to go into the city and talk to David. It was the only thing to do.

I smiled. "I don't actually have *any* religious background. My family was sort of antireligion. My father, anyway. You know, like a lot of Jews."

He nodded.

Still, it would have been nice not to have to go. At that moment I could almost have wished that there were no such person as David. I was so contented, here in this lovely house in the midst of the cool green countryside. The city would be humid and ugly and at this time of summer the pavement wouldn't cool off until ten or eleven at night.

What really would have been nice, of course, would be if there were no such person as Walter Stamm and it were David sitting opposite me offering me himself and this house and the rest of it. Not that I didn't like and admire Walter Stamm. On the contrary, I could see myself quite contentedly married to him. Hadn't we lived together in harmony for a good portion of the summer, between long weekends and these last two weeks, when he had stayed there with Boris and me? And hadn't his presence been not only pleasant but highly therapeutic? Still, David was David. For many years after the time when I was three or four years old and had been advised with finality that I couldn't marry Martin when I grew up, I had taken it for granted that David would be my husband. And even as I grew up and became gradually aware of the possibilities open to each of us, some part of me had always believed that whatever we might do in the interim years it was our manifest destiny to be married to one another. A sigh escaped me.

"I think," I said, ". . . would you mind very much if I went into the city for a day?"

"Of course not," Walter said gallantly.

"I have some things there to . . . it really is . . . it's that it's hard for me to think up here. It's too . . . I need to be someplace else to think." A lie made so effortlessly that I barely caught it myself. The subtle suggestion that I intended not to be swayed by what he was offering me beyond himself.

"May I drive you?"

"I'd rather you didn't. Although I appreciate it. It's just . . . I think I want the long bus ride as much as anything. Does that sound silly?"

"Not at all," Walter said. "I'll drive you into town before noon. The bus leaves just about at noon."

I called the Landau apartment from the terminal in New York the following evening but there was no answer, and after a moment I decided that it was just as well, I would go to Thea's. It was obviously an idiotic idea anyway, to have thought of descending upon David out of the blue with my marriage offer. So I went to Thea's, and there was nobody home there, either, and so I sat on the front stoop, trying to decide whether to wait for Thea to come home and when I had been sitting there for a while, she came walking toward the house with David. His arm was around her and they were both laughing.

She stopped, stricken, when she saw me. "Oh, Ruth," she said, "I started to write you last night but I didn't have time to finish. I wanted you to know we'd gone out a few times. Just so you'd know it didn't mean anything."

How could I be angry? She believed it.

I smiled at her. "Of course, Thea. Please don't worry about it. I understand perfectly."

David smiled at me. There was nothing in his expression that could be read as an apology.

"Listen," Thea said after a moment, "I'm going to run back to the corner and get some ice cream. Why don't you two go into the house and wait for me? I'll just be a few minutes." She handed David the key. "My folks are on vacation," she explained to me.

Thea's parents went to the mountains each year for a week—an annual distinction that set them apart from their neighbors, although they would modestly have denied that they were better than their friends by virtue of the air they breathed for one fifty-second of a year.

I nodded and Thea turned and walked quickly away from us. In silence David and I walked into the house. I waited as he unlocked the door and reached past me to switch on a light. The living-room walls were dark green; Thea's parents had been exposed to the middle classes and learned rapidly. The furniture was massive, dark, comfortable. Too large for a house built as a slum. I set down my small valise on the floor, walked toward the armchair nearest the window, almost sat down in it, but then perched instead on one of the arms.

"You're looking good," David said.

You always look good to me, David.

"It's a good life." I smiled. My words, like David's manner, had a studied quality.

Thea looked so happy. She was having such a good time with you.

He leaned against the front door, arms folded in front of him.

"Was this when you were planning to come back?" he asked casually. "Or are you early?"

"A little early."

I'm glad you're uneasy, too. I'm glad I'm not the only one.

"I had some thinking to do and I couldn't do it up there."

He smiled. "Crickets get on your nerves?"

"No . . . I . . . Walter Stamm asked me to marry him."

"Congratulations, kid." Deadpan. "I knew you'd swing it."

"Oh?" Fake casual as my heart set up a dreadful beat inside of me. "How clever of you."

"Not so clever," he said. "It was obvious."

"Not to me."

"Oh, come on, Ruth." Ultrareasonable. "You're not a moron. You knew what you were doing when you said you'd go up there with him."

As though the threads of my life were not, like other people's, woven partly by chance. As though the middle sister of the three fates took a coffee break each time I had a decision to make.

"I knew I'd have to make a choice," I said. "I didn't know what it would be."

"Like hell you didn't."

"You'd like to believe it, wouldn't you, David?" I said angrily. "I knew everything in advance. I knew before my mother died I was going to the country."

"You're not going to use that as an excuse, are you?"

"I knew before I went to the country that I'd marry him," I went on, ignoring him. "I knew when I came back a week early I wouldn't find you home because you were at a movie with Thea."

"Hah! I was waiting for that! I knew when you told her you understood perfectly it was a crock of shit!"

"It *wasn't* a crock of shit. I *did* understand. I understood that *she* thought it didn't mean anything. But you know better and I know better."

"All right," he spat out, "if you're so damn big on meanings, tell me what it means."

"It means that when I went away you took out my best friend, that's what it means! It doesn't have to mean anything else!"

"What the hell did you expect me to do? Cool my ass for a couple of months while you put out for your rich friend?"

"He's the beginning, the middle, and the end, isn't he?" I asked furiously. "He's responsible for everything that happened to us. If it weren't for Walter Stamm we might have gotten married and lived happily ever after."

"I don't know," he said. "It's possible. If I made a lot of money and you never had to eat me for dinner. It's entirely possible."

"Never!" I screeched. "Never in a million years!" And realized, only as the words tore up my throat, that they were true. I was almost sorry that they were out; I might have preferred to leave him with the illusion of having lost something he wanted. But no. He used the illusion not to salt his own wounds but to deepen mine.

"You never thought for a minute you'd marry me! You want to look at me, screw me, fight with me! Anything but marry me! I could be the neighborhood whore, for all you've ever really thought of marrying me!"

He stared at me. I wondered if he, too, had become suddenly conscious of our surroundings. I listened for Thea's footsteps in the hallway, but the house was quiet. Thea was lingering to give us time. David no longer seemed angry. He looked bewildered—or perhaps just thoughtful. The fight was gone from him.

"All right," he said quietly. "I'm sorry."

"And the truth shall make ye free," I murmured bitterly.

He smiled. He was friendly toward me now. His guilt-edged friendliness sickened me. It was one thing to shout the truth in someone's ears; another to have him hear it and smile. He sat down on the sofa, his arm resting casually on the ivory-lace antimacassar that was pinned to its back.

Thea came in and said she hoped she wasn't interrupting anything. I looked at David because I didn't know if we had more to say to each other. David told Thea that on the contrary, we had been waiting for her return so that I could tell them both about the summer. Thea said she would just dish out the ice cream and David asked if her parents might not have something to drink around the house, and she could put the ice cream in the freezer for now.

"Is something wrong?" asked Thea, in whose mind booze still represented a barometer of disaster.

"Not at all," David told her. "As a matter of fact, I thought we could have a sort of celebration."

She didn't ask if it was my return we were celebrating. I wished I were ten years old again so that I could stick out my tongue at him and say, "Nyah, nyah, think you're so smart!" Thea went into the kitchen. I lit a cigarette and sat on the Morris chair facing David, who would not look at me. Thea returned and set down on the coffee table a tray on which there were three gold-rimmed wine glasses, a half-filled bottle of Cherry Heering, and a nearly full cut-glass decanter of heavy purple Jewish wine, the sort of wine my father would sullenly down at someone's house, nothing decent and alcoholic being available, then upon leaving the house, spit out an imaginary residue, wipe his mouth, and say something about the host you could cut with a knife. Involuntarily David's eyes moved from the decanter and met mine. I smiled slightly; he looked away. A petty triumph, my knowledge that it would hurt him just a little to lose what we did have—perfect understanding on everything unimportant to our lives. We all chose the Cherry Heering.

"It's good to have you back, Ruth," Thea said.

"Hear, hear," David said. "And all best wishes for the future." He took a sip of the Heering, made a face. Thea looked at me, puzzled.

"He's just being coy, Thea," I said. "I'm getting married."

She stared at me, open-mouthed. In the interest of being casual, I sipped at the Cherry Heering. Its cough-syrup sweetness was particularly repellent on this warm summer night.

"Oh," I said, "you're surprised, too. I thought I was the only one. David seems to have known all along."

When did I know? Did I ever really make a decision, or was it made for me just now by David?

"Known? Known what? Who, Ruth?"

"Walter Stamm."

Her head swung abruptly toward David. She watched for the pain she knew he must feel.

David shrugged. "I've lost her to a better man," he said gravely.

"Oh, Ruth," Thea said tremulously, "are you sure you're doing the right thing? You and David are . . . David is so . . ."

And of course it was a tremendous temptation to let it stand that way forever. I had at least a normal share of vanity. It was my vanity, though, that would not permit David to turn me into a fraud.

"He could have had me if he wanted me."

"She's too modest," David said. "After all, how could I compete with this man? He has wealth, position, edu——"

"Oh, why don't you cut it out?"

"But I'm serious."

"I came back to talk to David," I told Thea. "When Walter asked me to marry him I said I'd have to think about it, and I came back to talk to David."

"Walter," said David.

"Yes, Walter!" I flashed out furiously. "Does that make me a whore, too—to call him Walter?"

He whistled softly, as though he had intended no provocation. I vowed that I would not let him trap me again. Silence. The Cherry Heering in my glass was gone. I refilled the glass and passed the bottle to Thea, who didn't take any more but poured what was left of it into David's glass. She sat again, raised her glass.

"I'm very happy for you, Ruth," she said. "I'm sure he's a wonderful man."

"He is," I said quickly. "He is wonderful. He's wonderful and he's rich."

"Atta girl, Ruthie," David said.

"Oh, David," Thea said apprehensively.

"Don't worry about it, Thea," I told her, suddenly magnanimous. "It doesn't bother me. Honestly, I don't care."

"She should worry," David chanted softly, "she should care. She should marry a millionaire."

"My goodness," Thea said, turning to me with a smile of recognition, "I'd forgotten that one. Remember they used to say it for you, and now it's true?"

There was no irony in her voice.

I stood up abruptly. "I'd better be going. I said I'd come back as soon as I could."

"Of course," Thea said.

David was silent.

"I'll be back after Labor Day, Thea," I said. "I'll be in touch."

Thea kissed my cheek. "Congratulations," she whispered.

"Thank you," I said.

David said nothing.

I picked up my valise and left. I walked briskly toward Second Avenue but when I reached it, was suddenly indecisive. I didn't really want to go right back to the country. I wanted very badly to talk to someone. I went into the candy store and dialed the hallway phone at the Mattracorne, but an unfamiliar voice answered and when I asked for Rita, I was told she was still on vacation with her family in Chicago. I hailed a cab and gave the driver Helen Stamm's address on Ninth Street. But in the lobby of her building, I was suddenly afraid. As though she might tell me that the decision that had been forced upon me was a bad one, after all, and in saying it, leave me with nothing. I left her house, half-running lest she see me from a window and call me back, and went up to the Greyhound terminal, sitting on a hard wooden bench in the terminal for most of the four hours until the bus was ready to leave, getting up once to have a sandwich and coffee in the terminal luncheonette, unwilling to set foot out of the terminal onto streets that led in too many directions.

It was five-thirty in the morning when I got off the bus; I waited until six to call Walter and would have waited longer had the morning not been cold and damp. It turned out that I needn't have waited. Walter had been up all night and answered the phone on the first ring. Twenty minutes later he pulled up at the depot. On the phone I had said, "I'm at the depot in town, Walter. The answer is *yes*, if you want me to." He had said, "I'll be there in a few minutes, Ruth. I'm very happy."

I myself felt unexpectedly happy when I saw him. He got out of the car and came over to me in the gray dawn light. He looked tall, and handsome, and safe, and the feeling I had for him at that moment seemed to me not remote from love. He kissed my cheek lightly, and seeing that I was shivering, gave me his cardigan. It was gray cashmere and after putting it on, I wrapped my hands around myself and rubbed them slowly back and forth over the soft luxurious wool. He put my valise in the car and we began the drive back to the house.

"How's Boris?" I asked, as though I'd been away for a long time.

"Fine." He smiled. "At nine o'clock last night he announced that it seemed as though you'd been gone for three days instead of three hours. He wanted to know if I couldn't give him a closer idea of when you'd be back."

"I hope he's still sleeping," I said.

But he was wide awake and wondering where his father was.

"Boris," Walter said, "I have something very pleasant to tell you."

Boris looked at me, then back to his father. From his expression I suddenly realized that he had no inkling of what he was going to hear.

"You're going to have a new mother," Walter said, smiling. "A step-mother, I should say."

"What do you mean?" Boris asked blankly.

"I mean," Walter said, "that Ruth and I are going to be married. And she'll be like a new mother to you."

We waited for happy recognition to dawn. How naïve we were. For when he did understand, the expressions he registered were of shock. Horror.

"But she's too young," cried out my sweet Boris in the first un-diplomatic throes of his agony. "You're too old!"

"Well . . ." Walter paused to consider his answer, "we thought about that, Boris. But you see, at our ages, the difference doesn't matter as much as—"

"She's practically *my* age!"

I put my arm around him. "Not really, sweetheart. Ten years older. That makes a big difference when you're young."

"But—but—" he began, and then unable to find the words for his anguish, he ran out of the house and disappeared for two hours. At the end of that time he came in to say shyly, dutifully, that he was sorry he'd been silly, that it was great, about our getting married. I kissed him and he burst into tears.

CHAPTER SEVEN

Walter was surprised at my not wanting a big formal wedding. He'd apparently looked forward to a talk in which he would patiently, sympathetically explain to his unsophisticated young fiancée that a sumptuous wedding wouldn't be appropriate in the circumstances. Poor Walter. He was so sure he was ready for a wife who would lean upon him, a twitty, frivolous creature who would alternate between awe at what he'd bestowed upon her and trepidation over the things she had yet to learn, who would bring home outrageous little hats which he would have to tell her would not do, whereupon she would become terribly contrite so that he would have to assure her, most graciously, that it was simply not the sort of thing one had to think about twice. The hat would be given to the maid, and little wife would weep in gratitude.

How then could he have fallen in love with me? I suppose it wasn't with me, but with a generalized fantasy-sort of poor girl. If so, I'm the last person who should be critical. His fantasies of the dependent poor were no more extravagant, after all, than mine of the independent rich.

It was Walter who first mentioned my father. We had set the last Sunday in October as our wedding date and we were making up the guest list one evening. Thea was to be my bridesmaid. Carl Simpson would be Walter's best man; the idea gave me no pleasure, but it wasn't until the day of the wedding that I realized just how distressing it was. Then there were several other friends of Walter's, a couple of men from his office, Lou Fine and his wife, although I didn't really expect that they would come, Selma and her husband, Rita. I hesitated over Jerry Glickman and a couple of others from the old neighborhood and decided against them, although Walter kept reminding me that I should have anyone at all I wanted.

"Ruth," he said, when the list was more or less complete, "I've been thinking about your father."

"So have I," I said. "It seems strange to be getting married with no family around."

"Do you want to invite him?"

"I don't know," I said truthfully. "Part of me does and part of me doesn't. Thea says he's still in bad shape. Depressed. Acting as if he's only half-alive. She wants me to go to see him. But I wouldn't know what to do if I went. I know that must sound ridiculous, not knowing how to act with your own father . . ."

"Not under the circumstances," Walter said softly. "Not at all, Ruth."

"That's just it," I said. "The circumstances. It's as though he isn't my father. If he seemed like my father to me, I think I'd still hate him. But if you could have seen him at the funeral, Walter . . . Just some broken old man. Of course you didn't know him before, so maybe you wouldn't've . . . Before, he was . . ."

What was he before? Bigger? Younger? Nicer? Before, he loved me, that was all.

"I worshiped him," I said. "He was always wonderful to me, but even so, when I think of it, it's hard for me to understand how I worshiped him."

Walter smiled sympathetically. "Well, Ruth," he said, "I don't want to press a decision upon you."

"I wish you would."

"Well," he went on reluctantly, "as I say, it's your decision to make. But it seems to me there's very little to lose by inviting him. If he comes, why, then you'll know he probably has regrets, too, about what happened."

So I sent him an invitation, and sent one to Daniel and Rose as well, and told Thea, when I talked to her again, that I couldn't go down, but that she should talk to him for me, and say that I really wanted them all to come. She called me a few nights later to say that they would all come together. Two weeks before the wedding I conveyed to him, through Thea, Walter's invitation to dinner on a night when Thea was coming up. (I was still sleeping at the Mattracorne but most of my time was spent at the apartment, getting things ready for the wedding.)

He was better than I'd thought he would be, from Thea's description, and that made me wary. If the past year had aged him, it had not destroyed him. His suit hung loosely but he could wear it. His manner was subdued but not humble.

"Hello, Ruthie," he said. "I'm pleased to meet you, Mr. Stamm."

"It's very good to have you here, Mr. Kossoff," Walter said.

Thea and I walked ahead of them into the living room. The two of us sat on the sofa, my father in an armchair, while Walter made the drinks—a martini for himself, Scotch for my father and me, sherry for Thea. Thea tried to make conversation, something about her new teaching job, but it didn't work; my father and I were concentrating on appearing at ease and couldn't even pretend to be attentive.

"Well," Walter said, smiling down at us benignly, "happy days!" He raised his martini glass.

"*L'Chayim*," my father said.

"I beg your pardon?" Walter said.

"*L'Chayim*, Mr. Stamm," my father said solemnly. "You don't know this word, yet? Ruthie, shame on you."

So that's the way it's going to be. I was mildly amused and mildly irritated. And I suppose mildly curious as to how Walter would react to the *Yiddishe Poppa* act he was obviously going to get.

"*L'Chayim*, Mr.—I can call you Walter?"

"I'd be delighted."

"It means 'to life,' Walter. The most important word of all. Life. What you and Ruthie between you should produce plenty of, God willing."

"I'll drink to that," Walter said, gratified and unsuspicious.

God willing, indeed. Mama drove you into a rage when she forgot and used that expression by mistake.

Thea, too, seemed pleased.

We drank to life. The maid brought in hors d'oeuvres. I followed her back into the kitchen for a moment to check on dinner.

"Every night," my father was saying when I returned, "every night that chicken slept on his special pillow on my bed. And when it came time for the slaughter, I sneaked from the house with it early one morning, and when they found me in the woods, I stood up with the chicken in my arms and I said, 'Kill me but don't kill the chicken!' Ah, Ruthie." He turned to me as I sat down. "I was just telling your—ah— fiancé, here, one of the Keidan stories."

One of the Keidan stories. If I'd heard the name of my parents' home town ten times in my life, it was a lot. I smiled, wondering how he could bear to be such a hypocrite with me there, knowing. The evening proceeded in this pleasant, artificial vein, Walter and my father establishing a slightly drunken camaraderie; Thea looking at me delightedly every once in a while as though to say, "See, Ruth, I told you that people were basically wonderful"; I feeling alternately relieved and irritated at the easy intimacy of the two men. I left the apartment with my father and Thea and my father shook my hand before I headed up-town.

We were married in the living room by a rabbi Walter insisted upon having out of deference to me, a young crew-cut blond who had developed to a fine point the art of performing a religious ceremony without actually seeming Jewish. He delivered the few Hebrew passages with a diffidence that suggested he could be lip-reading in the Columbia law library; his speech afterward was a small nonsectarian ethical cultural humanitarian gem, the burden of which was that in people like us, as well as in people unlike us, lay the world's hope for peace.

Lotte was there, under protest; Walter had told her it was very important to him that she come. She'd arrived five minutes before the ceremony was to begin, wearing a black-silk dress that made her look ten years older than her age and in mourning. Her manner, though, was anything but mournful. She was suffused with a gaiety and sweetness that were so patently contrived as to make me squirm in embarrassment while Walter's friends told her what a lovely young woman she had become.

"Ruth," she said, "how beautiful you look. You could be on the cover of a magazine, honestly. I've never seen such a beautiful bride."

And I squirmed in my white-crepe dress, and I said, "Thank you, Lotte. We're glad you could come."

The only time she dropped the façade was during the moment when she was introduced to my father.

"Lotte," Walter said, "this is Ruth's father, Mr. Kossoff."

Abruptly her smile vanished, her face drained of blood.

"I'm pleased to meet you, Lotte," my father said.

She stared at him.

"Lotte?" Walter prodded gently. He was puzzled but I wasn't.

"You dirty old man! He killed himself because he couldn't stand to come home to you. Ask anyone, you dirty old man!"

The rabbi came over to Walter then, sparing him further embarrassment. It was almost time to begin. I squeezed Lotte's arm.

"They changed the rules too quickly, didn't they," I said.

But she would have none of my sympathy. She turned and left us. I brought my father over to Thea and then joined Walter.

Strangely, I was a great deal more tense than Walter seemed to be. He was gay and charming, introducing friends of his I'd recently met to friends of mine—to Lou Fine, who to my surprise had come with

Lillian ("I'm very happy for you, Ruthie," Lou said, shaking his head slowly. Lillian, queenly in her wheelchair, said that Lou had never told her how pretty I was); to Thea and my father; to Rita, who had turned away from me when I told her I was marrying Walter but who had brought herself to come to the ceremony, tight-lipped and unhappy but polite, nevertheless; to Selma and Jerry. Almost as big as she had been when she was pregnant (the baby was five months old) Selma was wearing a pink-organza dress and looked like a mammoth sign for a cotton-candy concession. I was inexpressibly happy to have her there. Jerry, dwarfed by her pink hugeness, smiled amiably at me and said I would have to come up soon and see the baby, as though he was fairly certain that I never would, which I assured him was not the case. During the ceremony I barely listened but kept thinking of the people in back of me. I thought of Carl Simpson, who had congratulated me in a way that made it clear that he was acknowledging not my engagement but my acquisition. Of Thea, who wore a pale-pink dress which, together with her soft brown hair, accomplished the miracle of making me feel that my white dress was somehow a little too white, my lipstick a little too red, my hair a little more black and curly than the editors of *Bride's Magazine* would have decreed that it should be. Of Boris—remembering how, as I rode back to New York that night in August to talk to David, I had tried not to think about things but to concentrate on scenery and sleep, and how in spite of me, one thought had persisted—

If I don't marry Walter, I might never see Boris again.

Of Martin.

Of my mother.

Of David.

Of Helen Stamm.

The ghosts of my wedding. I think I half-expected to see one of them walk in. At one point before the luncheon I was standing in the main hallway near the door to the apartment, and the door opened slightly—I suppose the lock hadn't caught earlier. When no one came in I felt uneasy and had to go to the door and peer out into the hallway, holding my champagne glass inside the apartment as though an unfriendly presence in the outside hall might knock it from my hand. I closed the door firmly, turning the top lock. Then, not yet ready to face everyone, I wandered into the library, reminding myself that I had to get another ashtray to replace the one Helen had taken from the desk when she left. Sipping at the last drops of champagne in my glass. Wondering uneasily why the nervous tightness within me hadn't dissolved with the ceremony. Walking over to the bookshelves, noticing the empty shelves from which Helen had taken the books she wanted— reference works, mostly; looking at the shelves that held Walter's books —on architecture, industrial design, graphics, interior design, antiques, flower arrangement, painting, sculpture. (Helen, months later: "You might say we divided responsibilities. Walter was in charge of aesthetics and I was in charge of life.")

I went back to the dining room, where guests were helping themselves at the buffet table. The bartender gave me more champagne. Walter had been looking for me. He asked if anything was wrong and I said no, that perhaps I was just feeling a little overwhelmed. He smiled at me fondly and I thought of David again and dropped my glass, which crashed on the highly polished wood that bordered the Kirman rug and shattered into more bits than had the ceremonial glass Walter stepped on during the ceremony. Walter moved me away while one of the catering-service maids cleaned up the glass, then he asked if he could get me some food.

"I couldn't," I said. "I'm too excited."

He nodded in sympathy. "More champagne, then."

"I don't know if I should," I said, knowing that I should not. My head was already light.

"This is your wedding, my dear," he said. "You're to enjoy yourself."

I smiled gratefully.

I'm afraid if I get drunk I'll say something terrible.

How silly. What would I say?

I'll say, I hate you, Walter.

Ridiculous. Not true. I'd never say it, because it isn't true.

"I *will* be up to see the baby," I said to Selma and Jerry, standing by themselves in a corner, while Walter went to get me more champagne. "Tell me his name again. I know it's awful, but I've forgotten."

She looked at me strangely. "Gregory Martin," she said.

The Martin struck me then as it had not when I received the announcement. I repeated the name after her.

She nodded vigorously. "The Gregory is from G, for my father. He died only two years ago and he didn't have a name. The Martin is for your brother, they should both rest in peace."

I started to cry.

"What's the matter," she said, "you didn't read the announcement?"

"I read it," I said tearfully, "but not . . . you know, it never occurred to me."

"Don't cry now," she said, "everyone'll think you're a crying bride."

"I can't help it."

"I bet you didn't have a thing to eat."

"That has nothing to do with it."

Walter, deep in conversation with one of his friends, pressed a glass of champagne into my hand and drifted away.

"I'm getting you some food," Selma announced, looking disapprovingly at the glass in my hand. "Jerry, give her the pictures to bury her nose in. Look at the baby pictures, I'll be right back."

So Jerry took out his wallet and I looked at pictures of Gregory Martin Weinstock, a fat, chinky-eyed, adorable five-month-old, while Selma piled up a plate of food for me, then came back and led me out of the dining room, through the hallways, and to my bedroom, where I dried my eyes and tried to eat some of the food heaped on my plate while Selma called home to make sure everything was all right. As she hung up, I dropped a forkful of lobster Thermidor on the skirt of my dress.

"You're maybe a little high already?" she asked, rubbing at the spot with a tissue.

"I'm maybe a little high already," I said.

She got a soapy washcloth and worked over the spot, which was still visible, though not conspicuous.

"Why don't we just get some cleaning fluid from the kitchen?" I asked.

"Everyone has to know," she said, "that you got a spot on your wedding dress?"

"Selma," I said, yawning, "I'm so glad you're here." I finished the champagne and carefully set down the empty glass on my night table.

"It's a very nice wedding," she said politely.

I smiled sleepily. "A little dull, but nice, huh?"

"Don't put words into my mouth," she said. "It's a beautiful wedding."

I nodded. "A beautiful wedding. Everything perfect, except maybe the bride and groom." I hadn't particularly meant to say it, but there it was.

She gaped at me, stricken.

"Oh, don't be upset, love," I said, unable to ignore her expression or to retract with a complete lie. "After all, nobody's perfect. That's what I meant. Nobody's perfect." I sat back against the bed's headboard.

"We should get back in there," she said.

"I'm tired," I told her.

"You wanna rest a little while? I'll wake you up in a half hour?"

"Keep me company," I said. "I don't want to really sleep."

She sat down on the chaise and I stretched out on the bed.

"Do you loathe me?" I asked, unable to keep my eyes open.

"Don't be foolish," she said.

"I was just trying," I explained, "I was trying . . . No, I wasn't trying to tell the truth, but it came out anyway."

"Don't worry about the truth," she said. "You're drunk. Go to sleep."

"The truth," I muttered, "is a very strange thing."

"Yeah, yeah," Selma said. "We know all about it."

"For example," I said, "the truth of the matter is—"

"Ruthie," Selma said, "go to sleep. This is no goddamn time for the truth."

Walter forgave me for not waking up again to see the end of my wedding day. There was in his forgiveness none of the martyr's forbearance that I would later come to find intolerable. I apologized more profusely than he thought necessary, doubtless because I had a better idea than he did of why I had drunk myself into a stupor.

We went to Bermuda for our honeymoon, staying two weeks. Walter had wanted to go to Europe for a month or two, but it had seemed to me that it was a bad time for us to leave Boris for so long, and Walter had acted grateful for my willingness to postpone the trip for his son's sake.

It was a honeymoon in the classic ironic sense. Escaped from the early-winter cold to an atmosphere of physical luxury a great deal more extravagant than anything I'd ever known; free of the necessity to make decisions or to force one another to make them; away from all the people who set up anxious counterpoints in our lives, we were pleasant, if not very passionate, lovers. I could be grateful for what he had given me; he could be pleased and proud as I reveled in the life there more joyous and obviously than I had in the relatively mundane luxury of his life in New York.

When I try now to recapture the feeling of that first Bermuda visit, I must go not to the trip itself, for the sharpness of that first pleasure has been muted by subsequent visits. I must go instead to a dream that I had often in my childhood. I am walking down a corridor in school and pass a door that isn't like the others but is covered with red velvet. I push open the door; it isn't a classroom but a bedroom. The walls are covered with pale-blue satin and the rug is white fur. At the dressing table, wearing a blue-satin gown and slowly brushing her waist-length blond hair, is a lady who looks much like my kindergarten teacher, Miss Holman, except that she is more beautiful. Waiting patiently, adoringly, nearby, is the tuxedoed man whose pictures I have seen so often in bus ads for the Arve Dance Studio. Unaware of my presence, the handsome dark-haired dancer fondles Miss Holman with his eyes. I am unbearably happy.

We came home on a Sunday night. Esther, the maid Walter had hired just a few weeks before, opened the door for us, although we'd had the doorman ring upstairs and we'd expected that Boris would be waiting. It seemed Boris was at the movies.

Walter frowned. "He knows we're coming home tonight, doesn't he?"

"Yes, Mr. Stamm," Esther said. "He know." She eyed me cautiously. With a woman living in the house it couldn't be quite as pleasant as it had been, but she wasn't sure yet whether it would be possible to stay.

"Has everything been all right, Esther?" I asked.

"Yes, ma'am," she said. "Boris dodn't give me no trouble."

She was nineteen years old but not new at the job of taking care of children. There were eleven of them at home, not counting her two older brothers.

Walter asked her to make us some tea and we went into the bedroom, the only room where we'd made changes. His desk had been moved into the room on the other side of the bath, which for ten or more years had been Helen's bedroom. Her dresser, now in our room, was, like Walter's highboy, mahogany inlaid with rosewood. They had been designed and used by Walter's father, who had left them behind (along with most of his other possessions) when he set out for a new life in California, no more sentimental about discarding the furniture he'd shared with his wife for forty years than about leaving the city where they had always lived and the son whom they had raised. We had purchased twin beds and given Walter's old bed to Esther's boyfriend, Wallace, a big virile-looking black man who had come with a friend to pick it up, his manner pleasant and casual, and had taken the mattress over his shoulder and grinned at me and said, "No bedbugs in this one, eh, miss?" The wallpaper had a gold background and geometric design executed in white. The bedspreads and the curtains were white, the carpeting, gold. The chaise, his mother's favorite resting place, was one of the few pieces, aside from the chests, that Walter had consented to take from his parents' apartment. It was covered in an antique maroon velvet that was lightly streaked with metallic gold thread; when the material had begun to go a couple of years earlier, Walter had had it patched and repaired, rather than have the entire piece recovered.

I changed into a bathrobe before tea, a plaid viyella robe that Walter had bought me in the weeks before we were married, when every day that I saw him I would be greeted with some lovely new gift—clothing, usually, because he was determined that I should have a proper wardrobe by the time I became his bride. His taste was flawless, and it was a matter to me first of bewilderment and then of resentment when some time after our marriage he almost ceased to buy me clothes or jewelry at birthdays and such times, and began to bestow upon me such feminine necessities as electric appliances, encyclopedic cookbooks, and subscriptions to progressive weekly magazines.

Boris came in while we were having tea, kissing each of us dutifully, then sitting on the floor near the chaise to drink the milk and cake Esther had brought in for him.

"So," I said to him, "tell us what you've been doing. I feel as if I haven't seen you for months."

He shrugged. "Nothing much."

"That's hardly an answer," Walter said sharply.

Boris looked at his father.

"It doesn't matter," I said quickly. "I can wait."

The next day Boris's headmaster phoned to inquire as to why Boris had been out of school for two weeks. He assumed, he said, that Boris hadn't been seriously ill, as several phone calls had failed to reach anyone at home. On the other hand, parents who were taking children out for vacations normally notified the school.

Some deep-seated, long-established, antiauthoritarian instinct prevented me from blurting out my surprise. Instead I asked if it would be possible to hold the line for a moment, then I got myself a cigarette, settled comfortably in the chaise, and picked up the receiver again.

"Perhaps I should introduce myself," I said. "I'm Boris's stepmother, Ruth Stamm."

"How do you do?" said the deep discreet voice which was obviously accustomed to this sort of information. "Mr. Stamm did mention at the beginning of the term that he and his wife had been divorced. I wish we'd known about the marriage. The children do react to these things, of course."

"Of course."

"May I ask," the voice went on, "how long . . . ?"

"Two weeks," I said. "We've just come back to town and—actually, I've been planning to come in one day and talk to you. I'm eager to know if there's anything I can do to help Boris with his work."

We made the appointment and the headmaster hung up without

remembering to ask if Boris had been out of town with us. I put the receiver back in the cradle.

Miss McMann, you have stood me in good stead.

I smiled to myself. Miss McMann. Was she Martin's fourth-grade teacher, or fifth? No, it was Miss Krieger in the fifth. I was in the sixth grade by then, and had to fake awkwardness in writing his excuse notes, lest my handwriting be suspiciously better than my mother's. I wore out the pages of Thea's parents' *Fishbein Home Medical Encyclopedia* searching for unheard-of diseases of short duration, and when he was questioned one day about one of my more exotic discoveries, I began to rely more heavily on my own ingenuity.

Dear Miss McMann: Martin will not be in school today. He dropped the free-milk can on his toe and I have to take him to the clinic. Sincerely, Rose Kossoff.

I was momentarily doubtful. Were you supposed to lie for kids in fancy schools or were even the ground rules different? What would Walter say?

Don't tell him.

I assured myself that the very idea was absurd. I hardly had to lie to Walter on Boris's behalf.

That's hardly an answer, Boris.

Certainly not a terrible thing to say, yet there'd been something in Walter's voice I hadn't heard before. It was a reprimand for an infringement that hadn't been made. Boris had sensed it, too. He had looked at his father as though he almost, but not quite, understood what was happening.

At three-thirty I went into the library to wait for Boris. I sat behind the desk and I thought of Helen. I stood up quickly and thought of Thea on the day of Martin's funeral. I moved around the room to avoid them both, and I thought of David. I left the library and wandered through the house, finally landing in the kitchen, where Esther was sorting the clean laundry into Iron and No Iron piles. I asked her a couple of household questions. She answered politely but made no attempt to prolong the conversation.

Boris came in then. We were a little shy with each other, or rather he was shy with me and I was not sure how to deal with his shyness. I leaned over to kiss him, but he moved away from me. Esther set out some chocolate cake and milk for him, and I asked if he wanted to have it in the bedroom while I did some things in there.

"It's okay," he mumbled. "I'll have it here."

"Please," I said. "I really want to talk to you."

He picked up the glass and plate and followed me down the hall, but when we got to the bedroom door it occurred to me that he might prefer to be in his own room, on more familiar grounds. I asked him and he nodded. I let him go past me and lead me into the room. He sat at his desk and I sat in his brown-leather easy chair.

"Dr. Farmer called," I said, "about your not being in school."

His eyes met mine for the first time; he was holding back tears.

"I think I understand why you did it. I mean I don't *exactly* understand, but I know you were upset. And it doesn't seem so unreasonable to me that you should be upset."

He held my gaze steadily, although he seemed almost to tremble with his effort not to cry.

"How'd you spend all that time?" I asked. "In the movies?"

"Mostly."

I took my cigarettes from my robe pocket and lit one. There was no ashtray. He handed me his plate with most of the cake still on it.

"Not hungry?"

"Uh-uh."

I took the plate, resting it on my lap. There was really nothing more I could say to him. Preaching would be foolish because he knew perfectly well he had done something he shouldn't. Punishment was pointless; he wouldn't do it again, with or without punishment. As far as the work he'd missed was concerned, it was early enough in the term so that he could easily make it up with my help. I could even pleasurably anticipate a heavier schedule of work with him. For if I was not yet oppressed by the feeling of futility and uselessness that was to trouble me later on, I had already wondered just what I was going to do with my time for the rest of my life.

"Will you go tomorrow?" I asked.

"Yes," he said.

"Try to find out what you missed," I told him. "And we'll start going over it."

He nodded. I mashed out my cigarette in the layer cake, then stood up.

"I have to tell your father," I said. "I'm sure he'll understand."

He averted his eyes. I think that like me, he was less certain of Walter's reaction than he would have been a month or two before. I went over to him and kissed the top of his head. Then I left the room. I brought the cake plate into the kitchen and deposited it in the sink. Esther wasn't in there. I looked in the cupboards, examining the various sets of china and glassware—the white wedding-band pattern that had been Walter's parents'; the stark white Rosenthal china that he and Helen, now he and I, used every day; the heavy cutglass stemware, the cocktail glasses, the long graceful highball glasses, and so on.

Peanut butter, my mother would write on the store list, *Kraft, for the glass.*

I took an orange from the refrigerator and brought it into the bedroom with me, peeling it with pleasurable care. It was just past four. I looked down at the bathrobe I was still wearing and almost laughed out loud. It must have been the first time in my life I'd stayed in a robe all day without being ill. And I was almost never ill; Martin was the one who had colds, and tonsils, and adenoids, and appendicitis. I finished the orange and washed its sticky juice from my fingers. I wondered what Boris was doing. I looked out of the bedroom window. It was a clear day. The park trees had lost almost all their leaves, but there was still green grass covering the ground, and the footpaths looked inviting. In the playground, children in bright snowsuits ran around, swung in the swings, dug in the sandbox. On the slatted benches ringing the playground sat the nannies, already wearing their black fur-collared winter coats. Nannies, and the occasional mother whose unfashionable conviction it was that being a mother involved more than giving birth and handing over your kid to some strange lonely woman to be raised. I marveled at their ability, all of them, to sit on those park benches for endless days, weeks, years, doing nothing but watching the children move about, speaking an occasional nothing to each other, or at best mindlessly knitting sweaters and embroidering small pieces of linen in delicate crewel. The whole park was around them and they never moved.

I got dressed in slacks and a sweater and knocked at Boris's door.

"Boris," I called, "I'm taking a walk in the park. Wanna come?"

"I'll be right out."

"Do you have a Spaldeen we can throw?"

"In the hall closet. I'll get it."

He opened the door. He'd changed into a sweater and jeans. We got the ball and left the house, crossing Fifth and entering the park. We didn't talk at all. When we'd been walking for a while we came to a good flat place on the grass. We threw the Spaldeen back and forth, and when we got tired of that, we found sticks and batted it. We had to stop after about half an hour because there wasn't enough light left to see the ball coming through the air. It was about ten to five.

"Come on," I said, "I'll buy you a Coke. Your father won't be home, yet."

Happily we walked over to Madison, drank our Cokes, returned to the house. Walter was home. He was sitting in the living room, having a martini. He had taken off his tie and jacket and was wearing a tan cashmere cardigan that I had bought for him in Saks one day when he sent me out to buy night clothes for my trousseau. ("My dear," he said, "you really needn't worry about *my* wardrobe, you know.") He looked quite handsome.

"I'm sorry," I said, going over to sit next to him. "I didn't realize you'd be home so early."

"I thought I'd surprise you," he said, his expression just a trifle chagrined. "Will you have a drink?"

"All right. Same."

"Walter," I said, when he'd brought me my martini, "Boris has apparently been more disturbed about all of this than we realized."

("I think maybe you should tell him yourself," I had whispered to Boris in the hallway. "No, you," he had begged, and walked quickly away from me, down the hall to his room.)

"Oh?"

"Dr. Farmer called today. He's been playing hooky."

"From school?" He frowned. "That isn't like Boris."

"I know."

"For how long?"

"Since we've been away. I mean, you know, since the wedding."

The look of horror on his face would have been appropriate had I just told him that his son was an axe murderer.

"I don't think it's cause to be horribly upset," I said quickly.

"You don't?" he said.

"No, not really. I mean, if he'd done it just out of the blue, I could see being more worried about it. But he was upset about something in particular, you know? Something very big in his life. Something that's not going to happen again."

"Do I gather," his speech slow and deliberate to convey the false impression of an open mind, "that you consider our marriage reasonable cause for my son to stay out of school for two weeks?"

It was the first moment that I ever disliked Walter. His obtuseness, his self-righteousness, his sudden proprietary emphasis on *my* son, his sudden failure to sympathize with his son, now that Boris no longer had to be championed against an unloving mother. At that early naïve point in our marriage, I found the feeling of distaste that flooded me almost unbearable. I tried to push it off, to keep its traces from my words.

"Not exactly reasonable, Walter. But understandable."

"On what grounds?"

"Well, just the fact of its being such a big thing in his life. And he seems to have had something of a crush on me . . ."

"A *what?*" He stood up so abruptly that half the liquid in his glass spilled onto his pants. "May I remind you, Ruth," he said, rigid with anger, "that you are talking about a twelve-year-old boy?"

And there's one for your side, Helen.

"Walter," I said, "it seems so awful to be arguing like this at the end of our first day home."

This appeal, less to sense than to ceremony, he was willing to consider.

"I *did* talk to Boris. He *does* know that we consider it a serious matter. He *has* promised that he won't do it again. Even if you don't approve of the way I handled it, couldn't we forget it for now? Declare a sort of general amnesty? I'm sorry that I've upset you. Maybe the whole business should be chalked up to my inexperience." I smiled winsomely. "I *am* inexperienced, you know. I've never been married before, and I've never been a mother."

He sat down, but not willingly. He let it drop, but not graciously. He would not insist upon fighting it out, nor would he ever let go of his cause for battle. He wouldn't laugh and say that I was right nor would he battle to force an admission that I'd been wrong. He wasn't ready to stop arguing so he feigned readiness, but retained a sort of stiffness to his words during the rest of the evening.

I don't believe he ever spoke to Boris about those two weeks. Nor did he ever quite forgive him. (For months, at least, that was the most charitable explanation I could find for his new lack of sympathy with Boris.) He never again mentioned the incident to me. Yet he would come upon Boris and me sitting together on the sofa, reviewing some school text, and his expression would make it obvious that he was wondering what kind of unwholesome notions I might be entertaining now.

He has never hit me in anger; nor has he ever hugged me in impetuous warmth.

On Election Day in 1952 I walked into the voting booth at P.S. 198 and raised my hand to press the levers along Row A, to vote the straight Republican ticket. I was wearing a black tweed suit and a black cashmere sweater. In my left hand I held my purse and a pair of French kid gloves. When my right hand was less than an inch from the first lever I became simultaneously aware of the buttery luxury of the kid gloves in my hand and the soft warmth of the cashmere on my voting arm. The arm froze in mid-air and for a moment my entire body was rigid. Then I began to shake, first in my stomach and then all over, with a silent, uncontrollable laughter. I must have stood there, helpless to move, for a full minute or more, laughing silently as a series of images paraded through my head: My mother, crying on a clear spring afternoon as the news of Roosevelt's death came over the radio, my father, making fun of Dewey's mustache with a savagery that suggested that the mustache might as well have been responsible for the passage of the Taft-Hartley Act ("What are you talking about," he once demanded of Uncle Daniel, "with your good Republicans and bad Republicans? La Guardia's a Republican like I'm a Republican!"); Jerry Glickman's father, a student of science fiction, depicting for us one election eve in gory terms the horrors that would befall New York if it should ever through some freak of fate fall into the hands of the Republicans ("A hundred dollars a month you'd pay for rent, like that!"—with a guillotine-like snapping of the fingers).

I became aware of feet shifting restlessly outside the booth. Through the tears in my eyes I made out the Democratic line and pressed down the levers. Then, head down, I left the booth, walked through the building and out to Ninety-sixth Street.

It was the first time I had ever had the sense of myself as a ludicrous human being. I was almost twenty-two years old and had been married for a year.

It is difficult for me to understand how I got through our first year without developing that vital sense of myself as a worthy victim of the cosmic comic. How could I have failed to be just a little amused at the endless stream of inane provocations and senseless rejoinders that we directed at each other from day to day?

I despised Walter for opening the morning paper to the death notices; he read the obituaries as though they were the closing figures and he were a stock broker. But I thought it not at all strange that I should read the market closings first.

When did Walter first look at Boris and me, as we ate a hearty dinner in the dining room, and smiling with fake fondness, say, "You two are eating me out of house and home"? I think it was before I signed our first joint income-tax return and learned that his combined income from his salary as president of Stamm Realty and his dividends from the various syndicates and holding corporations that it controlled, as well as from the large number of other good stocks that he owned, was well in excess of a hundred thousand dollars a year. I loathed him for his incongruous self-preservative concern. But never wondered at my own necessity to keep, and to hide, the bankbook I'd had since my first job, and to maintain and enlarge the account that it covered.

When did cleanliness become an open issue between us? Helen had once referred to her husband as fastidious, but certainly it hadn't occurred to me that with a full-time maid in attendance, he would walk around the house, lips ever so slightly puckered, picking up the gloves I'd left on the hallway table or the sweater I'd draped over a chair. I tried to be neater and he thought I was mocking him. Like a thwarted child I became spiteful and left things where I knew he would notice them.

I understand my sense of betrayal at the fondness which Walter developed for my father and which my father professed to feel for Walter. I sensed in the harmony between them an emotional conspiracy against me. But how could I have failed to see any humor in the evening when my father came up to borrow money from Walter and walked away with what amounted to an outright gift of eleven thousand dollars?

He had been up a few times since the wedding for what he liked to call "dinner and a little chat." Until that evening I hadn't understood why he wanted to come. It wasn't as though we had any real feeling left for each other; if the hatred between us had been buried, that didn't mean the love could be restored. I would have preferred him to stay away entirely; his pious new aura made my memories doubly disturbing. He was going to synagogue regularly now and talked as though he had never spent Saturday mornings any other way. Deliberately or accidentally he found the things to say that would please Walter and bother me. During one of his early visits he praised Boris and then said something about the blessing of children, particularly sons. Finding Walter responsive and me disconcerted, he made it a point to play on the children theme each time he came.

"We have a saying in the old country," he would tell Walter gravely. "'In a perfect life a man eats the labor of his hands, his wife is like a fruitful vine, and his children are like olive plants around his table.'"

"Beautiful," Walter would murmur wistfully. "And true."

"They used to say," my father told him another time, "God forbid I should have only one child or one undershirt."

And one evening, not long after Walter had loaned him the money, he launched into a sickening, fraudulent monologue involving his long-time desire for a large family, but how could you insist upon it (with a deep sigh), when it was the woman, not you, who had to bear the child and the pain?

It must have been then that I realized that he was making fun of Walter in addition to teasing me, for the story was such a blatant lie as to make a conspirator of me, who knew the truth.

Boris always claimed an inordinate amount of homework on nights when my father came, and when Walter permitted him to do so, had dinner in his room. On occasions when Walter insisted that he dine with us, Boris was withdrawn and uncommunicative, and I knew he was wondering why I chose to join in the communal hypocrisy after the unforgivable way in which my father had treated me. The only answer I had was that this was the easy way out.

Not that I took full part in the gaiety. Often after dinner I too would find some reason to leave the two men with their drinks. A tiring day. A need for fresh air. Some such thing. Walter would come into the bedroom hours later and perhaps wake me up to tell me, in a somewhat drunken manner, what a wonderful human being my father was.

I don't know why I stayed around on this particular night, unless it was because I sensed that my father was eager to be rid of me. He said once or twice that I seemed tired and perhaps I needed a good night's sleep, and when I said that actually I was feeling fine, he winked at Walter and made some comment about my unwillingness to miss anything that was going on, although until that moment it hadn't occurred to me that there could really be anything to miss.

"If you don't mind, Walter," he said, when it became obvious to him that I was staying, "I have a serious business to discuss with you tonight."

"By all means," Walter said easily.

"Ruthie?" A last obvious attempt to get rid of me. "You have things to do?"

"Nothing at all, as a matter of fact," I said blandly.

"That's what I mean," he said to Walter with a shrug and a smile. "In Lithuania, the woman who saw her husband was going to discuss a—"

"You're very big on Lithuania this year, aren't you?" I interrupted irritably. "I didn't even know which part of Russia you came from until I had to ask you for a school composition."

"Ruth," Walter said in mild reproof.

"Maybe," my father said, terribly hurt, terribly dignified, "maybe I knew you weren't interested, Ruthie. You don't talk to people about things that don't interest them. What I was going to mention—"

"It's about money," I said suddenly—realizing it and saying it at the same time. "It must be about money."

"You're being rather crude, aren't you, Ruth?" Walter asked.

"No, no." My father put up a hand in protest. "It's all right, Walter. A smart girl, my daughter. She sees I'm embarrassed, so she knows it's a favor. I'm not a man accustomed to asking favors. She knows this. And what favor would I ask of you, if not money? Not," he added quickly, "that I'm asking you for charity. It's a business proposition I want to put to you. Straight business. A loan. But I wouldn't even take it from you unless it was straight business. On paper. You don't think it's a good deal, you tell me. No hard feelings. If that's not understood to begin, I wouldn't even tell you the rest."

"Of course," Walter said. "Of course . . . Abe."

It seemed that the building Daniel's grocery was in was up for sale. It had fifteen apartments, Daniel's store, and a small appetizing store, as well, adding up to an annual income of over twelve thousand dollars. The building was in good condition and the asking price was just fifty thousand dollars, although it could probably be gotten for an even four times the rent roll. It could provide a man with a steady income, he wouldn't have to worry for the rest of his life where his own rent was coming from (if Walter noticed the implied threat that we would have to support him, there was no sign), but you couldn't touch it without eleven thousand in cash. He showed Walter the offering sheet. Thoughtfully Walter took a pencil from his desk and made some calculations in the margin.

"Well, Abe," he said after a few minutes, "it looks all right to me. I *would* like to have a couple of men from the office look it over, if that's all right with you."

Generously my father said he would be grateful for expert opinion.

"Excuse me," I said abruptly as they began to discuss the details of the loan. "I'm going to take a walk." Not understanding why I was so angry with the whole thing.

"Ruthie," my father said, "you're not going to stay and drink a toast with us?"

"A toast," Walter said. "What a nice idea." And he went to get the bottle to refill the glasses.

"You should be ashamed of yourself," I whispered to my father.

"I don't understand you, Ruthie," he said, shaking his head sorrowfully. "You see things in a funny way. I don't understand you at all."

I got up to go but Walter was back with the bottle already, and rather than make a scene, I stayed.

"*L'Chayim,*" my father said. "Our lives should all be enhanced by our little business venture."

I glanced at Walter to see if I could find even a hint of annoyance at this presumption, but Walter was, as ever, willing to play it straight.

"*L'Chayim,*" he said seriously, trying very hard to get enough guttural into the *ch* sound, but not quite making it.

"I can't pretend to understand your attitude," he said to me later, when my father was gone.

"I'm sure you can't."

"Do I gather that you wouldn't have wanted your father to have the money?"

I thought about it for a moment and I couldn't answer him.

"I don't know, Walter. It's not just a question of the money."

"No, it's not just money," he said. "It's a question of doing another human being a favor. It could be money, it could be anything. But the human being happens, among other things, to be your father."

"I guess I don't really feel as though he's my father any more."

His eyes narrowed. "At one time," he said, "you gave me the impression that you wished the breach between the two of you could be healed."

It was too late already, though, Walter. By the time we were married it was too late.

"You're a young girl, Ruth," said my husband, the philosopher and philanthropist, "you shouldn't find it so hard to forgive."

If Walter surprised and repelled me, Boris astounded me in the way he blossomed. I was without the specific vanity that would have made me assume he would begin to exploit his intelligence more fully when I became his stepmother. Yet that was what happened, in spite of his changed and disappointing relationship to Walter. His math and science work, always good, became excellent, and while his language aptitudes never equaled them, they became, gradually, more than adequate for a boy whose primary talents lay elsewhere.

I was certain that both of them had changed and that I was the same, but this could not have been so. Or why, for example, would I have found that once I was the second Mrs. Stamm, the image of the first Mrs. Stamm was no longer larger than life? She had always been good to me, yet I'd been prevented from feeling gratitude by the fear and discomfort I'd experienced in her presence. Now that very presence was a comfort to me, and my pleasure in seeing her was abetted, I suppose, by my guilt at wanting to.

My friendship with Helen, during the years that it lasted, was one of the things Walter held most strongly against me, and while he couched his objections in terms so vague that I could pretend not to comprehend them (he could not help but find it "strange" that I should want to renew our association) I knew always that he was accusing me of disloyalty and that he had good reason to do so. There were, as he said, plenty of interesting people around, if one wanted good conversation. But I needed *her* wit, because whenever it was directed its secondary object was Walter. Her perceptions fortified mine, as did her illusions. Even in our disagreements there was no bitterness. Leaning on either agreement or dissension, we climbed conversationally over Walter's dead body.

She had taken a two-bedroom apartment in a house on Washington Square. One of the rooms had been furnished for Lotte, who now used it only when she came in from Vassar for holidays and an occasional weekend. The rest of the place had been done in a modern style so stark as to be unsettling, with black-leather chrome-legged chairs, glass and chrome tables, and draperies in a beige, black, and white block print. That it was less like a home than a doctor's office, or some futuristic classroom, was appropriate, for I went there less as a friend than as a student or patient. The arrangement suited both of us. I have never been a great talker and in that first year of bewilderment and adjustment I was less inclined than usual to talk, to argue, to postulate. While Helen was the eternal teacher. No more interested than I was in a true exchange of ideas, she was not happy unless she was dispensing some highly edited knowledge to the less knowledgeable; unless some pretentious person or fatuous philosophy were being punctured by her considerable wit; unless there were people around, generally people younger than she and less knowing, listening wide-eyed, volunteering by their presence to let themselves be battered by her verbal violence. She preferred the appearance of argument to the reality. On the rare occasion when one of her young friends could document some argument for, say, public relief, she made no attempt to respond on the same level but would resort to some outrageous generality, the wit of which filled in the gaps left by its deliberate simplicity.

"It is a well-known fact," she would announce, "that man's primary characteristic is a tendency to bite the hand that feeds him. Only a

sophist, or a madman, or someone running for office and thereby proving himself a little of both, would dare to suggest that you can earn the
gratitude of the lower classes by putting them all on relief."

I was soothed by her assertiveness, comforted by her generalities. Life
seemed a great deal more complex than it had in the days when my decisions were large and still before me. I was less interested in exploring
those complexities than in neglecting them in favor of simple solutions
to more sweeping problems.

I had gotten into the habit of going out after dinner—perhaps because I got tired of sitting in the living room with Walter for a couple
of hours without a word passing between us; if I interrupted his reading to make some little comment we invariably got into some discussion
that ended up in petty bitchery. Instead of trying to draw him out, I
would restlessly stalk the other rooms for a while, then put on a coat
and announce that I was going to take a walk. After the first few times
even this became a bone of contention.

"You never change to a robe in the evening," he said one night. "As
though you have to be prepared to escape at any moment."

"I get restless," I said.

"That's fairly obvious."

"I've always been that way, Walter," I said. "You know I've always
been a walker."

He said nothing.

"If you want to come with me, that's fine. I'd be delighted. I just
have to get out sometimes at night."

"I'm tired in the evening," he said. "I do work hard all day, you
know, Ruth."

Something in his voice suggesting it was the financial burden he assumed when he married me that necessitated so much time and energy
at the office.

"I understand that, Walter. That's why I haven't invited you along
before. I just thought . . ." I let it trail off.

Later, irresistibly, I would leave the apartment, heading downtown
on the park side of Fifth. Usually David was with me on these walks.
Walter had vanished, possibly in an airplane crash, or perhaps he had
never existed. Sometimes we walked in silence, sometimes we argued
good-naturedly. There was bitterness neither in our silence nor in our
arguments. Somehow we had come to understand each other. When
we got to Fifty-seventh Street, though, it was more difficult. David

would vanish in crowds. I wouldn't be ready to go home. I'd hail a cab and give Helen's address on Washington Square.

"Ruth," she said excitedly when she saw me one Tuesday in March. "Come in. Listen to this. Yes, take off your coat, of course, but I have to read you this." Waving a book at me. "Billy is driving me crazy by steadfastly refusing to appreciate it."

Billy was her new ward. She'd picked him up around New Year's time at Bloomingdale's, where he had endeavored to improve upon a post-Christmas sale of cashmere mufflers by slipping one into the pocket of his pea jacket, and had been noticed at the same moment by Helen, who was examining some sale pajamas at the next table, and by the salesman, who was trying, rather halfheartedly, to attract the attention of a store detective across the floor. Helen had suggested that in the interest of saving everyone trouble, she add the muffler to her purchases— she handed him the six pairs of pajamas she'd selected for herself—and they could then call it a day. The salesman had willingly assented and in short order she and Billy were out on the street, where she had given him the muffler, bought him a cup of coffee, and ascertained that he had been in New York for a week, had spent in five days the money he thought would do for a month if it should take him that long to get a job, and had slept in doorways for the previous two nights. He had gotten a job as an usher in a movie house, but it wasn't to begin until the following week and he wasn't sure what he would do in the meantime. She had brought him home and installed him in Lotte's room, which had just been vacated until the next holiday. He would have to hit the streets whenever Lotte came home, but otherwise he was welcome indefinitely. She was not the least bit concerned about the room's condition, for Billy was neat as a pin and, as a matter of fact, picked up after her constantly.

He was nineteen years old. He was small and slight, with an olive complexion, oily black hair, and big dark doe eyes, the effect of which was largely destroyed by hollow gray half-moons underneath. He would have looked altogether appropriate standing at the dock of some Italian seaport, offering to lead tourists to his sister; he was from northern Maine, where his family had been farming for six generations.

Helen deposited my coat on a hall chair and led me into the living room. Tuesday was Billy's night off from the theater. He was sitting on the sofa, knitting a sweater. He had been knitting it for weeks. It was supposed to be for Helen but it was coming out too large.

"Hi," he said. "I like your blouse."

I thanked him.

"All right," Helen said. "Here it is." She began reading from the book. "'And here's another Don Quixote of enlightenment has founded a school. Well, what can be more useful for a man than to know how to read or write? But this is how he manages things. The peasants from the village come to me. "What's the meaning of this, sir?" they say, "our sons have got completely out of hand, they won't help us on the land, they all want to be clerks, but you know there is only one clerk wanted." So that's what it comes to.'" She read a bit further, snapped the book shut, and gazed at us triumphantly. "*That*," she said, "is a Russian writing in the first half of the nineteenth century. What has the world learned since then? Nothing. I tell you, Ruth . . ."

I listened contentedly, nodding once in a while to indicate comprehension. If I had reservations, I felt no need to express them; if I had questions, I didn't ask them unless she paused and seemed to want prodding. After a little while I made myself a drink at the sideboard, and at his request, I made one for Billy, too. Helen never drank. She'd said it stopped her from thinking. I thought of that now and smiled, because she had precisely the same effect on me.

"Do you think it's funny, too, Billy?" she asked, misinterpreting my smile.

"You know something, Helen?" Billy said dreamily. "You remind me of my grandfather."

She turned back to me with a grimace. "It's hopeless," she said. "You two are about as political . . ."

I grinned at her mischievously. "Walter's very political these days. He goes to meetings at the Democratic club. He has his secretary mimeograph letters for Stevenson."

"How touching."

"It is, in a way." Blandly provocative. "I mean, they're all very excited about Stevenson. He's apparently a very unusual type, not like a politician, at all. They say—"

"In the words of Mr. Justice Holmes," she cut me off with a yawn, "'Liberals drool.'"

When I came home Walter was reading in bed. I'd decided that if he asked, I would say I'd dropped in on Thea. He liked Thea and approved of my seeing her, although I found that I didn't call her as often as I might have. The idea of her was no less important to me than it had ever been, yet there was a static quality to our meetings which ended up in making me turn back in upon myself. Walter didn't ask, though, and I offered no explanation. I undressed in the bathroom, showered, got into bed. My eyes closed before Walter had turned off his reading light.

It was June before I saw Lotte again. She had finished her first year at Vassar and come home for the summer. All year she had insisted that if Walter wanted to see her during her city visits, he must meet her someplace and take her out to dinner. And Walter did want to see her —every time she came in. I could have sworn, as a matter of fact, that he was a great deal more concerned about Lotte than he had been in the days when he was married to her mother, that in those days Boris had taken up the full measure of his paternal sympathy while Lotte had been more or less left to her mother's attention. In any event, she called and instead of coldly saying hello and asking for Walter, she said that she would like to come up that evening. She came for dinner, looking chic and pretty in a tailored blue-linen dress and high-heeled patent-leather pumps. Her hair was cut short around her head in a style that would have been like mine had her hair been curly. She'd turned eighteen since our wedding.

Walter wasn't home yet. (I'd called him to say Lotte was coming at about five and he'd been very concerned that he couldn't leave the office early that particular day. Five minutes later he'd called back to ask me to have Esther make veal Parmesan because it was Lotte's favorite dish.) Boris was still playing ball in the park with some school friends. I led her into the living room.

"You must be thirsty," I said, "traveling around the city in this heat. Would you like a lemonade or something?"

"I'll have a gin and tonic, please," she said, unsmiling.

"Excuse me," I said. I made the drinks and brought them to the sofa. She took hers with a nod and sat there, apparently prepared to drink it without conversation.

"So," I said, "have you decided what you're going to do for the summer?" My voice just tight enough to force me to acknowledge that while I had reached the stage of easy enjoyment with Helen Stamm, I was still unsettled by her daughter.

"I'm not sure," she said. "I might work, if I can get an interesting job—you know, publishing or advertising or something like that. I'm not going to work just for the sake of keeping busy. There are plenty of other things I can do."

I nodded. She contemplated her drink.

"We're going up to the lake early," I said. "It's so hot, we might as well. Boris and I will be there all summer."

No visible reaction. The house had remained in Walter's name, Helen having announced that she was at a time in her life when she didn't care to be encumbered by possessions and responsibilities. The agreement, however, was that the house was Helen's to use during the skiing season, with Walter continuing to foot the bills during that time.

"I hope," I said, "that you'll feel free to come up during the summer if you want to."

"Oh, I'm planning to," she said, a little too quickly, a little too forcefully, betraying her eagerness to show me how little she cared whether I wanted her there, in her own father's home. She flushed.

"Good," I said. "I'm glad."

She looked away from me. We sat for a moment in uneasy silence.

"I have some friends," she said, "who're going to be around there this summer."

"How nice."

"Mmm." She lit a cigarette.

Boris came in, and as he walked through the hallway I called to him that we were in the living room. He came in, sweaty and tired from his ball playing, probably having forgotten I'd told him after school that his sister was coming.

"My God," Lotte gushed loudly, "how you've grown! Come here and give me a kiss!"

He looked at her in stupefaction. He was twelve years old and the same height as Lotte. He and his sister had lived in the same apartment for nearly eleven years and during that time a combination of factors—the natural gap caused by the six-year difference in their ages, Lotte's own inward disposition, perhaps an unthinking tendency to imitate her mother's attitude toward Boris—had caused her to be quite indifferent to him. There had been no contact between them since the time their father had married me. Besides, twelve-year-old boys didn't kiss *anyone*. I tried to smooth over the awkward silence by saying that Boris's kisses were scarce that year; but while Boris looked at me gratefully, Lotte's face became frozen in an angry mask that suggested that all five feet six inches of her brother would be in her lap at that moment were it not for my presence. I turned around and left the room. Boris made matters worse by following me.

"Where are you going?" I whispered to him in the hallway.

He shrugged. "Where're *you?*"

"Just to the kitchen," I said. "I want to see how Esther's doing with dinner. Do you want a Coke?"

He nodded.

"I'll bring it in to you."

"I'll come in," he said.

Walter opened the front door.

"Hi," I said, relieved to see him. "Lotte's here. She's in the living room."

"Is everything all right?" he asked nervously.

"I guess so," I said. "Can I make you a martini?"

"Yes, please. Have you given Lotte something?"

"Yes, Walter," I said, very slowly, with exaggerated patience. "I have given Lotte something. I have given Lotte a gin and tonic, which is what she requested." Aware that she might be able to hear me, some little thing in his voice having driven me past the point where I cared. "I have also conversed politely with her and assured her of our eagerness to have her at the lake this summer. All of which doesn't explain why she's sitting in there looking as though I tried to eat her alive, but no doubt the two of you between you will be able to find some reas——"

But he didn't wait for me to finish. He dashed into the living room, clearly terrified of what he might find there. "You forgot your first-aid kit!" I shouted after him.

A murmur of affectionate voices reached me from the living room. I looked at Boris. His eyes were almost level with mine. In another year he would be taller than I. "I'm going to take a walk," I said. I turned around and walked out of the apartment. He came out while I was waiting for the elevator.

"You better go back, love," I said. "Your father'll be angry as it is."

"Why can't I come?"

"I didn't say you can't." Knowing it was what I *should* have said. "I just think you *shouldn't.*"

The elevator doors opened. I walked in. He followed me.

We went up to the lake the following week and had been there for two or three weeks when, on a sunny afternoon as I lay reading a magazine on the dock, I heard footsteps on the shore end of the dock and sat up. A man was walking toward me. I was alone, although far out on the lake I could see Boris and his friend Arthur Loeb in one of the boats.

"Hi," the man said.

I nodded. He wasn't really bad looking but he was dirty and sweaty, his white shirt and army pants looked not merely rumpled but gray and greasy, a toe poked through one of his sneakers, and his face showed the heavy stubble of a gray beard although the hair on his slightly bald-ing head was still brown.

"I'm looking," he drawled, "for the Stamm fiefdom." He squatted down on the dock, a few feet from me, casually looking me over.

"You're in it."

"That right?" He tore his eyes away from my legs for long enough to look quickly around him. "Nice," he said, his eyes coming back to my face.

Both curious and irritated, I said nothing.

"The kid around?"

"The kid?" I was startled. "Which kid?"

"How many are there?"

"Now, look here," I began angrily, but he put up a hand to stop me.

"Okay," he said quickly. "Peace. I apologize. I surrender uncondi-tionally. Don't be mad at me. Lotte. I mean Lotte. I'm a—a friend of hers. Name's Tom Krause."

I remembered Lotte's telling me that friends would be staying near the lake, and I stared at him, wondering where amidst the pure green hills of Vassar she had dug up this battered specimen. He held out his hand. I ignored it.

"I'm sorry," I said. "Lotte's in New York. She said she'd be up some-time during the summer, but I don't know when."

He nodded, unperturbed. "I didn't expect to get up so early," he ex-plained affably. "I figured on the end of July."

I didn't reply.

"My legs are getting cramped," he said. "Are you going to bite off my head if I stretch them out on the dock for a few minutes?"

"Nothing in the world," I said, "could persuade me to bite off your head."

He whistled softly and stretched out across the width of the dock, letting his feet, still in their sneakers, trail in the water.

"A lake, a country manse, and a beautiful girl beside me," he said, "squelching me in the wilderness."

I stood up, picked up my towel and magazine, stepped past him, and began walking the length of the dock.

"Whom shall I say called?" he shouted after me.

"My name is Ruth Stamm," I said, without turning around.

"Ruth Stamm, Ruth Stamm," he said. "Cousin Ruth? Sister Ruth? Miss Ruth—hey!" The last with such force that it made me turn around to face him. He was sitting up, grinning hugely. "Not Stepmother Ruth! You're not Stepmother, are you?"

"I'm married to Lotte's father, if that's what you mean," I said stiffly, prepared to stand priggishly on my twenty-two-year-old dignity rather than give an inch to his insolent ebullience or admit to myself for a moment that I was flattered by his surprise. I turned away from him again and walked across the lawn and into the house.

I called Walter that night and asked him to tell Lotte that her friend Tom Krause had come by. Lotte came up with her father that weekend. Her room was set up for her—I'd even asked Mrs. Bannion to put the linens on the bed that week. But Lotte asked, with that shy manner she was more inclined to adopt in her father's presence than in mine alone, if she might use the cottage, instead. Walter was momentarily disturbed by the idea—afraid, apparently, that I had made his daughter feel like an intruder. She explained to him that after a hectic school year she relished the idea of some solitude, and since it never occurred to him that solitude was precisely what she did not want in that cottage, he finally consented. I offered to help her get the cottage in shape; she rejected my help so quickly and intensely as to suggest that I had attempted a total invasion of her life and privacy. Then she went over to clean up the place before lunch, which we delayed until past two so that she could eat with us. She left the house again immediately afterward.

"How did this fellow seem to you?" Walter asked me when she'd gone. "Lotte seems to think a great deal of him."

"He was only here for a couple of minutes."

"Still, you must have gotten some impression," said Walter, who in the past months had found several occasions to wish aloud that I would not react so quickly and so strongly to people. "You're good at first impressions."

I shrugged. "I didn't like him."

"Oh? Why is that?"

"I don't know, Walter. Anyway, what's the point of talking about it? If Lotte's involved with him, you're sure to meet him soon, maybe even this weekend, and you can decide for yourself."

"There is," Walter said, "an ominous quality to your use of the word *involved*."

"I'm sorry," I said, finally irritated out of my good intentions. "He's a good ten years older than I am, and he looks as if he's had more women than baths in that time. If you can think of a more circumspect word, I'll use it."

Walter blanched. I immediately regretted the words.

"Are you quite sure of what you're saying?" he asked.

"No," I said. "I'm not sure. I could be wrong. Maybe I exaggerated. You know me. Sometimes I get carried away."

"He's got a decent enough background," Walter said. "His father is one of Lotte's professors—sociology, I think she said. His mother's a psychologist, or one of those things. Writes some sort of syndicated column. Marriage and the Family. Something like that. His uncle's Judge Krause, the well-known liberal."

(The phrase had become a favorite description of Walter's with his interest in Democratic politics that year.)

"The Judge has a place in Wilksboro. That's where the youngster's . . ." The words trailed off as he remembered that Krause was apparently not a youngster. He waited for either argument or reassurance, but I had no inclination for either, and we sat in silence for a while until Boris came up from the dock to find out why we hadn't put on our suits yet. Glad of the excuse, I changed and went down to the water with him. We'd been swimming for a while and were trying to decide whether to take out one of the boats, when I noticed Lotte and Krause walking on the lawn near the house.

"Still want to take out the boat?" I asked Boris.

He nodded.

"Okay. Let's take the canoe."

We went to the far side of the dock, where the boats were moored, and got into the canoe. In the boat's rear, I deliberately directed us around the bend that would hide us from the house, for I had no desire to make our escape obvious. We paddled contentedly around the lake for some time, eventually heading home because the sun had gone behind some big clouds and we were chilly in our damp suits.

They were on the lawn near the house, wearing bathing suits, chatting amiably. Nina Loeb was there, having scented out Lotte's arrival. She and her mother had come to the lake even earlier than we had that year, an event connected to Nina's advanced state of pregnancy. Nina had gone off to Hofstra College the previous fall, insisting upon rooming near campus although her home was a twenty-minute drive from school, and she'd received a shiny red convertible for her eighteenth birthday. She had managed to attend school for two months before getting herself knocked up (in early November), married (during Christmas vacation), and granted a year's leave of absence (in January). I knew all this because in Lotte's absence I had been granted the privilege of receiving alternate confidences, unrequested and undesired, from mother and daughter, always with the stricture that I not tell the other what I knew. ("Mom wanted me to have an abortion but daddy said he'd divorce her and marry me first, don't for Chrissake tell Mom I told you." "My daughter's going to give birth to the biggest seven-month baby in history. Would you believe it, Manny wanted poor Irwin to beg for Nina's hand in marriage, just so the kid didn't think he was doing anyone a favor?")

"Ah," Walter said jovially as we came across the lawn, "here are our wanderers."

"I'm sorry," I said. "I didn't realize we had company. Hello, Nina, Mr. Krause."

He looked better than he had the first time. He'd shaved, and he was clean after his swim, and with a bathing suit on instead of filthy clothes, his build looked good enough.

They were drinking.

"May I make you a drink, my dear?" Walter asked, some touch of warmth or gallantry in his manner that hadn't been there for months. He seemed to be really enjoying himself.

"Thanks," I said. "I'll make it myself. I want to go in and change, anyway."

Lotte never looked at me, or for that matter at anyone but Krause. She looked at him as a year and a half earlier she had looked at Martin, with a concentration that excluded everything in the world that could not be found in his face. With an adoration that was an end in itself for it suffused her in a greater warmth and happiness than she would ever receive from him.

"Yes," Krause said as I walked away, obviously picking up the strands of a conversation, "there is that tendency, to think of California as another country. Which it isn't, it's only an exaggerated version of this one. More stupidity, more lunacy, exaggerated degree of cutoff from tradition. The East is their Europe, you know. They talk about New York the way New Yorkers talk about Europe, only with hostility instead of admiration . . ."

I had stopped to listen in spite of myself. Now, suddenly self-conscious at the way I was standing there with my back to the group, I quickly went into the house. Upstairs I got out of my suit and still chilled, put on black woolen slacks and my long-sleeved red cashmere sweater. Then I brushed my hair and put on lipstick for the first time in many days, although it didn't occur to me to wonder why I was doing it. I went down to the kitchen and made myself a drink, then went out to the porch; but I felt reluctant to join the group on the lawn. I had a sense of alienation from them, a feeling that was no less

upsetting than the one I'd had in the old days, when I'd never felt excluded from anything except for reasons of money.

Poor Irwin came over to fetch his Nina home. A nice-looking, broad-
shouldered, tortoise-shell-spectacled young man, he looked as if now, in
the eighth month of his wife's pregnancy, he was still not certain of
what had happened to them. Nina arose with a nearly magnificent
combination of awkwardness and indifference, yawned in his face, reluctantly said goodbye to the group, flashed at Tom Krause a smile that
was distinctly an invitation, however impractical, and walked down
the gravel drive several paces ahead of Poor Irwin. I retreated to the
kitchen and a few minutes later Walter came in to say that of course
young Krause would be staying for dinner.

"I don't know," he said, "when I've had such an interesting conversation."

"Mmm," I said.

"Have you had occasion," he asked, slurring the word so that I realized that he was already a little high, "to revise your opinion of him,
now that you've seen him again?"

"He looks better today," I said.

Walter took a pitcher of sours from the refrigerator and walked out
of the kitchen with it.

"You can start the fire," I called, "whenever you're ready."

"Thank you, my dear," he called back.

They'd changed and moved on to the porch by the time I'd finished
preparing for dinner. Lotte was wearing blue jeans and a thick black
turtle-neck sweater, having apparently abandoned the pinks and
powder blues of yesteryear, along with the pony tail, as unworthy of
her current degree of sophistication. The effect, because her face had
lost none of its round and freckled prettiness, was reminiscent of a doll
my father had won for me once at Coney Island, during the war, its
painted yellow curls, blank blue eyes, and bright cupid's-bow lips made
ludicrous by the miniature regulation WAC uniform in which it had
been clothed. She glanced at me for a moment when I came out to the
porch, then quickly looked back to Krause to reinforce her conviction
that he made her impervious to me. Krause himself was not impervious
to me, as he made clear by an absolute refusal to look directly at me
while they were looking at him.

We had three bottles of wine with dinner, and a great deal of brandy
afterward. Walter passed out at about ten o'clock, during an attempt to
continue a conversation about Stevenson's chances of being drafted at
the coming Democratic convention. He had become highly expansive,

and increasingly jovial, during dinner, and had described to Krause in detail his memories of how the Democrats had gotten out the Yorkville vote in the old days. After dinner, as his drunkenness had become apparent even to himself, he had attempted to fight it off by becoming earnest and politically concerned. I was glad of the change, for I felt that I was somehow an observer of his geniality, rather than a participant in it, and that my presence, if anything, took the edge off their collective enjoyment. Boris went to bed and a short while later Walter roused himself sufficiently to say good night and retire. Lotte leaned heavily against Krause's shoulder.

"They're dropping off like flies, Stepmother," Krause said. Lotte, unable to suppress a smile, forced open her eyes to see how I'd taken to the title. She was markedly oblivious to any undercurrent between Krause and me. I went into the kitchen to do the dishes. Lotte must have given in and fallen asleep a little while later because Krause came in to the kitchen, holding his snifter, freshly stocked with brandy.

"Alone at last," he said, pulling a chair over near the sink and sitting down to watch me work. I ignored him, grateful for the work that made it easy for me to do so, and for the good feeling of the warm water on my hands.

"Talk to me," he said after a few silent moments.

"I don't feel like it," I said.

"Tell me of your life, your trials, your tribulations. Tell me, in short, how you got to be such a hard cookie at such a tender age."

"You can go to hell," I said.

"But that has nothing to do with you."

"*You* have nothing to do with me. Why don't you leave me alone?"

"Because you fascinate me," he said.

"You know you've got a lot of gall?" I asked, aware of a stridency in my voice. "Aside from the fact that I'm married, I happen to be married to your girl friend's father, and you happen to be a guest in his house."

"See?" he said. "That's just what I mean. A girl of your age should be able to quiver with moral indignation, and on you somehow it just doesn't come off. I can't get over the feeling that if you liked me we'd be out rolling in the hay someplace right now, and you wouldn't give a small hard turd for my child-friend or her father or his house or anything else."

My anger had increased as he began and then, unexpectedly, even inconveniently, subsided in the face of the bearable half-truth. Calmer, I went back to the dishes.

"If you know I don't like you," I said, "why don't you just stay away from me?"

"It's my nature," he said. "I lust for approval. Particularly from women. I like women."

"Really?" I said. "I hadn't noticed."

He shrugged. "A man takes what he can get. The kid chased me around the campus like I was free, white, and twenty-one. She goes for fuck-ups. What're you gonna do? She'll grow out of it."

"Nothing," I muttered. "I'm not going to do a thing. It's none of my business, anyway."

"Good," he said. "Let's drink to that. Can I get you a drink, Stepmother?"

I hesitated.

"I swear I won't take it as a sign that you've weakened," he said, succeeding in making me feel foolish. "You hate me. I'll write it on my cuff so I can't forget."

"All right," I said. "Make sure that you do."

He came back with my drink and sat at the big table as I finished the dishes.

"Okay Stepmother, what shall we talk about?" he asked when I sat down facing him.

"You talk."

"I'm afraid I'll bore you."

"I'd rather listen and be bored than talk and be bored."

"Let me see," he said, "what can I tell you that's interesting? What has brought me to this advanced stage in life?—twenty-eight years old—"

"You look older."

"—possessor of a half-finished manuscript on Daniel Webster, possibilities for completion of which fade, for e'er and e'er when I move . . . or don't move . . . object of the marital ambitions of a sweet-faced eighteen-year-old heiress—"

"The what?"

"Oh, the kid's serious. She wants me so much she's even ready to make it legal."

"You wouldn't do that, would you?" I asked, aware even as I did of how little my apprehensions became me.

"Who the hell knows?" he sighed. "I'm not totally immune to the kid, you know. Or to all this. Not to speak of the kid's stepmom, to whom I have no immunity at all."

"Maybe," I said, "you'd better cut it out."

"I was just—"

"I know, I know. But talk about something else, anyhow. Tell me about your life." I smiled sweetly. "Your trials, your tribulations. Tell me how you got to be such a crumbly cookie at such an early age."

"Ouch." He grimaced. "You win that one, don't you, kid?"

"You're getting me mixed up with someone else. I'm not Kid. I'm Stepmother."

"Sure, sure." He tilted back his chair so that the back rested against the wall, put his hands behind his head. "All right. Safety in history. Here goes. I was born in Minnesota, raised in San Diego and Los Angeles, moved to the East when my old man finally made it with the job at Vassar. That was in 'forty-two, the year I also hit eighteen and got dragged into Uncle Sam's olive-drab boys for a period of slightly over three years. My sainted mother didn't come East with Dad, she stayed in L.A. for a couple of years. Good old Sincerely Sarah was under the misapprehension that there'd be no market in the East for the shit she was peddling in the West."

"Sincerely Sarah?"

He laughed shortly. "Now I know what's wrong with you, Stepmother. You don't read the ladies' magazines. How the hell you gonna turn into a lady if you don't read the ladies' magazines? Sarah's got an advice column."

"You're kidding."

"You're surprised. You're making the reasonable error of confusing her progeny with her output. No, I'm not kidding. We were the reason she got into the racket in the first place. We were still in Minnesota when she discovered she couldn't cope with her own kids and home worth a damn. So she got herself a job on a German-language paper out there telling all the other hausfraus how to cope with theirs. *Die Mutter Henne*, it was called. Mother Hen, to you. You know the kind of thing. *Liebe Mutter Henne:* For years der kids was happy sleeping in der same room mit each udder, but now all of a sudden der girls say they got to have privacy, we should put der six boys in der udder room, but then der pigs got to sleep outdoors in der cold weather, makes lean der *Wurst*. *Liebe Küchleins:* For each of the *Kinder* take one orange crate. Cover each crate with a pretty piece of oilcloth, if possible different colors, and put the name of each on one of the crates. Tell each of the *Kinder* he or she now has a little room to keep his or her most precious belongings and they are to keep their fingers out of each other's crates. This will give them the feeling of privacy and identity that they long for. Your loving Mother Hen. When we got to San Diego she made the big switchover to English and became Sincerely

Sarah for a chain of suburban papers in southern California. She got more sophisticated. She stopped reading my dad's sociology textbooks and started relying on her great intuitive wisdom. Dear Divorced Mother: Tell grandma to go back where she came from if she doesn't want to help with the kids, etc." He eased his chair back to the table, sipped at his drink. "Let's see, where was I? After basic training I served for three years in Intelligence for reasons which you no doubt would find incomprehensible. Discharged honorably, to the astonishment of Sincerely Sarah and various other idiot-savants, at the end of 1945, bummed around the country for a year or two to the astonishment of no one at all, entered Yale fall of 'forty-seven, finished in 1950 . . . am I beginning to bore you?"

I shrugged.

"You're wonderful," he said. "Beautiful. All the things I fought for."

"I'm tired," I said. "What am I supposed to do? Beg you to keep talking?"

"Oh, no, that wouldn't be you, Stepmother. I don't want you to step out of character on my account. Stay as sweet as you are, and all that."

Abruptly I turned off the water, dried my hands and walked out of the kitchen, through the living room and out to the lawn. The air was cold and crisp. I heard him come out, so I kept walking across the lawn toward the road. When I got to the road I started down it, toward the spot where it almost touched the lake shore but then curved around it instead. He caught up with me after a moment.

"I feel like a dentist," he said. "I'm jabbing away at this big beautiful hard-as-a-rock tooth, and all of a sudden just when I'm sure there are no soft spots, the patient jumps to the ceiling."

"You don't look like a dentist," I said, smiling to myself in the darkness. Remembering.

Ruth: I feel like some ice cream.
David: You look like pistachio.

Ruth: I feel like a wreck.
David: You don't look too bad for your age.

Ruth: I feel like a movie.
David: You don't look like a movie.

"I suppose I don't," Krause said. "I just don't smell of Sen-Sen, that's the trouble."

We walked along the road in a silence he couldn't maintain for long. The moon was bright and the shining lake under it was all peacefulness and beauty. I was fully awake now.

"How long have you been married, Mrs. Stamm?"

"Eight, nine months," I said. "The end of October."

"Happy Halloween," he said softly.

"You have one fucking big mouth," I said bitterly, furious because I myself had thought of Halloween for the first time as I told him.

"No offense intended."

"Like fun."

"Not to you, anyway."

"I don't need you to insult my husband," I said. "If I want to insult him I can do it myself."

"Actually," Krause said, "I don't know why I should insult him at all, except that I find his wife very desirable. He's a pretty decent guy, far from stupid. He's been much more hospitable to me than I had any reason to expect he'd be. He's a little soft, but what the hell, that's par for us of the master race. Anyway, it's not the kind of thing you hold against a guy. Not if you're a reasonable type."

"And you're a terribly reasonable type."

"Only on Wednesdays."

We'd reached the Loeb grounds. They weren't out on the porch, but somehow I didn't want to take even a small chance that one of them would see us. I turned and began walking back.

"Hey, what happened?"

"Nothing. I just want to go back. It's cold."

He put his arm around me, rubbing my arm with his hand. I knew that I should move away but I was really cold, and it was too pleasant.

"You're going to be up here all summer?" he asked.

"Probably."

"You don't get bored?"

"No. I love it here."

"Love getting away from—uh—" (the pause was deliberate and obvious) "the city for a while?"

"It's more than that. I mean, it's not just a negative thing. I love this house, and I love the country. This was the first place I ever lived where the grass didn't have sidewalk around it."

"It has some pretty unhappy memories for you."

"What do you mean?" I was genuinely puzzled.

"Oh," he said, "Lotte just told me about your kid brother."

"Oh, I didn't . . . I never think of it as having happened here." I *never think of it. Period.* "The house looks entirely different in the winter. In the fall the housekeeper takes down the curtains and puts up heavy drapes, and she takes off the flowery slipcovers from all the up-holstered furniture and puts down woolen rugs in the bedrooms. And the outside's entirely different too, of course. Most of the winter you can't even tell there's a lake there, it's covered with a sheet of ice. And the trees are covered with snow, or else they're so bare you can see half-way to town. It could be any one of a thousand places around New England just as easily as it could be this one."

"So," he said after a moment, "it works."

"Anyway," I said, "I never come here in the winter."

"So it works when it's summer."

"There'd be no point to my coming in the winter," I said quickly. "I don't ski. I never did, not even before, if that's what you're thinking."

"Okay, don't get upset, I believe you."

"I'm not upset," I said, although he had made me conscious of the urgency in my voice. I forced a little laugh into the tree-rustling dark-ness. "Is that what Lotte called him—my kid brother? He was nineteen and I was twenty. I guess she likes to think I'm a hundred years old."

"Understandable," he said. "You're a lot of competition for a nice young girl to have to face all of a sudden."

"I'm not in competition with her," I said, and became newly aware of his arm around me, of his fingers, gently caressing the cashmere that covered my arm, and remembered how I had put on lipstick before din-ner although I hadn't worn lipstick in days, and was grateful for the night that concealed my burning cheeks. "Anyway," I said, the new tremulousness of my body somehow coming through in my voice, "I don't see what good it'll do her to tell herself that I'm a hundred years old and hideous."

"No one said it would do any good."

"I'm damn well not going to get that way any faster just because she wants me to."

"We all do it at one time or another—" he said softly, "try to get rid of something upsetting by making believe it doesn't exist."

It was too pointed to be missed, or ignored. Nor did I have an an-swer for it. I considered telling him that it was different with dead peo-ple, there was no point in trying to face things with dead people; but he would have some answer for that, something that I couldn't antici-pate, which would seem terribly obvious once it was said; I didn't want to encourage him to make new inroads in my memories. We reached the point where the dirt road split off to our driveway and curved back to the main road. I moved away from his arm's embrace.

"Sincerely," I said, "Sarah."

He groaned. "Why don't I hate you, Stepmother? You say such terrible things to me."

"Maybe you do and you don't know it."

"No, I don't. I swear I don't." He paused. "You don't believe me, I can tell. What can I do to convince you? What sacrifice can I make? Should I remove myself for the rest of the summer? That'll get the kid out of your hair, too. Would that please you?"

"Lotte bothers me," I said, unwilling to tell him how part of me enjoyed having him there, "far less than I bother Lotte."

"Still, it must be a strain. Having someone around who thinks you're the original Wicked Witch of the West."

The house was quiet; there was no one moving around in the living room.

"This is a stupid conversation," I said.

"We aim to please."

"Haven't you said that before?"

"It's still true."

"What makes you so noble, then?" I asked, turning to him. I could just make out his features in the light from the windows.

"Noble?"

"Self-sacrificing, I mean. If you leave your uncle's house, who are you going to sponge off for the rest of the summer? If you think you're going to live at the apartment with Lotte, forget it. There's a sleep-in maid there, which makes subterfuge pretty difficult. And even Walter isn't—" Even Walter isn't blind enough to have you as a house guest, I'd been about to say, and I'd stopped myself because of the beginnings of a smile on his face as I started to slight Walter.

"I'm aware that there are limits to your husband's hospitality." Blandly debonair. Yet always a certain nakedness. A visible hunger. As if he couldn't help but hope that I would like him for this one. "Actually, what I had in mind was doubling back here and enjoying yours."

I squinted at him in the near darkness. At first I wasn't quite sure that I'd understood him; once I was sure, I was as angry as though I had never put on lipstick for him, never enjoyed his arm around me, never thought to myself, he isn't so bad, but he isn't David; wondered how it would be to sleep with him.

It is almost impossible for me now to have the feeling of myself as I was then. Quivering with outraged pride and righteous indignation. Sophisticated enough to know why I'd married Walter, naïve enough to think I knew all the reasons. Proud to recognize the truth that I was capable of deceiving Walter, vain in my anger at Krause's temerity in thinking it might be for him. It is difficult to restrain the older me from adding some gratuitous touch of a humor that wasn't really there. A giggle escaping through pursed lips. A mocking reminder from somewhere within me that I was forgetting too much too easily. Some sardonic Jiminy Cricket perched on my shoulder, pointing out that I was pretty snooty for a kid who not two years before had walked tight-legged out of the house in the morning to pee in other people's toilets.

But there was neither humor nor humility. To view my situation with humor would have been to admit the possibility of imperfect solutions. To view myself with humility would have been to accept the justice implicit in the idea that only imperfect solutions were available to imperfect human beings.

I said, "You can't believe that I really despise you. But I do."

And I stalked into the house and up to my room, and got into my pajamas, and lay down in my bed, and pulled the covers up around me, and reproached myself. Not for the vanity that made me consider myself beyond his reasonable expectations of conquest. Nor for the cruelty that had made it important to me that he know exactly how little I thought of him. No. I chided myself for having been sufficiently friendly so that he could forget my dislike. (A reproach actually aimed not at myself, but at Krause.) I chided myself for having married a man who left me in need of other men's attentions. (A reproach actually aimed at Walter.) I chided myself for being soft enough to be put in a position where Lotte and her friends could condescend to me. (A reproach aimed solely at Lotte.)

And then I wept copiously, not for any of them, but for their victim.

Lotte and Krause got married at the end of August, in Tennessee, en route to Mexico, with Walter's official blessings, if not enthusiasm (he was concerned about her completing her schooling), and without my knowledge until it was over, as Lotte had specifically requested. With the money that Walter gave them as their wedding present, Krause selected a brownstone on St. Marks Place which they purchased and renovated. It was one block away from my old home. It was a while before I could believe the truth, that his choice was a coincidence, that there had been neither malignance nor collusion but simply practical consideration (the house was in decent condition and went for a low price) coupled with Krause's appreciation of the neighborhood, its convenience—Lotte would be attending N.Y.U.—and Lotte's willingness to let him make the choice. When they returned from Mexico at the end of September, Krause took a part-time job driving a cab, and during the rest of the time worked on his manuscript. This industrious phase lasted until the warm weather came the following spring, when Krause and his manuscript disappeared. Two months later Lotte got a postcard from Granby, Colorado, saying that he was working on a dude ranch out there, he wished her the best, and she could use the postcard address in the divorce proceedings. Walter had promised her not to tell me about the card, but he was too upset to contain himself. I made an attempt to comfort him by saying that it was just as well the whole thing had ended quickly instead of dragging on for years. At the time he seemed to think I was being particularly callous, but by two years later, when she married Edwin Bafford, III, he was inclined to agree with me.

CHAPTER EIGHT

Thea got married in February of 1953 to Murray Goodman, a neighborhood boy I knew only vaguely who had gotten a medical discharge from the Army after having a breakdown in Korea, and had since become a dress buyer at Klein's. She brought him up to dinner one night and the evening was so dull and stilted that even Walter admitted he'd been depressed by it. When she told me a few weeks later that she was going to marry him, I was so upset that I seriously considered finding some excuse to avoid the wedding, although Walter said, and I knew he was right, that it would be a terrible thing to do. What Walter didn't realize was that my dismay over the marriage was complicated by a new reluctance to see David, who had also been invited. I suppose it had to do with my altered view of myself—having recently come to see my situation as somewhat ludicrous, I assumed others would see it with the same clarity. Particularly David, who had always understood more of me than I wanted him to. I was sure I couldn't conceal my unhappiness from him, and it didn't occur to me that it would cause him to feel anything but triumph. An assumption which, of course, did him a grave injustice.

It was a big formal wedding that had cost Thea's parents most if not all of their savings, which was the way they wanted it although Thea had pleaded with them to spare themselves the expense. It was held at a big, sleazily elaborate catering hall on Second Avenue with a chapel that had about as much religious atmosphere as a beauty parlor on a Friday afternoon. The ceremony was to be at noon on Sunday, and at four o'clock Saturday afternoon I went into a sudden panic as I looked through the large closet that held my clothes and decided that it held nothing that would be exactly right to wear. I dashed down to Saks where in the twenty minutes before closing time I picked out three dresses that I brought home without trying on. The one I finally selected to wear was a pink-brocade sheath; but then on Sunday morning, when I had put it on, I became uncharacteristically concerned with the unruliness of my hair and with the problem of which earrings I should wear, the result being that we didn't arrive at the hall until noon. David was standing in front of the building, all alone, smoking a cigarette. My heart was pounding as Walter helped me out of the cab. I walked over to him as Walter was paying the fare.

I said, "Hello, David."

He said, "Hi."

I said, "You look a little different."

"You, too."

"How?"

"I don't know. Older, I guess."

I nodded.

He smiled for the first time. "Not *that* old."

I heard the cab move away, then Walter came to my side.

"I think you remember my husband," I said, without taking my eyes from David's face. "Walter, you remember David Landau."

"Of course. Good to see you again." He held out his hand and David shook it.

"Am I running fast?" Walter asked, looking at his watch. "I have just past twelve."

"That's probably right," David said.

"Are you waiting for someone?" I asked.

"No," he said. "I think everyone's inside."

"Well, then . . ." Walter took my arm and the three of us walked into the hall. As we neared the chapel I could hear the organ beginning to play the bridal march. Quickly we took off our coats and went in, the man at the door handing Walter and David yamilkes which they both put on. We slipped into the empty last row, and a moment later the procession began. Thea's grandparents. Thea's ugly first cousin, the maid of honor. Murray's brother, the best man. Murray, small, sallow, nervous, escorted by his parents, also small and sallow but apparently enjoying the occasion more than their son. And why not? They were turning him over to Thea with the knowledge that when he had his next breakdown he would be in good hands. Then Thea, between her parents. A very proper bride in a gown so bouffant and virginal as to make the Grand Street merchants swell with pride, a face so sweetly pretty as to be seraphic, and an expression so utterly serene as to make me doubt in the split second that I saw it that she was making the most dreadful mistake of her life. It was all I could do to focus upon the procession, or to remember Walter, sitting on my right, while on my left side sat David, shiny white-satin beanie perched precariously on his wavy black hair, shoulders straining against the blue serge of the old suit that was still his good suit.

The ceremony was entirely in Hebrew except for the marriage contract, which the rabbi read also in English so that Thea and Murray could repeat it after him. It might have been in Hebrew, too, for all I really heard of it. I felt very warm and slightly nauseated, a reaction perhaps to the combination of my excitement over David's presence and my feelings about the wedding itself. An interminable time later the procession made its way back out of the chapel, and along with the others, the three of us stood up and headed slowly toward the banquet room. Walter left us briefly to check our coats, suggesting that David and I go along ahead.

"So," David said, "what's new?"

"Nothing," I said. "Absolutely nothing."

"Oh, something must be. You must've learned to cook French food or something."

I shook my head. "The maid cooks. Most of the time we eat out on her night off."

Someone in back of me stepped on my heel so that my shoe nearly came off and I had to drag it along with my toes as I walked.

"How's school?" I asked, frantically trying to get the shoe back on without being stepped on again.

"Lousy," he said, "but at least I can tell myself I'll be through in a few months."

I got the shoe on but then someone's elbow jammed into my arm. "Sorry, honey," the man said. "Sorry. Are you from the bride or groom?"

"Bride," I said.

"*Mazel tov*," he said. "I'm Murray's third cousin Harry from St. Louis."

"How do you do," I said, turning back to David. "Are you working?"

"Still doing research for Morse."

"You've lost a little weight."

"Mmm. Between classes and Morse and Law Review there's no time to eat."

He extricated a pack of cigarettes from his pocket and offered me one, which I took.

"When did you start smoking?"

He shrugged. "A while ago."

We were embarrassed. We looked straight ahead. We reached the banquet room where he could move freely enough to light both cigarettes. I held his hand as he lit mine and had to force myself to pull it away when he finished. In one corner of the room was a huge table heavily laden with appetizers and hors d'oeuvres. In the other was a bar. We got drinks and wandered through the crowd, exchanging meaningless pleasantries with people we knew and smiling vacantly at strangers. Walter found us then.

"Ah, there you are," he said.

"So, Walter," I said, "now your life is complete. You've seen a real Jewish wedding."

He laughed uneasily and the three of us stood there not quite knowing what to do or say.

"Well, Landau," Walter said finally, "how are your studies coming along? You were in law school, weren't you?"

"That's right," David said. "I'm finished this term."

"Congratulations. Any interesting prospects ahead?"

"A couple." He glanced at me, then looked quickly back to Walter. "I've got an interview in San Francisco coming up."

"San Francisco?" I echoed, as shocked as though he had made some commitment to me, as scared as though I'd never learned to live a week at a time without him.

"Morse used to practice out there."

"I remember," I said mechanically. "Before he got involved with drafting the U.N. Charter."

"Right. Anyhow, he's recommended me for a job with his old firm when I graduate."

"In San Francisco." Momentarily oblivious to Walter.

"They say it's a great town."

"They?"

"People. You know, you hear talk about places. I've been thinking about getting out of New York. Morse thinks San Francisco's a great town. He really wants to go back, as a matter of fact, but his wife's a New Yorker and he can't get her to move again."

Walter coughed a small attention-getting kind of cough.

"Morse," David explained, turning to him, "is the professor I've been working for at school. He's a specialist in international law. A fascinating guy."

"He's certainly right about San Francisco, from my point of view, at any rate," Walter said. "It's probably the most civilized city in the United States. And certainly one of the most beautiful."

"You sound as though you're delivering a sales pitch, Walter," I said.

"In fact," Walter told David, "there have been times in my life when I rather fancied I'd like to move out there, myself. If my roots weren't down so firmly in New York, my business, and so on, I think I'd have seriously considered it." A small tuxedoed waiter thrust himself into our midst and refused to leave until we had each taken a hot-dog-in-a-blanket. "My father is out there, you know," Walter said to David when the little man had left—as though there were any reason in the world why David should know. "Retired and built himself a home in Carmel."

"You don't say." David was politely attentive.

"Mmm. I've been meaning to get out there for years."

"Will you excuse me please?" I said. "I'm not feeling very well. I think I need some fresh air."

Walter offered to come with me but I said I'd prefer not, that it would be better if at least one of us were there. I took the check from him and got my coat from the checkroom, taking a great deal of time to put it on and find my way through the hallway so that David could find me if he wanted to. When I had no further excuse for delaying, I simply stood at the glass doors in the front, looking outside at the cold gray day. After a few minutes he came up beside me.

"It looks awful out," I said.

"You should've worn your mink."

I smiled. "I know, but I was self-conscious."

"Want to go anyway?"

"Will you come with me?" I asked.

"Think it's a good idea?"

"I don't care," I said. "I miss you terribly, David. Much more than I thought I would."

He was silent for a moment. Then he said, "Come on. Let's get out of here," and took my arm and guided me out to the street. To Second Avenue. We began walking uptown and I had a fleeting sense of playing out a fantasy—as though this were one of my solitary night walks and David weren't really with me.

"I was pretty upset about Thea," I said after a while.

"Mm?"

"About Murray, I mean."

"Why?"

"He's a creep."

"Plenty of girls marry creeps."

I looked up at him but there was nothing in his expression to prove he'd been talking about Walter. We reached a crosswalk and I shivered as the wind cut through me. He put an arm around me and I burrowed as close to him as I could.

"It seems funny to be here," I said. "Right back in the same place."

"I'll buy you a cup of coffee," he said. "And then we'll go back."

We went into a candy store where we could see the coffeepot full on the portable stove, and sat on the stools, hunched over our coffee cups. After a while he swiveled on the stool so that he was facing me.

"I don't know what to say, Ruth."

"Tell me it's good to see me."

"My San Francisco interview was supposed to be this week," he said. "I could have gotten out of the whole damn wedding."

I was far too happy to speak. I sat there looking at him, blinking back tears, even forgetting, for the moment, the implied threat of San Francisco.

"Let's go, Ruth. We'd better get back."

Reluctantly I stood up, walked out of the candy store ahead of him, tried to take his arm when he came out, and had my hand put back at my side.

"Time," he said, "to start making believe you're married."

We were silent until we reached the hall, where we stopped in front of the entrance, neither of us wanting to go in.

"What happens now, David?" I asked.

"I'm not sure," he said. "There are a lot of complicating factors. Aside from the obvious one."

"Such as?"

"Such as the fact that the goddamn city is full of hotels and I don't have the price of a room."

"I do."

He smiled. "That's what I mean."

I searched his face, trying to determine how serious he was.

"In the old days," I said, "it didn't bother you when I had money and you didn't."

"That was *your* money."

"I have my own money," I said, feeling inspired. "I still have my bank account from before. I never closed the account when I got married." I didn't have to mention that I'd added to it.

He didn't reply. Absently he ran a hand over my head, pushed the curls back from my forehead, remembered where we were and pulled his hand down.

"Would it please you if I only used *that* money, David?"

"It would please me," he said slowly, "if we could keep the bullshit out of this. If we do it, we're screwing on your husband's time and your husband's money, and no amount of finagling with bank accounts that you wouldn't have been able to hold on to if you hadn't married him is going to change the fact. Is that understood?"

"You're right," I whispered, ashamed to look at him. "I don't blame you for despising me."

He propped a finger under my chin and pushed it up so that I had to look at him. "Oh, yeah," he said. "Sure I despise you. That's why I'm in San Francisco right now."

"Will it matter that you didn't go?"

He hesitated for a moment. "No. Not really. I can go any time in the next couple of months. It just would have been more convenient because of intersession."

Disappointed, but determined that he should not see it, I turned and walked into the hall ahead of him. I checked my coat and we walked to the big room. The crowd had begun to move from the buffet to the banquet tables and it would have been entirely possible for Walter not to realize that we had been together, had he not been standing right near the entranceway, looking rather alone and uncomfortable, when we walked in.

"Hi," I said.

"Hello, my dear," Walter said. "Are you feeling any better?" Not looking at David, as though by pretending not to see him he could negate the fact of his being there.

"Yes, thanks," I said. "I took a long walk. David was nice enough to come with me."

"Ah, yes," Walter said—a little relieved that I had chosen to offer some sort of explanation, however little it explained. "You two must have a lot to talk about."

"Mm," David said.

"I think," Walter continued manfully as we moved toward the dinner tables, "Ruth told me once that you two had known each other
since early childhood?"

"That's right," David said.

I laughed. "As a matter of fact," I said, "there are people who swear
that David's mother hated me before I was born."

I saw him often in the months before June, when he left for San
Francisco. I'd planned to rent a room at some place like the Mattracorne, but we were spared that sordid edge to our meetings when
David found, through Columbia's rental service, a comfortably furnished three-room apartment on the Drive that someone on the college faculty was subletting for the spring term. The couple that had
sublet it had gone to Europe for several months, the husband having received a study grant, and had left behind everything but their clothes—
thousands of books, an overwhelming collection of records to play on a
music system that looked as if it had cost more than the foam-rubber
sofa and the rest of the furniture combined, dishes, linens, plants David
had promised to water faithfully.

There was an obvious danger to all this warm and easy domesticity.
A hotel room would have been in itself a perpetual reminder of reality,
a fact to be forced out of my consciousness before I could satisfactorily
act out my fantasy of living with David in married bliss. While in the
midst of this unknown couple's cigarette-marred tables, frayed upholstery, Russell Wright earthenware, and wildly sprouting philodendron
and sweet-potato vines, it was all I could do to remember that our being
there had nothing to do with real life. That on the contrary I had to be
very careful about my meetings with David if I wanted to have anything of what *was* my real life left when he went to San Francisco in
June. For I never fooled myself that he would decide not to go, nor did
I have any real hope that he would ask me to leave Walter and go with
him, although I had let myself dwell on the second possibility long
enough to decide that I would do it if he asked me to.

We could talk about the past easily now. About Martin. About my
parents. About the neighborhood. The present lent itself less easily to
conversation. He told me in March that he'd accepted the San
Francisco job; there was nothing to discuss. Nor did I want to talk
about my marriage with him; if my motives in marrying Walter had
been somewhat more complex than David had been willing to admit,
the results had been no less disastrous than he could have predicted.

What was there to say? I couldn't reasonably expect David's sympathy, even if I'd been inclined to court it.

I only knew when our last day had come because from the first day of June I'd half-assumed that each day was our last. It was a warm, sunny day during the second week in June. David was asleep in the bedroom. The windows were open and a lovely cool breeze was coming in from the Drive. I got undressed and stretched out on the bed beside him, but after a while I was cold so I got under the covers.

I lay there for a little while, just looking at his handsome peaceful face, wanting to touch him but wanting him to stay asleep, too, so that I could keep looking at him. Finally I leaned over and kissed him. Without opening his eyes, he rolled over on top of me, fumbling for my breasts.

"Don't you have time to undress?" I whispered. "When is the plane leaving?" It awakened him. He stared down into my eyes, kissed the bridge of my nose.

"Tomorrow morning."

"Congratulations." Keeping it light. As though I'd really fully believed it all along. "Will you send me a picture postcard?"

"No."

"Is that nice?"

"No." Abruptly he rolled off me and lay staring up at the ceiling.

I propped myself up on one elbow and stared at him.

"What is it, David?"

He laughed shortly.

I moved closer to him, playing with his hair.

"Tell me."

"You're not under the impression that I particularly want to be three thousand miles away from you, are you, Ruth?"

"Then why are you going?"

"Because I think I should."

"Then why haven't you asked me to go with you?"

"I'm not sure," he said slowly. "I'm going to be making a big seventy-five bucks a week for a while. That's one of the reasons."

"I could work," I said. "I can teach. I have the ed credits, I could probably get a license pretty easily."

He smiled. "So let's say for the sake of the argument that you could teach. So between us we could make a hundred and fifty bucks a week. Six hundred a month. What does your husband pay per month for that shabby little joint you sleep in?"

"Not as much as you think," I stalled. "It's under rent control."

"How much?"

"Four-fifty a month," I admitted, flushing. "But I don't see that it's particularly relevant."

"All right. Let's try something relevant. How much did you spend on clothes last month?"

"But I have them now. I could take them with me."

"How about your full-time maid? Will she come along for the ride?"

"I don't *need* a maid," I said. "I *like* having her, but I don't *need* her. I need *you*, David."

"Yeah, yeah," he said wearily. "Right now. Here. In bed you need me. But when it comes time to cook a meal or clean out a toilet bowl, then what? You used to go crazy when your mother worked on the toilet in the hallway. What if you had to do it yourself?"

"It's not the same, and you know it," I said quickly. "It's not—"

"You're wrong, Ruth. The difference is quantitive."

"But quant——"

"Look," he said—but then cut himself off, too. "Oh, Christ, what's the point of all this?" In one movement he was off the bed and at the window, looking down at the Drive. "It's too complicated. There's no damn point at all in talking about it."

"All right," I said. "Only there's something else. There's some other reason you're leaving out. I won't argue any more if you'll just tell me what it is."

He stared at me thoughtfully for a while, came back to the bed, sat down on the edge. "Okay," he said. Instinctively I sat up and leaned against the headboard, trying to be ready, not altogether certain that I wanted to hear what he was going to say.

"You terrify me, Ruth. You always have. That probably sounds crazy to you." I nodded slowly. "It's true, anyway. I'm not sure how much of it is you and how much is me . . . but I feel . . . You're a cannibal, Ruth. That may be cruel but it isn't casual. I thought about it a lot . . . after . . . you know, after you told me you were marrying Stamm."

"After I told you," I corrected him automatically, "that he'd *asked* me to marry him."

"I was upset. Much more than I let you see. But I was relieved, too. I was trying to figure out why, and I remembered something I'd said to you, I don't know if you even remember it, but I said if you got hungry enough you'd eat me for dinner. Well, I was being vicious, then, trying to hurt you when I said it, but it was still true. I've always had that feeling about you."

"My God, David," I said.

"Part of me," he went on, looking through me as he spoke, "wants to be devoured by you. Part of me feels as though it had something torn out of its skin when it doesn't see you for a year and a half. But the rest of me . . . the rational man . . ." he smiled wryly at some place behind my head, "the rest of me wants to go to San Francisco and become a partner in a good respectable law firm . . . and marry a nice blond *shiksa* who thinks Jewish boys are the nuts, even if she doesn't understand their jokes . . . who I won't have to rip myself away from after I make love to her . . . and have three nice blond blue-eyed kids with no U's in conduct on their report cards . . . and—" He seemed to catch himself suddenly. His eyes met mine and he laughed. "—and die gentile," he finished. The smile went and we just sat there, looking at each other. The tension was gone; if I was drained of hope, I was drained of anxiety, too.

"Well," I said, "I wish you luck."

He reached out and touched my bare shoulder, cold with the cool air from the Drive. With the flat of his hand he caressed my neck, my ear. Then he pulled away as though he weren't certain that I wanted him to touch me.

"I must've known all along," I said. "I just didn't know that I knew."

He leaned forward, kissed my forehead, moved back, began to unbutton his shirt but stopped, his hand still on the top button. Staring at me as though he'd never seen me before. Or perhaps simply as if he would never see me again.

"Come to bed," I said.

He left before I'd awakened that evening. That night I threw away my diaphragm. Three months later I became pregnant with Andrea.

CHAPTER NINE

Andrea was born on May 14, 1954; Philip on September 20, 1957; Susan on December 3, 1960. These three dates constitute a bare but not unreasonable summary of my life during the years that they span. Soon I will give birth to David's child. A postscript. Not a substitute for life, but the result of it.

To catalogue those years before David's return is to experience again the shame I felt when he asked me that day three years ago whether I had just been having babies and playing with my money. I reveled in my love of the children, yet it was born not just out of warmth but out of desperation. I was proud that I spent more time with them than any of the mothers I knew spent with their children. Why, when it was the only thing I wanted to do with my time? I was proud of the places I went with them, the things we did together, of my ferocious concern for their well-being. I despised those women whose idea of motherhood was to spawn children only to leave them permanently in the care of some stiff European nanny or resentful young colored girl. But never thought to despise myself, whose idea of being a woman had come down to the narrowness of motherhood.

I hugged them to me to keep myself from falling.

Once carrying Andrea, I did not want her taken from my body. I didn't want to share her with Walter. I was awakened early in the morning by the first contraction preceding her birth, but I didn't get Walter up, nor did I call the doctor, who had made a five-dollar bet with me that I would call him too soon because all first mothers called too soon. I turned on the dim light on my night table and lay on my back, as I had every night for months, watching my big belly jump wildly with each of her caged motions. When the contractions began to come often enough to count the minutes between, I closed my eyes and bent up my legs so that my knees were against my belly, as though by this method I might contrive to hold on to her a while longer. My stomach ached not so much with the pangs of labor as with the effort to prevent birth. When Walter's alarm went off he took one look at me, said, "Good God, Ruth," and reached for the telephone. Then, suddenly uncertain, he asked if he should call, and I nodded because by this time the contractions were coming steadily every five minutes.

Andrea was born twenty minutes after we reached the hospital, just as the anesthetic I had been given was beginning to take effect. I awakened hours later with a dual sense of pleasure and loss; I remember massaging my stomach to ease the unpleasant hollow feeling inside of me. Walter sat near my bed, looking very happy. *His happiness should please me.* It was my first thought, but the truth was that my feelings had long since ceased to be in any way contingent upon his. My pregnancy had made me not simply indifferent but impervious to him, perhaps to the whole world. It was a feeling I enjoyed, and would continue to enjoy during the whole strange first year of Andrea's life, when my happiness depended entirely upon her moods, when I was sad on her unhappy days.

I fired the nurse on my first day out of the hospital. I hadn't wanted her, anyway. I'd pointed out to Walter that with Esther there I had no need of a nurse, but he'd seemed terrified at the prospect of my taking care of my own child. She was a German, a large, gray-haired, granite-bosomed grandmother who made me unwelcome in the baby's room out of her majestic assurance that since she knew so much more about babies than I did, my presence there when I was not actually nursing Andrea was unnecessary, and even frivolous. As a matter of fact, she seemed to rather resent my breast-feeding the baby, as though it were some unnatural whim that interfered with her own prescribed duties.

We had a bang-up fight that night, Walter and I, the first of many during that year, this, like most of them, being concerned with what Walter termed at various times my rashness, my grand conceit, my possessiveness, and my primitive exclusion of everything in the world that was not myself or my baby. Specifically, him. Most of such judgments being delivered in a tone I found less suggestive of an outraged husband than of a supercilious eunuch in a *Times* ad for hundred-and-twenty-five-dollar men's suits.

I pitied him, but my pity was not without malice. I chose to forget the reason I had let myself become pregnant and remember only that if it had been Walter's choice, I would have been pregnant much earlier. Even when David left, it had been less a matter of my wanting a baby than of needing to fill the emptiness inside of me. It was after I became pregnant, not before, that I was certain I wanted to be a mother; having Walter's child constituted in my mind not a beginning, but an end, and I'd had no idea of how I would relish that end. Of how, when Andrea began to grow up and be a little free of me, I would need to have another baby, and when Philip reached that same age, during his second year of life, I would feel it once again, the need to be part of that magic cycle that made me impervious to the rest of life. That made me complete.

If I inclined to omens, I would find it retrospectively ominous that I was in the park with Philip and Susan on the winter afternoon a little over three years ago when David returned. Andrea was eight, then, and in school all day, but Philip was in morning kindergarten and Susan had just turned two. We were making a snowman with the gray snow-ice that was left from the storm the week before. We were the only ones around, the nannies and other mothers not particularly caring for the park when the air was cold and the playground benches too damp to sit on. We were kneeling on the snow-covered grass, absorbed in the snowman's head, and I wasn't even aware that someone had come up behind me until Philip said, "Mommy and me's making a snowman," and I turned around to see whom he was talking to. And looked up into David's face. And burst without warning or preamble into violent, uncontrollable tears.

"Mommy, Mommy, Mommy," Philip said.

Susan began to cry.

"Oh, my God," I sobbed, "they've never seen me cry before."

"I'm sorry," David said.

Susan's crying got louder. I held out my arms and she ran into them, knocking me off my knees so that I was sitting in the snow.

"Why'd you make my mommy cry?" Philip demanded.

"I'm not crying," I said, my own tears subsiding just a little as Susan's sobbing accelerated toward hysteria. "I mean, *he* didn't *make* me cry. I was just surprised. I didn't know he was there. I mean, I didn't know anyone was there." Unable to stop crying altogether, hiccuping now, as well, I struggled to my feet, holding Susan, David supporting my arm as I got up.

"Hey, Susie Q," I said to Susan, who was still hysterical, "hey, it's okay." My lashes were matted with cold tears, my nose was running, and on Susan's face mucus and tears were competing for space. I wiped my nose on the shoulder of her snowsuit. "Come on, Susie," I said, hiccuping, "Mommy's okay."

"You have the hiccups," Philip said helpfully.

"Mommy's okay," I said again to Susan, ignoring Philip, lifting Susan's arm to wipe her nose with the snowsuit cuff. "I hurt myself a little, but I'm okay now."

"Where'd you hurt yourself?" Philip asked.

"Philip," I said, hiccuping again, the tears gone but my voice still shaky, "I'm just trying to make Susan understand. It's hard to explain things to a two-year-old."

"What things?" Philip asked.

"Oh, Jesus," I muttered, meeting David's eyes. He was laughing silently. I smiled. And hiccuped. Gradually Susan quieted down.

"Now you know," I said to David, "how I got to look this way."

"You look wonderful," he said.

"I'm old."

"You look wonderful," he repeated.

"You, too," I said.

"How come you're here?" Philip asked with disturbing relevance.

"Well," David said, "I was walking by, and I saw there was someone here making a snowman, and I came over to watch."

"Wanna help?"

"Sure."

"All right," Philip said. "Go find rocks for the eyes."

"That was supposed to be your job," I said.

"But *he* came."

"You'd better do it," I said, shifting Susan in my arms. "You know where the good ones are."

"He can come with me."

"What's the sense?" I asked with forced nonchalance. "Why should two people do the work of one?"

Reluctantly he left us for the hunt.

"Mommy crying," Susan told David.

"She looks like you," David said, smiling at her.

"Why Mommy crying?" Susan asked.

I nodded. "My older one does even more."

"Philip?" His eyes disputed me.

"Andrea," I said. "She's eight. I have three children. I had Andrea right—the year after you went."

Philip called out something unintelligible about the pebbles and I called back without turning around that he should do as well as he could. David was handsomer than he'd been nine years before. Visibly older and a great deal handsomer for it. I put down Susan, who began playing in the snow again.

"Do you have any children, David?"

"A girl."

"Blue-eyed?"

He smiled. "Yes, as a matter of fact."

Philip came back with some pebbles and, somewhat guiltily, I told him they weren't large enough. He trudged away to find more.

"How come you're here?" I asked.

"I'm in New York because I have to come in on business occasionally. I'm at Ninety-sixth Street and Fifth Avenue because for the past year or so, I've been walking around here every time I came to New York on the chance of running into you."

Nine years. As though for nine years we'd existed in space but not in time.

"These better be good," Philip cried from a distance, "or I'll be mad."

"It's hard to talk now," I said. "Philip is old enough to understand a little."

"When can I see you?"

"I could take a walk tonight. I still take walks sometimes."

"Around here?"

"I'll be down at about eight-thirty. As soon as I get all the kids off."

He wheeled away from me as Philip returned.

"How come *he's* still here?" Philip asked.

"He isn't," I said. "He's gone."

And we went back to our snowman.

Walter came home when Philip and Andrea and I were in the living room listening to a record. He made himself a drink, and asked how we had spent the day, and Philip said, "A man made Mommy cry in the park and she hurt herself and he talked to her."

"Good grief, Philip!" I forced a laugh. "Your son," I said to Walter, "has a flair for the dramatic." I had been trying to decide whether to say something to Walter just to cover myself, and had decided against it, since I might simply be creating problems—so often the children would forget to mention even momentous events in their lives.

Walter looked at me questioningly.

"I thought we were alone in the park," I said. "A man came by; I don't know who he was, but I think I've seen him around the neighborhood. I didn't hear him come, we were making a snowman, and he was in back of me, and then . . . I guess I turned around too quickly and I wrenched my back."

"Is it better now?" Walter asked.

I nodded. "A little."

"The park seems to be full of strange people these days."

"He was a perfectly respectable type," I said, more patiently than I might have said it in other circumstances. "In a suit and a tie. Just taking a walk."

He was sitting on one of the benches when I finally got down—closer to nine-thirty than to eight-thirty because Andy and Philip, having sensed my eagerness to be finished with them, had been correspondingly unwilling to go to sleep. He stood up when he saw me crossing Fifth Avenue.

"I'm sorry," I said, keeping my hands in my jacket pockets so I would remember not to take his arm. "I couldn't get the kids off."

"Too tired to walk?"

I shook my head. We started walking down Fifth.

"So," he said after a while, "what have you been doing all this time? Having babies and playing with your money?"

"I guess so," I said, feeling that I must be a ridiculous person, it being possible to summarize so fast and neatly nine years of my life.

"Enjoying it?"

"I enjoy the money, yes—or at least I wouldn't know what to do without it. And I enjoy the kids—maybe too much. I have trouble letting go of them when it's time. I catch myself not wanting to let Andy go someplace by herself, and it's really just that I want to go with her because there's nothing else I feel like doing. The rest of it . . . there is no rest of it. There's nothing else. The rest of me hasn't existed for the past nine years." I laughed shortly. "Corny but true."

Of course it was true. It was why I'd cried when I saw him. I was crying over his departure.

There were people in the streets—most of them walking dogs. We cut into the park at the next entrance.

"No guys?" he asked lightly. "I thought you moved in a good circle for that kind of thing."

"As a matter of fact, I don't," I said, wondering why the question didn't anger me. "As a matter of fact, we don't particularly *move* in *any* circle, in the way you mean it. Walter's friends . . . someone should do a study of them. How to be rich without ever getting hip. . . . Not that I really mind that part. I've seen just enough of the hip crowd to know I don't like them, either."

"How about your own friends?"

"I don't actually have any," I said truthfully. "I don't want them. I'm not sure why, except that they're a waste of time. The women I know mostly use their friends just to get away from the kids. I see Thea a couple of times a year, and Helen Stamm once in a while, not as much as I used to. In the past couple of years she's begun to bore me. Every once in a while someone in the building, or maybe a mother of one of the kids' friends, asks if I play bridge, and I say, 'No, I'm terribly sorry, I never did learn.'"

We were well into the park now. He put his arm around me and I put my right hand in his coat pocket instead of my own. A wave of excitement passed through me.

"I'm staying at the Roosevelt," he said. "At Madison and Forty-fifth. I'm supposed to go back tomorrow afternoon."

"I could come down in the morning," I said.

"Too late now?"

"It's not that," I said. "I want to. But Susan's been waking up with nightmares the past few nights, and Walter can't calm her down when she's like that."

He stopped walking and turned me around so that I was looking up at him. He smiled at me.

"You've turned into quite a mother, haven't you, Ruth?" he said.

"I don't know," I replied, troubled. "If I'm such a good mother, what am I doing here now?"

"One thing," he said, putting his arms around me, kissing my forehead, "has very little to do with the other."

"I know," I said. "That's what I mean."

But he wasn't listening to me. He was kissing my eyes, my nose, my cheeks. I put my arms around him, clutching the back of his coat, pressing myself into the warmth of his body as though I'd been cold for nine years. A dog barked someplace not too far away and we broke apart and began walking again.

"Do you like San Francisco?" I asked.

"It's all right," he said. "It's fine, actually. Everything they say about it is true. Beautiful, civilized, hip. Just like—"

"Like what?"

"Like Europe, I understand." But I was sure it wasn't what he'd been about to say. "It's a very European city. My wife tells me parts of it could pass for a Mediterranean seaport without any changes at all."

My wife. That was what he'd almost said. *Beautiful, civilized, and hip. Just like my wife.* He'd stopped out of loyalty, the impulse to list attributes implying the existence of attributes not on the list. David's wife left something to be desired . . . me, apparently.

"Is she Jewish? Your wife?"

"Aha! You can take the girl out of the East Side but you can't take the E——"

"But is she?"

"Her father is."

"Do they have money?"

"Enough. They're not rich, if that's what you mean. He's an engineer."

Respectable. Middle class, respectable. I almost said it aloud but thought better of it.

"I should get back pretty soon," I said. Wordlessly he steered me around and we headed back out of the park. There were other questions I wanted to ask him, but I held those back, too. I wanted to know about his work, more about his wife, something about his daughter. Not because I could pleasurably anticipate complaints about any of them; even if David were truly unhappy, and I didn't assume that he was, it wouldn't be his style to complain. It was simply my desire to fill in and thus have more of him. Until now I had known only what Thea had told me nearly eight years before, when she had run into David and his new wife, whom he had brought to New York to meet his parents. The girl seemed, Thea had assured me, very nice; no, Thea couldn't remember for certain whether her hair was blond or light brown. At once unhappy at the news and frustrated by its sparsity, I had told her that she wasn't to relay any more word of him to me.

"After Thea told me you were married," I said, "I told her not to tell me any more. Any more news of you, I mean."

"There isn't that much more to tell."

"Do you mind when I ask you questions?"

"Yes," he said. "I don't know why, but I do."

"It doesn't matter," I said. "I won't if you don't want me to."

We walked in silence until we were back on Fifth Avenue, heading uptown. It was colder, now, and there were fewer people on the streets.

He said, "My daughter's three years old."

I said, "That's usually a pretty good age."

He said, "She's adopted."

I said, "Oh."

He said, "She looks about as much like my wife as she would the other way."

I said, "People make too much of resemblances, anyhow."

We reached Ninety-fifth.

"I guess this is my stop," he said. "Will I see you tomorrow?"

I nodded.

"I have a nine o'clock appointment," he said. "I'll be back by eleven. Room four-twenty." He smiled and began to walk away.

"David," I called softly, as much to keep him from going so quickly as because I had anything to say. He turned back to me.

"Mm?"

"You seem different."

He smiled again. "You, too," he said. "But it's the same old story. I can't tell how much of it is you and how much is me."

CHAPTER TEN

How much has any of us really changed? Only my father, of the people who know me, held out against the idea that I had become a different person, and took pains to inform me, several years ago, just retiring to Florida, where he married a widow with a pension, that it took more than clothes to make a fine lady, that skim milk often in this world masqueraded as cream, and that as far as my suspicion that he took advantage of Walter at every opportunity was concerned, I knew as well as he that evil was in the eye of the beholder. Lotte, in this case, would not agree with him.

Lotte says that I have changed in recent years. Lotte hasn't changed, except that she wants to be my friend. She has a daughter of her own. Margaret. Margaret was born in 1960, several months after I gave birth to Susan. When Lotte and her husband want to go away for a weekend, they bring Margaret to stay at our house; frequently Lotte brings her up during the day to visit with us for a few hours. Margaret, an only child, loves to stay with us. Like her parents she is quiet, inward; she rarely expresses her happiness, yet Lotte tells me that every morning her first question is whether she can visit us that day after nursery school. She worships Andy and Philip but they are at school for the full day, and since she and Susan were three, they have played well together. Susan is talky and bubbly and inventive, and particularly bossy in the hours when Andy and Philip are at school and she has more room to swing in.

"I wish," Lotte says, "that I'd had children sooner. I wish to hell I could get pregnant again. I wish . . . I think we're going to find a place farther uptown—you know, closer to here."

Lotte's husband is a broker in Walter's office. Edwin is tall, nicely built, and reasonably good looking, having been turned out in the Anglo-Saxon mold that allows for anything but startling ugliness. His face displays all the character and tension of a wash-and-wear shirt, and one could spend days with him without being aware of the bitterness and conflict those pleasant features conceal. Which is why, although Helen once told me that she lost all respect for her daughter the day

Lotte brought Edwin to meet her, it seems to me that the two of them have a great deal in common.

Edwin was raised in Wilmington, Delaware, without being a Du Pont, until his family moved to Boston without being Roman Catholic. Shortly before Edwin's high-school graduation, Edwin's father, an engineer, was offered a good job in Manhattan, so that the family moved to New York City, where for the next four years Edwin attended City College without being a Jew. Through these circumstances, and possibly with the help of a deeper inclination, he has come to consider himself the eternal outsider. He supports the same political clichés as Lotte's mother, and Edwin has indeed posed a problem for Helen, who had handled Tom Krause with ease.

Edwin did not attempt, as had Krause, to be urbane while demonstrating to Helen that it wasn't the depression thirties or the wartime forties but the McCarthy fifties that had done the greatest harm to the United States. ("He's a dirty old man," she'd blustered at Krause. "He could have done every damn thing he's done and gone, further, too, without all this uproar, if he weren't a slob. Looks did Chambers in too, you know. Who could believe that Alger Hiss, that well-dressed choirboy, was lying? God save us from television! Any crazy Red can try to blow up the country, but no one protects the patriot with five o'clock shadow.") With Edwin the problem became more complicated; he proclaimed her beliefs with a passion that disconcerted us all. ("Orwell said it about socialism," she once told me when we were alone and discussing Edwin and Lotte, "and it's true of just about every damn form of organized human endeavor you can name. Their greatest weakness lies in the people they attract.") In company, though, she still tries to be careful with Edwin. A gardener laboring earnestly in the fields of political philosophy, she wishes to crush no flower of conservatism, however delicate, however badly it measures up to the brilliant hearty blooms she had in mind.

It is impossible to gauge the extent of Lotte's agreement with her husband, or her mother. She doesn't argue with them, and she seems to participate willingly in Edwin's political efforts to remold the Lower East Side in a Young Republican image. Yet always when she is listening to him, some part of her is holding back inside, not quite believing. For apart from her brief fling with Martin and her months with Krause, Lotte, more than anyone I have known, is the true outsider, the person who never commits any part of herself without first making sure another part is in reserve. I can't understand why she is willing to entrust herself to me now. I am made uneasy by her overtures; her trust is grounded in ignorance, as were her suspicions.

I myself am mistrustful of the idea of change.

Walter is goaded by his wife of twenty years to divorce; to gratify his illusion that he desires change, he marries a girl who, unlike his wife, is young, who, unlike his wife, comes to him poor, who, unlike his wife, is attractive. And finds, whether or not he has ever chosen to acknowledge it, that the differences in the women are largely circumstantial.

I can find few differences between Helen and me that neither appearance nor background could account for. She is far too manly to accept a man's love, but a man's love has never been offered to her, not even her father's. She has told me enough about her childhood to let me know that. Her father was a debonair, irresponsible, sexed-up version of Walter, who wanted no part of the difficulties in raising a child, who disappeared from home for months at a time only to come back and stare at Helen in dismay—as though he'd let himself hope for a while that she had grown less fat and homely in his absence. "Good God," she'd once heard him exclaim to her mother, when she'd finished performing for them a little dance she'd learned at ballet school, "why don't you give up and send it to military school?" "Sssh," her mother had said, frightened lest Helen hear and be angry. She needed Helen's good will, for she was a reticent person with few friends, and during her husband's next lengthy absence she would need to speak into her daughter's half-comprehending ears, in a remote and childlike voice, intricate descriptions of her womanly ailments, nostalgic reminiscences of her maiden days.

Neither of our minds has a true talent for compromise. Her fanaticism is more obvious because she chooses to make everything about herself obvious, and because, her personal possibilities having proved themselves so limited, she has transferred that fanaticism to social and political spheres.

So Walter changed wives to implement an illusion, or to adorn reality with a more pleasant façade. If he has had great pleasure from that change, I am unaware of it. He tells me now that I have changed; but the change in me is superficial, as was the change in wives. I replaced my lust for wealth with a lust for love, a nostalgia for communion and sensuality. Except that I was no more rid of the old lust than Walter was rid of his need for a Helen. It was simply that my money-greed being momentarily satisfied (always that satisfaction seemed momentary, subject to change without notice), I could focus, in moments of dissatisfaction, on other needs. I have never been really free of the need for wealth as I have been free, say, of all sexual desire at times after David has made love to me.

If the changes in Walter and Lotte and me are negligible, what of Boris, who was more drastically and more happily affected than his sister by my marriage to Walter? He gained a loving mother in the process. And he did blossom. The intellect that had seemed to take easy comfort in his real mother's notion that it did not exist, gradually became an instrument that functioned not simply with clarity in scientific matters but with clarity in all subjects and with brilliance in his scientific studies. By the time he entered high school in 1954, help of any kind from me was a thing of the past. In his senior year he won an honorable mention in the countrywide Westinghouse contest conducted among high-school students, for an original experiment involving hamsters and electric currents which he patiently explained to me in great detail and which I failed to grasp beyond the realization that it was very complex and I had good reason to be proud of him.

He was six feet tall by that time, and terribly handsome, looking like Walter except that his frame was much larger and his expression was somehow more open, or so I fancied, as though his features expressed what was inside of him, instead of concealing it. I stood on my toes to kiss him when he came home from school, flushed and proud, to tell me about the award. He permitted the kiss (he usually shrugged me off if I so much as attempted to place a hand on his arm as we sat together) and then rubbed it off his cheek and paced around the room, trying to act casual but betraying his excitement by asking when his father would be home, although it was just past four in the afternoon.

Andrea came in from her room, then. She was four, and still tiny—the size of most of the three-year-olds in the park. Boris scooped her up and kissed her noisily, then whirled her over his head while she giggled with delight until she began hiccuping, and I told him to set her down. He adored Andy and does still. He felt free always to lavish upon her the affection that he was embarrassed to display toward me.

I tugged him into the kitchen, where I called Walter. When I tried to give the phone to Boris, Boris shook his head, saying I should tell. Walter told me he was extremely pleased and said that the three of us would go out to dinner to celebrate.

At dinner that night Walter, after expressing his pride, cautioned Boris against developing a complacency that could hinder his scientific research.

In the fall of 1958 Boris went off to M.I.T., which had been his first choice among colleges. He wrote infrequently, but during the first months he came home when he had the opportunity. We didn't know how much of a social life he led but gathered, from his conversation, that he dated girls at least occasionally, and that he attended parties and school functions. In June of 1962 we flew up to Cambridge for his graduation. He met us at the airport, driving the red convertible he'd bought after his twenty-first birthday, when he had come into a good portion of his maternal grandmother's estate, and introduced us to Tanya Lensky, the girl he planned to marry.

Tanya was—is—a short muscular girl with a face that might seem pretty were her entire head not too large for her short frame; legs that look as if they could be harnessed to plow the south forty; and the voice of a television toothpaste pusher—deep, mellow, and not quite right for the rest of her. A sociology major. The very model of. She is a nice girl and I cannot dislike her, but she is a cliché and she bores me. I am a cliché, too, but it is easy for me to penetrate the simple sordid facts of my own existence and find at least the outside corridors of the bewildering maze beneath, while within Tanya I can find only faith and good works.

Boris is doing graduate work at M.I.T. now. They are living in Brookline, with Tanya's widowed mother. Between Tanya's salary and the steady income Boris receives from his grandmother's estate, together with the various stocks that Walter had held in trust for him, they could easily have taken an apartment near the college. But, as Tanya had confided, "We decided there was no point spending the money when Mom's been rattling around in the house since Dad died." Careful as always to say that it was "we" and not she who had decided. Not out of deceit—Machiavellian manipulations would be totally foreign to Tanya, who is as open and aboveboard as only the very dullest people can be. The effort to suggest that Boris has a hand in such decisions is an effort to convince herself that this is so, that he has not acquiesced simply to please her or because he is so sure he can rely on her judgment.

Her judgment is doubtless good. They have no need of an apartment of their own. He would never chase her, naked, down the hallway or take it upon himself to test the old legend that there was something great about making love under the kitchen table. She is humorless. Wit has never been Boris's strong point, and doubtless her lack of it is irrelevant to him. But I will never forget the way, when I proposed a toast at dinner that first night to those of us doing missionary work in wiping out the pure white Protestant strain in America, she looked at me with stricken eyes and said, "Oh, I don't really think of it that way, do you?"

"Oh, I most certainly don't, Tanya," I said quickly. "Please forgive my joke." Without looking at Walter. "It was in bad taste."

"Really, you don't have to apologize," Tanya assured me earnestly. "The statement isn't quite accurate, anyway, you know, because of Boris's great-grandmother on his mother's side."

Aside from her mental limitations she is a benevolent version of Helen Stamm. And it was this resemblance that kept me lying awake all that night at our hotel in Cambridge, examining at length, for the first time in over ten years of marriage, some of the fallacies of my life. As a matter of fact, I had a fleeting sense, more than once during the night, that I was about to die—as though that life itself had been an error and my discovery of this fact guaranteed that I would cease to exist.

I had used Boris to answer so many questions whose answers he only partly provided, to escape so many others that weren't related to him at all. Before the birth of my own children he had sometimes seemed to be the sole justification for my existence; as they came, my concern was divided between Boris and them without diminishing in intensity. I'd been proud, not only because of the intellectual achievements I'd encouraged, but because these achievements had seemed to stem from a deeper change within him, from a new confidence and a growing manliness. Less dependent for approval on teachers and people outside of home, he made his way more easily, and having made it, ceased to concern himself with failure. I had seen the number of his friends grow with his assurance and unconcern, and seen the subtle change in his relations to each new set of friends, how he had changed from a follower to an equal, from an equal to a sometime leader.

Now here was Tanya, to disabuse me of my vain notion that I had helped a boy grow into a man, that there had been a change in Boris that was not simply from the neck up (I asked myself now, for the first time, if he might not have come out of his intellectual shell if he'd never laid eyes on me, if I hadn't perhaps just happened to be around at the time when it was beginning to happen). Here was Tanya to prove, in her hairy-legged, social-worker's innocence that my son's needs were those of a boy, not a man. Friendliness, not romance. Sincerity, not sexuality. A sturdy creature who could be depended upon to get him through difficult times; not a woman, sometimes strong but sometimes so fragile that it was conceivable he might one day need to pick up the pieces of her life for her and put them back together again.

We went home the next day, after we had been taken to Tanya's mother to be inspected for fleas of either denomination and Walter had told Boris for the hundredth time how heartily he approved of his choice. ("Fine young girl," he'd said repeatedly after we'd returned to the motel the night before. "Fine young girl." He even acted fondly toward his son for the first time in years.)

We arrived home in the early afternoon, and an hour later I took Andy and Philip to the zoo. The next morning it was raining; I took the two of them to the American Museum of Natural History in the morning and a movie in the afternoon. Susie, having napped through most of the rainy day, was up through the evening, when Andy, Philip, and I baked cookies. For three days I went on like that, frantic with activity; thinking up things to do when the children would have been just as happy playing in their rooms; reading soft-cover mysteries until late at night, then tossing in my bed until it was close to the time when Walter's alarm would go off; reminding myself of all the things that were wrong with divorce. Once you had children you stayed married. It was one of the reasons, I must remember, that I had wanted to wait before having them. My sophistication had never extended to a point where I was undismayed by the endless succession of half-brothers, stepsisters, boys with different names than their parents, whom Boris—and later Andy and Philip—brought home with them from school. If the curse of money involved the too great freedom it bestowed upon unwise people, then the children of rich people suffered doubly under the abuse of that freedom, for they were our victims as well as their own. It was an idea I would have laughed off once, that the poverty which limited my childhood also protected me from unwelcome change. I thought about David a great deal—often daydreaming that he had come back to me and things were as before, only better, not having any idea that in a few months he would do exactly that and things would be so much better that they would cease to resemble before. Finally, close to the time when Walter's alarm was due to go off, I would fall into a troubled sleep that lasted until the alarm, or the kids banging around in the hallway, or some unbearable dream awakened me.

On the fourth morning I could not get out of bed. I tried to force myself up into the clear sunny day, but my body would not respond. It turned out that I had a raging fever, a severe intestinal infection, and various other maladies that made the doctor Walter summoned (his doctor; I hadn't been ill since we were married) wonder how I could have been walking around until that day. I knew quite well, however, that it wasn't an infection that had made me cease to function, but the fact that the vacuum that was my own private existence had loomed so large upon me that I could no longer pretend that my children filled it. Some day they would all go, and I would have nothing. I would have been jealous had Boris brought home some quiveringly beautiful young flower. In picking Tanya he had not only made me unnecessary to his future life, he had proved me superfluous to his past one.

I was in bed for the rest of June on a simple schedule, once the fever had subsided, of sleep and vitamins. At first I had nothing to do but read while I was awake, and I couldn't concentrate on anything but mysteries. Then Walter brought me some wool and a knitting book; and although I began by being amused and a little irritated at his attempt to initiate me into the mysteries of creative femininity, after a couple of days I began toying with the wool, finding with pleasure that I remembered how to cast on stitches although I hadn't knitted since I was twelve years old and had made for my father, in school, a muffler of scratchy government-issue beige wool which turned out to be so short that it barely tied around his neck. I ended up making a sweater for Andy and then, because there was wool left over, I began one for Philip with the same green-tweed wool.

Over the July Fourth weekend, Walter and Edwin moved the four of us, along with Esther and Lotte and Margaret, up to the lake, where we spent a quiet summer. The doctor had told me I might gradually resume activities as long as I stopped immediately when I found myself getting tired. Boris and Tanya came frequently on weekends, it being just a two-hour trip from Brookline. The house and guest cottage were filled to capacity then, since Edwin and Walter were also there; but I didn't mind, for I had made a limited peace with myself on the reassurance that now wasn't the time for me to cope with major issues. I had a baby at home who wasn't yet two years old. When she was old enough to begin school, then I would do something—get a job, divorce Walter—something to alter the static quality of my life. But the nature of this pact was such that I needed to keep busy to avoid examining too closely its terms, and since overactivity was temporarily forbidden, overpopulation would do to fill the gap.

Boris and Tanya were married in the fall as soon as the Jewish holidays were over: Tanya in a tailored white suit that would have been almost as appropriate for standing on the Israeli border picking off Arabs with a shotgun; Boris unbelievably handsome, sweetly serious; neither one displaying the slightest nervousness or hesitation over the ending of their separate lives. I came back to New York feeling that I had passed a milestone by simply surviving the wedding. It was a little over two months from that day that David found us in the park.

CHAPTER ELEVEN

In 1965 Walter was fifty-two years old and I was thirty-four. We had been married for thirteen years; David had been my lover again for two. I had seen him only a few times in the first year after his return; but then, in the year just past, he'd begun to come in more often, so that frequently less than a month passed between visits. It was in June of that year that Walter decided it was imperative his father meet me.

"I've been thinking," he said one evening, in the ultra-casual tone he always adopted when discussing something of deep importance to him, "that it might be nice to go out to the Coast this summer."

"The West Coast?" I asked, stupidly, caught entirely off guard, West Coast having in my mind only one meaning: David.

"Yes, of course."

"How come?"

"Oh, I don't know." He tapped his pipe against the outside of the ashtray. "Does there have to be a special reason?"

"No. I was just curious."

"Well . . ." with infinitesimal care scooping out the charred tobacco remains in the bowl, "as a matter of fact . . . there *was* one thing on my mind." Bringing over his humidor from the top of the console, uncapping it, packing the tobacco into the pipe bowl a strand or two at a time.

"What was that, Walter?"

"As you know, I've always hoped to bring you and the children out to Carmel, sooner or later. To meet my father."

As I knew. What I knew was that for thirteen years he had avoided taking advantage of any opportunity to do just that, and because David was in San Francisco, I had been unable, unwilling, to beg the question. I knew that several times Walter had gone to Los Angeles to look at property, and that one of the times he'd mentioned that he might fly up to Carmel. I'd asked if he thought it might be nice for me to come along.

"Oh, I don't know, Ruth," he'd said—so nervous as to make it obvious that he knew he wasn't making sense, "I don't think this is really a good time, do you? I mean, I thought we'd make a real trip some time, with Andrea." There was no point in a reply, but I must have looked puzzled, for he'd added, "It's not really too likely that I'll make it, anyway. It was just a thought."

And not another word about his father had passed between us for the next eight years except that every year in October he would remind me, as he had in the years before, to send a birthday card to Carmel.

"Yes, of course," I said. "But how come *this* year?"

"He's eighty-eight years old, Ruth." As though his father had been seventy-eight the year before. "He couldn't have much longer to live."

It was unarguable. My only argument was an instinct against the trip, a feeling that we should do nothing that might upset the delicate but harmonious balance that currently existed between us, and a concern that I might miss one of David's New York visits while I was there.

"How long would we go for?"

"I thought I might take some extra time from the office," he said. "A month or so. We needn't spend all that time with him, of course. We might fly out to Los Angeles, rent a car there, and take the drive up in a leisurely manner, perhaps spend a few days in Santa Barbara, then up the Pacific Coast Drive—it's spectacularly beautiful, you know. And then, when we've left Dad's, we might spend some time in San Francisco, and even drive through the Sierras and the Rockies."

"Do you mean with all the kids?" I asked doubtfully. "It's a lot of driving for them. They don't enjoy traveling that much."

"I don't say we have to do it that way, Ruth. We can see how it works as we go along."

Utterly reasonable. Sensibly stated. None of the quiet hostility that suggested my life was an unending effort to thwart his dreams. As there was in me none of the irritation at being misunderstood, the anger of sexual frustration. The tension between us had lessened since I'd begun again with David.

I smiled at him. "All right, Walter. It does sound good."

"Are you sure, Ruth?" he asked, suddenly a little apprehensive. "You're not saying it just to please me?"

"No, Walter," I said. "I'm not. I really like the idea."

He kissed my forehead. Smiled at me fondly. "Good. I'm glad. I'm looking forward to the trip enormously." He smiled. "The trip, and showing off you and the children."

I couldn't resist teasing. "I thought it was only the children you wanted to show off."

I'd expected a simple denial, but instead he looked at me thoughtfully for a moment, then said, "That might have been true once. But it isn't any more."

I stared at him curiously, half-anticipating what was to come.

"You've changed, Ruth, you know. I don't know if you're aware of how much you've changed."

"It must be motherhood," I said, amused and a little uncomfortable.

"No. It's more recent than that."

I was tempted to ask him to set the time, but there was no point to it, for I knew what he would say.

"Well, as long as it's a change for the better," I said.

"No question of that," he assured me.

What he was telling me, of course, was that he had not wanted to take to Carmel a wife who despised him. And certainly it was true that while motherhood had increased the distance between Walter and me, David, by increasing it further, had enabled me to be kind. The necessity to argue betrays a certain reliance on the person one needs to convince. With David's return Walter had shifted from the focus of my discontent to the periphery of my consciousness. Where he thrived.

Occasionally we slept together. I had no need to make believe that he was David; our intercourse was less disturbing than it had been in the years when no one was really making love to me. In any event, there was little possibility of confusing the two. Walter's sexuality was that of a small boy promised a reward he is too timid to collect. Even his lean body seemed ludicrous, unmanly. While David's large strong body forced itself into mine with a power that stopped just short of cruelty, and the intensity that enveloped the two of us seemed barely of our own making.

So I smiled at Walter. And I stopped arguing with him about silly things. Ceased to feel compelled to drop the one line that would provoke him to wrath and me to the temporary illusion that we were both alive. And I never went out at night, except when David was in town. I never held my future against Walter because the present entirely filled my thoughts.

And Walter wanted his father to meet me.

I did not like Rudolph Stamm. It was a surprise to me that this should be so. It made me realize that I had been even less fair to

Walter than I believed. For I had assumed that I would like the old man simply because I knew, from everything Walter had said or left unsaid, that the old man despised his son. I had taken this negative bond between us as tacit proof of a positive one. What actually happened, though, was that Rudolph Stamm's conspicuous contempt for his son, coming as it did at a time when I was less hostile to Walter, anyway, than I had been in the past, had the effect of increasing my sympathy for him, and filling me with disgust toward the old man.

The house hung over a palisade at the ocean. Modern. Self-consciously rugged. With no other homes in view to destroy the illusion of total power. The outside was redwood and glass. Aside from a white cast-iron boy who stood next to the footpath and spat water into a small goldfish pond, it offered no hint of the lunacy within.

We had called from San Luis Obispo the night before. Now I was tired and had a headache after the beautiful but terrifying trip up the high and winding coast highway. The children were restless, as always after a couple of hours in the car. Susan had fallen asleep, and although she was able to get out of the car and walk to the house, she wasn't fully awake yet. Walter rang the front bell. The woman who came to the door was large, gray-haired, and without cordiality, although she did unbend to the extent of letting us know that she, too, had expected us. Her name was Wanda and she had been with Mr. Stamm for some years in New York, before the death of his second wife. Walter said hello in a friendly way, but she gave him no particular sign of recognition. We were asked to walk into the house quietly because He was taking a little nap; but as it turned out, He awakened as we came into the main room, and struggled out of the hammock which was hung from balcony posts near the glass wall that faced the ocean.

He looked considerably younger than his age, although I could never bring myself to please him by saying so. He had wavy white hair, a complexion that was florid—or sunburned—to the point of absurdity, and he was very wrinkled, but his manner was youthful and his voice much less cracked and old than I would have expected. His age should have made Walter seem young, yet next to him, strangely, Walter seemed for the first time his full fifty-two years.

"So," he said to Walter, "it's good to see you, my boy." He turned to fix me with his dazzling white-on-red smile. "And this is your lovely wife. I must say, my son's taste is improving with age." I think he was about to kiss me. Instinctively I held out a hand, which he shook. "And the trip," he said. "How was your trip, my dear?"

The children had been standing quietly in back of us—even Susan, who was rarely still for two minutes at a time but was not yet fully awake—but at this sign from him that he was going to continue to ignore them, I felt them growing restless in back of me.

"It was all right," I said. "Let me introduce you to the children."

"Ah, yes," he said, without enthusiasm.

"This is Andrea, who's ten now. This is Philip, who's almost seven. And Susan is three and a half."

With a whoop, Susan ran to the far side of the living room.

"You are the image of your grandmother," the old man said to Andrea, whose resemblance to me was almost uncanny.

"Do you think so, Dad?" Walter asked.

"No question about it," the old man said.

"Thank you, sir," Andrea said, and I stifled a laugh at this inspired bit of corn from my older daughter.

"And who's this? Philip, you say? How old are you, Philip?"

"I'll be seven," Philip said shyly.

"The boy's got a little of you in him, Ruth," said the old man of Philip, the only one of the three who looks anything like Walter.

"Can you find me, Ma?" Susan called from behind some piece of furniture.

"Where are you?" I called obligingly, noting that Wanda stood in the doorway regarding us with stolid disapproval.

"The idea is to *find* me," Susan called. "I'm *hiding*."

"Why don't you sit down?" the old man said. "You're tired after all your traveling. I'll have Wanda make some tea." As though he'd pressed a button, Wanda vanished from the doorway.

"Are you really my grandpa?" Susan called.

He smiled, without amusement or interest. It was one of the things that made me look forward instantly to getting out of his house—that very obvious failure to be the least bit charmed by the children. They were fascinated by both him and his home. They wanted very much to be treated like grandchildren, a privileged status which some of their friends enjoyed and talked about. My own father had been crazy about Andy, and it was she who'd made him waver about the move to Florida, even if she couldn't remember him now. Several times he had almost come back to see the children, or we had almost gone there, but my father's health had been poor since his remarriage and always sickness or something else had prevented our seeing him.

"Grandparents," Andy had once written in a composition for school, "are something like parents except that they *always* like you."

And here was this old man who ignored them most of the time, who at best forced a smile when they tried to be amusing (Philip tried to do riddles with him and he flatly refused) and who seemed to feel, in some generalized but terribly obvious way, that their presence in his home constituted an invasion. They behaved so beautifully—and received, for their efforts, judicious comments to the effect that children were more wild than they had been in the old days. "In the old days," I once irritably replied, "people thought their children were just more pieces of furniture around the house. Now they know better." He only smiled.

The old man followed Wanda into the kitchen. Walter and I sat down on one of several sofas. Andrea asked if she and Philip might go outside and watch the goldfish, and I said it would be all right. Susan was too busy investigating the room to even notice when they left. And there was a great deal to investigate. I'd been much too intent on the old man to really look around me, except that I'd gotten a vague feeling of the room's size and opulence. Now I could be simultaneously amused and overwhelmed.

The main part of the house was one huge room, about sixty feet square, with a beamed ceiling at least forty feet above our heads. About twenty feet above us, a balcony ran around the entire room. (The bedrooms branched off it.) The furniture was primarily California Mission and there were huge quantities of it lost in that room—massive green and orange sofas and armchairs, trestled tables, sturdy dining chairs. There were Mexican Indian rugs scattered around the floor. A huge, free-standing copper-flued fireplace dominated the center of the room. Aside from the glass wall that faced the ocean, there were two bay windows on each side wall. Every bit of wall space that was not glass was covered with mural art. On either side of the bay windows stood potted trees and vines in ceramic buckets. Where the vines had not extended along trellislike sticks to lush heights, the mural artist had picked up their patterns and carried them farther up the wall with green paints. Blue skies dotted with neat white clouds began where the painted foliage ended and ended where the balcony floor began. Between one set of bay windows a painted waterfall plummeted to the floor. In the waterfall's foreground a wild boar slaked its thirst. The staircase that led to the upstairs balcony led also, on the wall, to a stone castle built on sturdy rock ramparts. On the opposite wall a Swiss chalet graced the banks of a meandering river. I met Walter's eyes and smiled.

"Leave it to Dad," Walter said, his expression uncritical—even admiring.

"Look, Ma," Susan called from the far end of the room. "Look at this big bunch of seashells!"

I walked over to her. In front of the glass wall was a depressed area filled with thousands of shells. And stones. And more potted plants. A stone wall about a foot high enclosed this area; Susan sat on it. I looked through the glass wall and decided there must be some madness to it— the necessity to enhance a view such as this, of clear-blue to turquoise ocean, of sandy beach curving around below us, and to the sides and the back, slopes covered with ice plant and manzanita, and back still farther, acres of evergreens. The mountains farther south had been dry and brown, but up here the green didn't disappear.

The old man came back into the room.

"Can I touch them?" Susan asked me.

"Can she touch the shells?" I called to him. "If she's careful?"

"Well, if she's very careful," he called back, walking toward us. "Those shells are from all over the world, you know. Cuba. Virgin Islands. Have a little lady in the village who gets them for me."

"Handle them carefully, darling," I said to Susan. "They're delicate, you know, the shells are. They can break very easily."

"In my day," the old man said, "we just told the kids what to do, we didn't bother giving them a lot of complicated explanations about why they should do it."

"I think they don't mind obeying so much if they know the reasons," I said.

"In my day," he grinned at me aggressively, "we didn't worry about whether they minded or not."

"Ah, yes," Walter said, coming over to us. "Well, times have changed, haven't they?"

Neither of us replied.

"So, Dad," Walter said, "tell us how you've been spending your time."

"Oh, I'm busy, all right," his father said. "Sometimes I don't know why I bothered to retire, spend just as much time on the house and matters around here as I used to on the business."

I glanced at the hammock, stretched out partly over the stones and shells, partly over the dark-wood floor, angled in such a way as to catch the afternoon sun.

"What's taking so long?" the old man demanded of Wanda, who was setting the long table in the dining corner of the room.

"It's ready," Wanda grunted.

"Look, Mommy," Susan said excitedly, "look at this beauty. It's striped."

"Mmm. Lovely."

"What'd she say? What'd she say?" asked the old man.

"She was just admiring one of the shells," I said.

"All right, all right. Let's have a bite to eat."

The table was loaded as though for a banquet. This was to be the case at every meal, including tea. There was a ham, and several kinds of cold meat and sausage. There were sardines, pickled oysters, and caviar. There was Limburger cheese, Swiss cheese, and Liederkranz, and in the center of the table a large bowl of sliced onion flanked by a basket of bread on one side and a bowl of fruit on the other. I had never seen anything quite like it, not even at Helen Stamm's abundant table. After the first meals, though, I began to resent that loaded table as I resented so many things in his home. There was something aggressive about his determination to ply us with food. I sometimes felt as though he were trying to physically bury us, and the fact that he ate very little himself contributed to my suspicions. At that first "tea" he had one orange, all the while urging cheese and meat and onion upon us. At dinner Wanda served a stew that smelled heavenly and turned out to be made of all those innards most calculated to repel anyone who hasn't eaten them since childhood. He had a broiled lamb chop. When I barely touched the stew he insisted that Wanda bring in some alternate food so that I would not starve to death—even though I vehemently assured him that after our afternoon repast I had no appetite, anyway—and he was highly and continually critical of me for permitting the children, none of whom would even sample the stew, to fill up instead on bread and butter.

After tea we were taken up to the balcony for a tour of the bedrooms, which were small and spartan, as well as the old man's "study," in which stood a massive desk, a file cabinet, and a rowing machine.

He patted his waistline. "Weigh ten pounds less than I did twenty years ago," he announced proudly.

That, I thought, *is because you are shrunken, old man.*

We stayed for a week, which was a compromise because I wanted to go after three days and Walter thought such a short stay would offend his father, when we'd tentatively planned for two weeks there. Walter was sweet and sympathetic, saying that he understood my reaction but he couldn't help wishing that I liked his father more. I said I couldn't help wishing his father liked our children more, and Walter reminded me that his father was quite old, and old people were often impatient. I said I had the feeling that the old man had always been much the same as he was now. Walter changed the subject—as though after all these years he still could not bear to face his father's indifference.

We made love every night, a fact in itself surprising. What was more strange to me was that there in his father's house, three thousand miles from our own home, in a not-quite-double bed on a too-firm mattress in a small room sandwiched between the one where all the children were sleeping and the one that was the old man's, Walter seemed to feel, and he aroused in me, an ardor stronger than anything I had felt for him before. Perhaps it was part of the reason he was reluctant to leave. He may have sensed more readily than I did that our passion was in some way related to our being there, to the fact that we were away from home, to the fact that I disliked his father while his father had gone out of his way to express to Walter his approval of me, to Walter's being cast, for the first time since our marriage, in the intermediary-peacemaker role for which he was so eminently suited. He may have known that once we were back in our home, his passions would subside again, and with them his ability to arouse me beyond the most basic level.

I, more peculiarly, feared the reverse. Not sensing the transient nature of our communion, I was afraid that we'd entered some new stage where my rapturous pleasure with David would be complicated by strong feeling for Walter. It was only in the past year, as I had begun to get along with Walter, that I had felt guilt over David. I had restrained these guilty feelings partly by reminding myself, however ironically, that my love affair with David had actually caused the improvement in my relations with Walter. Now, absurdly, I was confused by guilty feelings about betraying David—not only David, but myself as well—by letting myself love Walter just a little. During one of those nights I dreamed that I was riding on a train with a man I couldn't identify but who must have been Walter. The train never stopped at any of the regular stations, but hurtled through to the end of the line, then charged through the brick wall at the end and began to fall. I awakened with David's name on my lips, yet I knew David was not in the dream. I wanted desperately to see him. I *needed* desperately to see him, to be reminded of the love for him which as far back as I could remember had been the one certifiable fact of my existence; to be reminded that what Walter now touched in me, David had long since made a part of himself. I was terrified by the groundless fear that my love for David might diminish, for in some strange way I associated not loving him with death and oblivion—punishments I should have thought reserved for more obvious crimes, like betraying one's husband.

I think the old man might have persuaded Walter to stay longer. Had he tried.

We drove up to San Francisco on Sunday morning. The children, having spent a good portion of the week restraining their natural energies, were wildly uncontrollable in the car, and by the time we reached the Hopkins I was thoroughly exhausted. Walter, still exhilarated by our good week in Carmel, took the children out sightseeing. I took off my dress and stretched out on the bed, meaning to nap but instead becoming wide awake with thoughts of David, whom I had vowed not to call while we were there. Without getting up, I reached out for the phone book, found his office number and under it his home listing. Relieved that it was Sunday and I could not call him at his office, I put back the book. If I called, I reminded myself, I would only be more eager to see him. Walter had told me that he would have business to attend to during one of the weekdays that we were there, but there were still the children. I was unwilling to leave Andy even briefly in charge in an unknown city. And to risk any meeting, however brief, however casual, while the children were with me, would be foolhardy in the extreme. Nor could such a meeting offer any great pleasure to either of us. Certainly it could not be worth risking the warmth that had so recently developed between Walter and me. No, I wouldn't call.

But I couldn't sleep and only succeeded in becoming drowsy a short while before Walter and the children returned, the result being that one martini before dinner destroyed whatever little energy I had, and I fell asleep immediately after getting the children off to bed at eight.

We spent most of Monday sightseeing. Walter made some business calls late in the afternoon when we returned to our suite, but he didn't mention them to me until we'd gone to dinner, returned, and gotten the children off for the night.

"I've arranged to look at all the property I want to see tomorrow, dear," he said then.

"But what will I do?" I asked quickly. Untypically helpless. The question really meaning not what can I do but what might I do that I should not, if I am given the time and the opportunity. But Walter was far from displeased by the suggestion that I would be at a loss without him.

"Well," he said thoughtfully, "if you're really concerned, I can probably get one of my associates' wives to show you around, or perhaps a young man from one of their offices."

"Someone I don't know," I said, idly beginning to unpack the things I'd left in the suitcases that morning.

"On the other hand," Walter said slowly, "there might be someone you want to look up. What was your friend's name—the one who came out here? The lawyer?"

"David Landau," I said, peering into the suitcase as the blood rushed to my face and my heart hammered wildly inside me.

"Yes. Would you like to call him and say hello? He's in the phone book."

I stopped unpacking and looked at him curiously. He smiled.

"You see," he said, "I really did remember his name."

It had never occurred to me until then that Walter could know. But there was no hint of suppressed rancor in his voice or his expression.

I shook my head.

He was still smiling. I waited. In the next room Andrea screamed at Philip and Susan at the top of her lungs that they were keeping her from falling asleep.

"I thought you would want to," Walter said.

"It's too long ago," I told him.

He nodded. I watched him. He took his pipe from the dresser top, filled it, lit it.

"You'll never know what it did to me, Ruth," he said, dragging slowly on the pipe as it began to smoke steadily, "seeing the two of you come into the wedding hall that day."

I'd tried to anticipate what he would say next. Still, I was startled.

"I don't mean that you were together," he went on, his manner almost abstract. "I mean the way you looked. It's impossible to describe. The physical resemblance is part of it, of course, the obvious part, even if I hadn't seen it before . . . just as I'd never realized . . ." He took the pipe from his mouth, stared into the bowl. "I was very nearly destroyed by the way you two looked together."

Terribly dignified. Without self-pity. I started to walk to him, remembered the implicit lie in our conversation, remained where I was.

"I'm sorry, Walter."

"There's nothing to apologize for. As a matter of fact, that day was the first time I ever felt sympathy for you, felt a little sorry for you, I mean. It was the first time I ever had the sense that you'd given anything up when you married me."

Tears welled in me. For myself? For him? For both of us.

"Until then I'd only thought of it the one way. That I'd rescued you, you know, from squalor." He put the pipe back in his mouth, but it had gone out. He didn't seem to care. He put it in the glass ashtray on the dresser. "But you knew all that, of course. You made fun of me."

I'm sorry, Walter. I'm truly sorry.

"I thought you a very callous young lady."

"You were right," I said. "I was a lousy kid."

What am I now, for all our confidences?

He shrugged. "I was a rather obtuse young man." He smiled. "Or, rather, an obtuse not-so-young man."

Our eyes held each other. A mixture of affection and embarrassment seized us both. Why was he saying this now? Why was any of it happening? Because of where we'd been, or because of where we were then? I sat down at the end of the bed. He came over and sat down beside me. He took my hands in his and raised them to his lips, kissed them gently, brought them down to rest in his lap, stroked them.

"I love you, Ruth."

I looked at him helplessly. I couldn't say it. Even if it were more true than it was, I couldn't have said it to him.

"I can't, Walter. I'm sorry. It's me. It has nothing to do with whether I love you or not. I just can't say it."

He nodded. And released my hands. The room was very quiet. I'd been dimly aware of the children's voices in the adjoining room, but now they, too, were still. I stood up.

"I guess I should finish unpacking."

He was silent. I began transferring clothes from the suitcase to the dresser. "I'll manage about tomorrow," I said. "I don't want to impose on someone's wife. We'll help turn the trolley around again. The trolleys should be good for half a day. Then lunch. Then maybe I'll let them make some phone calls from the Chinese booths. We can even call someone in New York. That should give them a thrill . . . Don't you think?" I turned to him and he did the sort of double take one does when queried after only half-listening.

"Mmm," he said, "of course, my dear. Whatever you think best." He got his pipe from the dresser, tapped the bowl against the ashtray, put his tobacco pouch in his pocket. "I thought I might go out for a bit. Take a little stroll, see the city at night. Have a drink someplace. You don't mind, do you?"

"Of course not."

He hesitated. "I'm not running away from you, Ruth. I'd be delighted to have you come with me."

I told him, truthfully, that I would like to come. We called the desk but there were no sitters available just then. Walter said he supposed I wouldn't want to leave the children alone.

"It's just that they wouldn't know," I explained. "If I could leave a note where I'd be sure Andy would see it . . ."

"We could attach it to the night-light shade."

Andy might miss it. Still, she was a very capable, self-possessed eleven-year-old, and it was entirely likely that if she were to wake up, or be awakened by Philip or Susie, she would immediately grasp the situation and take charge.

"They probably won't wake up, anyway," I said. "They're exhausted."

"I'm sure you're right," he said, obviously pleased that I wanted to go.

"Good." I took off my bathrobe. "I'll get into my slacks if you'll write the note."

We spent five more pleasant days in San Francisco. A couple of times Walter and I got a sitter and went out in the evening, but more often we were tired after our touring and went to sleep not long after the children did. We flew home on Sunday morning to a blazing hot New York July and decided, within a few minutes of leaving the airport, that we would move up to the lake as soon as possible.

There was a long list of messages from Esther when we reached the apartment, one of them being that a Mr. Segal had called and would call again. That would probably have been David, our arrangement being that any time he came to New York he called and, if someone else answered, left a name—a different one each time. So I *had* missed him. I regretted now not having tried him in San Francisco. On our next to the last day I'd almost called and then, at the last moment, it had occurred to me that he might not want me to contact him there. We left for Quanthog three days after arriving in New York.

The rest of July was hot and beautiful. We did all the things we always did at the lake. Walter came every weekend and occasionally during the week as well. Our relations continued to be pleasant, if more vigorous during the day's activities than during the night's. But then, during the last week of July, a damp cold descended and remained with us through August, dominating the month and our spirits by keeping us from doing all the things we enjoyed most. Lotte, despondent at her continued failure to become pregnant again, went off to Europe with Edwin at the beginning of August, leaving Margaret with us for the month. But Margaret's presence, rather than creating the extra ac-

tivity I might have welcomed, relieved me of the necessity to amuse
Susan at times when Andy and Philip went off without her or simply
didn't want her around. As the gray coldness remained with us I became more and more restless. I went to the movie in town as often as it
changed. I haunted the lending library but failed to get through the
books that I borrowed. Out of boredom rather than ambition I began
baking a few things beyond the simple cookies I occasionally made
with the children, and cooked a few dishes that were more complex
and exotic than the broiled meats and fish I'd learned to do on the char-
coal grill the second summer that I was there. Boris and Tanya had also
gone to Europe and were planning to meet Lotte and Edwin at various
points in the trip. The four of them got along well in spite of occasionally violent political quarrels between Tanya and Edwin. I half
wished they were all there with me to relieve the boredom with one of
their silly arguments over whether the right wing was dominated by
psychopaths.

In the third week of August, Walter came up on Wednesday morning and David called on Wednesday afternoon. I'd so little expected to
hear from him that for a moment I didn't even recognize his voice.
Then I said, almost whispering because I was in the kitchen but I
didn't know where Walter was, "Is that you, David?"

"It is I," he said. "Young Lochinvar come out of the West."

"Where are you?"

"I think I'm about twenty miles from you. A place called The
Lodge, at Mantinoc. You know it?"

"I'll be over," I said quickly, barely waiting until the words were out
to hang up because I heard footsteps coming down the stairs. But it was
Esther, coming into the kitchen to begin advance preparations for dinner. I got a list from her of the things she could use in town, put on a
sweater, and left the house without telling Walter I was going so that I
wouldn't have to lie to him.

Mount Mantinoc is less than half an hour's drive past town. The
road leading to the two peaks which house the lodge and the chair lift
respectively is a narrow, winding one which strangers looking for Mantinoc often pass without noticing the fieldstone entrance posts or the
small black-lettered sign for the lodge that hangs above one of them. I
had been past the posts many times, but had traveled up the road only
once before. Strangely, I found as I drove up now that I remembered it
in great detail—the winding blacktop barely wide enough for one car to
pass another, the sharp curves, the sudden clearing at the base of the
smaller peak where the lodge was situated—and beyond it, slightly to

the left, Mantinoc itself, the chair lift now bringing up summer tourists who wanted to see the three-state view. I drove up the long driveway and left the car in the lot in back of the lodge, then walked into the big central hall. Sofas and armchairs were scattered around. At each end a massive fireplace held a blazing fire to warm the room and burn off the pervasive August damp. I got David's room number from the desk clerk and took the elevator to the third floor, then walked the length of the carpeted corridor to the far end. He opened the door when I knocked. I came in quickly and shut the door behind me. He was holding a half-finished drink.

"Did something happen?" I asked.

He grinned at me. "I wanted to see you, that's all."

"I was scared," I said. "I don't know why. It seemed so odd . . ."

"What do I do at this point?" he asked. "Apologize for missing you?"

I shook my head. "Walter's at the house, that's all."

He whistled. "Sorry. I called his office late yesterday afternoon, when there was no answer at your place. I asked for him and the switchboard asked me to hold on, he had another call, so I just hung up. I figured you'd be up here without him."

"He came up this morning. He's been coming up sometimes in the middle of the week."

"How friendly." He seemed a little disgruntled.

I smiled. "How long can you stay?"

"Dunno. Couple of days."

I looked around. It was a pleasant room. Green grass-cloth paper on the walls, blond furniture, a bright orange-and-green striped spread on the bed, two Swiss travel posters on the wall. A local paper was spread out on the bed and next to it sat a plate with half a sandwich. I walked to the window and looked out. I don't know why I did it, but I found myself looking at the clear side of Mantinoc, where there was no chair lift. Just grass, and dirt, and here and there, a tree. David came up behind me and put his arms around me. Without turning, I reached back and hooked my thumbs into his belt.

"This is where Martin killed himself," I said. "Right over there."

"I didn't know."

"Of course not." I turned around in his arms. "Anyway, I don't feel anything about it. Except . . . I sometimes . . . the exact moment when he went into the tree. Every once in a while I can be lying in bed . . . or maybe just waking up . . . and I get a kind of physical memory of it. As if I was right there. *In* it."

He kissed me, his hand finding the back button on my slacks, pulling down the zipper.

"Horny old David," I said. I leaned against the window sill to keep my slacks from falling down, trapping his hand between my buttocks and the sill. He looked down at me speculatively.

"What's up?"

"Nothing," I said. "I forgot my diaphragm. I rushed out of the house."

I nodded, but involuntarily I glanced over my shoulder at the mountain in back of me. David picked me up, carried me across the room, deposited me on the bed, pulled the newspaper out from under me and threw it on the floor, and put the sandwich on the night table.

"Close your eyes," he said, "and you're screwing in Italy." With care he took off his white business shirt and dark pants and folded them on a chair.

"Business suits look so funny up here," I said. "Walter always looks so strange to me when he comes up without changing."

"I didn't expect to be here," he said, a little irritably.

"I didn't expect you to be, either," I said. "But I'm glad you are."

"That's nice," he muttered, sitting down on the bed. "I was beginning to wonder."

"How could you wonder?" I asked. Perfectly serious. Because as usual I understood less of what was happening than he did.

"Forget it."

"David?" I reached out a hand, caressed his thigh, inviting him to lie down beside me. "I was so upset when I missed you in June. You *were* Mr. Segal, weren't you?"

"I suppose so. Something like that."

"I didn't even want to leave the city. I had a feeling you'd be coming in."

"Where were you? Up here?"

"Uh-uh. California."

He started.

"That was the crazy thing," I said. "Walter took it into his head that I should meet his father. In Carmel. After all these years. Not just me, I mean, the kids, too. And then we went up to San Francisco for a week, and every day I wanted to call you but I didn't know how I could arrange things; and then I almost did it anyway. And then it occurred to me you wouldn't want me to call you—you know, in your home territory, sort of." I briefly considered whether to tell him that Walter remembered him, had even suggested that I call. And decided against it because he was reacting strangely to everything—had I not known him better, I told myself, I would almost have thought he was a little jealous.

He stared at me intently for a while. He looked almost as though he were trying to decide whether I was telling him the unvarnished truth, but the truth was that it wouldn't have occurred to me to lie. I had no idea as yet that I had reason to lie to him.

"Did you have a good time?" he finally asked, his manner dry.

"No," I said. "He's a terrible old man. I hated him."

He kept staring down at me, motionless, his mind seeming thousands of miles away. I played with the hair on his arm, gently tried to pull him down beside me, but still he didn't move or speak.

"What is it, David?" I asked.

And then, suddenly, he was all over me, kissing me with a violence that was not new to us so much as it was very old, feeling my body like a blind man making a last desperate attempt at Braille, tugging at my clothes with a wild unconcern that forced me to remind him that I would have to put them on again in a little while, thrusting himself into me before I was ready, but quickly communicating his passion to me, carrying me away with him so that by a moment later I, too, had forgotten everything in the world outside.

It wasn't until a week or so after the time when it could have occurred to me, that I first suspected I was pregnant. It was September, and we were back in the city. From the moment I thought of it, I knew it was true. And I remember with a ghastly clarity the very next thought I had:

Thank God I've been sleeping with Walter. He can't know.

My feelings about the baby itself changed from day to day, largely according to my current estimate of how David would feel about it. There were times I was afraid he would be angry with me; at such times I would take the stand in my own defense to remind me that I'd told him I didn't have my diaphragm. (Q.—And what about the next day, and the last one? A.—offered lamely—I know it sounds silly, but it didn't seem to pay to bother, somehow, after the first time. I just sort of forgot about it.) There were other times when I knew quite surely that with all the difficulties involved, some part of him would have to exult in the news, be proud that I'd conceived his child, even if his wife had failed to do so. Then I would chide myself for being smug. Remind myself that it was only his relation to me that kept David from talking about his daughter; people who adopted children were traditionally more, not less, loving than natural parents. Tell myself that it ill became me to compare myself to a girl I didn't know whose particular misfortune it was that for reasons unknown to me she was unable to bear children. None of which admonitions to myself worked for a moment. After all, I had been jealous of David's wife from the moment Thea told me he had one. It would have been quite beyond me not to revel in the fact that I instead of she had become pregnant by him.

I didn't tell Walter until I was in my third month. I'd assumed he would be pleased with the news that I was pregnant, as he had always been in the past. An assumption fortified by his growing closeness to the children. Things had changed between them, too, in the months of our peacefulness. In the past, Walter had wanted me to have children, and care for them, and bring them to him, scrubbed and polished, to be held on his knee for a few minutes before the dinner hour, particularly when there was company. It had been the idea not the fact of being a father that appealed to him. While I had enjoyed being a mother far more than I'd enjoyed being a wife, and thus added to the distance between Walter and the children. It was only in recent months that he had come to welcome their confidences; that he willingly gave them advice when they requested it; that he occasionally took them places without me; that he had volunteered to see Andy's and Philip's teachers at conference time in late spring, and to be an assisting parent when Susan's nursery-school class took a trip to the Central Park Zoo.

Yet his reaction was not of unmixed pleasure but of quiet apprehension.

"What's the matter, Walter?" I asked. "You don't seem pleased."

"I don't know," he said. He seemed upset—even confused—by his own reaction. "I think it's . . . I'm afraid . . . I'm fifty-two years old, Ruth."

I nodded.

"Doesn't that seem old to you? To be the father of an infant, I mean?"

"You seem younger to me now," I said truthfully, "than you did ten years ago."

He smiled. "Well, that's very pleasant to hear, of course. But if you don't mind my saying so, dear, it's partly because you're older. You're not a young girl any longer. You're a young woman. And there's a great difference there, you know, in vantage point."

"Maybe," I said. "But it's not *just* that." I kissed his cheek. "You're aging very well, Walter. Really. I guess practically everyone does these days, as a matter of fact. Being in the fifties isn't the way it used to be; it's more like being in the early forties was in the old days."

Again the troubled smile. Not disbelieving me specifically. Almost as though he knew. No, that wasn't it. If he knew, there would have to be some suggestion of repressed wrath, of anguish at betrayal. It was more as though he *almost* knew, but not quite. As though he were mentally casting about to find what it was that really troubled him about my having a fourth child at a time when he'd finally come to genuinely enjoy the other three.

"Not only that," I said, "but I think you're a better father than you used to be."

He was silent.

"I'm sorry, Walter. I'm truly sorry. I wish I'd known."

He patted my hands absently. "I should be the one to apologize, Ruth," he said. "I shouldn't be troubling you with these foolish worries of mine. I'm sure I'll get used to the idea."

David didn't come in again until the end of November, when I was entering my fourth month. I was still taking a morning nap during that time and I was asleep when he called, so that I was startled despite the fact that for over a month I'd been anxiously waiting for him, half-expecting to hear his voice each time the phone rang.

"How're you fixed for time, kid?" he asked.

"I've got the whole day," I said. "Susie's in school until two. I don't even have to be here when she gets back, because Esther'll be."

"Good," he said. "That makes two of us. Why don't you trot right down here?"

He sounded unusually buoyant and I assumed his mood was a result of the day's freedom. Catching his excitement, I showered quickly and put on one of my prettiest dresses, a flowered-wool shift that wasn't maternity but left room for my expanding waistline and my belly, which was just beginning to conspicuously swell. My hair was a little longer than I usually permitted it to be—it curled down my neck and caught in the back hook of my dress, until it was closed. I wore a red-wool coat although it was cold for early winter—I hadn't even taken my furs out of storage, anticipating the warmth that always came with pregnancy.

"Hiya, Gorgeous," David said when he opened the door for me. He grabbed me exuberantly and gave me a big loud kiss, helped me off with my coat, spun me around, held me at arm's length and said, "Hey! You really *are* gorgeous!"

I felt my cheeks flush.

"Jesus Christ," he said delightedly. "You're blushing, Ruthie. I never saw you blush before."

I felt confused, happy, and—absurdly—embarrassed. He sat down on the bed and pulled me down on his lap.

"Now," he said, "what's going on? What have you done to yourself? Why do you look so different?"

I smiled. "Why are you *acting* so different?"

"Who, me? I'm feeling good, that's all. Can't I feel good if I feel like feeling good?"

"Of course."

"Anyway, you're changing the subject."

"My hair's a little longer than usual."

"Very nice. But that's not it. Wait a minute. You had a nose job." He felt my nose, considered. "No, that's not it. The bump's still there."

"Oh, David," I protested helplessly, laughing, putting my arms around his neck.

"Say that again," he demanded.

"Say what?" I asked into his neck.

"Say, *Oh, David,* the way you just said it."

"I can't. You made me self-conscious."

"I made you self-conscious," he repeated softly. "I made you self-conscious."

I kissed his neck and his arms tightened around me.

"I'm pregnant," I whispered. "From you. From the summer."

His whole body tightened around me then, so that I could barely breathe; nor did I want to, any more than I could have thought of breathing during an orgasm. When his grip finally loosened it was as though we were breaking away after sex. Gently he transferred me from his lap to the bed, made sure my head was on the pillow. Then he put his hand on my belly and, unsmiling, began to rub it in a slow circular movement.

"You can't feel anything yet," I said contentedly. "In another month or two you can feel it moving."

"You feel okay?"

"I always feel wonderful." It was a subtle form of boasting. I wondered if he knew that.

"August," he said. "What's nine months from August?"

"May. I'm due around the end of May."

"I wish I'd known sooner." Still massaging my belly rhythmically.

"I know. But it's not as if there was something to do."

His hand stopped moving. It rested on my belly, motionless, for a moment. Then, abruptly, he stood up and walked away from me. I watched him anxiously, wondering whether he was surprised that I was asking nothing of him. He lit a cigarette, leaned against the dresser, inhaled deeply, blew a set of smoke rings and carefully traced their evolution and disappearance.

"The reason I haven't been in until now," he said slowly, "is that Sara was in Nevada getting a divorce, and I didn't want to tell you about it until it was final."

"Sara," I said. He'd never mentioned his wife by name; I'd assumed it was out of a half-logical, half-mystical desire to keep me out of that part of his life. Something sacred. "You never told me her name."

"My plan was just to tell you about the divorce," he went on, ignoring this irrelevancy. "To let you know I was free. Make it clear that I didn't expect anything from you. That I didn't get my divorce on the simple assumption that you'd pop into court and do the same."

My mind, which until that moment had been occupied with the registration of his words, began to comprehend what he was telling me. I sat up.

"What are you saying, David? Are you saying you want to marry me? Did you get this divorce because of me?"

"Yes and no. It's something I should have done even if I never saw you again. I don't know whether I would have or not."

"You don't love your wife?"

"What the hell do you think I've been breaking my neck to get away for? Love of my wife?"

I felt my cheeks flush. "I thought you had to come in for business."

He said nothing.

"And then I thought . . . sex. In the old days . . . well, there was always sex between the two of us . . . even if you . . . even without love."

"In the old days," he said, "I had a clearer idea of where sex ended and love began." He smiled wryly. "Old age has tended to blur the distinction."

"What about your daughter?" I asked after a moment.

"What about her?"

"It must be hard for you to leave her."

"As a matter of fact," he said, "it isn't." Again the wry smile. "I'm sorry to disappoint you."

"I'm not disappointed. I'm surprised."

He shrugged. "It's not really so surprising. I married the kind of girl I wanted to marry. A nice, pretty, intelligent, genteel kind of a girl. I thought I loved her just enough to marry her. I never gave any great thought to having kids. It wouldn't have particularly bothered me if we didn't have them. But Sara . . . women seem to have the idea they don't exist unless they have children."

I felt a momentary pang of sympathy for Sara, who loved David and couldn't have children.

"I didn't want to adopt a child. I don't mean that I was indifferent to the idea. I was repelled by it. By the idea of pretending someone else's kid was my own. I brushed her off the first time she raised the question, wouldn't even talk about it. She didn't argue with me. She waited —like the nice, smart girl that she is—and six months later she still hadn't conceived and she brought it up again. And again. And finally I gave in. So we applied for a kid and I said the right things; and it took a while, because we had to go through an agency that handled mixed-marriage kids because Sara wasn't certifiably Jewish—her mother's Protestant. Then we got Sally. She was four months old. A couple of days after we got her she developed something that looked like severe diarrhea and turned out to be celiac. You know what that is?"

"I've heard of it. One of the children in Susan's nursery had it. He came to her birthday party but he couldn't touch any of the food."

"We were lucky. It was a fairly mild case. It was gone before she was three and even while it lasted it wasn't severe, as these things go."

"Still," I said, "it can be pretty difficult."

A fleeting smile. "I can tell from the way you said that I must sound full of self-pity. If I am, I have no right to be. Sara left me as free as was humanly possible. She wasn't always palming the kid off on me, pulling this bit some of her friends pulled—waiting until I got home to do the shopping and other stuff. She never tried to turn me into a baby sitter. She had a maid clean once a week and if she had things to do that she couldn't do with Sally, she did them that day. She's crazy about the kid, about being a mother. She doesn't complain—she never complained if I was late at the office, or if I went out to have a drink at night with a buddy, or when I went swimming a couple of nights a week at the club. Even at times when she was having a rough time with the kid. Actually, she never considered that she was having a rough time. Sally's a pretty agreeable kid, they get along better than most of the mothers and daughters I've seen—not that I make a hobby out of observing these things. But they're pretty much like pals, most of the time." He paused, looked around the room restlessly, ran the fingers of one hand through his hair, stared at some place far beyond me. "Two well-dressed, well-mannered, blue-eyed pals. When they come to visit me they both wear white gloves. When I go to visit them . . . I don't feel any further away from them when I'm here than I do when I'm there, sitting in her living room."

He was finished. He lit another cigarette, inhaled deeply a couple of times, put it down on the ashtray.

"David," I said, "I love you so much."

"That's not the question at this point," he said. "The question is whether you're willing to do something about it."

"I'm a little overwhelmed. It's hard for me to sort out things in my head."

"Tell me something, Ruth." A change in his manner. He became a bit lawyerish now. Efficient. Supervisory. "Would you say Walter has any suspicion at all about the two of us?"

"No," I said slowly, "I don't think so. Things have been too— He knows about the once-upon-a-time of it. He told me a few months ago . . ." *He told me he was nearly destroyed by the sight of us together.* "You remember Thea's wedding, how we—he was very upset when he saw the two of us together. He said he real——"

"Does he know about the baby?" He cut me off, uninterested in the details of Walter's unhappiness. "Not that it's mine, I mean, but that you're pregnant?"

Reflexively I touched my stomach. "Yes, of course. I had to tell him. I mean, it never occurred to me *not* to tell him."

"That's going to make it harder. Damn it." Forgetting the cigarette in the ashtray and lighting another. "Damn it, I wish you'd told me first."

"You mean because he'll want the baby? Because I'll have to tell him it's not his?"

"It's not just a question of the baby, Ruth. Don't you think it's much more likely this way that he'll fight you for *all* the children?"

"Oh, no!" It was an automatic response, not even to his question but to the fact of its being asked. A protest against consideration of the *possibility* that the children could be taken from me. I looked around me. I was standing, although I didn't remember the act of having gotten off the bed. I looked at David. He was watching me. Very carefully. As though I were some kind of specimen. Or an exhibit at one of his trials.

"Why are you looking at me like that?"

"I'm trying to see what's going on in your head."

"What's going on in my head," I said excitedly. "Do you know what you're talking about when you talk about a custody fight? That's what's going on in my head. How many custody fights have you seen in your little Marin County paradise?"

"We've had a couple in the office," he said calmly. "They're ugly."

"Ugly!" I cried. "Ugly isn't the word for it! They're unbelievably horrible, ghastly messes! They reduce everyone in them to a common denominator, and you know what it is? Shit! That's what! Shit! It's a terrible horrible shitty mess and no one ever recovers from it! Not the parents, not the kids, not anyone!"

He stood motionless, his arms crossed in front of him. For a moment I wanted to strike out at him—do anything to get a visible response—but then that feeling passed, leaving me subdued but still resentful.

"You're just staring at me. Why don't you say something?"

"What do you expect me to say, Ruth? Do you really think you're telling me something I don't know? Given that you're being a little melodramatic, making it worse than it is—if that's possible—basically what you say is true. If you and he fight for the kids, it could be a messy business."

I sat down again. "I don't even know how I'd tell Walter," I said after a while. "Things aren't the way they used to be, you know. They're better. Maybe that sounds funny to you, but . . . Walter's different. He's *nicer*. We're both nicer, I guess. He's much better with the kids than he used to be. Much closer to them. That's one of the reasons it would be so— He still doesn't like to be the one to discipline them; but before, he didn't want any of the responsibility at all; once they were born he was sort of through with them, except that they were showpieces, proof of something. I don't know what. Not virility, that's for damn sure. He's never been much in bed." *Almost never. There was a week when we came close.* "I used to hold it against him very strongly, the way he was with the kids—even Boris, from the time we were married. He'd been so attached to Boris, and then he got terribly unsympathetic. Disapproving, but in a vague, disinterested kind of way. Do you know what I mean? Remote. As though he—"

I don't feel any further away from them when I'm here than I do when I'm there, sitting in her living room.

I cringed at the memory of David's words. He caught the motion and he tilted his head slightly.

"What is it?"

"Nothing."

"That's a ridiculous thing to say. It was almost as though something struck you physically."

I smiled. "It would be a very great strain to be married to someone who can read my mind."

"Has it been so easy being married to someone who can't?"

"All right, David. I was wondering whether you'd feel the same way if we were married and we had the baby together. Feel the same way as you did with your wife and daughter. The way you described it—it's not so different from the way Walter used to be. Maybe neither of you really likes children."

"Maybe neither of us ever felt as if the kids were his own kids. For different reasons."

"Maybe."

"And maybe it's worth taking a chance, because we'd be together. And whatever else is open to question, it's damned well certain it hasn't worked out, our being apart."

"What if we stopped loving each other?" I asked suddenly. "Us, I mean. Forget about the baby. I'd die if you stopped loving me. Not that you've ever told me you did."

"All this," he said, his gaze level, his tone still reasonably calm, "is bullshit, Ruth. You're bullshitting me again. And yourself. Creating all kinds of imaginary obstacles to cover up—"

"That's not true!" Self-righteousness propelled me to my feet. "I'm not! I'm just trying to anticipate—"

"Anticipate, bullshit!" he shouted. "Complaining that I never said I loved you, when I'm ready to turn my life inside out so I can marry you."

It stopped me for a moment, but then I said, "I don't see where you're turning your life inside out." Thinking I must be right because I sounded so reasonable. "It's not as though you gave up something you loved when you gave up your wife and daughter."

"Well, I happen," he said, his voice still raised, "to have given up a hell of a lot of dough I haven't even made yet in the bargain. And furthermore—" he began, but saw that I was startled and quieted down. He smiled at me bleakly. "You see? You don't have to waste your time making up difficulties. There are real ones you haven't even thought of yet."

"You mean money," I said dully.

"I mean money."

"That wouldn't stop me by itself."

"I make fifteen thousand a year, Ruth. Sara's getting a hundred and twenty-five a week from me. That leaves a hundred and seventy-five. If Sara remarries—and there's no reason to believe she'll do that very soon;

as a matter of fact, she swears she's not going to at all, but I'm allowing for a change of mind because I'm basically an optimist—then the payments will be reduced by more than half, but there'll always be the money for Sally, always for the next fifteen years or so. As far as your end is concerned, you obviously wouldn't get alimony. Assuming for the moment that you got custody of the children, it's reasonable to suppose that you'd be able to get generous support payments for them, too."

"You say it so casually. *Assuming for the moment . . .*"

"That's tough. I'm sorry if you don't like the way I express myself. I'm not concerned with being delicate, I'm concerned with showing you what's involved."

I nodded. "A hundred and seventy-five a week plus whatever I could get for the children. That's about what teachers make these days, isn't it?" Despising myself for dwelling even briefly on money, yet knowing it was futile to pretend it didn't concern me at all.

"In that range. Some a little more, I suppose. Some less."

"Can you live on that these days?"

He smiled. "I imagine that if you looked around hard enough you could find someone living on even less."

"Don't make fun of me, David." My lips trembled; suddenly I was steeped in self-pity and fighting tears. He sat down on the bed and beckoned me over to him, but I didn't want to go. I was afraid he would make me forget the realities I needed to remember and reckon with. The course he wanted me to take was fraught with danger and with him, in bed, I would forget the danger and remember only how much I wanted him. Insistently he patted the bed next to where he was sitting. I went to it with some reluctance, but he pulled me down on his lap instead, and I snuffled on his shoulder.

"It's what goes by the name of Real Life," he said into my ear. "You work, you eat, you screw, on Saturday night you go to the movies. You keep wishing for your husband's first wife to drop dead or remarry so he can stop paying alimony. When she does, you find you're as broke as ever. Now that first wife's out of the way you fight with him a little more because his salary doesn't seem like as much as you thought it would. You make up in bed and he gets a raise and then you fight again and you fuck again."

I looked at him through blurry eyes, resentful of his conjuring.

"You make it sound like a game. Like fun. The people I've seen who live that way don't have so much fun."

"They're not us," he said. "*We* have fun."

I got up from his lap although he tried to keep me there.

"Do you know what it would do to Walter, David? It would kill him if it happened now."

"People don't die that way, Ruthie. It would hurt him very badly. Like living with him for the next twenty or thirty years would hurt you."

People don't die that way. But Walter had long ago died from less than what I was considering doing to him now. Walter had died once with the knowledge that I didn't really want or need him. It was a thought I'd had so many times that year—that no matter how strong his will, Walter could not have flourished on what I had offered him. I pushed away the thought now; it added a new and difficult dimension to my conflict.

"If only I could tell him in some way that wouldn't make him angry. Wouldn't want to get back at me."

He shrugged. "I'm not sure it'd be possible. Nothing would change the fact of what you've done and what you want to do. If you kick a guy in the nuts because your foot needs exercise, how much good'll it do if you explain it's nothing personal?"

I turned to look at him again. "What you're really telling me is that you're just as sure as I am that he'll fight me for the children."

"I suppose I am."

"What are the chances he would win?"

"It's impossible to say. The mother almost invariably gets custody. On the other hand, a good lawyer could make out a pretty strong case against you."

"As a mother?"

"As a wife—and by inference as someone who's not morally fit to raise children. Figure it out. Poor girl marries rich guy much older than she is. Pregnant by childhood boyfriend. Any smart lawyer would have a detective agency check back for evidence that we'd carried on without substantial interruption for the whole time of your married life."

"No."

"It's a distinct possibility. And it's also a distinct possibility that he'd be able to collect enough scraps from the times we *have* been together to make anyone believe that the rest of the time we'd just been too smart to leave tracks."

Feelings of futility and nausea engulfed me.

"Why are you telling me all this stuff?" I moaned. "It's as though you don't really want me to do it."

"Nonsense. You're trying to put me in the position of lying to you. I won't. Aside from any other reason, if I don't think of the worst now you'll only think of it yourself, later."

David. I need you so much, David. There's no one else I can't lie to.

"All right, then." Trying to be steady and sensible. "They might make me out to be a whore, and if they do, Walter might get the children. Where does that leave us?"

"It leaves us together, with one child and generous visiting rights. And the decent prospect that Walter would remarry and there'd be a mother for the children. Or even that in a year or two you could get them back, especially if they seemed to be reacting adversely."

"Oh, my God!" I cried. "Do you know what you're saying?"

"I'm saying that life is hard, Ruthie. I'm saying there are times when you get something without giving up something else, but this may not be one of them. My own opinion is that the kids won't be that much worse off if you fight and lose than they'll be if you don't fight at all. Because if you don't fight, you're going to hold it against them for the rest of your life that you didn't." He hesitated, seemed to be making up his mind about saying something. "I'll also tell you this. I'm willing to move to New York—whether we get custody or not. I've already made inquiries and there're a couple of good places open for me here if I want them. The salaries are a little better than I'm making but I think it costs more to live here, especially if we lived where your kids could go to the same schools, so it would be about the same thing. And that way there wouldn't be such an upheaval involved for the kids. No school transfer, even if you got custody; and if you didn't, you'd be close enough to see them very often."

"You're very sweet."

"I'm not sweet." Impatiently. "I'm trying to get what I want."

"You don't really want my children."

"Not as much as I want their mother. I don't even know them. It'd be a little ridiculous for me to go swearing that I'd learn to love them, even if I think I will. Even if I think I would have loved Sally, adopted or not, if I'd ever been in love with her mother."

We were silent. Everything he'd said whirled around in my brain together with the things I'd left unsaid. I was terrified at the prospect of doing what he wanted me to—nor could I contemplate the alternative.

"David, you said before you *want* me to get a divorce, but you don't necessarily *expect* me to."

His smile was grim. "The mood is right but the tense is wrong. I said that was what I'd been *planning* to tell you. Before I knew you had something of mine."

"Now you expect me to."

"That's right."

"When do I have to decide?"

"Now."

"Now!"

"That's right."

"But why, David?" An anguished cry. "How can it make any difference if you give me a day or two?"

"That's exactly the point. I don't think it'll make any difference at all. So I'm sparing both of us a lot of agonizing."

"What will you do if I can't do it, David?"

"None of your business. Nothing I do'll be any of your business. Ever."

I looked at him helplessly. "I'm afraid."

"Of what?"

"Of everything. I'm afraid of not getting the children. I'm afraid of your not loving them if we do get them. I'm afraid you'll stop loving me. I'm afraid of not having enough money. I'm afraid—"

"All right, all right. I get it. You're afraid."

I hung my head, shamefaced. Like a kindergarten child who's just confessed to wet pants.

"Do it anyway, Ruth. Plenty of people do things they're afraid of." He came over to me and put his arms around me and stroked my hair, kissing the top of my head, gently massaging the back of my neck. "You won't be alone, you know. I'll be there, doing a lot of it for you. I'll help you explain. The kids aren't so young you can't explain anything."

"They might insist on being with me. I mean they might tell Walter they wanted to, and then maybe he'd . . ."

"They might. He might."

And then he might die. If no one of us wanted him, he'd die. The best I could hope for would be the thing that would hurt him most terribly.

"I can't." A petrified whisper. His body stiffened, almost convulsively, and then he let go of me, kissed my forehead lightly, pushed me away. "David." A plea, but for what? "David, please . . ."

"Go home, Ruthie." He turned his back to me. A terror greater than any I'd felt before engulfed me. I had lain down to rest in a coffin and he was sealing the lid.

"How can I leave here like this?"

"What do you want, Ruth? A consolation prize? It's at home."

I put on my coat, picked up my bag, dropped it, picked it up again. *It's not too late. You can change your mind now. It won't be over until you leave here.*

But what was the point? I couldn't tell him that I was willing to lose the children; I could only ask for a respite he wouldn't give me.

I said, "I love you, David."

He said, "You know what you can do with it, Ruth."

And I left.

CHAPTER TWELVE

For a time I could not believe in the future seriously enough to think I might have to plan for it. When I tried to think of what I would do after the baby's birth I invariably thought of death, yet I thought of it not as a punishment but as an escape from whatever it was that I would otherwise need to do. Then, at the end of my fifth month, as I began to feel the baby's movements inside of me, I could see that eventually I would have to do something. People don't die simply because they do not know what to do next, any more than they die because their wives leave them. Since I am going to live, it will be necessary to find the best possible way to go on. Still, it will be very difficult.

I've become friendly with a girl I got to know in the park. I noticed her first because she played with her children as though there were fun in it for her as well as for them, and I was therefore doubly surprised to discover that she was not their mother but their governess. Maria. She is Dutch. Born and orphaned during the last year of the War, she was raised by English cousins and came here at seventeen under a contract to care for the new-born girl who is now five and the oldest of three children who call Maria their mother and address their mother by her first name. A state of affairs their mother finds distressing but which she has thus far been powerless to change. Maria has become so attached to the children, the oldest one in particular, that she is unable to decide what she would do if their mother were ever to make good her oft-repeated threat to stop working and care for the children herself. It is the obvious bond between us. We sit in the park and talk long past the time when the other mothers have gone home. She expects that some day she will return to England. Occasionally one of us says that it would be nice if we could somehow arrange to take a trip there to-gether, perhaps with the children, or Maria could even accompany Walter and the children and me. A silly idea, perhaps, but some sort of daydream seems to be necessary, and my actions have made my old fan-tasies ludicrous.

Walter is often home by the time we get back. For a long time I could not bear the sight of him. It was far worse than in the old days, when I'd been able to easily hate and casually despise him. He'd been an alien object to me then—remote, refined, Anglo-Saxon, devoid of strong feeling, able to smolder at best, never to burn. In those days I'd looked at David and seen myself; now I saw myself in Walter and I could not bear the sight.

Often I went to bed immediately after dinner. Occasionally I went to a movie, either with Walter or with Maria. On the rare evenings that I spent with Walter in the living room, reading or watching television, I avoided conversation, but would find myself gazing at him surrep-titiously. I was embarrassed if he caught me then because I was unable to return his smile. What I was trying to do was to gather strength in myself to hate him again. I had the feeling that if I could hate him I would once again know who I was. I would mentally list my grievances against him, but they turned out to be as much about what I had with-held from him as about what he had not given me. I would catalogue his faults but then recognize them as the various disguises of fear, and I knew as well as he what it was to be dominated by fear.

Naturally Walter was confused by the change in me, by the lengthy depression whose grip I could not break because I could summon nei-ther love nor hatred to fill the void that it would leave. He wasn't happy either, of course. In the old days he'd retreated into himself when he was sad but now he seemed to rely increasingly on the chil-dren to divert him. Which was just as well, because during that time I had nothing to offer them. Susan was wetting her bed every night. I knew that if I had divorced Walter and she was with him—or even if she'd been living with me—I would have assumed she was wetting again because she'd been upset by the divorce. Instead she was wetting her bed and I was married to Walter. Andrea was subdued at home—perhaps reflecting my own depression—but difficult and rebellious in school. David would have known what I should do about her but Walter was reluctant to take any disciplinary action, and how could I blame him? Years before I'd convinced him with my monumental self-assurance that he didn't know what was best for the children. Of the three only Philip seemed relatively serene and perhaps he would have been serene in any event. If not, David and I could have handled him; David, after all, was the one I used to go to for help with my brother, and Philip is nowhere near as difficult a person as Martin was. The only indication he gave of being remotely aware of my condition was that occasionally, as I sat staring into space, he would ask what I was thinking, and when I said that I wasn't thinking of anything at all, he would hesitate for a moment and then run off to play.

I couldn't even feel guilty at my withdrawal from all of them. The relief of death, after all, involves the absence of guilt, and I was not convinced I was alive.

Then one night at the end of my fifth month, Walter, Andy and I were sitting in the living room, Philip and Susan having gone to bed, Walter having finally decided to talk to Andy on the subject of her behavior at school. I was stretched out listlessly on the sofa, as he sat in his armchair with Andy perched on one of its arms, listening to him a little more patiently than she sometimes did. I observed in a remote way that the two of them, slim and handsome in such different ways, made a rather pleasant picture. Andy began to explain earnestly that it wasn't that in the morning she made *plans* to be fresh to the teacher, it just always turned *out* that way, and as I watched them I felt the first distinct kick inside my belly and it excited me, and I said without thinking, "Sssh, the baby!"

Andy stood up abruptly and flounced out of the room to show her displeasure at being interrupted. Walter smiled at me fondly, came over and sat on the edge of the sofa and put his hand on the mound of me. I was pleased by the kicks but I felt guilty at having interrupted him and Andrea in one of their rare moments of communion. And guilty that the baby whose kicks he could not yet quite feel was not his. And then a momentary peacefulness came over me; it was the first time since I'd left David that I had a sense of the baby as a living force inside of me and, by extension, the sense of myself as the living creature that sheltered and nourished it.

In the weeks that followed I felt the pain of losing David more keenly than I had before. It was as though I had fallen from a very high place and had lain immobile for weeks, not dead but not able to get up, either. Now, as I moved, I fully felt my bruises for the first time, could begin to understand the difficulties ahead. But I understood, too, that for all the danger and all the pain, I must not lie down again.

Nine Months in the Life
of An Old Maid

For Dorothy Shapiro Perelman

The author wishes to express her appreciation to the Theodore Goodman Memorial Fund of The City College of New York for financial assistance received during the writing of this book.

Part One
JULY–OCTOBER

A nightmare is terrifying because it can never be undone. A piece of paper tore with an incredibly loud screeching noise. My eyes opened. Then what? If the paper had torn while I was awake I could have taped it but if the tearing of a dream paper tore me then I was torn forever. I could scream for my sister Mimi and she might or might not hear me and come in to find out what was wrong, and if she did come my fear might be somewhat allayed, but nothing she or anyone else said could ever make that piece of paper whole again because it had torn in a world where we were powerless.

While in the beautiful well-ordered lie of our everyday lives there was almost nothing we could not do. We commanded the flowers to grow and within the more or less predictable limitations of soil and weather, they obeyed our commands. We turned wool into rugs and sweaters, crab apples into jelly, wood into fire. We put screens on the windows and summer came; we replaced them with storm windows to permit the snow to fall. Our lives denied our nightmares, which was why I stayed awake for all but four or five hours each night.

I looked at my clock. It was just past four. The house was very quiet but outside the bluejays and grackles were already making their harsh daytime noises. I felt exhausted and I would willingly have gone back to sleep but the dream that had exhausted me had also left me full of vague fears that made sleep impossible. At five o'clock I opened the curtains and pulled my rug over to the window and then, in the gradually brightening morning light, I hooked woolen remnant strips into the rug canvas until I finally heard Mrs. Cushman walk through the hallway and go downstairs to make breakfast.

A while after breakfast I walked up to the road to get the mail. It was the very end of June and the last blooms had long since gone from the azaleas and rhododendron in the interior garden, but alongside the winding driveway the peonies and sweet william were in full bloom and the woodlands were shot through with orange daylilies, yellow butter-and-eggs and here and there a clump of violets or delicate white trillium.

The mailbox was full of flyers and business letters, at the bottom of which I found a postcard from Vincent saying that he would arrive the following week. I was delighted; Vincent always had exactly the opposite effect on me that he had on most people.

I walked back to the house and showed Mimi the card, which pictured a lighthouse on a beach at Cape Cod.

"Cape Cod," she groaned. "Only Vincent would spend a year in Europe and then go up to Cape Cod *before* he came here."

As though she were in a hurry for him to arrive. She hated his visits as much as I loved them.

"I wish he were here now," I said, thinking that Vincent might be able to drive out the evil spirit that had possessed me during the night. I sat down at the kitchen table. I was so tired by this time that I had a physical sense of coming apart. As though I were a piece of putty that might, if my brain couldn't get control of my body, spread out and spill over the chair seat.

Barney came down then. Barney, whose hair had been grey for years, always looked entirely grey in the morning.

"Vincent is coming," Mimi said.

"Mmm," Barney said. "Why don't you cry now and get it over with?"

"Ohhhhh." She poured his coffee and sat down again, a small roundish pink mass next to the lanky grey mass of her husband. What a picturesque trio—I slender and sallow to the point of yellowness.

"I'll never get anything done for as long as he's here," Mimi said. "I never do. No writing, no housework, nothing."

Not because Vincent interfered with her work but because his very presence threw her off balance.

"Why are you looking at me like that?" she asked. "You know he's impossible, Elizabeth. You know it's not me. Everyone is upset by that lunatic, everyone but you and Barney."

This was true. Most people were disturbed by the naked quality of Vincent's needs. He at once lusted for their understanding and bitterly disliked them for his dependency. He demanded comprehension with a violence that taxed people to close their minds for safety. We had in the attic the first letter Mimi had ever received from him. Written from Vincennes in 1943 when Vincent was eighteen and Mimi eleven, it begins without salutation: "I am your half brother. I suppose you know *that*." It was typical of Vincent that the letter neither reflected his age nor catered to hers. What Vincent had to say was said without regard for such trivialities. "I suppose I should ask you how my mother is but the truth of the matter is that if she can't even bother to tell me herself then I don't care."

Poor Vincent. If she had troubled to write him she would not have been Lily. Lily wanted us, her three children, to be her three friends—but never friends in need. We were to be gay pals. She didn't hold it against Vincent that she'd abandoned him and his father to run away with Josh. Why did he have to refer to all that unpleasantness when he wrote to her? Why couldn't he just tell her about school, send news of people she knew in Vincennes, instead of begging her for snapshots of herself and describing how he and his father split the housework between them? Lily. Lily the chair without arms. Mimi and I had survived Lily's friendship more easily, Mimi because she was herself and I because I had Mimi, who was five years old when I was born and already sure of the way things were done.

"My father was called back into active service after Pearl Harbor," Vincent wrote. "I just finished high school here in Vincennes, living with my father's father, and now I've been drafted, which is okay. Soon I'll be shipped someplace, I don't know where. I need someone to write to who'll always be in the same place, not moving around like my father and me. If I write to you will you save the letters and answer them, not all of them but enough so I know you're still in the same place? There's no time to waste so let me know right away. Vincent."

There was never time to waste, even now, so many years later. Always there was that urgency. To talk to someone. To find out something. For Barney and me Vincent's visits were pleasant diversions from our own inwardness but for Mimi it was maddening to have in the house someone who very nearly bristled with need yet would take nothing from her, who only needed to give.

"I feel like getting out and doing something," Mimi said. "You want to go to a movie, Barn, or go have a drink with someone?"

"All I want is another cup of coffee," said Barney, whose mood was apparently uncompromisingly sour.

"You know what I mean," she said, giving him the coffee. "I mean tonight. What do you think?"

"I think that you're confronting me with major decisions when I haven't even had two cups of coffee."

Barney of course detested making decisions at any time of day, not just in the morning.

But they did take a drive to have drinks with friends, and Barney got even more drunk than usual so that he couldn't drive, and Mimi drove home, or nearly drove home, because at the point where she was to turn off Sugar Hill Road and onto our drive she instead ran the car into the culvert that runs beside the road and under our drive where they meet. They had to leave the car there and walk to the house, where I was waiting for them, having tried to sleep but been frightened by a vision of a huge bald and bloody head suspended outside my bedroom window. Mimi called the garage right away but it was two in the morning and of course no one was there. They went upstairs in a marvelous mood, giggling like a couple of naughty children, leaving me sitting at the kitchen table feeling neglected and disgruntled, for I'd looked forward to chatting with them over tea when they came home.

I must have been sitting there for an hour or two, paralyzed by a fear of sleep and a lack of interest in doing anything else, when there was a knock at the kitchen door. I peered out through the top panes and standing there was a man—a tall blond prince out of some fairy tale. I opened the door on the foolish assumption that men who look like fairy-tale princes couldn't be dangerous.

"Hi," he said, "I'm sorry to bother you at this hour but I saw the light on. . . . I just smacked into a car up near the end of your drive."

I nodded. "My sister's car. She went off the road and it was too late to get the garage."

He smiled. "The trouble is, she didn't go all the way off. She's nearly halfway across it and without any lights on I didn't see it in the dark."

"Oh, God," I said, "I'm sorry. I don't think they realized."

We stood looking at each other, not knowing what to do.

"My name's Max Merganser," he finally said. "I live up the road about a mile."

I was startled. I knew almost no one outside of family friends since I seldom left our grounds—yet it was inconceivable that this particular person should live nearby without my knowing him. Silly.

"My name is Beth Cane," I said.

He nodded. "I know your brother . . . half brother."

"Vincent?" I was puzzled. Vincent had lived such a solitary life when he was with us after the war. "How do you know Vincent?"

"We met the first year he came to live here."

"How long have you lived in Welford?" I asked incredulously.

He smiled. "All my life. Except for the past few years. My father had Otto's, you know? The butcher shop in town?"

This too seemed incredible.

"He died a few years ago," Max Merganser said. "I've been living in L.A. but my mother died in April and I came back to fix up the house and sell it."

Suddenly I felt very foolish at keeping him standing there in the doorway.

"Would you like to come in?" I asked.

"Maybe for a few minutes, thanks," he said. "I guess there won't be anyone at the garage yet but I can try."

I put up some tea while he was ringing them without success.

"I left one of those lanterns on the back hood," he said. "But I guess it isn't that dark, anyway."

"I never even realized Vincent had friends in Welford," I said when we sat down. Thinking that Max must be at least ten years younger than Vincent.

"Oh, sure," Max said. "It was a whole bunch of us, although I guess I kept seeing him longer than the others. We weren't exactly friends at first, we were all still in high school when he came back from the Army and we thought he was pretty old and experienced."

There was only a few years' difference, then. Yet Vincent was nearly forty-two and Max looked like a boy.

Max smiled. "At first we couldn't make him out at all. We'd be walking home from school, you know, and he'd just sort of appear near us and get into an argument about the football game or something like that and then somewhere around here he'd disappear into the bushes. For a while we didn't even know he came from Ye Gods. . . ." He hesitated, uncertain whether he'd offended me. I smiled and he went on. "He'd make up these crazy stories if we asked him about himself. The only thing he told the truth about was the Army. He'd ask us all kinds of weird questions like how much sleep we got at night, if our mothers were good cooks, did we get bawled out when we didn't get good marks, things like that. At first we thought maybe he was some kind of crook wanting to blackmail our parents." Max laughed at the memory. "Then one day we saw him coming up the drive here and when we asked him if he lived here he said as long as he'd been caught he'd have to admit it, his mother worked in the big house and he lived in the gamekeeper's cottage. It was always like that, if he finally told you something about himself it turned out to be a joke or a lie, not a lie, really, because he didn't think for a minute that you'd believe it. I remember we couldn't get over it when we found out who he really was."

"Who was he really?"

Max blushed. "I mean, you know . . . that he was your brother."

"But you didn't know me." Fighting the realization that I was known by strangers. The crazy girl who stayed up on the hill.

Max shrugged. "I used to see your sister around once in a while. She was only a few years behind me in school. I knew . . . you know, it's a small town."

"I never thought about it," I said slowly. "Maybe you think it's stupid but it's true, anyway. I assumed if I wasn't interested in other people they wouldn't be interested in me."

He smiled at me in a friendly way.

"I'm not crazy," I said—perhaps more fiercely than I meant to. "I don't stay here because I *have* to, I stay because I *want* to. I'm happy here. Does that seem so crazy to you?"

"Nope," he said, "it seems fine to me. This is a beautiful place."

We were silent for a while. He said he'd better try the garage again but when he did, there was still no one there. We had tea and when he admitted to being hungry, I made him some bacon and eggs.

"It's a rough year for selling houses," Max said. "The mortgage market is very tight. I suppose you don't know about stuff like that."

I shook my head.

"Well, it's complicated. The part that matters to me right now is that people can't get money from the banks for buying old houses. It's a crazy old house, anyhow. It needs a lot of work. I'm doing a lot of it while I'm around. I'm a contractor. Know what that is?"

I said I guessed I did, it was like a builder, and he said that was right, that others made the plans and he executed them.

I smiled. "You execute old houses."

He thought that was funny but he was concerned that I not misunderstand—what he did actually gave old houses a new lease on life. I said I thought that was wonderful. He asked if I meant that and I said that I did.

"My folks were pretty upset about it," he said. "I mean that that was what I wanted to do. My mom, especially. She used to go wild every time she saw me fooling around with a couple of sticks of wood and some nails. As far back as I can remember I remember her telling me not to waste my time. She thought I ought to be a doctor or a lawyer or something like that." He grinned. "*Anything* like that."

"What does your house look like?" I asked.

"Oh, it's great looking from the outside," he said. "I mean, not like this place, it's not a mansion, but it's real pretty. Inside it's a little dark. One of the things I'm doing, I'm putting in a new kitchen and making a glass wall in the back."

I must have grimaced without knowing it.

"Don't look like that," he said. "It'll be beautiful. There's a stone wall in back of it, complete privacy. You'd love it."

I was doubtful.

"You'd have to see it," he said. "I'll tell you—" but then he stopped and I had to prompt him by asking what he'd tell me. "I was going to say I'd take you there and show it to you but I don't know if you . . . you probably wouldn't want to go."

"Yes I would," I surprised both of us by saying.

"Great," he said. "In a few days I'll come and get you. There's just a couple more things I want to do before anyone sees it."

A few minutes later he went up the drive to meet the men from the garage, who'd promised to be right up. Later that day he called to talk with Barney about insurance but since I never answer the phone, I didn't speak to him. I asked Mimi if she had ever known him and she said oh yes, of course she knew who he was. In school plays he'd always been the messenger of the gods, or the sweet young boy who got killed in the war, or something like that, because he was so beautiful that everyone loved him. At first he'd been a full four years ahead of her but then he'd been left back a year somewhere along the line so that she'd already finished her freshman year of high school when he graduated. She remembered that even then he used to insist on calling himself Max, his father's name, instead of the name his mother had given him—Marsden or Maximilian or something terribly unusual and elegant like that—and his mother had made a tremendous row at the school when she discovered he'd been permitted to list himself as Max in the yearbook.

Lily called from Beverly Hills to find out if we'd heard from Josh, which we hadn't, and to say she would be here in a couple of weeks. It wasn't like her to give that much notice; I thought she must be having some new private disaster. The departure of some young boy she could no longer afford; the death of some old man who for years had come

once a week to talk about the past. Bought as a sanctuary not for us but
for Josh and Lily, Yiytzo was little more than a prison in her eyes, or at
best a temporary refuge. Not that she didn't love the place, not that she
didn't think it was beautiful, not that she didn't think it was the most
marvelous place in the world. For children. Hollywood, in contrast, was
no place at all for children to grow up. We were taught this long before we could understand that Hollywood was on the West coast of the
United States while Welford Heights was three thousand miles away
in the East. It was the reason we didn't live with our parents. It was
necessary for Josh and Lily to be there most of the time but Hollywood
was no place for children to grow up. So we lived in the home Josh had
purchased in 1930 from the estate of a financier who'd been a Depression suicide. For the house and land together he had paid eight thousand dollars, a good portion of the money earned from his first (and
only) novel, *Our Blood, Their Tears,* a reasonably early drop in the
flood of anti-war novels between the two world wars which received a
sizeable advance and also was bought for serialization by the Hearst
chain.

They'd called the place *Yiytzo,* Russian for *the egg,* because it was to
be their world within a world. The use of Russian constituting a sort of
magical invocation for the good will of the Party penates who might
otherwise be displeased. A vow that if their tastes leaned toward the
North Shore their hearts were still full of the Soviet communion. Its
thirty-two acres took in the main house and guest cottage, set in two
formally landscaped acres near the north end of the property; a lengthy
winding drive leading to the house and then splitting off in back to the
cottage; a stable that could accommodate six horses and had a groom's
residence on the upper floor; several acres of riding paths cut through
otherwise uncontrolled foliage; elm, locust, birch, maple, oak and alder
trees whose bark was made invisible for a portion of each year by the
Virginia creeper and honeysuckle that twined their ways up every
available trunk and branch; thorny elderberry, blackberry and raspberry
bushes; billions of blades of chive, known to us as onion grass; thousands of seedlings of the large trees; monumental stumps long since
overgrown with prickly weeds and vines that made them impossible to
sit on; an occasional animal grave, its small headstone visible only in
the brief brown times before the first heavy snow of winter and after
the last; innumerable streams running into a large pond; and beyond
this the ten-acre dairy and vegetable farm run then by Mr. and Mrs.
Okada, later by Mr. and Mrs. Facciolo, who lived in the small red
farmhouse set between the barn and chicken coops and the planted

acres of the farm, and who still managed to supply us and themselves with fresh vegetables for five months out of every year and sell their overflow, along with their eggs, to other local people.

So Yiytzo was to be their world, Josh and Lily's, when the fund raising parties got too wild, the arguments too vicious, the justifications too arduous. To the extent that they had to venture into the outside world, Yiytzo would be their nourishment and their refuge.

Ironically, however, it had developed that whatever the place gave them in spiritual nourishment (a problematical question, anyway, in Lily's case) it more than took back in physical upkeep. While the house, for example, had stone interior walls a foot thick and exterior walls over two feet in depth, both of which tended to keep the heat out in the warm months and in during the winter, it also had ten rooms in which the ceilings ranged from twelve to twenty feet (in the living room) high, so that during the cold months it took an enormous amount of heat just to warm up the rooms in the first place. There was a staff of three, aside from the Okadas. They slept in the cottage and their salaries were low but nevertheless, they had to be paid regularly and in cash. Relatively little was required in the way of furniture, for Yiytzo had been sold them with most of its furnishings intact. But then there were the visitors. True, Josh had bought Yiytzo out of a yearning for peace and solitude, but how much peace and solitude could be tolerated by a couple who'd lived on Barrow Street in the middle of everything that was happening for several years and whose previous idea of a country outing had been a picnic lunch in Washington Square Park? Then, too, if in their one-room Barrow Street apartment they had felt unable to refuse a friend who needed a place to sleep for the night, just a blanket on the floor would be fine, how were they now to turn away the homeless artists, the itinerant anarchists, the unpaid organizers who flocked the fifty miles from Union Square to Welford Heights even before they knew the extent of Josh's good fortune or were certain they could count on what he later called his *gelt* guilt to make him their permanent host?

Josh's expenses being what they were, how could he have refused the offer to make a filmscript of *Our Blood* when it came? They didn't think of the move as being permanent. (I have read since that nobody did.) There was an absurd quality to the very thought of living permanently in a place like Hollywood. On the other hand, it was the bleak beginning of 1931 by this time and it would have been preposterous to thumb one's nose at the moguls of the West. Josh's book had been published a little over a year before and the reviews had been excellent but a combination of factors—greatly reduced book buying due to the Depression; a sudden glut of pacifist novels—had cut short its selling life. Lily was pregnant with a child she later claimed to have miscarried and their plan was to come back here for its birth, to stay for a few months and then to leave the child at Yiytzo while they finished out their Hollywood term. They could feel particularly easy about such an arrangement because Josh's parents were coming to live at Yiytzo. Josh's father, Hyman, had lost his job as a cutter a couple of months before when the cloak and suit house he'd worked for failed. Josh had talked about doing something for them; the job situation was hopeless and Hyman was getting old, anyway. Leah was a quiet person with nothing of the old country disciplinarian about her and there would be a nursemaid at first to fulfill the more arduous demands of a baby.

So Josh and Lily went to Hollywood forever, coming back often to Yiytzo, always the gay visitors who descended upon the household, sometimes with an entourage of their own, but always in either case being deluged with visitors when word got out that they were there; sometimes for a particular reason (Mimi's birth; Hyman's death; my birth; some mystical illness of Lily's which she could trust no Los Angeles doctor to treat; my four incarcerations in the madhouse), sometimes because from the vantage point of Hollywood they became convinced that at Yiytzo they could really get some rest. Sometimes they swore that it was because they couldn't stay away, they missed us so terribly. A new batch of snapshots or some clever remark of Mimi's transmitted by Leah, who wrote about us copiously (they kept her letters in looseleaf notebooks which were bound permanently when they became full, Josh and Lily's way of possessing our childhoods without living through them). In any event they had less of mine than of Mimi's because I didn't talk until I was four years old and after that I was seldom conspicuously clever—some such reminder would make them realize they hadn't seen us in months and then they would whirl into our lives like two Method actors cast in the role of parents, question Leah closely about our diets and tonsils, beg for hundreds of kisses and yearn verbosely for the day when they could afford to get out of the rat race and come back home where they belonged.

Now Lily would waft in on the three-thirty train and Mimi would pick her up at the station, carrying to and from the station wagon her numerous valises, transporting her to Yiytzo, and Lily, in a pink linen dress a bit too jaunty for a woman of sixty-one, high-heeled black patent pumps setting off legs that had lost some of their flesh but none of their shape, a net kerchief keeping her hair in place, would stand in front of the fireplace, raising her arms in a theatrical gesture that was meant to be all-embracing, and say with a voice that had stayed younger and more tremulous than the rest of her, "My God, it's good to be home! You have no idea how good it is to be home!"

"No," I'd say. "How is it, Lily?"

But Mimi, with a warning look in my direction, would put an arm around Lily, squeeze her affectionately, say, "Of course we do, love, and it's marvelous having you back."

Having her there was *unbearable*. I hadn't had a breakdown in many years but the times I felt closest to falling apart were the times when Lily was around; I didn't know how I would manage if my bad dreams and strange moods hadn't passed before she came. In the old days, no matter what the ostensible reason for their visit, she had spent most of her time with us in bed, being waited upon by Mimi and the others, visited by doctors as well as various friends who knew that if she had any illness at all, it wasn't something they would ever contract. Now stunningly healthy in the years when she had a right to occasional illness, she fluttered around the house until someone took her someplace for an appointment, hovering at the ends of our nerves, waiting for Josh, who for nearly fifteen years had refused to live with her. Needing to be there so that when Josh called Mimi would tell him not to bring one of his girls. Hoping to lure him back into her future through a nostalgic voyage to the past. To the twenties, to the thirties, the forties—the very beginning of the fifties, if need be, but never any closer than that to here and now. "Ah, Lil," Josh teased her, "it's your only departure from type—you'd rather revel in the past than bury your age."

He had never divorced her. Their marriage certificate lay in a yellowed envelope in the bottom drawer of the massive living-room desk where Mimi did the bills. It was hard for me to admit what was obviously true, that what the certificate symbolized still existed in part, that something was still there. They weren't woven through time to this or any place but parts of them were woven together into time. Nothing they said to each other was simple; they spoke a sign language perhaps more perfect than it had been when they were together and one or the other often chose not to understand. Single words had complex shared meanings. Lily's father had been a fireman in Vincennes and her first husband had been a fireman in Vincennes and the word fireman invariably set off smiles, jokes, reminiscences. Once during one of their reconciliations Josh had showed up at Yiytzo in a red sports car with ladders strapped to the sides. Names evoked places, years evoked events. 1926. Oh, yes, that was the year that twenty-six-year-old Josh Cohen had zigzagged through the United States, stopping in Vincennes overnight and at an all night diner introduced himself as Josh Cane to a pretty young waitress who turned out to have a husband who was a day-shift fireman and an eleven-month-old baby at home but who left Vincennes with him forever the next day anyway. Fireman, oh yes, did you ever hear the joke about the fireman who . . . remember the fire at the hotel in, when was it, thirty-eight . . . Mimi loved them to reminisce but for me their stories had the quality of a book someone reads you aloud while you are trying to concentrate on something of your own.

Not in my earliest memories do I remember missing them when they weren't around. Nor did I feel anxiety when they were about to leave after a visit. I never called them anything but Josh and Lily; I think that until I understood the biological meaning of parenthood I didn't believe they had any closer relation to us than the numerous adults, some nameless, others friendly to me, who lived in the guest cottage, coming and going independently of us. As a matter of fact, I think I may have preferred the others, for they did not invade the big house itself, and even as a child I had strong feelings about privacy and outsiders. I can remember quite distinctly (although Mimi swears it isn't possible as she swears many of my memories aren't because she has none of her own) the first time she brought a friend home from school. I'd only begun walking around the time of my second birthday but when school began for Mimi I would walk with Leah the length of the long driveway, arriving at twenty past three, when the school bus let off my sister at the entrance. It was a girl named Carol who came home with her that day; they were in second grade. Mimi put down her briefcase and picked me up and kissed me, as she always did, then said (she always talked to me in a normal way, understanding that I understood even if I never responded in words) that she wanted me to meet her friend.

"No!" I screamed at the top of my lungs, my first and last words until another two years had passed. My foot lashed out at Carol's shins and then I wiggled out of Mimi's arms and ran into the woods where I hid for so long that a good part of Carol's visiting time was used up in the effort to find me. And eleven years later when in her first year of college Mimi began to bring Barney home weekends my reaction was very much the same except that instead of shouting I sulked. And when she and Barney married early the next year and Barney came to

ive with us, it took me a year to regain some semblance of my usual
elf, a year or two more before I could accept his friendship, longer for
ne to really care about him.

Now I was occasionally eager to see who Mimi would bring home to
ne yet always some remnant of that early resentment persisted, some
eeling that an invasion, however pleasant, had occurred. There were
eople in the house who didn't belong there, even if I was happy to
ave them. When they left, both the house and I would return to our
ormal selves.

Vincent, on the other hand, could not exist without people around
im, people to declaim at, people to question, and when I try to imag-
ne him growing up in Vincennes, or Chicago or Los Angeles or any of
he various places that he and his father tried for very brief periods
fter Lily ran away with Josh, I cannot understand his surviving a time
when he was so isolated as to need to write to an eleven-year-old girl
vho was a stranger to him lest he have no one to write to at all.

After the war things changed, of course. Vincent lived with us for
hree years while he was writing his first novel, *Celebration's End*, a
ymn to the older forms of combat, which was published in 1949 when
e was twenty-four and had an immediate if limited success. The book
egan as a parody of Josh's pacifist novel, although all but one of the
ritics failed to see this, and that one an old political enemy of Josh's
who took great pleasure in praising Vincent at Josh's expense, a lengthy
iece called "Beyond Pacifism" the burden of which was that in Josh's
ook one felt a savagery undermining the ostensible plea for peace,
while *Celebration's End*, a *war* novel, was permeated with a love of
nan as he really was that belied its young author's surface bellicosity.
Stapled to the clipping of the article (Josh, like all of us, always kept
his records in the attic of Yiytzo, part of our shared feeling that what
was there was permanent) there was an index card with a copy of the
inswer Josh sent to the *Times*, which of course was never published:

> *In many a pacifist a warrior's heart*
> *'Neath many a nun's veil a manqué tart*
> *In many a soldier a peaceful part*
> *'Neath many a critic a fat old fart.*

But at the time of the book's publication we hadn't seen Vincent in
more than a year, for from the day he had come home from the war to
live with us, he and Mimi had proved totally incompatible, and once

the manuscript was finished and Vincent wasn't shutting himself away for the great portion of each day, the squabbles between the two of them—invariably provoked by him—had become frequent and increasingly bitter until finally Vincent had left and taken an apartment of his own in New York City.

I was eight when he came back at the end of the war; Mimi was thirteen and had been carrying on a steady correspondence with him since his first letter to her. It was I, not Mimi, who was apprehensive, for aside from my usual fears, the two of them had become tremendous friends through their letters, and although Mimi had tried to include me in their long-distance warmth—always detailing my activities as carefully as her own—Vincent had failed to display interest in even the barest facts of my existence and had even expressed his concern that no one should be permitted to get in the way of their intimacy.

Mimi's last letter to Vincent:

I've asked Lily and Josh if it's all right for you to stay with us when you return and Josh thinks it's a wonderful idea, Vincent. Beth and I have been embroidering pillowcases with your name on them. Beth is already better than I am at the chain stitch and the feather stitch although Mrs. Cushman says it is very unusual for a child of eight to be doing decent embroidery at all! I am so excited to be meeting my brother!!!

And Vincent's reply:

I don't think you know what I need. I need a bed and food—at least one meal a day—and I need to talk to you, not because I think you'll understand my ideas any more than you understand my needs but because I require a sympathetic presence and not necessarily a piercing intelligence. You are to be a sort of extension of myself. I have a lot of things to say. Some of them I've partly said in my letters although I don't expect you've understood them, only that you've saved them as I told you to. You don't understand me when I tell you that war is to men what sex was to the Puritans, the forbidden pleasure, but it doesn't matter, it only matters that you're there so I can tell it to you. If I said it to anyone here I'd get thrown in the hospital if I was lucky and the stockade if I wasn't. I hope your house is big with plenty of room where two people can get away and talk and not always be getting interrupted. I hope there's a decent bit of land outside where we can walk and talk. In Vincennes the house had two feet on each side of it so the old lady next door heard me when I talked to myself and told everyone I was crazy.

That was the entire letter. No word about when he would come, no suggestion that if he was aware of my presence at all I could be anything more than a hindrance to his work. He appeared at our front door on a cold grey November day and without saying hello to me when I opened the door, asked for Mimi. When I told him my sister was in school, he got something to eat from Mrs. Cushman, then went to sleep with instructions that Mimi should wake him instantly when she returned. My diary for that day reads:

Vincent has starey eyes and stiff hair. Mimi kissed him to wake him up and he sat up so fast he hit her she said she was sorry to friten him she couldn't wait to see him she was so exited and he asked her was she always like this and she cried and said she was not always like this. Mimi says Vincent does not like her. He tells her not to fuss over him she said she only wanted to make him happy he said nobody can so don't knock yourself out. She sent me out to look for him because he did not come to dinner. He asked me when does Lily come I said I don't care. He said why I don't care I said Mimi takes care of me and Mrs. Cushman. He asks me did I know if his father was a fireman and a very good man not like Josh. I said I didnt know that. He asks do I know what is war I tell him Josh wrote a movie about that he says Josh does not know anything about anything. Mrs. Cushman does not like how Vincent talks.

Mrs. Cushman didn't really like anything about Vincent, and doesn't yet. I remember Mimi's reassuring her, that first day, that she would come to like him. As she had reassured Mrs. Cushman on the day three years earlier when Josh and Lily had come East to attend Leah's funeral and hire a replacement for her, had found Mrs. C. and brought her to Yiytzo, and Mrs. Cushman, widowed during the first year of the war, had watched their car move up the long driveway as they headed back toward the airport, and burst into tears with the words, "I don't know if I can stand it here in the country."

"Oh, you'll love it here, Mrs. Cushman," Mimi promised, putting both arms around her. "I promise you will. We like you already, don't we, Beth?" And Mrs. Cushman believed her. As Josh believed her when just before leaving he had gone through the motions of feeling guilty about leaving his children in the care of a stranger they'd known for four days and Mimi said to him, "Oh, but we'll be all right, she's such a nice lady and it'll be an adventure and we'll be just fine, won't we, Beth!" (How many months later did I find the courage to ask Mimi where Leah was? She told me Leah had gone to live with the plants and the flowers.)

We always believed Mimi. All of us except Vincent, who went to the opposite extreme. "I will not die happy," he once said, "until I wring from your sister a confession that she hates my guts." And even with less than my total recall I would have to remember the fantastic scene that preceded his departure after his three-year stay with us, when Mimi was all of sixteen and I was eleven. Vincent chasing her around the living room, brandishing the bread knife at her, shouting, "Admit it, you little teenage whore, why don't you admit you hate me?" And Mimi sobbing, saying, "I don't hate you, Vincent, I feel sorry for you, I think you're very sick, but I don't hate you." And then Vincent calling her, as I wrote in my journal, a sanktamoneous little slut who didn't know the difference between love and hate, who was dead from the neck up and probably from the waist down, too, and Mimi stopping short, staring at him wildly, finally and utterly stupefied. She collapsed into a chair then, limp and drained, and sat in the chair for hours, unable to move or speak, which terrified me and made me angry with Vincent for the first time in all the three years, for we had become very close and I had from the beginning been Mimi's substitute as the passive recipient of Vincent's ideas. He left the following morning, his duffle bag over his right shoulder, the valise containing his manuscript in his left hand. I doubt he even knew yet where he was going. He just left, promising me I would hear from him, which I did, but not for almost two years, until his book had been published and well received and he had an advance on the next one in his pocket. And ever since his visits had been very much the same, with Vincent goading Mimi and Mimi making every effort to please him until finally he brought her to anger or tears.

Right after Vincent's card came, Mimi had begun having trouble with her new mystery. She was puzzled by this difficulty, for until the week before she'd been moving along very well, having written the first three chapters in the month of June alone.

"I can't understand it," she said. "Virginia's never deserted me so early in a book."

Virginia Bonnett, the cheerful, no-nonsense New England spinster who teaches Latin in Salem and is called in by the local police (when all else has failed) to solve the knotty crimes committed during the tourist season. While Josh still paid the basic expenses of Yiytzo, it was Virginia who had paid the rest of the bills for the past eight or nine years, Barney's teaching salary providing us with what he referred to as the petty cash, his scholarly essays providing us with satisfaction but of course no money at all.

"It has nothing to do with Vincent," Mimi said. "You can believe it or not, I haven't thought twice about Vincent. It's not that I'm upset, it's just that nothing comes when I sit down to work."

"There's something happening," I said. "Don't you feel strange? Don't you feel as if you're looking for something?"

"No," she said. "No, of course not. I don't know what you mean."

Barney, on the other hand, in spite of the fact that he was drinking noticeably more than usual, was having a spurt of creative activity. His paper on the women poets of the Lowell school was going very well and a long poem he'd had half-finished in his desk for years was coming into his head at moments when he least expected it to. I had been seeing much less of him than I usually saw when he was on vacation and maybe this was contributing to my sense that things were not right, because Barney and I enjoyed that special understanding that came from his being married to Mimi while being temperamentally much more like me.

Vincent looked marvelous. He was deeply tanned after his weeks at Cape Cod, in addition to which he seemed, for the first time in the twenty-two years that I'd known him, not to be underweight. The hair in his beard was partly white but the hair on his head was still reddish brown.

"Hey, there she is!" he said when I came out to meet his cab. "There's my little girl." He slammed shut the cab door and picked me up and whirled me around as though I were ten years old. "Where's Mother Courage?"

I laughed. "My God, Vincent, you're not going to start in so soon!"

"When do I ever start in?" he asked, and then we both laughed. He took his suitcase and we went into the house. Mimi was still having breakfast. And reading the paper. She looked up and said hello. *Very calmly.* Not at all in the way she usually greeted Vincent—a combination of anxiety and dismay with a little hope she could never completely conceal that this visit might end up differently.

"Hi, Mimi," Vincent said. "Where's my breakfast?"

"In a little while, Vincent," she said, still seeming genuinely indifferent. "When I finish my coffee."

"I remember a time," Vincent said, "when you had to eat a meal before you were allowed to walk in the front door."

"My apologies," Mimi said.

"For then or for now?" he asked.

"Take your pick," she said coolly.

It gave Vincent pause. "Where's your husband?" he finally asked.

"Barney's around," she said. "I guess he's in the study."

"When's Lily coming?" he asked. "I have to ask her some questions."

Always he has to know when he will see her and always he must provide himself with an excuse for his need.

"She said she'd be here in a week or so."

"Mmm. Were they here during the riots, do you remember?"

Mimi's calm didn't disappear but some of its surface opened up a little. "You mean the Peekskill riots? In '49?"

"Well of course I mean the Peekskill riots," he said impatiently. "How many riots have there been around here?"

"Just those two," she said slowly, "if you don't count the business in '53. Josh and Lily weren't here for the first one but then they flew in that week and they were here for the second."

"Naturally," he said. "Every Red in the country flew in for that one." As though he didn't know Josh had broken years before. "I wish I'd been here." He grinned at her provocatively. "If it hadn't been for you I probably still *would've* been."

Mimi pretended to yawn.

"But you were both here."

Mimi nodded.

"In Welford the whole time, or did you go up to hear Robeson?"

Mimi glanced at me uneasily. An old wound reopened. She went up to the grounds the first time Robeson was supposed to sing, leaving me alone with Mrs. Cushman, whose sole flaw was a tendency to fall to pieces in any emergency. I was twelve. That night a telephone call came saying we should stay indoors because men were patrolling the hill with shotguns. Mrs. Cushman got hysterical and ran through the house turning out lights and then we huddled together behind the living-room sofa for the rest of the night. Mimi came in during the early hours of the morning, with a boyfriend, and I cried as soon as I saw her and kept crying the whole following day and night until finally she had to get a doctor to put me to sleep for a while.

"I went up for the first one," Mimi said uneasily.

"Tell me about it," he ordered.

"Later," Mimi said. "You just got here. I'll give you breakfast first, okay?"

"No," Vincent said irritably. "First talk and then give me breakfast."

"But I don't *feel* like talking, Vincent," she said softly. "I *never* feel like talking in the morning. You'd know that if you knew me at all. If you'd ever tried to talk to me in all the hundreds of years since I met you."

He stared at her thoughtfully.

"As a matter of fact," she said, "I happen to be particularly tired this morning. I didn't sleep well. So if you'll excuse me, I think I'll go back to sleep. I'm sure Beth will be happy to make your breakfast. Or Mrs. Cushman, if you can find her." And she rose majestically and sailed out of the room.

"What got into her?" Vincent asked. Not angry, just curious.

"I'm not sure," I said. "Some kind of evil spirit has been hovering around, messing up things, giving me bad dreams."

He looked at me the way people look when they'd only thought they wanted a truthful answer. "It's funny," he finally said. "I came back with a certain idea about this place, about its not changing. I somehow had a different feeling about it after being out of the country. You can't really understand how crazy it is, the way this place doesn't change, and it still doesn't really, not the way other places do, but this business of Mimi throws me, I don't know why. She has no importance to me. What the hell."

I waited.

"I came here right from the airport a few weeks ago," he said after a long time. "How does that strike you, kid?"

I smiled. It was an unvarying pattern of Vincent's never to come directly here from Vincennes or Los Angeles or wherever he happened to be, but always to make some stop-off first. In New York, at Fire Island, Cape Cod, someplace where he had a friend he could talk to.

"I took a cab from the airport and I gave the guy the order and then I read the newspaper to keep from thinking about whatever it was I was doing. Or not doing. When we got to the bottom of Sugar Hill I put down the paper and started looking out the window, getting tighter and tighter, wondering if anyone was here, and so on, and when we got here I had the guy turn down the drive, but when we got to the turn-around, without even thinking about it I said to the driver, 'I changed my mind, take me to the city.' Then when we got to New

York I called Richard and asked him if the house at the Cape was being used, and he gave me the keys and I had it to myself most of the time except he was up for a couple of long weekends. I can't tell you how beautiful it is up there when it's empty. I kept thinking of you, I kept thinking, Beth has never seen the ocean. Maybe I can get her to come here with me some time when there's no one else here." He waited for me to say something but of course there was nothing I could say. The idea of the ocean is frightening to me. "So," he finally said, "so what else is new, Beth Elizabeth?"

"Nothing much, I guess. Barney and Mimi had a little accident last week, the car went into the culvert and then someone went into it in the dark. He said he knew you, the man whose car it was. Max Merganser, something like that."

"Maxie?" Vincent seemed pleased. "What the hell is he doing around here? He was on the Coast, last time I saw him."

"His mother died," I said. "He's fixing up the house to sell it."

"His mother died," Vincent said. "Maxie's mother—Maxie had the mother of them all. I don't know how he kept from getting flattened, she was a steamroller, but Maxie would just smile at her and go do whatever he wanted to do. But Jesus, that was the bitch-cop-mother of them all."

"I never even realized you made friends in Welford, Vincent," I said. "I thought you used to just go and take long walks all by yourself."

He laughed and said there was a great deal I didn't know about him. I said, perhaps a bit truculently, that I didn't doubt it, whereupon he became apologetic and said I shouldn't be angry with him. It was true that he had kept his lives in and out of Yiytzo secret and apart and he wasn't sure why he had done it, but it seemed important at the time.

"So," he said when I didn't respond. "Old Maxie. Is he as handsome as ever?"

"I suppose so," I said, not looking at him.

"All the girls were crazy about him," Vincent said. "Every afternoon you could see this bunch of giggly girls following Maxie and the others up the hill, twenty or thirty yards behind. The others called it his fan club."

That was irritating to me. It made him seem silly. I had to remind myself how long ago it had been.

"Old Maxie," Vincent said again. "I'll have to give him a ring."

Barney, drink in hand, came down from his study to see Vincent. Terribly fond of each other, their fondness was hedged with doubts, qualifications, animosities. Vincent's anyway. For Barney there was only the occasional discomfort of enjoying someone who despised his wife—a discomfort which would have been more severe had Barney not been amused by the entire situation. For Vincent it was a different matter; his liking for Barney had always involved a perpetual challenge to his own professed beliefs.

"A college teacher she met at a campus HUAC protest," Vincent wrote when I told him of their coming marriage. "An intellectual. A liberal. Great. Perfect. That is all ye know and all ye need to know. I can sculpt the guy just as well as write about him—a great big Welford-type egghead and no balls at all. This is completely appropriate since his head will have to serve for both of them and as far as balls go, she wouldn't know what to do with them, anyway."

And then a lengthy diatribe on the liberal Eastern intellectuals of Welford Heights as opposed to the bedrock Midwestern conservatives like his father ("By definition an intellectual is someone who isn't capable of undying loyalty, just as by definition a Catholic like my father is someone who is") ending with a promise to visit me soon to rescue me from the tedium. (I was fifteen years old and of course tedium was not my problem when Barney came into the household.)

And then finally they met and so much of what Vincent had assumed about Barney was true, and the only thing Vincent hadn't counted on was that Barney knew it all and could make better jokes about it than Vincent could.

"I don't trust your sense of humor," Vincent told him.

"Because it robs you of your target," Barney said. "And you can never be sure that somewhere down inside I don't take myself very seriously. Don't worry about it. If it's true, the somewhere is so far down that I don't have access to it myself."

"Hey, hot-stuff," he said to Vincent now. "How you doing?"

"Okay, okay," Vincent said. "How you, Barn?"

Barney shrugged. "My wife tells me that after all Mr. Guggenheim's done for you you've gone and gotten hung up on Peekskill U.S.A."

Vincent laughed. "Maybe it was partly being in Europe. Mainly I think it was because I started noticing how different the school kids are now, there and here. They're philosophically liberal but they've picked up some of that low class right-wing personality that always appealed to me. They don't sit around for hours picking the nits out of America's pubic hairs, they—"

"You're always so worried about the harm the intellectuals did," Mimi broke in from the doorway. "What about what the others were doing? What about the ones who were overturning cars and calling Paul Robeson a dirty nigger and patrolling Sugar Hill with shotguns? What were they doing?"

"They were defending a symbolic threat to their country, that's what they were doing."

"Symbolic threats should be defended symbolically," Barney said.

"This country's too big for any symbols but violent ones to matter," Vincent said. "That's something this generation found out."

"And what were they doing when they frightened my sister half to death?" Mimi asked angrily. "Was that for their country's sake, too?"

Long pause. Vincent glanced at me, considered, decided to play dirty. "What were *you* doing when they frightened your sister half to death? That's a better question."

"It's not!" Mimi cried out. "It's not at all. You're being completely unfair!" She was on the verge of tears.

"Hey, Vin," Barney said, "you're setting some kind of record. How long have you been here, an hour?"

"All right, all right, I'm sorry," Vincent muttered.

But I did find myself wondering, not so much about what Mimi had been doing during the day as why she'd come home as late as she did. I'd never thought about it before. The day had been one mass of horror in my mind but it was true that the riots had been early and Mimi had come home very late. When I was far past the point of reason.

"Once we crept out through the field in the darkness," Mimi said slowly, almost oblivious to Vincent, "and went nearly up to the road and we saw a bunch of them going by, they looked like a lynch mob. When school opened a couple of weeks later this boy I knew, I mean we were friends, I'd gone out with him and we were still friendly, he came up to me in Tony's and he put his arm around me and he said, 'Hey, Sugar, I'm glad we didn't see you that week 'cause if we'd've seen you we'd've killed you.'" She shuddered. "It was what made me decide that I'd never have anything to do with politics."

"Atta girl, Mimi," Barney said. "You see, Vincent? They say McCarthy cowed Mimi's whole generation but my little cow here took her vows six months before he made his first headline."

"Except maybe for the little things that affect us right here," Mimi said. "Like the road."

It sent tremors through me. *A little thing like the road.* I would have known then that something was wrong if I hadn't sensed it for days. By what sudden shift of standards had the road become a little thing? Periodically the Planning Board talked about modernizing and widening

Sugar Hill Road. Always, no matter who brought up the plan, we at Yiytzo were affected in some way. Yiytzo and the few other large estates that remained along the road. Periodically Mimi led the battle against those people who wanted to ruin our land. For the time each battle lasted, it dominated our lives and thoughts. And now here was Mimi, referring to the road as an example of a small matter. As though she were hoarding her energies for something more important.

"What road?" Vincent asked. He had never taken the slightest interest in such things.

"Sugar Hill," I said. "Once or twice a year the Planning Board tries to push through a plan to modernize it. Every maple tree on it would be destroyed, not to speak of the other things."

But he still wasn't interested. For all of his sudden fascination with the Peekskill riots, Yiytzo would never be a part of Vincent.

I woke up early because Lily was coming and puttered around doing nothing until I finally asked Vincent to take a walk with me and he growled through his door that the fact that I was a compulsive early riser didn't mean I should shout him awake at any hour of the morning. It was almost eleven by then. I should have known better than to approach him that day.

"I know who she is, idiot! She's my mother!"

That is what I remember most clearly of Josh and Lily's first visit after Vincent had come to live with us. Mimi trying to overcome the embarrassment of those first moments by introducing Lily to Vincent in a humorous way and Vincent hitting her so hard that she fell to the floor and shouting at her, "I know who she is, idiot! She's my mother!" And Lily saying over and over again, "My God, he's a madman!"

There was a lot of excitement, then, until finally Josh somehow got Vincent to apologize to Mimi, although Mimi kept saying it wasn't necessary, she was all right. It was Christmas, the first Christmas after the end of the war. The tree in the living room came to the ceiling and there were pine ropes along the mantelpiece and around the arches. In my diary that night I wrote:

> *Josh asked Vincent how old he is. Vincent said if Josh wants to know how old he is he has to count the years since Josh ran away with his mother then add on eleven months. Lily asked isnt somebody going to stop the little beast. Then Lily said her head hurts but Vincent did not mind that he only said to her why did you leave me. Every body got quiet.*

How startling it must have been to Lily. Everyone, even I, my not quite nine-year-old self, had known what it was all about, this first meeting between Lily and her grown son, but no one had thought that what was underneath it would come out so readily. With Vincent the problem was never to bring out the truth but only to maintain the surface, which is also real.

Then, I wrote, *Lily got nice to Vincent.*

Surprised into forgetting her headache. Or perhaps she'd just seen that here, finally, was someone with whom her evasions wouldn't work. The illnesses that defied diagnosis and deflected criticism (and once had even made Josh change his mind about divorcing her) would not distract Vincent for a moment.

She said she was wanting to see him but now he acts mad at her so she is afraid of him. She kissed his two cheeks and he cried and then Lily got very jolly and said how good it is to be home.

How terribly confused he must have been. Years later he still didn't know what to make of his own mother—or rather would not make of her what he should have. He occasionally decided to address her as Mother, which drove her wild. He pretended to be indifferent to her indifference, but when he came up against it, could never believe that she herself wasn't feigning, that she truly felt neither guilt nor remorse over what she had done to him. He swore that the time when she could hurt him was long past but spent the hours before she came barricaded in his room, attempting to build up the extra strength that he needed simply to confront her. He maintained that he'd arrived at a certain objectivity in his view of her. Then, when he said that she looked remarkably good for a woman of sixty and I pointed out that Josh once when very drunk had given us a riotous account of one of her face-lifting operations, told me that the difference between me and Josh was that Josh wasn't to be trusted on any subject, while I was to be trusted on every subject except Lily.

Just after Mimi had gone to the station for her, Vincent emerged from his seclusion and penetrated mine.

"I'm ready to walk now," he said, as though I'd asked him five minutes before instead of five hours. I went with him but I felt obliged to point out that the mosquitoes were out in full strength, not that it mattered to me for the bugs never come near me.

"So they'll bite me," he said. "So I'll scratch. So I'll bleed."

I got up to go with him and he told me I looked pretty. I was startled. I was wearing the yellow lawn dress whose significance for me lay solely in the fact that Lily hated it and every time she saw me in it told me how ill it became me, with my sallow complexion. Always if there was some dress I knew she disliked I felt obliged to wear it when she was there, and when I was younger I used to become frustrated that she failed to notice what I was about and therefore failed to be offended.

"I know you hate it, Lily," I'd once said when Lily pointed out that the dress I was wearing was a particularly loathsome shade of green. "That's why I'm wearing it."

"Oh, Beth, you're such a funny girl," trilled the Patron Saint of Triviality.

She never cared enough about me to be hurt by anything I could say or do.

"Lily hates this dress," I said to Vincent and with a little smile he said, "Life is so simple for you, isn't it, Beth."

I knew what he meant. That he always intended not to try to please Lily but ended up trying in spite of himself and then getting hurt, for if he could please her at all it was only for a little time. Then, thinkingly or unthinkingly he would do something to make her aware that he was a human being and not simply an instrument of her pleasure, and as soon as that happened she retreated from him and he couldn't bear it, however much it was expected, however many times it had happened before, back to that first time when she'd finally kissed him and he'd cried and she'd begun to dance around the living room, saying how good it was to be home.

It was pleasantly cool outside. We walked to the brook, which was flowing well for the first time in several years because of the good rain we'd had all spring. Vincent at first was fairly relaxed—my small signs of Lily-hatred seemed always to have a benign effect upon him—but as we walked I could feel him tightening inside himself.

"Do you know how old I am?" he asked after a while.

"Of course I do, Vincent," I said.

"How old?" he demanded. "When is my birthday?"

"September 26th," I said. "You'll be forty-two on September 26th."

"For all the good it does me," he said fiercely. I didn't reply and after a while he went on. "I could be five years old for all the good my age has done me. I've never been afraid of getting old and I've never been afraid of dying. The only thing I was ever afraid of was not changing and naturally, that's what's happening, the thing I'm most afraid of. I keep waiting for the numbers of my age to have some significance. I keep waiting to be different and year after year goes by and the world is changing at the most fucking unbelievable pace, beyond all human comprehension, and I'm the same fucking Vincent." I touched his arm and he put it around me. "If she died I'd be different. I know that, I'm just not sure how. You can't really change while your mother's alive, they don't let you, they don't want you to, or else they don't give a damn and that has the same effect, maybe worse, because you can't break out of a prison with no walls, you can't wave goodbye if there's no one looking out of the window. Otherwise known as the parable of the forest. If the tree falls and no one's there to see it, did it happen? Does the tree exist? Sure the tree does, but you don't, you sap. What time is it?"

"Five past five."

"When does the train get here?"

"Ten past." He knew this, of course.

"Did you miss me while I was away, Beth?"

"Sometimes a lot," I said.

"When?"

"Mostly around two o'clock in the afternoon."

He laughed.

"But also sometimes in the evening," I said. "Or when things are happening. Like . . . I was terribly eager for you to come this time."

"Why?" he said quickly. "What's happening?"

"I don't know."

"It's not this road business you mentioned the other day."

"I don't think so. There hasn't been anything about that in a few months."

"Then what is it about two o'clock in the afternoon?"

"I don't know."

"I bet you do."

"When Mimi went to school, I used to keep myself busy all day, my tutor would come in the morning, and then in the afternoon I'd do things, keep busy . . . except around two I would get very restless. The waiting would come up to the surface from wherever it'd been all day, and those last minutes when I knew she was about to start home but she hadn't been let out of school yet were almost unbearable."

"It wasn't as though you were alone here."

"Oh, the whole house was different when Mimi came home. Leah and I . . . sometimes we didn't say a word to each other all day, not because we were mad, it was just that I didn't talk and she was very quiet. Then Mimi would come home, and she was always so gay, and she thought of good things to do. The whole house changed, really, it was like a physical thing, the rooms got brighter—warmer, even. Everything changed from not right to quite right. That's the way it's always been, that the three of us are *supposed* to be here, Mimi and me and Leah or Mrs. Cushman or someone like that. And when you ask me if I miss you . . . there are times when I want very much for you to be here, but when you're not here, or if Barney goes away for a few days or something, or anyone outside of the three of us, it's not as though there's anything missing."

We walked in silence for a while, reaching the place where the brook went underground but continuing on the path through the woods. As we walked I became aware, not for the first time that day, of irregular flutterings of my heart, and I put a hand on my chest to feel them better.

"I've been feeling my heart beat all day," I said, "in a kind of strange erratic way. Fluttery."

He asked if there was anything wrong with my heart and I said not that I knew of. Then he asked if I was aware that I'd talked more in the past five minutes than I usually talked in five days.

I smiled. "Well you know I've never been much of a talker, Vincent."

"Then why now?" The question frightened me because I had no idea of why, but when I told him that, he pointed out that I'd said the same thing about two o'clock in the afternoon, the first time he asked.

"Well it's more true this time," I said.

"You're so fucking careful with words, Beth," he said. "As if they cost you something."

"What I mean," I said, "is that I don't know what's happening any more than you do."

"Then what makes you think anything's happening at all?"

I shrugged.

"Come on, Beth," he coaxed. "You've said it more than once since I got here."

"It's a lot of small things, nothing anyone would notice. And I've been having dreams."

"Dreams?" he asked incredulously.

"I mean I've been dreaming that things went wrong."

He laughed shortly. "Did you ever dream things went right?"

"Oh, yes. Sometimes I have lovely dreams."

Silence. Then, "What was the dream?"

But I could no more give away one of my dreams than I could . . .

For Vincent things said were less frightening than those same things left unsaid, but for me . . . We had an argument about dreams, Mimi and I, the first time that I was ill. When I was eleven. I don't remember the early part of course but I do remember Mimi's telling me as I got a little better that the doctor wouldn't be able to help me if I didn't try to tell him my dreams. And then Josh, too, saying that I couldn't be treated at home if I didn't cooperate, that I would have to go back to the hospital. And so I took fairy tales remembered from my books and changed the characters to objects that moved like furniture in the house, and the doctor said, "I understand what you're doing, Elizabeth, but it's all right." And then I stopped talking to him but the doctor told Josh that I was apparently better off at home, anyway, than I would be in the hospital. And Josh went back to California, leaving a trained nurse in his place, and Mimi came into my room and cried with relief that they weren't going to take me away again, and at one point she said, "Forgive me, Bethie, forgive me." But she never said why.

"I couldn't possibly tell you, Vincent."

"Why the hell not? What do you think I'm going to do with it, for Christ's sake? Publish it?"

"No, it's nothing like that. It has nothing to do with you. I've never told anyone any of my dreams, not even Mimi."

He made me face him. "Is that true?"

I nodded and he released me.

"What about her?" he asked. "Does she think something's happening, too? Does she know the two of you are acting different?"

"No, she thinks I'm silly. You know, Mimi doesn't believe in anything she can't see."

"But you, sweetheart," Vincent laughed. "That's all you believe in."

"No," I said. "I do believe in the things I can't see. But I believe what I *can* see, too."

From far away at the house we heard the car horn honk several times.

"Oh, shit," Vincent said. But he turned and began walking back to the house so rapidly that it was difficult for me to keep up with him. Until we got to the interior garden, where he slowed down so that we were barely moving at all. I heard him take a deep breath before opening the front door and then we went in.

Lily was standing at the fireplace, looking around. Her unnaturally white-blonde hair piled high on her head. Her face bland and unwrinkled as ever, her loose wrinkled neck giving the lie to her face. Wearing a white dress and high white pumps, always high pumps, to set off her legs, no matter what the current fashion might dictate. Josh once said that if Lily took a fifty-mile hike she would wear high heels so the squirrels would notice her ankles.

"Sweethearts," she said, fluttering toward us so that everything inside of me shrank away from my skin in case Lily should touch it. "Vincent, darling, you look magnificent, what happened to you in Europe, you look positively handsome! I know, you've put on some weight. Marvelous. Very becoming. Oooh," she squeezed his arm excitedly, "it's wonderful to see you. It feels so good to be home . . . and Beth . . ." Her eyes clouded momentarily as she looked for something to say about me. "How are you, Beth, dear?"

I said that I was the same as usual because lies always came to me more readily than the truth when I was with Lily. Mimi came in from the kitchen with iced tea for herself and Lily. She asked if we wanted some but we both refused.

"Now," Lily said, dropping into the big armchair that we used to call Josh's throne, "tell me what's been happening. Tell me everything."

Mimi laughed. "Very little's been going on, really, Lily. But that'll change, now that you're here."

Lily giggled. "Where's Barney?" she asked. "Barney always tells me good stories."

"Not sure," Mimi said. "He said he was going out but he didn't say where. Probably just for a walk, he's been taking walks. Or maybe fishing."

"Fishing," Lily sighed. "Walking. Not Barney, too. Now everyone walks but me. When did he become a traitor?"

"I don't know," Mimi said. "The past couple of weeks, I guess. Maybe vacation boredom set in."

"He's been working harder than he ever worked on vacation," I pointed out.

"Mmmm," she said. "And Vincent's working on a new book, too, Lily."

"How exciting," Lily said. "I wish to hell I had some talent. I met a boy on the plane, a lovely young boy who's a writer. He asked me if it was true blondes had more fun and I pointed out that my hair is really white, not blonde, and he said he didn't believe it for a minute and why did I feel that I had to protect myself from him?" She giggled. "He writes for the ladies' magazines. He told me he spent his childhood waiting for his mother in the beauty parlor, reading ladies' magazines, and when he got out of school he tried selling them stuff but he kept missing until one day he noticed all the writers had two last names. So he changed his name, his pen name, to Brigid Pocatelli Smavarmt, something like that, and he swears that right away they started buying everything he could turn out. He was delightful, so funny. I gave him the number here but I don't imagine he could stand this place for more than an hour or two. He's not the type for the quiet rustic life." She sighed. "I do love pansies, I only wish they aged better. The fakes are all right, they look better than real men, more masculine, but the others, I don't know. Something happens to their mouths." She sipped reflectively at her iced tea. "It's such a relief to hear good conversation again. Hollywood has changed, you can't imagine how much it's changed. Lately I've even considered coming back to New York. Everyone I used to know practically is in New York now."

"That would be wonderful, Lily," Mimi said. "If you came back to the East Coast."

"Mmm," Lily said. "Well, I'll have to see . . ."

See whether she would confer on us this great favor, the very thought of which kept me from eating for the rest of the day. Vincent hadn't uttered a word through all of this but just sat there, almost succeeding in looking amused, an unthinking imitation of Josh in which he never really succeeded because unlike Josh, he had never accepted the truth about her. "I used to think your mother's ignorance was an affectation," Josh once told him. "After all, even in Indiana they have high schools. Eventually I was forced to face the fact that it's not only genuine but it's probably her most profound quality. Lily's politics change with the temper of the times and her tastes with the woman's page but her ignorance is always there to be relied upon." And Vincent said, "You think you're so fucking smart, don't you," and loped out of the room. Refusing to understand what Josh was trying to help him do, which was to take Lily less seriously. To care less. To get past the point of being concerned with Lily's reactions because to care for Lily's reactions meant, in a sense, to depend on something that didn't exist.

"I didn't tell you the most interesting thing of all," Mimi said to Lily.

The game. Find something to interest Lily. Amuse Lily. Please Lily.

"Mm?" Lily asked languidly.

"Vincent's new book is going to be about Welford."

"Ten minutes with your mother," Vincent said, "and you revert to type."

Mimi was baffled, naturally. "What did I do?"

"First of all you made a mistake. I'm not writing a book about Welford and I never will. I am writing a book and I am making some use of the Peekskill riots, which happened to occur near here and happened to involve many Welford inhabitants, a distinction you would assume if you were a writer instead of a hack."

"I've never had any illusions about what I write," Mimi said quietly.

"Ha!" Vincent began. "That's what—"

"Oh, dear, Vincent," Lily said with a yawn. "Why are you being a bad boy again?"

"Because that's what I *do* when I'm here," he said. "Or at least when you're here. Can't you see that? I'm Bad Boy and Beth here is Frail Waif and over in that corner, ladies and gentlemen, weighing in at I'd say a good twenty pounds more than the last time I saw her, is Resident Earth Mother, Eternal Hostess, Keeper of the Shrine, Pollyanna the Glad Girl and you'd better be Glad, too, or else. She was a little more bearable than usual until you got here, Lily, old Mom, I'll say that for her. But now you've arrived and she's talking Basic Press Release again. . . . And looking in on the happy little Welford Heights crew, Mom, we find your oldest son, in fact your only son, writing a book about that quaint little series of events known as the Peekskill riots. Now isn't that just too delicious? And—"

"Now that your looks have improved a bit, Vincent," Lily said, "you really should do something about your manners. I know your father never taught you any manners but God knows you've had plenty of time since then to pick them up."

"It would be too easy for me to hate you," Vincent said to Lily. "I resist the temptation. I worship you. The Goddess of Gall. Tell me what I can do for you, Goddess."

"You can stop talking nonsense," the Goddess fretted. "That's what. You can say something interesting for a change."

"Sure," Vincent said, "only tell me what'll interest you. Do you want to hear about Europe?"

"I suppose so."

"Europe is in a state of chaos. What else would you like to hear about? My new book?"

"If you like."

"I don't like. I never like to talk about my books."

She yawned. Uninterested in his irony. I felt a sudden change in his mood. He became afraid of losing her. Afraid that she would just get up and leave the room, thus destroying the pitiful illusion that of the two of them he was the aggressor.

"I'll tell you what I would like, though, Lil. I'd like to ask you some questions having to do with the book. How would you like to answer some questions?"

She shrugged.

"Not boring questions," Vincent promised. "Interesting ones. About *you*. Like why did you fly back for the riots when you'd been out of the Party for so many years?"

"Because of her," Lily said, jerking her head in my direction without looking at me. "She was having one of her breakdowns." Making it sound as though I still had them.

Vincent was unnerved. Naturally it hadn't occurred to him that an answer could hurt me. I smiled at him so he could see that I was fine.

"We wouldn't have come back just for that Robeson stuff," Lily said. "By that time there was nothing in Welford worth coming back for. It wasn't like the old days. In the old days everyone who wasn't in the city was here." Her whole manner had altered to a dream-fed melancholy. "Not just Westin," she said. "The whole crowd was here, from the *Masses*, everyone."

"You knew Westin?"

"Everyone knew him."

"What was he like?"

"Beautiful." She sighed. "He was a beautiful boy. He still is. I saw him the last time I was in. He's got white hair and wrinkles and he's still a beautiful boy. I told him so and he laughed and he said I was lying but it was absolutely true that I was as gorgeous as ever." She smiled wistfully. "That isn't true, though. I'm beautiful for a woman my age but that isn't the same as being a beautiful twenty- or thirty-year-old. You didn't know me when I was really beautiful."

"A remarkable observation," Vincent said.

"We were so happy here." Somehow implying that they'd been carried away by force. "We had the best parties, the biggest and the best. We raised more money for the Scottsboro boys than anyone. You were never bored. If nothing was going on up here you looked in the *Worker* for a What's-On. They had a whole page of them all the time and you could always go to a What's-On. Do you know what it's like never never to be bored?"

A starving orphan describing a magical land where children are never hungry.

"Actually," Vincent said, "there's more going on now in terms of the country as a whole. But it's all the kids."

"Ohhh . . ." Irritated at this unwelcome, frighteningly true interruption of her reverie. She stood up, yawned again, began fluttering around the room. "When is Josh coming?" Picking up a stone from the bowl of smooth stones I kept on the mantel. People always touched them but when Lily did it I wanted to scream, grab them back, hit her. I never did it, though, except for the one time she came when I was about to be ill. Around the time Mimi got married. Things were beginning to come apart, borders to fuzz, although Mimi hadn't yet noticed, I suppose she was too busy to notice. I was losing pieces of some of the days and my diary for that week was strangely fragmented—like a puzzle that had been pushed together in spite of the fact that pieces were missing.

"We haven't heard from him," Mimi said.

"I wonder why." Fretful again. "He always comes in the summer." Which of course was the only reason she was there.

"He doesn't always give a lot of notice, though."

"You never even called me when he came in the spring."

"He was working. He made us promise not to call a soul."

"Also," I said, "he had his girlfriend with him."

"Oh, Beth," Mimi said.

"He was very sparkling," I said. "She seemed to bring out the best in him, she was very intelligent. We had a wonderful time, no one was bored for a minute."

Silence thicker than milkweed chewing gum.

"I'm tired," Lily announced abruptly, in that way she had that made people wonder why they hadn't thought to put a bed under her. "I'm going to take a nap."

And she headed upstairs, taking it for granted that someone would carry up her bags. Two days later she left to visit friends in Westport with instructions to Mimi that she was to be called as soon as anyone heard from Josh.

Josh called and told Mimi he and Gilda were in Southampton and would arrive in a couple of weeks. I heard Mimi tell him that Lily was there and then there was a long pause and Mimi said, "It's not that you have an obligation, Josh, it's just a question of how Lily *feels*." Then another long pause and she said Gilda was welcome, we would all love to see Gilda, but not while Lily was waiting to see Josh. Then a brief pause and she said he was a darling and hung up.

"You told him not to bring her because Lily's here."

She nodded. "He said in that case he wouldn't be here until after Labor Day."

"We had a lot of fun last time," I said.

"I know, dear, but it wouldn't have been the same. I'd have to tell Lily, she'll be calling to check, I'm sure."

"You could keep her away if you wanted to," I said. Knowing Mimi, being Mimi, could not.

"Oh, Elizabeth," Mimi sighed. "You know I can't do that."

"I don't know anything of the sort. Tell her there's someone coming she wouldn't like. Why should she spoil our fun?"

"She doesn't spoil *my* fun," Mimi said. "Sometimes it's a little hectic if I'm trying to write but I don't seem to be writing, anyway. So what difference will it make? I won't mind having her here at all."

"Well you should! She only comes here to get pampered. All those years she had Josh waiting on her she never wanted to come back, she only came when he insisted, and now that he's not pampering her any more she—"

"He never did," Mimi said. "Not the way you think he did, anyway. You think he was such a perfect husband? You think he didn't have girlfriends even when they were living together? You never even try to look at it from her point of view, only from his."

"You're wrong," I told her. "I look at it from my own, and that's why I hate her and I hate having her around. I'm not the way I want to be when she's here. I'm some rotten hateful little girl that I despise. It's the same thing Vincent was talking about. When she's around I hate myself because I'm full of hatred."

"You upset me when you talk about hating," Mimi said. "You're the most gentle person I know, it seems all wrong to hear you say it."

"You think she comes because she loves you," I said. "She doesn't know what love is, she doesn't love you she only *needs* you."

"That isn't fair! How can you be sure? How can you even be sure they're two different things?"

"It's like a convalescent home when she's here," I said. Thinking, *this is what I meant, Mimi. This is what Lily turns me into. Someone who can stand here and try to make you see the truth about your mother even if you're the only one the truth will hurt.* "She rattles around the country, Hollywood, Chicago, Florida, New York, shopping, having her hair done, going to parties and parties until finally she's exhausted and she needs a rest or she wants to see Josh. What better place than here? With her slave Mimi? She wakes up and Mimi brings her brunch in bed. She wants to go someplace, Mimi drives her. She's bored, Mimi and Barney tell her stories and if that doesn't work, Mimi calls up some people to come over and amuse her. And if all this begins to wear her out Mimi runs her a bath, or picks up some of the trashy

magazines she adores, then plumps up the pillows so she can nap, or
. . ." I stopped. Not because Mimi was upset, although she was, but
because I suddenly thought to myself, *Oh, my God, I know what she's
thinking! She's thinking she does more than that for me and she never
gets rid of me, I'm always here. Maybe I bother her more than Lily
does!* And then my head was a blank except for the words, *Mimi hates
me, Mimi hates me,* over and over.

"What is it, Beth?" Mimi asked. "What happened?"

But I couldn't speak. *Mimi hates me.*

"Beth," she said, "speak to me, Beth, you're scaring me."

She hates me.

"Beth!" She shook me by the shoulders and that broke it. "What is
it, Beth?"

"Nothing. Never mind."

"How can I not mind?"

"I just . . . I was just thinking you do much more for me than for
Lily."

"I don't understand."

"Well . . ." I found myself picking my words with great caution for
no apparent reason. Like tiptoeing into a room where no one was
asleep. ". . . what I mean is, I know that I practically owe you my
whole existence."

"Nonsense!" Dismissing my idea at the split second that she began to
understand it.

"It isn't nonsense, Mimi. You know perfectly well that I couldn't get
along without you."

"Why should you? I don't even want you to. But you could if you
needed to. People do the things they have to do."

"*You* do the things you have to do. I do the things I want to do. It's
not the same thing."

"Ohhhh . . ."

"I don't blame you for getting annoyed with me. That's part of what
I'm talking about. I don't know why you don't get angry more often."

Ashamed a little because I was manipulating her. Evoking inevitable
responses with guaranteed lines.

"Because I love you, Elizabeth, that's why. Why should I get angry
if I love you and I don't mind doing things for you?"

No. Mimi hardly ever got angry. Even later—even *now*—she is a person of great patience and forbearance. But something had changed,
something to do with *needing* patience in the first place. Mimi had
never seemed to be controlling her anger and forcing herself to bear

with us; the anger seemed not to be there at all. One never had the sense that some final blow could suddenly make her explode. Now the anger was there and simply buried almost all of the time.

She had waited too long to tell me and then she told me too quickly. It was almost the end of August. She came down to breakfast, made some iced tea, which she'd been drinking all summer instead of coffee, spilled a little on her hand as she set it on the table, said nervously, "Beth, there's something I have to tell you. It's crazy but it's also wonderful and I hope you'll be pleased because I'm pleased." Looking as though she hadn't slept a minute the night before. Speaking in a way that made it clear she'd rehearsed every word. "I'm going to have a baby."

"I'll drink to that," Barney said, raising his mug.

"You've been drinking to that since before you knew about it," she snapped at him, and then she caught her breath and stared at him in a mixture of confusion and pain. She'd never talked to him like that— never in all the time they'd been married, certainly while I'd been around and fairly certainly when they were alone. He teased her or was querulous and she ignored him or responded but never with anger. It frightened her as much as it frightened me.

"God, I don't know what's wrong with me, Barney," she said. "I'm sorry."

Barney smiled. "What the hell, sport. It's taken fifteen years for the bitch in you to come out. You're entitled." She stood up abruptly and ran from the room. No. Sort of walked heavily, as she's so small anyway and had already gained weight. I'd noticed the weight and blamed the fact that she'd been eating big breakfasts instead of just having coffee in the morning. I just sat there, not even thinking about the baby, yet, because that would take time, to be able to even be horrified about the baby. Instead I just kept seeing Mimi snap at Barney. Over and over. As though the image were a stone skipped into a pond.

"So, Elizabeth," Barney said. "What do you think?"

"About what?"

You've been drinking to it since before you knew about it.

"About your baby brother . . . or sister . . . or niece . . . or whatever you want to call it. My own personal assumption is that it'll be a girl because there's not another male around with the guts to force his way into this matriarchy."

"I can't think about it, yet," I said. "I can't even believe it, much less think about it." I could think about the irises, about cutting them back, except that we were very likely to have another heat spell before the fall.

"Where the hell has the summer gone?" Barney said. "I can't believe school begins in a couple of weeks."

"It's because you've been working so hard," I told him. "I've hardly seen you all summer." Even during our rare quiet times together he'd sometimes abruptly left me to go to his study. Other times he and Vincent became absorbed in talk about Vincent's book and one evening, when Vincent had called Max and Max had come down to say hello, the three of them had ended up getting so drunk that I'd felt excluded.

"Miss me?" He reached over and smoothed the hair back from my forehead.

"You know I like to be with you," I said.

"Then say you missed me."

"When is Mimi going to have the baby?"

"Oh, shit," Barney said, "how'm I supposed to know . . . March . . . middle, third week of March."

"How long have you known?"

He shrugged. "We suspected almost a month ago."

"Why didn't anyone tell me?"

"She wanted to wait until she was positive . . . she wasn't sure how you'd react." He grinned at me. "Have you decided yet how you're reacting?"

"I don't know," I said. "I feel strange but that's nothing new. I've felt strange all summer. Now . . . my God, if I think about it at all, all I can think about is our lives being turned inside out. Our whole lives being changed. I couldn't bear that. . . . I hope it doesn't cry a lot. . . . There's a house on Main Street, whenever I pass it I hear a baby crying. Once or twice a year I go by and always there's that baby crying. For years and years . . ."

"Same baby?"

"I suppose not. I guess there're really a lot of them. I just never thought of it before. It doesn't matter, it's all the same in my mind." I shuddered. "I can't bear the sound of a baby crying."

"Poor Elizabeth," Barney said.

I began to cry. He came to the back of my chair and stroked my head.

"Poor little Elizabeth."

Mimi came back in and said, "Oh God, Bethie, I didn't want you to be upset. Why are you crying? Is it the baby? It won't matter, it'll be all right. Honestly, Barney, you haven't been sarcastic, have you?"

At that instant I felt that I could appreciate for the first time why Vincent couldn't stand Mimi. That is, I could sympathize with his anger at her determination to make him happy. Understand his resentment at her trying to dictate his emotions—even if her intentions toward him were always good.

"Your sister," Barney said, "doesn't like to hear babies crying."

"But it's not going to be that kind of baby, Beth," Mimi said quickly. "It's going to be a very happy baby, I promise you. I mean—I'm not saying she'll never cry, he'll never cry, whatever, because all babies cry a little but she won't cry a lot and when she does start to cry I'll pick her up right away and then she'll stop."

But I couldn't stop crying.

"Elizabeth isn't convinced," Barney said. "I think maybe we ought to drop the whole thing."

Mimi told him he wasn't being very funny and Barney told her he wasn't sure he intended to be. He said that actually now that I'd brought up the matter, he didn't think that *he* liked the sound of babies crying, either. He said he admitted that he hadn't had any unpleasant experiences in that direction, that he had been the crybaby in the house where he was raised by his mother and his older sister, but it seemed to him that that was much the better of the bargain and he should have quit while he was still ahead.

"Nobody *likes* the sound," Mimi said to me, then turned to Barney, "but most people just do whatever they can about it, they don't sit around worrying about it before the baby's even born."

Silence. No response from either of us.

"*Some* women," Mimi said quietly, "when they announce they're going to have a baby, everyone becomes very solicitous. Their husbands make them sit down all the time, and carry things for them, and hover over them."

There it was again. It was such a totally incongruous thing for Mimi to say. Mimi can't *stand* being hovered over.

"You're too late, Mimi," Barney said to her.

"What does that mean?" she demanded.

"It means," he said slowly, "that you're nearly thirty-five years old and I'm forty-two and we've been married for fifteen years and it's too late to decide that you want to be hovered over."

"What you really mean is that it's too late to have a baby."

He shrugged.

"It's not my fault it took so long," she said. "I mean if it *is*, I didn't *will* it this way, God knows I didn't. Ten years ago, even six and seven years ago, I was crying myself to sleep every night because I couldn't get pregnant." This was something new to me about Mimi. "I used to lie in bed wondering if . . ." She cut herself off.

"Wondering if what?" I asked.

"Nothing," she said. "I don't know why we're talking like this in front of Beth, Barney. I don't know why we're talking like this at all."

"It's called getting things out of your system," Barney said. "You've never been very good at it."

"I don't *want* to be good at it, I don't see why we have to talk like this. Ever. I don't see how it can do any good at all. I don't even know what we were talking about, so how important could it be?"

"You were saying," Barney told her, very slowly and deliberately, "that you used to think you were being punished for having an abortion."

She stared at him in horror. I stared at her in shock. Not possible. Not Mimi.

"That isn't what I was saying," she choked out.

"Sure it is. You were saying you used to lie in bed at night thinking you couldn't get pregnant because you'd had—"

"Stop it!" she screamed. "I don't know why you're doing this but stop it!"

"As a matter of fact," Barney said, "I don't know why I'm doing it either. Maybe Beth knows. Beth, do you know why I'm—"

"When, Mimi?" I asked, feeling as though I were dreaming. "When did you do that?"

"What difference does it make?" She was terribly upset. More upset than I was because she knew it was true while I didn't believe it.

"I didn't say it made a difference." A lie.

"Then let's talk about it some other time. All right? Bethie?"

Of course not, Mimi. Of course it's not all right. It's not all right that it happened and it's not all right that it was you who did it. You. Because in a sense my whole existence depends on the value that you place on human life. After all, I toil not nor do I spin. I inhabit this house very much as any living parasite inhabits a larger benevolent organism; my value lies in my existence. How could you think it would be all right? And if you really thought so, why would you have taken such pains to keep it a secret?

"I was in the hospital. I must have been in the hospital or I would have known something."

Mimi turned very pale. "It wasn't that." Denying what hadn't even occurred to me yet, that the burden of having me in the hospital in addition to a baby was what had made her do it. "We were just married," she said. "We weren't ready. We had no money."

Money. Money had never been a reason for doing something or not doing it.

"I know it's hard for you to think of it, Beth, we've never bothered you with all that stuff. But Josh only pays the most basic house expenses. Taxes, major repairs, a couple of service contracts. We have living expenses. I know you've never given any thought to things like that, I never wanted you to, but we do have them. Barney wasn't even an assistant professor then and it was years before I started Virginia."

"In point of fact," Barney said, "you started Virginia thirty-four years ago."

"Damn it," Mimi shouted, "haven't you said enough?"

There it was again. Mimi being angry. Being somebody else.

"None of this makes sense," I said.

"Since when are you so big on sense?" Barney asked me.

"You're all turned out, Barney," I said sadly. "Usually you're turned in on yourself and now you're turned out on us."

He stared at me for a moment and then he laughed his old inward kind of laugh. An announcement he'd turned back on himself. He went to the refrigerator and poured himself a glass of tomato juice, added a large quantity of vodka almost as an afterthought, and quickly drank it down. Then he made another one and left us. Mimi began clearing away the half-full breakfast dishes.

I said, "I always thought of Lily as a murderer."

Mimi said, "Well, you shouldn't have. It's ridiculous. Plenty of people have abortions. It's just not that big a deal. Anyway, you never should've known about it. Lily should never have told."

True. Lily should never have told. Lily should never have announced that she'd had an abortion before Vincent and one after him and the only thing she regretted was the one in between.

"It's a medical thing," Mimi said. "If you don't make a big deal out of it."

"Someone once told me that when a baby—a foetus . . . that two months after conception it has all the lines of its palms and fingerprints engraved in its skin already."

"Some nut, probably," Mimi said.

"No, it was a doctor. It was when I was in the hospital the last time. I asked him. He was interesting, he seemed a little more open-minded than the rest of them, not so quick to dismiss things. I asked him if he ever looked at people's palms when he was trying to understand them.

He said it would be like reading Sanskrit—the meaning might be all there but he wouldn't understand it. And he didn't believe the palmists did either. And then he told me about the lines."

"All right," Mimi said after a moment. "So Lily's a murderer and I'm a murderer. What do you want to do about it, Elizabeth? Lock us up?"

A joke. Jokes and abortions were unbecoming to you, Mimi. Long ago you agreed to be the mother of us all and now we were your victims as all children are their parents' victims. All parents being doubly victims in that they are victimized by both their parents and their children. Children. Babies. Why did I have to hear about the two things, the baby and the abortion, at the same time? One would have been enough to think about. As it was, the two things became hopelessly intermingled in my mind so that I couldn't react separately to them, feeling upset and horrified by both. That Lily had had abortions was upsetting because the nature of the act was upsetting. But it was neither surprising nor confusing because everything in Lily's nature prepared one for the likelihood that she could treat any form of human life in the most casual way. Lily had never been convinced that human life existed outside the boundaries of her own skin. Lily would not care what would happen to me when you had your baby, Mimi, a fact which I could easily accept when I was certain that you cared enormously.

In the afternoon Vincent came home from the Peekskill Library chortling that the Peekskill *Evening Star* was as big a rag as any paper in the Midwest. I'd been at loose ends all day, trying to embroider, trying to sort clothes, unable to do anything for more than a few minutes, and I was contented to let him try to absorb me in what he was saying.

"Listen to this, Beth, this is gorgeous, are you listening? It's an editorial:

"It appears that Peekskill is to be 'treated' to another concert visit by Paul Robeson, renowned Negro baritone.

"Time was when the honor would have been ours—all ours. As things stand today, like most folks who put America first, we're a little doubtful of that 'honor,' finding the luster in the once illustrious name of Paul Robeson now almost hidden by political tarnish.

"His magnificent voice, which thrilled millions, opened up a brilliant career for him that easily could have led to a place in the

halls of American fame. His influence with his people, properly directed, could have won a place for him beside Booker T. Washington and George Washington Carver, as truly great white niggers . . ."

"Pardon me," Vincent said, *"truly great Negro Americans.*

"Any possibility of such attainment is now, in the opinion of most Americans, lost to him forever.

"The time for tolerant silence that signifies approval is running out . . ."

"How do you like that for incitement to violence?" Vincent asked happily.

"But I thought you liked violence," I said abstractly, only half paying attention.

He stopped for a moment then he laughed. "It's the flaw in my position," he said. "I like the violence but I don't like most of the idiocy that causes it. Now you ask me, if I like violence how can I afford to be fussy about the causes . . ."

But of course I wasn't asking him anything at all. I turned away from him, walked aimlessly around the room, picked up a smooth stone from the bowl on the mantel, rubbed it, put it down, took another.

"Something wrong?" Vincent asked.

I couldn't tell him.

"What is it, Beth?" he asked. "Tell me what's wrong."

"Mimi," I began. Trying to say it.

"Mimi," he nodded. "Mimi what?"

"Baby," was all I could say.

"Mimi baby," he repeated, uncomprehending for just an instant. Then, "Mimi's going to have a baby?" Incredulous.

I nodded.

"Jesus Christ," he said, "you're kidding. Where are they? Hey, Barney, hey, old man, where are you, did you know your wife was going to have a baby?"

Max dropped by that night. Vincent met him at the door and apparently told him quickly because when Max came in he seemed uncertain of what to say. Vincent had been a little strange, himself. He hadn't congratulated Mimi or anything—at least not in my hearing—but his manner at dinner had been somewhat circumspect. As though the fact of her pregnancy made it less tempting to provoke her.

"I just wanted to tell you," Max said to me, "I finished the outside wall. I'll take you up any time you feel like it."

I nodded. My lips were very dry. "Thank you," I said stiffly.

"She's a little thrown by this baby business," Vincent apologized for me. "It's a big thing for her, you know, a big change. She's got to get used to it."

"Sure," Max said.

Pause. Uneasiness. Barney came in, so drunk that he was weaving. As often as he was a little drunk, I had never seen Barney in that condition.

"Hi," he said. "We're taking a poll here. How do you feel about babiesh?"

Max laughed. "Babies are babies."

"Babies are a pain in the ash," Barney said. "Check yesh or no."

"I guess so," Max said. "I guess they are."

"Thish baby should be dishposed of. Check yesh or no."

Max ignored him. Barney flopped down on the sofa.

"My mother delivered a few babies," Max said to Vincent. "When I was little. Her whole family was up in Peekskill, her three sisters, and she was midwife when they had their babies. I helped a couple of times."

Vincent gaped. I stared. It seemed incredible.

"You're kidding," Vincent finally said.

"Uh uh," Max told him, "I'm not kidding. I'd bring the hot water, you know, just like in the movies, and clean sheets and newspaper and stuff like that. I was around nine or ten for the last one. They started using doctors after that."

Barney seemed about to throw up. Gagged audibly. Then with some difficulty he got up and lurched out of the room.

"How the hell did you do it?" Vincent asked. "How the hell could you stand it?"

"I don't know," Max said. "I threw up the first time but after that I was all right. It was interesting."

Expecting Josh's arrival soon, Lily came back from Westport, her immediate concern being that Josh should return before her suntan had faded. Mimi said she had something to tell Lily but Lily said she simply wasn't in condition to hear anything, she was exhausted, maybe some mild form of sunstroke or something, she must take a shower and

a nap before she had anything to do with anybody. Then she swept up
the stairs, leaving Mimi staring up at her.

"She doesn't want to hear it," I said.

She doesn't want to hear it.

She doesn't want to hear it.

No one wants to hear it.

"What do you mean?" Mimi asked.

"I mean she doesn't want to know you're pregnant."

"That's a funny thing to say. She doesn't know what I'm going to
tell her."

"Then why doesn't she want to hear it?"

Mimi laughed as though I'd made a joke but later on, when Lily had
washed and slept and put on another dress and come downstairs, and
Mimi had followed her from room to room trying to talk but being interrupted by successive requests for a drink, a tissue, windows open a
little wider, and so on, I tried to catch her eye and finally realized she
was avoiding mine.

I was standing at the open terrace door in the living room when Lily
floated toward me on her way out.

"Lily," I said, without premeditation, "I'm going to have a baby."

Lily stopped short. Mimi laughed. Lily looked back and forth between us, gratifyingly bewildered.

"You're terrible, Beth," Mimi said, and came over and put an arm
around Lily. "She's teasing, Lily. *I'm* having a baby. That's what I've
been trying to tell you."

"What a silly joke," Lily said, frowning.

"No, I'm not joking," Mimi told her. ". . . Oh, you mean Beth's
joke."

Lily nodded.

"But I really am going to have a baby, you realize that, don't you?"
Mimi asked anxiously.

"Yes," Lily said, "well, that's all right . . . I mean, it's all right if you
want it . . . of course there's no rule that says you have to have it if
you don't want it . . . I know millions of people in L.A. who take care
of those things . . . if you feel you're too old . . . or you just have too
much to do . . . any reason . . ."

At first Mimi couldn't believe what she was hearing. When she did
believe it, tears came to her eyes and began rolling down her round
cheeks.

"It's nothing to cry about, dear," Lily assured her. "It's perfectly
harmless."

"Not to the baby," Mimi said, struggling to hold her voice together.

"But if you don't *want* the baby," Lily said reasonably.

"But I *do* want the baby," Mimi said. "I've wanted a baby for years. I'm *dying* to have a baby."

"Oh, well . . ." Lily shrugged. "That's all right, then." And she wafted past me out to the balcony.

Mimi began crying in earnest. I wanted to say something to comfort her but just as I was about to try I suddenly remembered her saying to Barney, *Some women, when they announce they're pregnant, everyone gets very solicitous,* and somehow that memory frightened me into silence, reminding me of that feeling I'd had of not knowing who Mimi was any more. Mrs. Cushman came in to say that dinner was ready and I finally asked Mimi if she would like me to cut some mums for the table but she didn't stop crying. Mrs. Cushman seemed about to go to Mimi but then she changed her mind and went back to the kitchen so I went up to Barney's study to get him. The door was open and he and Vincent were talking quietly. I stood in the doorway but they ignored me for a moment.

". . . no question of provocation," Barney said. "Of course the Reds provoked it. Especially after the veterans and the other idiots stopped the first concert and they realized what fertile ground they had here. But the Reds were smart enough to let the locals take the initiative . . . and also to stick with legal weapons. Baseball bats, can openers, cans of pepper, stuff like that. Josh was past all that by then, of course. If he went up there at all it was most likely to laugh." He turned and looked at me expectantly.

I said, "Dinner is ready. Please come down right away. Mimi is very upset."

"Are you suggesting," he asked after a moment, "that if I'm a good boy and eat my dinner my wife will cease to be upset?"

"No. It has nothing to do with that."

"What does it have to do with?"

"Lily."

"Lily? Lily doesn't upset my wife. Lily upsets my wife's sister but . . ." He trailed off and I could see he'd realized. "My wife," he said, "has told her mother that she is pregnant and has been disappointed with her mother's reaction."

I nodded.

"What happened?" Vincent asked with sudden intense interest.

"Mimi told Lily she was going to have a baby," I said. Knowing that what I was doing was evil. "And Lily said if Mimi doesn't want the baby she knows a lot of people in Los Angeles who take care of those things." Never taking my eyes off Vincent's face, although I heard Barney laugh abruptly, murmur, "Good old Lil." The outside of Vincent's body remained motionless. The inside curled up into itself until it didn't exist any more. I shuddered.

Barney put down his drink and came with me. For a moment we waited to see if Vincent would come with us. But he wasn't even there. Downstairs we found Mimi already seated at the dining table. Her eyes were red but she wasn't crying any more. She was eating a roll.

"Hey, sport," Barney said, bending over and giving her a kiss. She smiled absently. We sat down. Mrs. Cushman brought in the salad and Mimi began serving without asking where Vincent and Lily were.

"Where's Grandma?" Barney asked.

"Grandma?" Mimi repeated.

"Mmm. Grandma Lily," Barney said. "Or maybe it hasn't occurred to you that that's what she's going to be?"

"No," Mimi said. "I hadn't really thought of her that way."

"I don't imagine she thinks of herself that way," Barney said. "I don't imagine she wants to."

"Is that what it's all about!" Mimi exclaimed with some relief, but then her face clouded over and she said, "You told them, Beth. You told them what she said."

Vincent, or the body of Vincent, came downstairs and seated itself at the table. A moment later Lily came in and asked why no one had told her dinner was ready, she was famished. There was absolute silence around the table for perhaps a full minute, then Mimi said she was sorry, she'd assumed Lily knew and hadn't felt like coming in yet.

"I'm famished," Lily repeated, attacking her salad. "Everyone in Westport is on Weight Watchers, the food was ghastly. Dietetic soda and vegetables and some kind of fake dressing on the salad. Unbelievable." She shuddered but couldn't conceal her smugness at not having to diet.

"How is old Westport these days, Lil?" Barney asked.

"Dull," she said. "Incredibly dull. All they talk about is TV commercials and Vietnam. I don't know which bores me more."

"Vietnam, no doubt."

"I suppose so. At least they all have different accounts but they all say the same thing about Vietnam. That wretched little swamp has just about destroyed the art of conversation in this country. I don't even know where it is." Proudly. Lily was the only person who ever briefly made me feel I should take an interest in outside affairs.

"Lily," Barney said abruptly. "When did Trotsky's daughter kill herself?"

"Zina?" she said. " 'Thirty-three. Why?"

"Where?"

"Berlin. You know that, Barney. When they wouldn't let her come back to her husband."

"You see?" Barney said to Vincent. "That's what I was talking about before, about the things they remember and the things they don't remember. Even Lily . . ." but he trailed off because he'd failed to get Vincent's attention. Oddly, Barney was always quicker to catch my moods, or even Mimi's, than to understand Vincent's.

"That was when Josh broke, Barney," Lily said. "A little after then, you know that. It was so sad, her husband was in Russia and she'd gone to Germany for treatments, she was tubercular or something, and while she was there they took away her citizenship and wouldn't let her back in and finally she killed herself with gas. I remember we weren't supposed to think it was sad and then when Josh broke with the Party he came home and told me that now I could cry for her if I wanted to, and not be ashamed of it, and the hell with anyone who thought it was all right just because Stalin had done it. Then I didn't know which was sadder, that Trotsky's daughter killed herself . . . or that Josh had broken and no one would talk to us any more. Josh knew they wouldn't talk to us, that we'd be outcasts, none of our old friends would come near us . . . that was really why it took him so long to break."

Vincent stirred.

"Did you ever decide?" Barney asked her softly. "Which was sadder, I mean?"

"Oh, I don't know," Lily said. "Suicide, I suppose, because it lasts longer. After all, by the time of the Moscow Trials we had a few of our friends back and then after the Nazi-Soviet Pact we had almost all of them. In New York, I mean. On the Coast it was never as bad. There's always someone there who wants to talk to you more than you want to talk to them . . . but Trotsky's daughter was still dead." She giggled suddenly but when no one else laughed she became very serious. "Suicide is a terrible thing," she announced. "When you think about it . . . and don't think I haven't thought about it. There've been times . . ."

It had the desired effect, at least on Mimi, who quickly said, "Oh, Lily, don't talk like that," in a low, troubled voice.

"Oh but it's true," Lily said. "Ask Josh how close I came. Once it took him hours to convince me that I should keep living."

It was easier to conceive of Lily's pressing that button I once read about, to destroy the entire world, than to imagine her letting a razor come within an inch of her wrist.

"I don't have the courage," Lily said. "That's the thing. It takes an enormous amount of courage to—"

Vincent stood up so abruptly that he knocked down his chair in back of him, and stalked out of the house, slamming the door behind him.

"What on earth is wrong with him now?" Lily asked. Then, without waiting for an answer, "In the old days, people were plenty temperamental, but they were *interesting*. Josh was always slamming out of houses, especially after he broke, but at least he'd have a good fight first. We were still on all the mailing lists and we'd get all these invitations, you know, people would give private parties and you paid for food and the money would always go to something called Liberation this or Freedom that and then Josh would always get into an argument with someone about whether it was just a Party front, which was what it was most of the time, even if a lot of them didn't know it, and then Josh would get kicked out because he always won the arguments and they couldn't stand it. Or else we'd just slam out on our own and go get drunk. It was *fun*. He didn't just sit there like a zombie and then slam out for no reason."

I said, "Vincent had a reason."

Mimi said my name in a low warning voice but I ignored her.

"He didn't want to be in the same house with you. He thinks you're a murderer."

"Beth," Mimi said, "Beth, stop it. You don't know what you're doing."

"Oh, Jesus," Barney said.

"What is she talking about?" Lily demanded. "Will someone please tell me what the little witch is talking about?"

"It's nothing, Lily," Mimi said. "Forget it."

"Being a witch is like being royalty," I said calmly. "You have to inherit it from someone."

"Barney," Mimi said, "don't you think it would be nice if Beth went up to her room for a little while until we can all calm down?"

"Two of them," Lily said, her voice cracking with self-pity. "What have I done to deserve two of them?"

"C'mon, Beth," Barney said, coming over to take me away. "Let's go up, honey."

"Honey!" Lily screeched. "Will you please tell me how he can call her honey? She's a lunatic, a raving lunatic!"

"Please, Lily," Mimi said. "Please let it go. Everyone's upset."

"Damn right I'm upset," she screamed. "She always upsets me. The two of them upset me. Plenty of people have one crazy kid, hardly anyone has . . . In L.A. there are places to send them, I tell you, I can't stand looking at either of them, it makes me CRINGE when I have to look at them."

"Shut up, Lily," Barney said, his arm around me to help me. But I had put Lily thousands of miles away where she couldn't hurt me.

"You see?" Lily asked, still in that horrible hysterical screech. "That's why I can't stand to come here. She starts in with one of her crazy lunatic bits and he tells *me* to shut up! It's like a zoo or a nut house or something! L.A. is full of creeps but they're all out on the beach or put away someplace and if you want to get away from them all you do is go into your own house but here there's no place to go, I can't stand it here, why don't you put her away someplace, I don't know—"

"She's hysterical," Barney said to Mimi. "Smack her face."

"Don't you dare!" Lily screamed. "I have a very low threshold of pain!"

For a moment we all just stared at her in wonder but gradually I felt laughter welling up inside of me, taking over my entire body until finally it burst out in a wild trumpeting sound that I was powerless to stop. Lily rushed from the room and Mimi covered her eyes but still I couldn't stop laughing, although it was coming out a little more quietly now, and then I thought to myself, *they would hit me, now, if they hadn't been about to do it to Lily for saying they should put me away.* And with that thought I began to cry, and then after a while the crying ended, too, and then Barney carried me upstairs and put me to bed, where I slept through the night with my clothes on.

Vincent didn't come back. All his belongings, including his wallet, were in his room. I called Max, thinking he might have gone there, but Max hadn't seen him since our last evening together. In my dreams Vincent was a bird without wings. I willed him to fly but my will was insufficient and his heart burst when he tried. I wet my pillow weeping for him before I was awake and the dream was so real to me that as my eyes opened my hand touched the wet spot and I knew without thinking why it was there.

Josh arrived as Lily was packing to leave. Another half an hour and we would have been rid of her. He'd come on a motorcycle he'd rented in Southampton. The cycle almost but not quite concealed that he'd aged somewhat in the eight or nine months since we had seen him. Still it was hard to believe that he'd just had his sixty-seventh birthday. His hair was white and his paunch had grown a bit but otherwise he was as lean as ever.

"How's my punkin?" he asked, galloping from the cycle to the lawn, where I sat with my embroidery.

"I'm all right, Josh," I said. Which was true, I was tired but very calm. I got up so he could kiss me. Then we went together into the house, which was very quiet.

"Where is everybody? Where's your mother?"

Habit. He didn't really care if she was there, I was certain; I knew that sometimes he preferred it. But he had to know right away. For a moment I toyed with the idea of getting him to take a long walk so that by the time we returned Mimi would have taken Lily to the station. Then I realized it wouldn't work because of the motorcycle.

"She's upstairs packing."

"To go?"

"Mm. But she won't, now that you've come."

We went into the kitchen where he kissed Mrs. Cushman loudly and took a can of beer from the refrigerator then strode to the bottom of the stairs and shouted, "Hey! Poppa's here, where's *Momser?*"

"Josh! Josh!" Mimi called from the top. "Oh I'm so glad you're here!"

He turned to me. "Your sister says she's glad I'm here."

I nodded.

"Your sister always says she's glad I'm here but this time it has the ring of sincerity."

"Josh," Mimi called, "Lily's up here with me. Please come right up."

And with a puzzled look in my direction he ran up to soothe his much abused wife. Mimi came down a few minutes later. I didn't particularly feel like talking so I wandered outdoors, but she followed me outside and said I must promise not to start in with Lily again if she stayed.

"Do you want me put away, too?" Maybe it was some sort of measure of the unreality of my life that I could spend so much time eliciting specific known responses. On the TV set I saw war being waged; missiles being fired; cities being destroyed, none of which seemed to affect me although my brain, on those rare occasions when I permitted it to function, told me that eventually they all would. Certainly I never felt moved to even attempt to do something about them, if indeed anything could be done, but I did feel moved to ask Mimi if she wanted to put me away so that I could hear her tell me I was being ridiculous.

"Don't be ridiculous, Beth."

"Why are you so worried about her, anyway? She worries about herself enough, you don't have to do it, too. She puts everything else out of your mind. You haven't even asked me where Vincent is."

"Do you know?"

"No, I don't know. But *I'm* worried about *him!*" Because I didn't have the strong sense that he was alive.

"I don't think you need to," Mimi said. "He can just bum around. Men can do that, you know." She put a hand on her stomach, which already looked somewhat swollen. "I'm starvingly hungry. Want some lunch?"

"No."

She rushed to the kitchen as though there were an emergency.

I walked up to the mailbox just in case there should be word from Vincent, but there wasn't, only some letters for Josh that had been forwarded from California. And the *Weekly*, with a small item saying that the Village Planning Board had put on its fall agenda a discussion of the widening of Sugar Hill Road. So it was time again. Except that I thought of it as time for battle and I suddenly remembered the way Mimi had recently referred to the road. By the time I got back to the house they were having lunch and Barney had joined them. Lily and Josh sat side by side and his arm was on the back of her chair. She had on a great deal of makeup. She looked down at her plate when I came in.

"So I said to him," Josh was saying, "'Okay, baby, now *I* have a riddle for *you*. What is it that when you do it, you lose your identity and when you undo it you don't get your identity back, you only lose the one you scraped together in the meantime?' The answer's 'Marry a *schickser*,' of course, but the interesting thing was to see the answers the silly bastard came up with. What they amounted to was that everything he'd ever done in his lifetime was what lost him his identity. The one thing that didn't occur to him was that he never had one in the first place. There was someone there who knew him when he was six years old and swore to me that even then he was a total blank."

The whole thing would have been funnier had his manner not been so strained. Josh always dominated our conversation and almost invariably in an interesting way, but now there was a feeling that he *had* to. As though everyone else were made of stone and this would be apparent if he didn't keep talking. Lily looked at him adoringly. I could see through the makeup that she had been crying, could easily picture the touching scene upstairs where Josh persuaded her that the things families said to each other were meaningless and the best way to get over them was to push them out of your mind. "Come on downstairs, Lil, I've got some good stories for you."

I gave him his mail and he began opening it, making jokes about the various bills and letters as he read them, until finally he came to one, from some law firm with a series of names which he read aloud from the envelope, adding a few obscene ones for effect, but when he read the letter itself he was silent.

Barney clucked. "He's involved in another paternity suit."

"What is it, Josh?" Lily asked, trying to see over his shoulder. But he hid the letter.

"*I* know," Barney said. "*You're* suing him for paternity, Mimi. I knew it couldn't be my fault, they promised me when I had that operation . . ."

"What operation?" Josh asked. "What the hell are you talking about?"

"Your daughter is pregnant," Barney said.

"You're kidding," Josh exclaimed jovially. "Hey, that's great, I'm gonna be a grandpa! Jesus Christ! Hey, congratulations, sport!" He seemed genuinely pleased.

"My God," Barney said, "I can see it in the papers now. A Communist-incest-paternity case!"

"I am not now nor have I ever been," Josh said solemnly, "incestuously involved with my older daughter. She is one of my failures."

Lily giggled.

"Very funny, Josh," Mimi said, snapping off a big piece of her Italian bread to show what she thought of his joke.

"Ouch," Josh said. "You know that reminds me of a party I went to. You know the old bit, the girls coming out of a cake and so on, well—"

For some reason my mind went to the letter he hadn't joked about, which I now realized he was edging toward his pants pocket as he spoke. Lily must have noticed it, too, because as he had the letter at the edge of his pocket, she reached around and grabbed it playfully and swooped up from the table with it, ignoring Josh's command to give it back and opening it and reading it instead. She handed it back to him with a shrug.

"They've got some nerve."

"Someone's got nerve," Josh said. "Someone I just rescued from the depths of depression."

"Incredible," Lily went on, not noticing. "It was worth more than that ten years ago."

I still might not have understood what they were talking about if Josh hadn't glanced at me guiltily then. A dead feeling came over me. It was too much, this on top of everything else. If he . . . but it wasn't possible . . .

"So anyhow," Josh went back to his story, "instead of having the girls come out of a cake, Sam had them bust out of a huge black stew pot in the middle of the barbecue, all covered with soup and vegetables AND THEN . . ." Interruption. Laughter. They all laughed. Why didn't they ask? Why didn't they see what was happening? "Then he'd had these six-foot-long Italian breads flown in from Manganaro's . . ."

"Josh," I interrupted, "you've had an offer for the land."

"Forget it, honey," he said. "It's nothing to worry about."

"But you *have* had an offer."

"It's not an offer, it's a joke. Forget it."

"Are you going to forget it?"

"That's exactly what I'm going to do."

"What if they offer you more?"

"Don't worry about it," he said. "They won't offer me enough."

"What would be enough?"

"God damn it," he exploded, making me cringe. "What the hell kind of third degree am I getting?"

Barney whistled because Josh had never talked to me that way before. He was often casual—even sardonic—with Mimi, but he'd always treated me with tenderness.

"She has no idea, Josh," Lily said. Fantastically smug and self-righteous. "She has no idea of what's involved."

"Oh, I dunno about that, Lil," Barney said. "She knew it was the house that was involved, which was more than the rest of us realized."

"It's not the house!" Josh snapped. "They don't want the goddamn house. They probably wouldn't take the fucking monster house if I handed it to them on a silver platter."

"Is it only land then?" Mimi asked quietly.

"Of course it's land," Josh said. "What do you think they want? The suburbs are getting built up like crazy, or hadn't you heard? You kiddies knock me out. Hollywood is a hotbed of realism compared to this place, you live in a nice little dream world of your own up here. A nice *big* dream world, I should say. Thirty-two acres. Did you really think thirty-two acres an hour from Grand Central Station was going to go unnoticed forever?"

"No," Mimi said. "I guess I didn't think so. I mean, I guess none of us really thought about it seriously, at all. We knew there'd been offers in the past but we never took them seriously. The only time we ever got worried was when something like the road came up, something we might not be able to control, otherwise we didn't really think about it."

We assumed that we were safe.

"I *bet* you didn't think about it," Josh said. "You're all quick to grab lawyers' letters out of my hand"—as though it had been one of us, instead of Lily, who'd snatched the letter—"but no one ever bothers to sneak a look at my tax bill, *that's* just forwarded to California."

There was silence for a moment. Barney broke it.

"You're losing your posture, Josh," he said.

Josh glared at him but unthinkingly straightened his back.

"Not that one, J.C. I mean your liberal posture. Your Paying-Taxes-is-a-Small-Price-for-Living-in-a-Democracy Posture."

Josh laughed but he wasn't really amused. "Thirty-five years ago," he said, "I tried walking down the hill alone one night and I had my pants pulled off and my ass and dick painted red by a bunch of guineas who didn't know the difference between Leon Trotsky and Benedict Arnold." He paused, added irresistibly, "They only knew both of them were Jews. . . . Today I pay a small fortune every year to send their goddamn guinea kids and guinea grandchildren through public school. For what? No doubt I'm supposed to sit in Beverly Hills, holding my balls and paying Lily's bills and telling myself that if their kids have enough education their attitudes'll be different from their parents. But you know and I know that all that's so much horse manure. They get their attitudes from their lousy guinea parents long before they ever get to school and nothing they learn in school ever changes them."

"Listen to him," Barney said. "He hasn't been near a school in half a century."

Silence.

"What do you use it all for?" Josh suddenly demanded of Mimi.

"Use what for?" Mimi asked, confused.

"The land, Mimi," Barney said. "Your father wants evidence that you make good use of this land that he sacrifices to let you keep occupying. You know, how often you tread on each square inch of the acreage, what healing potions you make from the herbs thereon, that kind of thing."

"Josh," Mimi said, "there are ways to hold on to land without paying taxes. There's a group called Nature Conservancy, that's just one of them, and you can deed them the land and they leave it wild but you don't own it any more so you don't have to pay taxes."

I was completely bewildered by all this. We had never talked about any of it. But Josh pounced on it gleefully.

"Aha!" he said. "How interesting. I thought you never thought about such things, daughter mine."

She blushed deeply. An announcement that she thought about them more than I could have dreamed. She must have sensed long before that something could happen.

"I meant," she said lamely, "I hadn't thought about them in concrete terms."

"Oh, no," Josh said. "Nothing concrete. Nothing *profitable*, you mean. You just sat around and figured out a good way for me to get rid of all my land without getting a red cent for it. Your generalities bore me, sport, but I'll give you one of my own. Land around here's going for about six thousand an acre and I've got thirty-two acres, here, let's say thirty that could be sold for a grand total of a hundred and eighty grand."

"It's unimproved land," Mimi said quietly. "And you don't get that price when you sell a large parcel."

"Fine," Josh said. "Cut it in half and laugh off ninety thousand."

"Nobody's laughing off anything," she said.

"Well I'm glad," Josh told her. "Because ninety-thousand clams'll pay a lot of Bonwit bills and I've got a lot of Bonwit bills to pay, eh, Lil?"

She kissed his cheek.

"Hey," he said, "if I say that again will you do that again?"

It was repulsively mechanical. A parody.

"Look at them," Barney said. "Shirley Temple and Bob Hope."

"Are you serious about it, then?" Mimi asked Josh.

"I'm not serious about anything, sweetie," Josh said. "It's the secret of my charm."

I looked around at all of them. They had the air of having settled something, but I couldn't tell what.

I said, "I don't understand what's happening."

Lily laughed shortly as though to say I never did.

"We seem to have established that your father owns a rather valuable piece of real estate, even if one doesn't consider the land immediately around this house," Barney said, "and that his inclination is to take advantage of that fact, sooner or later."

"But why, Josh?" I asked, my throat aching with held-back tears. "Why should you do it? Are you punishing us for something?"

"Sweet Jesus," Josh said, smacking his forehead, looking unutterably pained. "What the hell can I say to a question like that?"

"Beth," Mimi said, "listen to me. We've got to be reasonable. He's not talking about selling the house out from under us." She hesitated, turned to Josh, "You did mean that, didn't you, Josh? About not taking the house or the immediate grounds?"

"What's going on?" Josh asked with an unsuitable bitterness. "What are you two trying to make me out to be? I can see it now—Junior, I want you to meet your Grandpa Josh who kicked us out of our house in a blizzard when we couldn't come up with the mortgage money."

"You see?" she said. "He has no idea of selling the house."

It had never occurred to me that he had. My mind simply never separated the house from the rest of it. "What about the farm? And the pond? And the stables?"

"The farm is half a mile down the road," Josh said. "The piece of land it's on is legally bound to this only by the fact that I own it all and someday you will, or the remaining proceeds therefrom. I fail to see why you should take more than a normal neighborly interest in it."

"Oh, come off it, Josh," Barney said. "If you're going to do it you're going to do it, but let's not have any of this fail-to-see stuff. You understand Beth as well as anyone does and you know how she feels about this place."

Did he? Did he understand that when he asked why I should care about having the other land as long as the house and gardens were left intact, it was very much like asking why I should mind having my limbs cut off, provided my internal organs were left alone?

"All right," Josh said. "I know, I know."

What we had was inseparable from what we were. Mimi used to get upset that so many people should be hostile to us without even knowing us but to me it seemed quite reasonable. Without it we would have been no better than they.

"Listen to me, Beth," Josh said.

The world is impossible. Nothing but madness and confusion. And in their crowded homes on tiny plots on paved streets they have no protection from its most casual violence. To say they should not resent us was to say that having nothing was as good as having everything.

"Beth?"

"I don't see why you bother, Josh," Lily fretted. "She's off in a trance, she won't listen."

Lily was always the one person from whom Yiytzo's protection was inadequate. And even with Lily the size of the land helped because she never ventured beyond the interior gardens so that when I found it entirely unbearable to be in the same house with her I could disappear into the forest.

"Beth," Josh said, "come with me. I want to talk with you." He took my hand and led me out to the terrace. "Beth, I have no intention of doing anything right now. If I sounded that way it was just because I felt as if I'd been put on the defensive. I'm not seeking out this thing. I haven't put it up for sale and I'm not going to. But I get constant pressure. It's too beautiful a piece of property, too big a piece to be neglected. There's one developer who's been after me hot and heavy for six years and I've been saying no all that time and I have no intention of saying yes in the near future, but I can't promise you that I never will, can't you see that?"

He seemed terribly earnest but I couldn't believe in his earnestness. Maybe it was the deep deep suntan and the white hair, which always made him seem a little unreal, anyway. Mimi and Barney had visited him once in Beverly Hills and reported that he seemed entirely different there. He looked just like everybody else.

"You've got this vision of me as some kind of millionaire," he said.

This wasn't true. I'd never thought twice about Josh's money, except to be grateful for that part of it which allowed him to support Lily away from Yiytzo and thus made possible my continued existence. Money never had any reality to me otherwise.

"It simply isn't so, Beth. I've made a lot of money and I've spent a lot of money. The only thing I've got that would make me rich by anyone's standards is this land, and it also keeps me poor. Not this alone, but after all, I maintain an expensive apartment for myself, I have to, and I pay Lily's hotel bills all year 'round, so I spend a lot of money just on places to live. And I don't mind. Not the part of it that's necessary, or even that adds substantially to our pleasure, any of us. I love you and I want you to be happy, you know that." Still very earnest. So many words without a single joke. Still playing the role of doting father. It was the first time I'd actually thought of it that way. "But to ask me to hold on forever to a piece of land that drains my blood without giving anyone very much in return, most of it, when I could make a small fortune by selling off a bloc of it and investing the money. That isn't fair to me. It isn't even fair to you. What would happen if I just passed it on to you? You couldn't afford to hold on to it, anyway. It takes most of my income from stocks just to pay the taxes and the basic maintenance costs and when I die you won't have that income because the stocks are going to Lily."

"She'll die, too," I pointed out.

He smiled. "Only you could say it with such equanimity. Anyway, I wouldn't count on it. She could outlive me by thirty years, probably will, and the place would bust you in much less time than that. There's a trust fund for the two of you but it just won't cover everything. I'd show it to you in writing if I thought it would help but I know it won't . . . would it?"

Help what, Josh? Your writing could only help you to show your reasons for what you were going to do, it couldn't change my reasons for not wanting you to do it.

"No."

"Is there anything that would help?"

"No."

People do what they are going to do. All my life I'd had fewer enemies than Mimi because I never asked nor expected anything of people. There was in Mimi's wholesale affection and eternal optimism an implicit demand that people attempt to fulfill their better selves. While lacking the belief in those better selves, I never summoned them to action.

"I guess I should stop trying, then . . . is there anything you want to say to me, Beth? Do you want to argue? I'll listen to anything you have to say. I don't want to be arbitrary. Talk to me."

That day you lost your partisan in this household, Josh. I can't say you betrayed my trust because that would suggest that I'd believed you would always protect my interests while in point of fact it hadn't occurred to me that I would need your protection. I'd only assumed that in any discussion with Lily of where our interests lay, you would be more likely to be on the right side. And of course it was true, it just didn't go far enough. It seemed strange later on that I'd never questioned further. It seemed strange now that the things you and Lily together did to us, I only blamed on her until that day.

"You only blame her," Mimi had said to me more than once. "Why is everything her fault?" Followed by a recitation of Josh's faults. "I don't mind that you love Josh, that's fine, but can't you have a little sympathy for her, too?"

I couldn't of course. Why should I have? Why should I have torn myself to pieces attempting to hate someone and sympathize with her at the same time? So, hating Lily, I sympathized with you until that day when your interests became hostile to mine. And then you lost me, Josh. As Lily had lost me years before from not caring, you lost me that day from caring but not nearly enough.

Part Two

NOVEMBER–DECEMBER

Finally I had a letter from Vincent. He was in Vincennes. He asked me to send his wallet and papers but to discard the clothing he'd left. (I brought it up to the attic.) Not a word about what had happened, of course. He was boarding with a family there, a woman and her son, and expected to stay for a while.

You know that I hate it here, Beth, but you must also know that aside from battle periods during the war it's the only place where I've ever been able to briefly delude myself that I exist. In all the time that I'm traveling—that is to say in most of the time of my life—I am looking for someplace else that will have this same effect on me. Not because I hate Vincennes—hating things has never bothered me in the least, I enjoy hating—but because it seems inappropriate that I should be the embodiment of that otherwise charming cliche, the small-town boy who's uncomfortable when he's away from home. Out of his element except in his—Oh, Jesus—except in his birthplace. His birthplace, his deathplace. Still, if it surrounds him he must be there. Why this more than any other place? Memories? 'Nothing that happens after the age of five has any importance,' one of those phony perpetually couch-ridden types once said to me as she spread her legs beneath me. But I have no memory of anything that happened in the first five years of my life, which taken to its obvious conclusion means that nothing of importance has ever happened to me or ever will, a conclusion which would be as laughable as the idiot who made the pronouncement if it weren't obviously true.
The identity thing has become the new groove, of course, groove

alias rut. Safe harbor for the TV walkie-talkie creeple peoples who get their kicks from rubbing up against half-baked potatoes and ejaculating sour cream at them. Identity is a bag and a gag. Yet it exists for me with all the force of a fatal disease. Obviously I'm here, a mind and a body. To say there's no proof my body exists would be arty and specious and if my mind is more ephemeral, less provable, the solution of being a writer with solid (touchable, tearable, burnable) books is as close as anyone has come to a perfect answer. The obvious reason that every asshole in the world wants to write. So. I'm here. But where do I end? I wasn't finished when I was born, a hole was left and most of the time I can't tell what part of my surroundings has seeped into the hole to masquerade as part of me . . . or vice versa . . . while the ancient—prehistory—dull familiarity of Vincennes makes me relatively certain that I would know if something were out of place.

It took me four days to hitch back to Vincennes, with good long night rides from trucks and shorter ones in the day. A surprising number from women alone in their cars. Particularly surprising since I've been given to understand that my appearance is generally formidable and I'd been without shower, clean clothes (or food, for that matter) since leaving you. I was picked up by teenage girls out driving daddy's Buick, by good-looking women in sports cars, and so on. At some point during the time I was in Europe—or maybe it began before then and I just didn't notice—women stopped thinking of rape as being something to avoid.

My last hitch was with this woman I'm staying with, Myrna. She was on her way to Vincennes with her kid, a great little nine-year-old kid named Steven. Her husband was killed in Vietnam. She was in a pretty bad way—I noticed how she was driving before I even realized she was going to stop for me. To do that, she cut from the left lane across the middle one in front of a little Jaguar that was doing at least sixty itself, and then to stop she braked so hard that the kid, who was sleeping on the back seat, was thrown onto the floor. It took a few minutes to straighten him out but he wasn't hurt. I don't suppose you'd go for her, Beth, it's hard to see how she'd fit into that little nineteenth-century convent that Pope Joan runs there, but there's something about her that gets me . . . her hands . . . maybe it's just those wild hands. She's got a lean muscular body and her face is as hard as a whore's. The general effect is of the lady villain in a Sunday comic strip. But her hands are very small, very soft, incredibly fragile, holding one is like holding a sparrow, there is the constant fear that you're going to break one of its bones. Or all of them. When I touch her hands I feel for her a tenderness that I've felt for only one woman—girl— female—oh, shit. You're the only person in the world, Beth, for whom I've ever willingly imposed even a little caution on myself.

I'll have to come back before too long because some of the information I need still isn't here. I keep stumbling on the goddamn details. I've never bothered with details, as you know, and that supposedly adds to the power of my stuff although in the old days every time I published a book some carping little academic bastard made sure to point out that if I did know what my hero looked like I was keeping it a secret. Anyhow. The symbols of the sixties have the purity of the Greek myths—Vietnam, the Blacks—while the symbols of the thirties were tied up in a thousand tricky little arguments and philosophies which only became purified in later years, the Peekskill riots being one of the better examples. I'm using the time-machine bit—right now I'm trying to work out a chapter called Lovestone and Shachtman Take a Trip—but I keep getting bogged down in details. In the thirties all the healthiest symbols—i.e. the Spanish Civil War—end up getting shot to hell and all that you're left with is betrayal. Betrayals are a dime a dozen. They bore me. My old man, who for some reason I suddenly wish you could meet although I'm sure you never will, it's all I can do to get the poor old bastard to see me once in a while, I make him uncomfortable . . . my old man gets tears in his eyes when he looks at the American flag and that single fact about him makes him more interesting to me than all the Josh Cohen-Canes in the world. I suppose that sounds pretty obvious and predictable but my feeling for the two set aside, I could probably make out a pretty good case that loyalty is more interesting than treason because the mental contortions it requires are far more complex, it's far more difficult to justify the actions of those you love than to simply betray them by loving elsewhere.

It is easier to betray than to remain loyal.
It takes far less courage to kill yourself than it takes to make your-
self wake up one more time.

*It's harder to stay where you are than to get out. (For everyone
but you, that is.)*

Myrna knocked around when she was in Vincennes and it was the
hardest thing in the world for her to come back and she nearly
didn't do it. I think I told you the way she was driving when she
picked me up. The first thing I asked her was if she was trying to
kill herself, why'd she have to kill the kid, too, and she didn't deny
it but said, "Why not? Do you have a better idea?" I couldn't answer her. It takes a certain dumb arrogance to tell someone else to
go on living. I just said if she wanted to kill herself she could let
us both out of the car and I'd look after the kid.

"What makes you such a big public benefactor?" she asked. I said
I wasn't, I just liked kids, I especially liked them better than I
liked crazy broads that try to smash them up in cars. Then she
pulled over to the side of the road and said if I was just going to
bitch at her the rest of the way, I could do the driving.

The setup here is pretty good for me. We have a floor-through in
one of those raunchy Greek Revival jobs that makes Vincennes
superficially distinguishable from the rest of Indiana. I work in the
kitchen right where all the action is—I'd forgotten how good it was
to work that way, how easily words came when I was in the middle of a barracks—with Myrna working and washing dishes if she's
home (she got a job in a laundromat a couple of weeks ago) and
Steve hanging around. He's a funny kid, tight and quiet, but with
plenty inside. He watches me writing the way old ladies watch an
artist at the seashore. As if any minute he'll be able to look at the
paper and see what I've been up to. Once when I looked up he
was staring at my beard as if the words were coming out of it.
I made some joke to that effect but I only succeeded in throwing
him for a loop. He doesn't know from jokes, this kid, he only
knows . . . I make it a point to be serious with him now . . . anyway, in Vincennes the juiciest puns come off like farts in an echo
chamber.

Don't write to me. I'm not ready for you to write to me yet. I'll let
you know when I'm coming and then all you'll have to do is let
me know if I shouldn't come, that is, if anyone's there beside the
three of you.

Meanwhile strangers began coming around. I would walk past the farm and see a car parked in the bushes on one of the dirt roads and two men in business suits standing near it, looking around them. Men with surveying instruments claimed to be lost when I asked if I could help them. A couple with children in the back of the car pulled up beside me on the road and asked if I knew anything about the farmhouse. A tightening network. I told Mimi and she said that I had become overly suspicious. But she did attend the next two town board meetings, although I first had to persuade her that no matter what happened with Josh, a highway right outside our drive would be as much a horror as it would have been five years or five months before. She came home from the meeting more absorbed in the fact that several people had failed to recognize her because of the weight she'd put on than in anything else, and I had to press her to find out that the road had come up and the Mayor had suggested they postpone real consideration since they didn't have the Planning Board's report yet.

"I had a feeling he might be stalling just because I'd turned up for the meeting," Mimi said—*but without indignation.* "During the question period I asked him why they needed a new report when last year's report said they could make it faster but not safer because all the twists and curves are too basic. And he just smiled in that sort of charming-disarming way of his and said they liked to keep up to date, but I had a feeling that if I hadn't been there, or one of the others, they might have slipped something through." She laughed ruefully. "I suppose I should be glad he recognized me. The town clerk didn't. Of course my hair's longer, maybe that's part of it. But it's not the whole thing, my face is as round as a . . . I don't know . . . I don't know what I'll do if I don't stop gaining weight. The doctor said I've already gained more than I should gain in the whole pregnancy."

She just sort of slid from one subject to the other, as though they were of equal importance. They *were*, to her. At best. There is a small oval area up at one point near the mailbox, created by a slight outward bulge of the land, obviously the sort of bulge that would be first to be straightened out when a road was modernized. In that oval, which is no more than six feet long, I once saw while waiting for Mimi to come home on a hot summer day: Queen Anne's Lace, buttercups, poison ivy and jewel weed, clover, chicory, daisy fleabane, a group of pinks, their tiny bright flowers just managing to be seen among the giants that surrounded them, and a large clump of wild lupine, their bright blue spires at the height of their glory. Lupine, perennial lupine, can't be moved, or at least I had never been able to do it. This was im-

portant. When I'd tried to move her, she'd died. If that oval patch of
land were destroyed, the blue lupine would be destroyed with it. Looking at the size of the roots one would assume she could survive all sort
of change, but the size of those roots was deceptive, they made her
seem less fragile than she was.

Of course Mimi, even the old Mimi, couldn't have gone to the Planning Board and argued against the road on behalf of the wild blue
lupine. In a world where natural priorities were ritually reversed she
would have been made to seem quite mad by the first self-righteous
matron who pointed out that her child had fallen off his bike at that
curve—even if in point of fact he'd barely bruised himself in the fall,
even if for all the talk over all the years about the dangers of the road
nobody has ever been seriously injured on it, people have simply traveled a little slower and arrived home a minute later. Perhaps I would
be a little less horrified than I am of children if so many terrible things
weren't done in their name.

"Will you go to the next meeting?" I asked.

She sighed. "Yes, Beth. I'll go to the next meeting, and the one after
that . . . but I can't promise to keep going much longer . . . for one
thing, if I get much fatter I won't even be able to leave the house, I
won't have a thing to wear."

"Someone has to go," I said, fighting panic. "They'll just slip it
through, otherwise. Will one of the others go?"

"I'm not sure," Mimi said. "Some of the others should be willing
. . . the Chernins would lose much more land than we would, but I
can't tell . . . I'll talk to them . . . sometimes in the last fight I felt
they wouldn't go on if it weren't for us."

Us. Who constituted us? Mimi. Me. Barney. Barney wouldn't go.
Aside from the fact that like me he lacked Mimi's ultimate faith in
human beings, he really didn't care too much. In a sense he didn't care
about anything. Not in the sense that he had no preferences, but rather
that there was no event or circumstance so lacking in interest or irony
that he couldn't enjoy its outcome on some level, however unfavorable
to us. Irony was mother's milk to him. I broached the road to him when
he came home from school that day. He laughed. I said I didn't think it
was funny.

"I wouldn't expect you to," he said. "Any more than you'd ever really expect me to grapple with the town jokers over the road."

"If you cared about me you would," I said.

"Not true at all," he said. "Doesn't follow. Any more than it follows
that *you'll* go because *you* care."

I was silent.

"Anyway," he said, "this whole 'You don't care about me' routine is very tricky. People never say it when they're trying to give you something and you won't take it. I've never come up to my room and found you waiting in bed and turned away and had you tell me, 'Barney, if you cared about me you'd accept my love.'"

"That's silly." Although I'd thought about it, Barney, I mean, you must have known it had occurred to me. I had dreams. I had dreams that made me terrified that Mimi would die the next day because I could never be unconvinced of the connection between my dreams and Mimi's death.

Barney shrugged.

I couldn't even imagine what would have happened if you'd tried to make love to me, Barney. For years you'd said little things like that but usually Mimi was nearby and how did I know what would happen if that weren't the case? It was easier to picture you making love to me than to picture you—or anyone—making love to Mimi.

Max came by that night and invited me again to see the house the next day, saying that most of the work was done now, but I was far too agitated to go any place.

"What is it?" he asked me. "Is something wrong?"

"It's the road," Mimi said. "She's upset because they're talking about widening the road again."

"Sugar Hill," Max said. "I just saw something about it in the paper."

"Mimi's the only one that stopped them from doing it before," I said. "Mimi and a few of the others but mostly Mimi, and now she doesn't want to fight them any more."

"Say, Max," Barney said, and I could tell from his expression that he wasn't trying to help anybody, only to make mischief. "That'll affect your land, too, won't it."

Max nodded. "As a matter of fact, I was thinking about it. It'll affect me worse, in a way, because the house is set much closer to the road, you know, the acreage is in the back, the house is only thirty, forty feet from the road." He shook his head.

"I should think," Barney said gravely, "that it would definitely be in your best interest to pick up the gauntlet, with the Board, I mean, fighting the road."

"Maybe you're right," Max said, unaware of or at least indifferent to Barney's ironic prodding. "I think I'll go to the meeting, anyhow . . . see what's happening. When is it anyway?"

Mimi sighed loudly. "Honestly, Beth," she said. "I promised I'd go to the next one. I can't see what all the fuss is about." As though the whole conversation had been staged for her benefit.

"When is it?" Max asked.

"I don't know," she said. "It doesn't matter, you don't have to go. I'll take care of it."

"If you tell me when it is," Max said calmly, "I'll be happy to pick you up."

Mimi looked at him with a combination of confusion and hostility. "But you really don't have to bother," she said. "If I go, and the Chernins and one or two of the others go, the usual ones, I mean, you don't have to bother."

He shrugged. "I'd like to go, anyway. I can find out when it is."

He wouldn't fight her nor would he let her tell him what to do. I think I had my first fond feelings for him that night.

But when the meeting came, they went separately, and the road wasn't brought up.

Josh didn't come for Thanksgiving and I knew it was a bad sign although Mimi swore it had nothing to do with the land but only with the fact that he was on location in Spain and would have had to make a special trip back. He had let Lily come with him. They had left Yiytzo together in a perfectly casual way as though it were the usual thing for them to do and apparently she'd succeeded in hanging on to him all those two or three months because he wrote that she was with him in Spain. I felt it had to do with my own sudden estrangement from him—something about a common enemy. His letter said that they would be home for Christmas, and I wrote this to Vincent right away.

Vincent came, not with the woman he was living with but with her son. Vincent was in an enormously expansive mood, more so than I'd ever seen him. The two of them had driven across the country together, stopping whenever they felt like it, and Vincent seemed more excited at having given the boy this adventure than the boy was at having had it. Although it was difficult to tell. He was very quiet and his manners were almost excessively good. This is carping, especially from me. Raucous children are very upsetting to me. But this boy . . . it was as though he feared that if he once forgot to say thank you he would be put out of the house. When he spoke at all his words were soft flat notes that struck the ear instead of falling into it. Vincent was dirty and rumpled when they arrived but Steven was immaculate, face clean and shiny, his light brown hair cut too close to his head to get sloppy.

His face long and pale and dreadfully serious (a description which I now realize has often been given of me). Mimi and I both greeted them at the door and Mimi kissed Steven and said it was good to have him and Vincent said, "Go easy, now, huh?" and Mimi retreated to the kitchen and Steven looked puzzled.

At lunch Vincent delivered an exuberant travelogue on their cross-country trip, complete with stories such as the one about a desk clerk in Fort Wayne who didn't want to give them a room, finally admitting to the suspicion that the bearded Vincent was illegally taking a minor across state lines. Vincent, who apparently has great patience with this particular form of stupidity, didn't stamp out and find another motel but instead got his suitcase, in which he had a paperback copy of his latest book, *Death of Roget*, with a snapshot of himself on the back, and when the man apologized profusely for his suspicions, autographed the copy and gave it to him. At three in the morning when Vincent had just gone to sleep there was a loud knock at the door. Groggily Vincent opened it and had the book thrown in his face.

"Next time," Vincent said, "he'll know better than to give a room to any writer, minor or not."

"The only thing that's surprising," Barney said, "is that he understood enough of it to know it was dirty."

"In Indiana," Vincent said, "books are dirty unless proven innocent." Mimi got up to clear the table and Steven got up to help her.

"Hey, Steve-O," Vincent said, "you don't have to do that."

"I want to," Steven replied, and Vincent shrugged but I could see that he was annoyed.

"Yes," Barney said to Vincent, "but what did he *find* in it? Part of the joke was not using any dirty words, yes? So what did he find?"

"He found my intentions, pal. Don't ask me how but they always do. Idiots always know when you're laughing at them. They may not know another fucking thing but they know that. Like the Nazis with their facial insubordination bit. Did you ever read anything about that? Some of their prisoners could be polite and completely unprovocative and still bug the hell out of the examiners. There was something in these guys that nothing could touch and it drove the Nazis crazy, there was some kind of reserve there, and when the examiners got down to that place and couldn't get any further, the image bounced back and they saw themselves instead and couldn't take it. The mistake people like you make . . . you Eastern intellectuals"—flashing a grin at Barney—"you assume these people don't read because they don't know that books would open a whole new world to them. But it's not new worlds that books open up, it's the old one, the inside of their own heads. And they want to see the inside of their own heads about as much as they want to see a cross section of their mother-in-law's tongue. If they read about people who're like themselves they're repelled and if they read about people who're better they're upset by the implicit contrast. Which leaves them with the people—or non-people, preferably—who're much worse than they are, specifically along criminal and sexual lines. The only decent books that sell are the ones that happen to have enough sex and violence to distract the general reader from the message. They give his mind something to light on before the wheels start turning too fast and he gets an unwelcome idea in his head."

Vincent always sounded entirely different when he talked about Indiana and the people there, in general, than he sounded when he talked about his father in particular, although he'd never said anything to suggest that his father was a misfit out there. On the contrary, he'd said more than once that his father's claim on his affections stemmed largely from his ordinariness, from his being what he was meant to be, a real person, born and raised in a real place, who'd taken a lot of shit from life and managed to keep being the same person, unlike—guess who—so unlike Josh, whom Vincent was fond of calling a geographical-historical freak and/or a hybrid gone to seed.

No one could find Steven after the meal and he turned out to be in the kitchen with Mimi, drying dishes as she washed. Vincent said he hadn't brought Steven a thousand miles across the country to do dishes but again it turned out that this was what Steven had *wanted* to do, not what Mimi had asked of him. He clung to her for the rest of the day, at first to Vincent's chagrin. But then finally, grudgingly, Vincent became pleased—and even grateful to her that Steven was having a good time. After the dishes the three of them walked down to the farm together to get eggs for breakfast. Mimi asked if I wanted to go but of course I didn't. Something about the boy made me uncomfortable. I didn't even know what it was. I didn't dislike him, I just . . . there was something at once sad and irritating about the way he clung to Mimi. He asked for nothing and yet I felt by his very presence that he was a beggar. I kept remembering the second time I was in the hospital, when I was thirteen. While I was out on the grounds one day a ragged old man came to the fence and stuck his hand through, begging for money. I would have readily given him money if I'd had it but of course I didn't. When I told him this, though, he ignored me and went on begging. I tried to move away but his whining demanding voice followed me everywhere I went and finally I began screaming at him, asking him what kind of a stupid old man he was not to be able to see that I had no money. Then he said that maybe I could give him food and I said I didn't have food, either, but by this time one of the attendants had come over and she gave him some saltines she had in her pocket and took me inside.

When they came back from the farm they rushed into town to pick up a few things for Thanksgiving dinner the next day and once home again, Steven helped Mimi prepare the stuffing, although they wouldn't put it in until the next morning. At night they played dominoes together. Every time I looked up I saw Vincent watching them carefully. When he put Steven to bed for the night he came downstairs and with a sheepish expression asked Mimi if she would go up and say goodnight, and she went and didn't come down for a long while. When she did, Vincent asked her what they'd been talking about.

"Oh," she shrugged, "lots of things. School, vacations, animals. Lots of things."

"You like him, huh?" To ask Mimi if she liked any child was roughly comparable to asking other people if they liked money or food.

"I'm crazy about him," Mimi said. "I wish he didn't have to go back. I wish he could stay here."

After a moment Vincent asked if Steven had talked about his mother. Mimi couldn't remember that he had.

"How about me?" Vincent asked.

"Did he talk about you, you mean? No, I don't think so. I don't think he talked about *people*, at all. Why?"

"I dunno," Vincent said. "Just curious." He stood up and began prowling the room. "I may marry her," he said suddenly.

I was stunned but Mimi jumped up and said, "Vincent, how wonderful! Congratulations! That's marvelous."

"How do you know it's marvelous?"

"Well, it's just . . ." she groped for an answer, ". . . I think it's great for you to be getting married. And I think it's great that Stevie'll have a father again."

"Not again," Vincent said.

"I don't understand. His father—before he was killed—"

"He never had a father. His mother's a whore—*was* a whore, I should say. If you believe that anyone who's a whore stops being one just because she stops peddling her ass. Personally, I think any broad who says she had a husband who was killed in Vietnam when she didn't is a whore." He smiled aggressively at Mimi. "What do *you* think?"

"I don't know," Mimi said in a low voice.

"Aw, come on," he prodded, "you must have some idea. Or at least . . . do you still think it'd be marvelous for me to marry her?"

"I don't know, Vincent."

"Well you must have some idea. Maybe you think it would be horrible."

"No, I don't think that. Not necessarily. Not if you love her."

"I don't love her. I don't love anyone. What difference does that make? I don't love myself but I've been married to myself for years. What the hell are you asking me, anyway, when you mouth all this garbage about love? Love is the direct opposite of hate. By *definition* it's something you can't feel for more than a few minutes at a time, so what's all this bullshit about loving somebody for the rest of your life? Marriage is about ninety per cent indifference, people just going along, doing what they'd be doing anyway, and who they're living with while they're doing it doesn't make a damn bit of difference. The other ten per cent is about nine per cent hatred and one per cent love. If you're lucky. Because love is a very unproductive feeling. It can't be channeled. It's got its object, its focus, and if it's deprived of the object, forget it, it can't turn on to something else, it just suffers. Hate is much healthier because you can use it in so many different ways. I write out of hatred—I don't even know why or what for. I don't have to. You don't need a particular focus for hatred, you can use anything that comes along."

He finished as abruptly as he'd begun. Mimi said nothing. Vincent stood there in a sort of suspended posture, waiting for her to respond in some way.

"If I'm only talking for posterity," he finally said, "I can go upstairs and tape it."

"It's not that I wasn't listening, Vincent," Mimi said. "It's just that I don't know what you want me to say."

"*Forget* what I want to say, just say what you *want* to say, if there's any such . . . no . . . wait a minute. I changed my mind. There *is* something I want you to say. I want you to congratulate me again and tell me it'll be marvelous for me to get married."

"Congratulations, Vincent," Mimi said levelly. "I'm very happy for you, if you're doing what you want to do. And I hope you'll be happy, too . . ." She smiled at him. "At least some of the time."

"You did it," he said after a while. "You really did it, didn't you? I mean, you managed to mean it. Didn't you?"

She nodded.

"Doesn't any part of you, any part you're aware of, I mean, doesn't any part of you say it hopes that nasty bastard Vincent gets what's coming to him? At least just enough to teach him a lesson?"

"You've had too much misery already, Vincent," she said.

Vincent's eyes filled with tears. He seemed helpless to move, nor did Mimi move, but just stood there watching him as the tears began to run down his cheeks. The weight of the room was unbearable. And then Mimi began crying, too, and I ran upstairs. Not thinking at the moment I ran, only knowing I couldn't bear to stay. Then, as I got ready for bed, telling myself I had run because Vincent would be embarrassed later on and it would be better for him if I weren't there. Trying to read but not able to concentrate. Turning off the light. But sleep wouldn't come. Useless to chase after it. I got out of bed, thinking that if Mimi were still downstairs we could talk for a while. But they were both there. Talking. Mimi's eyes were red. There was an air of intimacy between them which made me feel unwelcome. A sensation no one could have made me believe I would ever feel in Vincent's presence. They didn't even notice me at first, as a matter of fact, and when Mimi finally saw me she was startled.

"Hi, Beth," she said. "Is something wrong?"

"I just couldn't sleep."

"Come on and sit with us for a while."

But I fancied—although it could have been my imagination, it was such a rapid thing—that I saw a flicker of resentment on Vincent's face when she said this, so I refused and came back upstairs. Not wanting to be in the way. In the way *between Vincent and Mimi!*

I tried to sleep again but I was too tense to let myself fall into it. An explosion had to follow this unusual amity between the two of them. After all, the faults they'd always found with each other were still there, even if they were choosing to ignore them for a while. Sooner or later they were bound to come up again and then there would be new and more horrible anger. The idea wasn't pleasant, of course, it was much more pleasant—or should have been—to see the two of them being friendly for the first time in all these years. But on the other hand, such an explosion would have the virtue of restoring things to a more normal situation. This wasn't a time in my life when I could stand any more change. What was this frantic desire for movement and change, anyway? So often I heard people paying blind obeisance to change—as though it had some virtue of its own. Change or we will die. Change or we will stagnate. Evergreens don't stagnate. The perennials that year after year die down for winter then come up the following summer neither die nor stagnate, and if they change at all it is usually for the worse.

What were they talking about downstairs?

I finally fell asleep by gripping the brass sidepieces on either side of my bed, just below the mattress, and holding on to them as tightly as I could for a very long time until finally my grip relaxed, and the rest of my body as well.

When I came downstairs Thanksgiving day I found: the twenty-five pound turkey in the oven already; Mimi and Steven at the work table skinning pearl onions; Vincent on the high stool near the window, watching them. This, at eight o'clock in the morning. Barney, the only one besides me who usually got up early, wasn't around at all. I mumbled something about wanting to dress before breakfast and ran upstairs. After breakfast I tried doing various things since Mimi didn't need my help in the kitchen . . . Mimi didn't need help in the kitchen, she had so much help already . . . but I couldn't concentrate on anything and finally at about eleven o'clock I decided to take a walk. It was a cold nasty day. I put on my raincoat. My quilted raincoat I hardly ever wore because it made me look like someone else. Mimi had bought it for me in the spring and I'd been so surprised, it was unlike anything I'd ever owned. I disliked it, especially as it came to seem part of some larger pattern, a symbol of other changes being foisted upon me. But now summer had come and gone and everything was happening anyway and this was a cold rainy day so I wore the coat, which because of the quilting was warm. And perhaps because I was wearing it, I sneaked out of the house, walked quickly up the drive, and when I got to Sugar Hill Road, walked north toward Max's house instead of south toward town, my usual direction. Of course at the beginning I didn't know I'd end up walking all the way there, a long, mostly upward climb which took me over an hour as I stopped several times to rest. The name was on the mailbox, his car in the garage. I didn't want to knock so I walked past very slowly, which failed, but I kept walking and after going up the road some yards I turned and came back and this time he saw me and came out of the house.

"Hi," he called. "What're you doing up here?"

"Taking a walk," I called back.

He hesitated. "Do you want to come in and see the house?" Coming down the path to me.

I said, "You must be busy."

He said, "Not really. I'm going out later but now . . . I'm watching the Macy's parade on TV."

I said, "All right, then," and followed him in.

A strong smell of paint. The walls had just been done white. Dark and massive furniture, looking shabby now, and incongruous. He said he was leaving the furniture because it was easier to sell a furnished house than an empty one. I felt upset when he said it but I couldn't tell whether it was at the thought of his leaving or at the idea of a house changing hands. He turned off the TV set and we went into the kitchen. It was very large as he had made one big room out of a dining room and an ordinary kitchen. The appliances weren't there yet but the glass wall was. Perhaps, I thought, perhaps it will be all right in the spring when the outside is green again. The high stone wall around the back terrace did give some feeling of protection. (How little encouragement a female needs to feel proprietary. We sink our roots as though some magnetic force below pulled for them.) An electric percolator stood on the floor, bobbling away. He offered me coffee and I accepted and we drank it together (it tasted terrible) on the terrace. I told him I thought he was doing a beautiful job, and I told myself that the only reason I seldom lied was that the need seldom arose. He said he hoped I was right.

"Am I keeping you?" I asked.

"Well . . ." he said, "I guess I should take a shower, I'm going off to someone's Thanksgiving."

"Please go ahead," I said. "I don't feel like going back, yet, do you mind if I just wait?"

He said of course he didn't and went off to shower, coming back after a while looking radiantly beautiful in a white shirt and dark pants. He poured me a little more coffee and I held the cup and was startled to see my hand and arm next to his as he poured. His skin was very fair and the hairs that crept out under his cuff were even lighter than the hair on his head. While my skin, in contrast, was terribly dark and sallow, and the dark down on my arms was much more noticeable than I'd ever thought it. I could almost have sworn, as a matter of fact, that it was darker and downier than it had once been.

"Your skin is so fair," I said.

He laughed. "That'll be taken care of when I get back to L.A."

"When will that be?" I asked, once again saddened.

He shrugged. "After I sell the house, I guess."

"It seems a shame to sell it after all this work you've done," I said.

"But I only did the work so I could sell it," he said.

"Is it so much better in L.A. than here?" I asked.

"No," he said, "not really. I mean, there's no winter but I never minded winter that much."

"Then why are you going back?"

"No special reason," he said. "Do I need a reason?"

"It's not that you *need* one," I said. "It's just that I'd think you would *have* one before you did something big like leaving home."

"Couldn't the leaving *be* the reason?"

"I suppose so. If you were very unhappy."

"No, I mean even if you weren't unhappy. I wasn't that unhappy. My mother breathed on me a little hard but she didn't bother me that much. I had an apartment in the city for a while but she could drop in if she felt like it. Not that it's so horrible having your mother drop in on you but while she can do it you're still home, in a way, right? Maybe I wanted to get away just for the *idea* of it. Time is even different when you're away from home. Did you ever notice that?"

I nodded. "It stops."

"That's it," he said, pleased that I understood. "In L.A. time never weighs heavy on my hands. They say out there it's the weather and all, there's always something to do, but it's not just that. You can get plenty bored out there. Everyone goes crazy when it rains, there's nothing to do indoors. But it's not the same thing, being bored and being weighed on by time. I have this feeling when I'm out there that I can't die while I'm there because I'm outside of time. I can't die unless I go home. Does that sound crazy?"

"No."

"It would to most people."

"When I was little," I told him, "I had the idea for a long time that the clock on the mantelpiece was what made everything in the house work, even the people. Once a man came from the village to clean it and when I came into the room and saw pieces of it spread out on the table I was so frightened I got sick."

We sat in silence for a while and then Max said he guessed he'd have to be going. We walked around to the front of the house and he said he would drive me home.

"I don't think so," I said. I wasn't ready.

"It's past one," he said. "Don't you have to be back?"

"Have to be? No, I don't think so."

"Is something wrong?" he asked.

"No," I lied. "Not really."

"It's so funny for you to be here like this," he said. "I didn't even think it was you, when I first saw you go by. I thought it must be some girl that looked like you."

"It's this raincoat," I said. "I look like someone else."

"No," he said, softly persistent. "It did look like you. It was just that it *was* you . . . and on Thanksgiving. Thanksgiving's such a family day."

"Please," I said. "I don't want to keep you. You go ahead."

"I can't just leave you here," he said.

"Yes, you can," I said. "I'll be all right, honestly. I just can't go back there yet."

"I have an idea," he said after a bit. "You can come with me."

"That's a funny idea," I said. Thinking, *Wouldn't they be stunned if I had Thanksgiving someplace else?* Finding the idea had a distinct appeal. "I don't even know where you're going." *No. It's a crazy idea, really.*

"They're some old friends of mine. You don't have to worry about them, they'd get a big kick out of it. They worry about me. They like to see me with girls, they think it means I'm about to settle down."

"I don't think I'd better." Frightened by the thought. "You can drop me off at the beginning of our road and I'll walk in from there."

"But you don't *want* to go home," he said as we got into the car.

"I know, but I don't want to go *there*, either."

He pulled out of the driveway and we began rolling down Sugar Hill.

"You don't even know where I'm talking about."

I was almost annoyed by his persistence. When all was said and done I did things very much my own way at Yiytzo. A spoiled child in a permissive home. Mimi was impressive but it was I who dominated her, really, for the true center of any household is the person the others try to please.

"Look," he said, "I'll tell you what we'll do. I'll take you with me but you don't have to stay. I'll tell them you just came by for a few minutes and then if you don't feel like staying, or say if they don't invite you to stay, I'll drive you home. Okay? The minute you say so I'll take you home."

"Maybe they'll come and get me," I said. "Mimi, I mean. Or Barney or Vincent."

"I don't mind driving you," he said. "It's only a few minutes from your house to theirs."

"Still . . . I guess I'd better call them. They may be wondering where I am."

He laughed. "Did you just tell them you were taking a walk?"

"No," I said. "I guess I didn't tell them anything. They were all busy when I left."

That was why I sneaked out, Max, I wanted them to be worried. I wonder if you could accept the fact that I harbor such childish malice if I were to tell you?

"We'll call them when we get there," Max said.

I said that would be all right but things were in such a state of chaos when we got there that we both forgot. Children were swarming all over the place. If I'd known there were going to be children there I'd never have consented to go. Children blocked the entrance to the drive-way and wouldn't let us pass until Max said some magic password or another. Further down the drive children played rope and then, when we finally parked the car in back of three others, two little girls clapping hands against each other singing a ghastly little rhyme about a Miss Mary Mack Mack Mack all dressed in black black black, and so on, which Max seemed to find amusing for he just stood there until they'd gone through the whole thing.

In the house it was no better. Adults. Children. Children turn the people who surround them into nonentities. They tried to make me comfortable. They told me how much they all knew about the family, which only made me more uncomfortable. I thought of Max, that first morning, telling me he knew of me.

Here I am, folks, and I'm not even on my way to the hospital.

I found myself answering accusations that doubtless weren't even in their minds. I defied them to find that borderline which they presumed that I stepped over. *My mother,* I wanted to say to them, *Lily, has never been in a mental hospital. She carries her own around with her all her life. An invisible plastic bubble mental hospital in which she is the only patient and anyone who chooses to penetrate the bubble to amuse her can serve, at least briefly, as a doctor. What do you know about sanity?* Distinguishable from each other, they were indistinguishable to me from dozens of other such groups of people who had visited us at one time or another. The old man, head of the house, an old-time labor leader denouncing the aimless young radicals. The son-in-law, denouncing the reactionary ex-radicals in control of the unions and government. The older wife . . . pursed lips . . . Remember Joe

McCarthy . . . the younger wife a combination of apathy and disgust.

"I think I'd better go home," I said to Max.

"We only got here a few minutes ago," he said.

"I know," I said, "but I didn't call. And I think I'd better go."

I thanked them and Max said he'd be back in a few minutes and we waded through the children out to the driveway. I sank into the car seat, as exhausted as though I'd taken a trip around the world. Max looked at me and smiled.

"Mimi will be worried," I said, leaning my head against the back of the seat and closing my eyes.

"Mmmmm," Max said.

She burst out of the doorway before the car had even stopped and waddled frantically toward us; I became aware of the enormous bulk she had become.

"Beth, are you all right? Where were you?" she called.

"I'm fine," I said. I felt very calm and contented.

"We've been going crazy looking for you, Vincent said to try Max's house and I thought it was silly but I tried and nobody was there."

Barney and Vincent appeared in the doorway but didn't come after her to the car.

"We were there for a while," I said, "and then we went to visit some friends of his."

She hadn't acknowledged his presence and it was hard to know just how to refer to Max.

"Why didn't you call me, Bethie?" A touch of hysteria. "You knew I'd be worried, why didn't you call?"

Vincent stood in the doorway, one hand resting on the jamb, the rest of his body leaning on that arm. Watching.

"I meant to," I said. "I meant to call but then I forgot."

Vincent still watching. *He's turned his thinking onto me.* Suddenly in a panic. For I'd never fancied that I was a better person than Mimi but had only assumed that Vincent would continue not looking at the part of me which, if he examined it, he might find himself disliking.

I got out of the car, Mimi taking me by the elbow as though I were ill and guiding me back to the house. Max got out of the car and began walking with us.

"I don't want to be rude," Mimi said to him, "but I think Beth has had enough for one day."

Barney, looking amused, turned and went back inside. Max, not asking what it was I'd had enough of but simply touching my arm lightly, said he would call me. I stood there in my magic quilted raincoat, watching Vincent watch Max go.

What were you thinking, Vincent? Did you remember how toward the end of your first long stay when things between you and Mimi were so dreadful, you moved into the guest cottage, which you called the Gamekeeper's Cottage, and when I asked you why you called it that, you said I wouldn't understand, and when I said I'd like you to tell me so I'd know even if I didn't understand, you said it was because you were the Master of the Games? And because I came to Hesse in Josh's library before I came to Lawrence, I thought for a while that your fantasies had originated with *Magister Ludi*. Once, when Mimi was looking for us, we hid under the same bed.

There ought to be a law that having once had a certain closeness people are enjoined from turning on to each other that extra vision that is inimical to love. For twenty years you loved me and curbed your vision of me at a point short of where it might cause me pain; you consented to entertain only that vision of myself which it was convenient for me that you have. Why should I have to bear your scrutiny now— just because your capacity for love is limited, so that having come to care more for my sister, you now had to care less for me?

Mimi led me inside, made me sit down in the living room. Barney had sat down in an armchair and was pretending to read a newspaper. I looked around for the boy, whose name I couldn't remember at the moment, but he wasn't there. Through the archway I could see the dining table set for dinner. Vincent came in but stood near the archway.

"Where's the boy?" I asked.

"He's in the attic," Mimi said. "Looking at some of the old stuff. He loves it up there."

"Will he be careful?" I asked.

"Sure he will," Mimi said. "He's very careful."

I said nothing. Vincent was watching me.

"What happened, Bethie?" Mimi asked.

"This morning, you mean? Well, nothing really happened. I felt like taking a walk, and then I ended up at Max's house, *near* Max's house, I mean, and he saw me and came out, and then he was going to Thanksgiving at someone's house, I think you know them, I can't remember their name but the older ones know Josh, and then I realized I hadn't called and we came home."

"We were so worried about you," she said after a moment.

"Yes," I said. "Well, I can understand that."

"Oh. You can."

"Of course. I was doing something different from what I usually do. Disappearing like that for so long. If I expect you to take care of me then I guess I expect you to worry about me if I disappear."

"Then why didn't you call her?" Vincent asked.

I didn't answer him.

"It doesn't matter," Mimi said suddenly. "It's all right. I don't want to interrogate you, Beth."

"Nobody's interrogating her," Vincent said. "I'm just curious. As a student of human nature and all that shit. I've always been a student of human nature, haven't I, Beth?"

"Not of mine, Vincent," I said. And then, not wanting to talk to any of them, I went upstairs. I told Mimi I would come down when dinner was ready but then I found when she called me that I wasn't up to it, so I ended up eating from a tray in my bedroom.

The New Order. Mimi and I both received letters from Vincent but mine said nothing. They seemed written out of some desire for familial decorum, a most un-Vincentlike desire. I decided Mimi was encouraging him to write me. I hid away his meaningless notes. His letters to Mimi said everything he was thinking. She left them out for me to read. I ached when I thought of the closeness we'd once had, of the way we . . . particularly in the months after he'd first come. When he'd had no one else in the world to talk to. When we'd spent hours together, in the house, in the woods. It wasn't just that we talked, it was more than that. Mimi would leave for school and Mrs. Cushman would be busy around the house. Vincent would write during the morning while I worked with Charles, my tutor. (Vincent, who frightened Charles half to death, had been banned from his presence.) But then after lunch we would walk together through the snow, or later when spring came through the grass and high weeds and along the riding paths, Vincent talking the whole time, I never interrupting, never questioning, occasionally understanding. He was practicing his book on me, although I only realized it years later when I read *Celebration's End* for the first time and was startled by its familiarity.

"There's this myth of men needing women," says the hero of the book, in exactly the sort of speech that Vincent used to try out on our walks. "Sex and laundry, that's all we need them for. The food we can take care of ourselves. Maybe we don't take the crusts off the sandwiches. . . . It's only women that don't like war because they feed on lies and their biggest lie is that they may die but their children never will. While their sons are off enjoying themselves at war all they worry about is having their lie pulled out from under them. What if their son died in a bloody ecstasy at the end of a bayonet duel where he killed the other guy, too? What if he never thought there was anything so great about spending forty hours a week at a desk and mowing the lawn on weekends, then when you get too old for that sitting around waiting to die some kind of nice slow death? She doesn't give a shit if he'd die happier dying young, she only wants him to be there when she closes her eyes for the last time so she can look at him and tell herself that part of her isn't dying. Y'see what I mean? He can't even have his own life and death, he's gotta have hers."

And by way of reply I would pull off a piece of heather to tickle him with and he would brush it off absently as I reached his neck with it, perhaps talking again, perhaps silent. Then we would continue walking until we came to some favored spot—perhaps the place where the brook goes underground, perhaps the meadow in back of the point where the riding paths intersect, and we would settle down, Vincent as often as not holding me in his lap, for although I was a tall nine-year-old I was very thin and light, his arms around me. He would stroke my head or perhaps my arms and sometimes he would kiss me. And then, as often as not, we would nap together for a little while, a few minutes or maybe as much as half an hour, then we would awaken refreshed and walk contentedly back to the house. Except that one day, I think it must have been in the second spring, Mimi found us asleep that way and was distressed and told us it wasn't suitable for us to be sleeping together that way, and so we stopped. Not because I understood what was wrong but because it bothered Mimi.

His first letter after Thanksgiving said he was sorry we hadn't been able to talk more and that would be remedied at Christmas, when he'd be back for at least a week, perhaps with both Steven and his mother. His letter to Mimi was full of questions and strange details of his life with this woman. I don't mean that the details were strange but only that he wrote them to Mimi as though she would be able to fathom their significance.

What a pair we are. I make the beds because she has a phobia about bed-making. She'd rather iron for a week than make a bed. But then she complains that I've done a sloppy job, the sheets aren't taut, and I APOLOGIZE! You don't believe it; I don't believe it myself. I only know that at the moment I'm apologizing, I'm fully aware of but totally unconcerned with the ironies of the situation. The possibility that I'm an idiot for letting myself be shat on by a two-bit whore who wouldn't have a decent roof over her head if it weren't for me. My only concern at these times is to relieve her misery. She is quite possibly the most miserable person I have ever known.

Getting her up in the morning is an unbelievable job. I wake up like a challenger who's just heard the bell for the first round but Myrna . . . I've never seen anyone fight so hard against opening her eyes, not even in the Army. Maybe it's some kind of index of her life that she doesn't think anything in it is worth waking up for . . . ever.

His next letter was composed of lengthy arguments with himself about the desirability of bringing her here for Christmas; this was entirely uncharacteristic of Vincent, who in principle as well as practice had always done and said what he needed to say or do and only afterward, if at all, stepped back to survey the results. This woman from the beginning had made Vincent hesitate.

Should I bring her if she'll come? I know you'll be decent to her, Mimi, that's not what worries me. And it isn't Beth, either, because Beth keeps it all inside. Anyway, her dislike of people outside the family is never deep enough to rise to the surface. What am I worried about then? Who the hell knows? The only thing to come to mind is the analogy of introducing a foreign chemical into a given substance without having any idea of its effect. It makes me uneasy and yet I have an overwhelming urge to try it. Why? I don't know that, either. Except maybe that I feel as though you could help her if she were willing to accept your friendship. She has no one except me. If you tell me not to bring her, I'll understand perfectly. It may be a terrible idea. Tell me what you think.

Mimi wrote him that she thought it was a wonderful idea and that everything would be all right and he should make sure to let Myrna know in advance how warmly we all felt toward Steven. I was disgusted, but much too resigned to the whole loathsome idea to even argue with her.

Meanwhile I seemed to be virtually losing the habit of sleep. I got into bed at night and my eyes refused to close. Of necessity I acquired the habit of going into a sort of semi-trance, almost as refreshing as sleep itself but never with my eyes closed.

"But you *must*," Mimi said when I told her I couldn't close my eyes. "Everyone closes their eyes when they blink." Which was probably true, and after that she took several opportunities to swear that she'd just seen me blinking, but if it was true, I couldn't feel it, and I thought she might have made it up. She came into my room occasionally during the night to check on me. I lay silent in the darkness and when she turned on the little night light I smiled at her. She claimed that some of the times when she came in I was so sound asleep I didn't hear her but that I didn't believe at all, or why, when in response to her command to force shut my eyes, would I have been physically incapable of doing it? She called the regular doctor and he said there was no such sickness. She called Dr. Angstrom without telling me about it! I saw it on the phone bill.

Mimi got bigger and bigger. She was really enormous by this time yet she wasn't due for more than three months. Her obstetrician got furious about her weight every time she saw him and she would come home and swear she was going on a diet and not eat for several hours but then, when night came, the refrigerator door would slam and the cupboard doors creak even more often than usual. The maternity dress she'd bought in October for special occasions didn't fit her any more. Mrs. Cushman had her try it on to see if alterations were possible but Mimi got so uncomfortable from the tight neck and sleeves that she got upset while Mrs. Cushman was still examining it and ran upstairs and pulled it off, ripping it in order to do so. The next morning she drove to Lord & Taylor to get another but there was nothing in the entire store that fit her. She came home almost in tears and that afternoon took the train into New York to buy clothes, an almost unprecedented event.

Vincent wrote to say the woman didn't want to come but then the following week he said she would, and that they would fly in the day before Christmas and take a cab from the airport.

Max began dropping in frequently, always bringing regards from the people we visited at Thanksgiving, although Mimi was still a little stiff when he mentioned them in her presence. (Once or twice I felt he might not have bothered if she weren't there.) He told me his house was for sale but that he'd priced it on the high side and didn't expect to sell right away. Mimi asked if that wasn't a little silly, to price it too high when he wanted to sell, and he said he wasn't actually in any big hurry, he was kind of enjoying the snow and there were enough inside alteration jobs to carry him through the winter, if he wanted them. Mimi asked—in a way that seemed quite sharp for her—how come Max had no trouble getting work when some of the other contractors were starving due to the rotten mortgage market and Max said, in that open way of his that made you wonder if he could possibly be telling the truth, that the trick was to work for people who had the cash and didn't need the mortgages. Mimi flushed then as though she'd been caught at something red-handed, which was strange because it was natural for her not to have thought of that. Later Max told me that the people we'd visited wanted me to come back during Christmas vacation and he had some other friends who wanted to meet me, too. It sounded a little frantic and crowded, the way he put it, so I told him I didn't know, I'd just have to see what happened, we didn't even know yet who would be here for Christmas week. Max said it wouldn't be fair if I didn't find any time for him at all during the entire holiday and I said that he was welcome to come on New Year's or Christmas or any other time, that after all he had yet to be chased away. At which he smiled mischievously, and I said, "Not by me, anyway."

Josh and Lily were to be here three days before Christmas but they were delayed so that Vincent and the woman, arriving past midnight of Christmas Eve, were here first. Steven seemed younger in her presence. Slim, sullen and ugly she entered the house, a sinew of unpleasant matter in our midst. Wearing black. She always wore black or brown. Mimi, hugging Steven as though he were her own long lost child, told the woman how happy we were to have her at Yiytzo, how we'd been looking forward to meeting her ever since Thanksgiving, to meeting Steven's mother because we thought he was such a wonderful boy. The woman nodded dumbly. The string of pearls around her neck was extraordinarily ridiculous looking, as though someone spiteful had gone out of his way to make sure that even from a distance they couldn't be mistaken for real ones.

"Suppose you make us some toddies, Mimi," Vincent said, but then as he saw how laboriously she waddled toward the kitchen, he said maybe he'd better do it.

"Don't be silly," Mimi said. "You must be exhausted."

And he reluctantly allowed her to go. Vincent took their coats into the foyer. Steven and his mother looked at the tree.

"Is Mimi all right?" Vincent asked me when he came back in. "She looks swollen, has she been to a doctor?"

"Of course," I said. "She goes every month."

"What did he say?"

I shrugged. "She eats too much. She's terribly fat."

Mimi came back with the hot toddies and guggle-muggle for Steven.

"We always have good luck with trees," Mimi said to the woman, who was still staring at the tree and the presents.

The woman grunted.

"This one's even bigger than usual, though," Mimi said. "As a matter of fact, Beth was going to make some new ornaments, some new eggshell scenes, but they didn't work this time, they kept breaking before she even drained the insides, and then we meant to do some styrofoam balls with velvet and stuff instead, but I don't know, maybe we're all getting lazy."

Nothing. Even Mimi got a little nervous. She was sitting with Steven, her arm around him as he drank his guggle-muggle.

"Myrna must be exhausted," Vincent said. "She put in a full day before we even got to the plane, and then I won't describe what the plane ride was like."

Mimi nodded. Eager to believe that their difficulties explained the woman's sullen manner.

"And then we had to find a driver who'd come all the way up to Welford."

"I can imagine," Mimi said. "I guess we're lucky we're not travelers."

Steven twisted around to get a better look at the tree.

"I've only flown a couple of times," Mimi said to the woman, "and Beth never has." Silence. *Dead* silence. *Aggressive* silence. I began to feel a little sympathy for Steven, in spite of myself.

Mimi took Steven over to the tree to show him some of the special ornaments and his mother came to life.

"Don't touch anything!" she said sharply. Which might have seemed logical except that one of his hands was in Mimi's and the other hadn't left his side.

More silence. Vincent and I facing each other with nothing to say. Barney came down in his bathrobe, took a look around the silent room and said that he couldn't sleep because of the racket we were making. Then, scornful of winter toddies and such, he made himself a Bloody Mary. Vincent introduced him to the woman and he said that he was charmed but Vincent didn't seem to notice that it was the wrong thing to say.

The doorbell rang and I went to get it, even though I assumed it was Josh and Lily. It was Max, though, saying that he hoped I didn't mind his dropping by, he'd been coming home from a party and had only come down our drive when he saw that the lights were still on.

"Oh no," I said. "You couldn't have come at a better time."

So he took off his heavy boots and thick sweater and we went into the living room together. Barney and Vincent sat talking on the sofa, the woman nearby, neither talking nor listening but just sitting there. Mimi was talking and Steven stood looking up at her and as he listened, apparently oblivious to what he was doing, one of his hands began lightly, slowly, in a circling motion, rubbing Mimi's belly. Then Mimi stopped talking and rested a hand on his head except at that moment the woman looked toward them and said, loudly and harshly so that all other motion and talk stopped, "What the hell do you think you're doing, Steven?"

Startled and guilty in the same moment he pulled away his hand and stared around like someone coming into the light of a new and confusing place.

"It's perfectly all right, Myrna," Mimi said.

"Not with me, it isn't," Myrna said.

"But I don't think he even knew what he was doing," Mimi said, obviously terribly upset by the woman's tone.

"But *I* did," the woman said, staring Mimi down. "And he better learn to keep his hands to himself."

"Hey, Steve-O," Vincent said, sudden joviality forced out of him, "I bet you're shot. What the hell time is it, anyhow? This is a crazy time for you to be up, come on, we'll get you to bed. It's two in the morning, for Christ's sake!"

"And you can watch your language, too, in front of him," the woman snapped, not the slightest bit interested in his attempt to smooth things over. But Mimi looked at him gratefully and said she would bring up a snack for Steven.

"Fine, Mimi," Vincent said. "You do that." He waved hello to Max, who Mimi then seemed to notice for the first time although she didn't acknowledge him in any way, but just went into the kitchen to get Steven's snack. Max stretched out on the rug in front of the fire and five minutes later, when Josh rang the bell, was already sound asleep. (There was a small package in his back pocket. Every once in a while, as he was dropping off, his hand went to the pocket and touched the package and then fell back.) The house was very quiet, only an occasional clattering from the kitchen, crackling from the fireplace. And then surrealism burst upon us. Josh first, wearing no coat but a suit made of green plaid wool with a long jacket and flared pants, a huge red and yellow striped scarf around his neck and a green beret perched to one side of his white hair. Carrying a large purple velvet satchel.

"Heigh ho, kiddies, Mama and Tata Klaus are here!"

Lily in a fur coat belted and as short as a little girl's dress, clear vinyl boots that went up to her knees without concealing her legs, her platinum hair loose and on it a floppy red velvet hat.

I looked at Vincent; his expression was impenetrable. I couldn't even be sure he was concealing anything. I looked at Lily but Lily never looked at anyone when she came into a room, she was much too aware of herself.

"Merry Christmas," Josh bleated, "and a Chappy Chanukkah, God bless us every one!" There was a hostile note to his joviality. Maybe it had always been there but I'd never noticed it before, never found myself wondering as I did now whether something was behind each new wisecrack. I glanced at Myrna and was taken aback; her mouth was open, her entire body seemed limp with awe, but not the sort of awe such a spectacle might reasonably have induced. She looked as though the golden angels on the Christmas tree had come to life and were walking amongst us. Vincent saw it, too. He looked at her and then he looked away at some distant place. And Josh saw it.

"Whommmmm have we here?" he asked resonantly, sweeping across the room toward Myrna. "I don't believe, my dear, that we've been introduced."

And Barney had seen it. "Myrna," he said, "permit me to introduce Elizabeth Taylor and Richard Burton."

Lily giggled. "Oh, Barney, cut it out."

"Well," Barney said, "would you believe Barbara Payton and Franchot Tone?"

"Myrna," Josh said soulfully, "that is your name, is it not, Myrna, I should like you to meet my wife, Lily. And I am Josh Cane."

"How do you do," Myrna breathed.

"And may I ask what fortunate twist of fate brings you to us?"

"I brought her," Vincent said quietly. "And her son, Steven, who's sleeping upstairs."

"Ah, a friend of Vincent's," Josh said. "How delightful. Myrna, it is time you met the delightful creature who is Vincent's mother."

"His mother!" Myrna exclaimed, so thoroughly shocked as to eliminate any possibility that she was trying to flatter.

"I like this girl," Lily said. "What did you say your name was?"

"Myrna," she said respectfully. "Myrna Bauer. I'm pleased to meet you." Nearly curtseying.

And Vincent. Just watching. Knowing this woman had made an observer of Vincent. Now he watched things that went on between people instead of going inside himself for the truth and bursting out with it. He acted no more wisely than before but he thought so much more first.

"Goddamn it," Lily said, "these lousy vinyl boots stick to your legs like glue."

"And do you like our house, young lady?" Josh inquired in his new artificial deep warm basso-falsetto.

"For God's sake, Josh," Barney said. "You sound like a department store Santa."

"Ho ho ho," Josh said.

"Will someone help me get off these goddamn vinyl miseries?" Lily whined. I looked at Vincent; once he would have gone in spite of himself. Now Myrna went instead.

"I should've known better," Lily complained, "I bought them in this freaky little boutique in Beverly Hills that only has things you can't get in and out of without taking a trip."

"Speaking of tripping, Lil," Josh said, "you're tripping over your twentieth-century Hollywood vocabulary."

"Hollywood," Myrna said. "Is that where you're from? I should've known. You look like Hollywood."

"Did you hear that Lil?" Josh asked.

"Well of course I heard it," she said. "The girl's right here on top of me, practically." The tone was no longer adoring when she spoke to him; they'd been together for a couple of months and again she was taking him for granted.

"Do you think we look Hollywood?"

"Well of course we do, nobody in New York has a suntan."

"The original cosmopolitan kid," Josh said. "She knows from Hollywood and New York, nothing in between. Hey, Lil, is Chicago a suburb of New York or Hollywood?"

"Are you an actress?" Myrna asked Lily.

Max sat up groggily.

"No, dear," Lily said warmly.

"She used to be," Josh said. "She's too modest. You should have seen her do the 'I wore black when they hung Sacco and Vanzetti, black was my best color anyway,' speech from *The Glass Menagerie*. It was stunning."

But Lily wasn't listening. She had seen Max, who was looking around him in such a way as to make it clear he wasn't really awake. The little package was on the rug.

"Who," Lily asked softly, making my blood reverse directions inside of me, "who is that beautiful boy?"

"She reached for him hungrily," Barney murmured so that only I heard.

Max stared at her as though she were out of her mind.

"Well, now, let's see," Josh said, straining visibly. "It's not Hippolytus and it's not Adonis and it's definitely not Mickey Rooney because he's in L.A."

Which helped not at all, but fortunately Mimi and Vincent came in from the kitchen with eggnog at this point.

"Haven't you met Max?" Mimi asked. "That seems funny, he's been around so much lately. Max, these are our parents, Josh and Lily Cane. Josh and Lily, this is Max Merganser. Max lives up Sugar Hill a couple of miles."

"But who is he?" Lily asked. "What is he doing here?" As though she'd found him lying on a counter. His expression changed from confusion to embarrassment.

"He's just visiting, Lily," said Mimi, who couldn't understand what Lily was getting at and was therefore puzzled.

"As a matter of fact," said Barney, who understood and was amused, "he's visiting your younger daughter, basically."

"Beth?" Lily asked incredulously.

"Well I'll be damned," Josh said. "Elizabeth's got a gentleman caller."

Were you less careful with me than you'd once been, Josh, because it was too much trouble to be nice to someone whose trust you couldn't again have in any circumstance? Could you really have been angry, a man as sophisticated as you, that I had insisted upon being upset by your actions instead of soothed by your interpretation of them? Yes, you really were. You had always claimed to love the contrast between Hollywood and Yiytzo but instead you had turned us into another movie set of your mind. How convenient for you. How convenient for you if we had not existed in several dimensions. When the cameras stopped, how deeply had the Gish sisters ever been wounded?

My eyes went to the purple velvet satchel which he had so carefully put under the dining room table and which was too small to contain any number of regular Christmas presents.

How easy for you, Josh, to fly out of our lives while we incorporated this new wound into ourselves, and fly back only when the surface was closed again over the wound so that we were once again fit for the selective vision of your camera eye.

Max was groping for his little package.

"It's on the rug in back of you," Josh said.

Sheepishly Max picked it up, seemed about to pocket it again, then changed his mind and handed it to me.

"Merry Christmas," he said.

"Christmas," Josh exclaimed. "By God, the boy's right, it's Christmas!"

"Thank you, Max," I said. "Is it all right to wait until later to open it?"

He nodded gratefully.

"Where the hell's my satchel?" Josh asked. His gaiety just forced enough so that everyone got quiet without knowing why.

Lily trotted around the room searching for it but it was Myrna who found it and handed it to her so she could bring it back to Josh.

He took it with a flourish, deposited it on a table, said, "Ho ho ho, what have we here?"

"Three colored handkerchiefs," Barney said, "and a rabbit in heat."
Lily tittered. She almost *tilted* with eagerness.

"Ah! Here we are!" From the satchel he took two big envelopes.
"Let's see. First, to the nominal head of the household—" he held out
an envelope to Barney, "Merry Christmas, Barney, to you and Mimi
and Beth and my grandchild."

"Why, thanks, old chap," Barney said with a fake casual British accent. "Is it all right to wait until later to open it?"

"Very funny," Josh said.

"But I wasn't kidding," Barney told him.

Mimi took the envelope from him and opened it, reading for an interminable time. Then she looked up, said quietly, "Thank you, Josh,
Lily, that's very generous of you." Dutifully she kissed each of them.
Then she came to me, whispered, "Bethie, listen to me, Bethie, it's
much better than I thought. Much."

It's happened. Sinking and tearing. It had happened, it was happening, it is happening, I can tell, Josh, reality being relative to time and
place, what is really happening, as opposed to what someone is telling
me I should think has happened.

"It's the house and more than an acre to the north," Mimi said, reading slowly through the legalities, ". . . and then everything right in
back of the house . . . all the way through to Reed Lane, and the guest
house and then south . . . how much is it, Josh? It's hard to tell exactly."

"Almost four acres, all together," Josh said. "There's a lease attached,
you lease us the guest house for life. I'm going to renovate it so Lily
and I can use it when we want to, instead of being on top of you here.
The rental I pay you will more than cover your taxes and the other
stuff I've been paying for."

"That's great, Josh," Mimi said with determined enthusiasm. "It really is."

"It really is, old chap," Barney said. "Thanks very much."

Silence. Josh and Lily looked at me. Barney and Mimi avoiding looking at me.

"Don't bother waiting," Lily told him.

"I thought you might go through the motions," Josh said.

"I don't do that," I pointed out. "Mimi does it for me."

He looked at me thoughtfully for a long time. Finally he smiled.
"You know the only thing I ever minded about being an absentee parent?" he asked. "The leverage. I never minded in the least not seeing
my kids every day, you'd have a hard time convincing me that most fa-

thers would mind a setup like ours. It's only the leverage I occasionally missed, giving up the right to take my kid over my knee when she acted like a spoiled brat. You know what I'm talking about, sweetheart? The pleasure of socking one to you?"

"I don't believe you even missed that, Josh," I said. "You're only making up a whole story about missing it now because right now you feel like hitting me."

"You see, Josh?" Lily whined. "You never believed me."

Josh nodded, never taking his eyes off me. "You were always such a sweet, quiet little thing. You never gave me any real trouble at all, expense, maybe, the hospital and stuff. But never anything I'd call trouble."

"You never handed me a piece of paper that said you were giving me something when you were really taking something away."

"Let's get something straight," he said angrily. "This was my land before you were born and it's been my land ever since. You seem to have the cockeyed idea that you acquired some kind of squatters' rights just by living here and maybe this is as good a time as any for you to get that one out of your head, because it's not true, it's not your land, except now a part of it is, only you share it with your sister and her family, and if you don't like it you know what you can do about it."

This land was what you gave us instead of yourselves, Josh, and having concluded that bargain you lost all moral rights to take it away. Having this land, I wouldn't cry when you died. When I explored the way I felt about Yiytzo I found a Van Gogh tree with its branches that didn't actually end.

I turned away from him, went to a far corner of the room and opened my little package. It was a tiny beaded bag. It looked quite old. The beads were in a floral pattern and its clasp and chain were gold. When I closed my hand around it my hand hid it completely. I had a good feeling from it. I could feel the individual beads and the metal of the chain. I knew that it must have belonged to someone in his family a long time ago. I felt he must be watching me. I didn't turn around but I touched the bag to my lips.

"Well," Josh said slowly, "here goes more of nothing." I turned around. He threw the other envelope to Vincent. "Merry Christmas, buster—and spare yourself. From you I don't expect thanks."

I thought Vincent would toss it back as it touched his hands. Instead he glanced at Myrna, took a deep breath, opened it, read the pages for what seemed a very long time. Then I could tell he wasn't reading any more but he still didn't look up from the pages. The crackling of the fire was the only noise in the room. Finally he looked up, and his face still devoid of expression, said,

"Thanks."

The room breathed.

Josh said, "Think nothing of it, sport," and smiled, but the smile didn't work. It looked more like one of Vincent's unthinking attempts to ape Josh's casual air.

"Josh!" Mimi exclaimed, peering around Vincent's arm to see, "I think that's lovely. Vincent, I'm so happy for you!" She hugged him excitedly, or came as close to hugging him as she could, his height and her girth taken into consideration. "Beth, Josh gave Vincent acreage just south of us, a couple of acres, whatever it is, I think it's just great, Josh, you did a wonderful thing."

"Yes, Josh," Vincent said. "It's just great, you did a wonderful thing."

"Okay, sport," Josh said irritably, "you pulled it off very well, now can it, huh?"

Simmer simmer, bubble bubble. I had a very strange sensation at that moment. Of evil spirits passing in the night. Of us as the stage set of your inner being, Josh. Not that we were created by your imagination but that we represented your various real limits and possibilities. It stood to reason that your life, or at least your possible lives, should be lived out while you only inhabited your pose. So perhaps, I thought, perhaps Mimi was your sense of duty, and I was that private, inward part of you which could not have survived the life you lead, and Vincent—Vincent was your anger, that's what started me on all of this— that at the moment when you threw Vincent the deed, expecting anything from smoldering fury to a lengthy diatribe on the impossibility of buying him off, accompanied by the deed's being thrown back at you, and Vincent failed to register any emotion at all, why then at that moment he had freed himself, he was no longer your anger, which thus passed back into you.

Lights off, lights back on again. A moment of stillness. We waited for thunder, but in the wrong season.

Josh stalked to the window. "We're not going to have any snow, goddamn it. I travel three thousand miles for Christmas and I get nothing but a few lousy patches of snow on the ground. I should've stayed home and screened a Sonja Henie flick."

"You haven't touched the eggnog, that's your trouble," Barney said, himself holding another Bloody Mary.

"I'm off booze and onto grass," Josh said.

"Ah, yes," Barney said. "I read someplace that it'd become very middle class."

"You know something, son?" Josh said. "If you put your pecker where your mouth is you'd be the biggest cunt man on the East Coast."

It was such a vicious remark, so out of proportion to Barney's sly needling, everyone was stunned. Even Lily's giggle was nervous.

Barney whistled. "Wow. Merry Christmas and No Holds Barred."

"Josh," Mimi said tremulously, "you have a way of saying these perfectly terrible things that don't mean anything but they sound so awful."

"Oh he means something all right," Barney said mildly.

"Sorry, buddy," Josh muttered, "you caught me at the wrong time."

"Sure, I understand," Barney said. "It's like playing Russian Roulette. The bullet's always there but this time it hit me."

I smiled in spite of myself. It was the reason Josh had made so many enemies over the years, not so much the people he'd insulted as everyone's feeling that the insult was lying there in wait in his mind, to be used at will, so that many people preferred him to be their enemy whom they never need see, rather than a friend who might eventually victimize them with his tongue.

"I could use a smoke right now," Josh said. "Do you have anything with you, Lil?"

"You told me not here, Josh," Lily said. "You know you told me not to bring it here."

He laughed shortly. "I suppose I did. It just goes to show."

"Show what?" Barney asked.

"Oh, I dunno . . . One man's Eden is another man's Elba. Or the same man's. Whatever." His good humor was temporarily restored. "Hey, I like that. Maybe I'll force down a drink, after all, none of that afterbirth-nog, a drink. Some scotch, some ice, some glass, some straw, ho ho ho, I feel the Christmas spirit upon me again. It must have begun to snow, look outside, somebody."

"Snow's all in here, Josh," Barney said.

"Ho ho ho," Josh repeated. "Did I ever tell you, son, that if you put your mouth . . . no, forget it."

Only Josh would attempt to neutralize an outrageous remark by repetition.

Silence.

"How long ago did you buy this land, Josh?" Vincent asked. Myrna was asleep, her head on his shoulder, looking far less lethal than she had when she was awake.

"I dunno. 'Thirty, 'thirty-one. Why?"

"Just curious. What was it like up here?"

Josh shrugged. "Dull. Just like it is now."

Things are dull when you look at them from too far away.

"Josh," Lily protested, "you know that isn't true. It was so lively, there were so many brilliant people, the conversation sparkled."

"Like Concord wine."

"He's just putting you on, Vincent," Lily said. "Josh, you shouldn't do that." At that moment eager that even the despised Vincent should understand.

Josh said to Vincent, "I've never seen anyone develop a landowner's mentality so quickly. Next thing I know you'll be tracing your family tree."

"Don't be silly, Josh," Lily said. "He's writing a book."

"A book?" Josh asked, suddenly bristling with suspicion. "A book about what?"

"About me. Everything I write is about me."

"Maybe that's your problem."

"Maybe," Vincent said. After a moment calmly adding, "On the other hand, it's a problem you have to be an artist to have. Only a hack can afford to concentrate on other people."

"Son," Josh said, "you're getting so fucking pretentious I can't even tell what you're talking about. Hey, Barn, be a good kid and get me another drink, will you? The stuff is good, y'know? Fattening but good. I forgot how good it is, that's pretty funny, isn't it? Jesus, I'm tired. What the hell gave you the idea of appropriating Welford, Vin? Welford has nothing to do with you."

Oh but you were so wrapped up in Welford, weren't you Josh!

"It has nothing to do with any of you, really, except as counterpoint," he went on. "Welford's just this cruddy little town full of Jewish reds and provincial blooze. Forgive me, it's a visual pun. I work in a visceral medium." He finished the second drink. "Jewish reds." He smiled nostalgically. "We used to get furious when they talked about the Jewish Communists. We were supposed to be Communists *instead* of being Jews." He held out his glass to Barney, who brought him the bottle. He refilled his glass, stood up very solemnly, found his beret, put it squarely on top of his head, and began reciting in the manner of a rabbinical chant: "In the social production which men carry on they enter into definite relations that are indispensable and independent of their will . . ."

At every point we came up against his clever unwillingness to understand us.

". . . The sum total of these relations of production constitutes the economic structure of society."

So funny. As if he'd gone past Marx to find out how the world really worked.

He bowed and took off the beret with a flourish. "What else do you want to know, sport? Maybe I should write the book for you."

"Maybe," Vincent said. "It's about selling out."

"Right," Josh said. "Selling out is what you do when you have something and someone wants it and is willing to pay your price."

Vincent smiled. "You're taking it in a narrow sense. I meant selling out as a function of betrayal."

"Betrayal, selling out, whatever you want to call it. It's what your friends say you did when you fall out of love with an idea they still have or a woman they still think is sexy."

Or a piece of land whose beauty you've never seen. With a flash of panic I realized the land he'd taken away had to include the whole pond. I looked at Max. He was stiff and bemused.

"I've been accused of selling out so often that it's made me realize what extraordinary resources people saw in me in the first place. It's why I can afford to sell out my ideas; I know something new'll spring up to replace the ones I'm unloading."

It was quite a set piece. Vincent had walked into a trap. I wanted to tell him that a pond was a world of its own, that a pond couldn't be replaced like his ideas, but I was afraid of getting caught in the trap, too.

"Actually," Josh was saying, "I fail to see how the concept of betrayal can apply to an idea, except for purposes of rhetorical convenience. How do you betray an idea? By seeing its fallacies? By expanding on it, by limiting it, by seeing that whether it's true or not doesn't make a fucking bit of difference? The whole concept of betraying an idea involves a kind of romantic personalization fantasy where ideas become people with feelings. People don't betray their ideas, they only betray themselves."

"Or others," Max put in, so quietly that I almost didn't believe he'd spoken.

"I drop ideas and people," Josh said, ignoring him, "when they don't interest me any more; I'd be betraying myself if I did anything else."

Later on Vincent would lie in bed awake and remember where it began and think of the things he should have said, but right then he couldn't cope with Josh's rhetoric. He could have done better if he were angrier; now, leaning against the back of the sofa, Myrna's head on his shoulder, he seemed not to care if he won. He wasn't really angry; he'd been goading Josh out of habit. He had been disarmed by Josh's gift—or perhaps only by his own ability to accept it. Barney could have answered if he'd cared enough but Barney was an expatriate at Yiytzo and he couldn't jeopardize his status by caring too much. By a choice made long ago his visa could be revoked if he participated in our politics. Or perhaps it would be more accurate to say he was a plant evolved to a point where it couldn't exist in its natural element but must remain warm and calm in the greenhouse of other people's lives. Barney had gone home once in all the time I'd known him. He was away for two weeks, lost ten pounds and took a full month from his return to recover his weight and a vestige of his humor.

"Josh," Vincent said, "would you mind if I nosed around in some of the stuff in the attic?"

"Stuff in the attic?" Suspicious again. "Which stuff?"

"I don't know," Vincent said. "I'm not really sure what I'm looking for until I find it. I thought maybe some of the old stuff from the *Masses*, things like that."

Long silence. Josh deliberating. He looked at the whiskey bottle, looked at his glass. His face already had a drunken slackness to it.

"C'mon."

"Where?"

"You wanna go up to the attic? So let's go."

"Now?"

"Why not?"

"Do you think this is really a good time, Josh?" Mimi asked. "With all of us here?"

"I think it's a *great* time," Josh said, drunkenly decisive. "Christmas Eve. We can make a bonfire with the *Masses* and sing Christmas carols."

I panicked—not because I took him seriously but because of the careless drunken violence of his mood. I could envision everyone tramping up there, papers getting torn and ground under heels, drinks spilling. Nobody ever went to the attic but Mimi and me.

"No," I said. "Don't go up there. Not now."

Everyone stared at me as though I'd said something unrelated to what was going on.

"Why the hell not, if I may make so bold as to ask?"

"Too many people," I said. "Nobody goes up there except Mimi and me. And anyway, you're drunk, Josh."

"Irrelevant and immaterial."

"Please, Mimi," I said. "Please don't let them go up now."

"Where do you get this 'let' shit?" Josh asked.

"In point of fact, Josh . . ." Barney began.

But Josh wouldn't let him say it.

"Screw the attic," he said. "There's nothing in the attic, anyway."

It must have been the first moment that he realized he'd given away the house. He could go up if he insisted, of course, and the stuff up there belonged to all of us, still . . . we had no more of the house than before, but he had less.

"Maybe tomorrow?" Vincent asked. "Or some other day?"

"I'll tell you what's in the attic, Vin." He staggered over and put an arm around Vincent, soddenly confidential. "A bunch of garbage. Old clothes, an overworked mimeograph machine, the kids' school stuff. Mimi's compositions. Did you ever see Mimi's old compositions? 'When I Grow Up I Will Marry Ferdinand the Bull.' What else? Lily's outgrown diaphragms, photo albums, a wicker bassinet, a couple of old guitars that need to be wired for sound, songbooks. More songbooks. *The Weavers Songbook*, the *People's Songbook*, the *Workers of the World Songbook*, the *Drudges of the Party Songbook*." A mad gleam came into his eye and he began singing. "*Oh the banks are made of marble* . . . remember, Lil? Come on, you remember it. *Oh the banks are made of marble, with a guard at every door* . . ." Together they began doing a sort of tap dance as they sang. "*And the vaults are stuffed with silver that the worker sweated for*." They stopped for a minute. "Jesus Christ, thirty years, more like nothing. Come on, Lil." And they went on again, a mad duet in green plaid and red velvet. "*I've traveled around this country, I saw the Western farmer, ploughing his sod and loam, I've heard the auction hammer just a-knocking down his home. But the banks are stuffed with silver* . . ." He stopped, out of breath and momentarily disoriented. They both collapsed on the sofa.

"Jesus," Josh said. "I'm nearly as old as I used to be."

Lily giggled breathlessly. "That was fun."

Max's face still told me nothing of his reaction. Aside from his one soft reprimand to Josh, there had been nothing to tell me anything. Myrna had awakened but her head was still on Vincent's shoulder as though she didn't want to interfere with this good dream of two beautiful singing dancing Hollywood stars entertaining her.

"But what do we do for an encore?" Josh asked Lily. "Hey! Wait a minute! I've got it, a voice from the dim past is coming to me!" He stood up, still unsteady but very excited. "I've gotta find something. Lil, you come with me." He bowed to me. "Assuming we have your permission, Madame Curator?" But without waiting for a reply he took Lily by the hand and headed upstairs. Myrna watched them go as though she were waiting for a curtain to drop so she could applaud.

Barney shook his head. "You really set him off on a rampage, kid," he said. To *me*.

"I didn't set him off on anything," I said.

"Sure you did. You let him see that you were prepared for anything and that made him feel free to do anything. The only thing that made Josh so benevolent to you all these years was his idea of your picture of him."

I closed my eyes. A combination of exhaustion and anxiety overwhelmed me. I wanted terribly to go to sleep but feeling as I did that the house was an occupied country, I knew that even if I went to bed I would stay awake.

"Just a minute," someone said. "I don't see how you can say that." Max. I opened my eyes. "Or at least if you can, you can say it about anyone and you can always blame anything anyone does on someone else." I clutched the beaded bag, now warm in my hand.

"Right," Barney said. "You've hit the nail on the head." Max was silent.

"You like them, huh?" Vincent said to Myrna, who was watching the steps for Josh and Lily's reappearance.

"How come you never said a word about them?" she asked.

There was a long pause then Vincent said, "It was a treat. I was saving it."

"You must be worn out, Myrna," Mimi said. "After that long trip."

"I'm all right," Myrna said resentfully, as though Mimi were trying to send her off to bed so she'd miss something.

Max put his arm around me.

"I'm exhausted," I whispered to him. "But I feel as though I'll never fall asleep with all of them here."

"You want to take a little walk?" he whispered back. "I could use some fresh air."

"Wonderful," I whispered. So grateful to him. I went to get my coat but meanwhile Josh and Lily came down, Josh triumphantly bearing an old book, one of the bound magazine collections, yellow pages of which fluttered to the floor as he waved it at us. I picked them up.

New Masses, 1929. The little bag dropped out of my hand and Josh scooped it up although he hadn't bothered to get the pages.

"Aha, what have we here?" he asked.

"Give it to me," I said.

"I do believe," he said, holding it out of my reach, "that we have here a bearded ridicule, I mean a beaded reticule." Max flushed. "You, sir, did you have my permission to give my daughter this beaded bag, which I believe from the look of it must have belonged to your mother? Did you give my daughter your mother's bearded reticule?"

"Leave her alone, Josh," Mimi said. "You're not being at all funny."

"All right, all right," Josh said, tossing me the bag. "Here we go, Lil. You be Harriet Tubman and I'll be John Brown. Here we go kiddies, an American Chronicle Play by Michael Gold. A lesson in selling out." He took both of Lily's hands, the book open on the coffee table in front of them. "'So this is Harriet Tubman! God bless you, you brave girl. You are the Moses of your poor people. I've long wanted to know you.'"

Lily giggled. "'I've also heard of you, Mr. Brown, as one of the most determined abolitionists among all the farmers in this region.'"

"You made your point, Josh," Barney said. "Don't beat it to death."

"Why not?" Josh asked. "It's something to do."

Barney groaned.

Max took my hand and we began gradually edging back and out of the room.

"Are my eyes deceiving me," Josh said, "or am I looking at two people walking backwards?"

"We're going to take a little walk," Max said.

"Backwards?" Josh asked, mock incredulous.

At which point Max steered me around and out of the house. He closed the door behind us and whistled. He put his arm around me and we began walking through the interior garden. The Christmas lights showed us the path.

"Wow," Max said. "I don't envy you, having to live with that."

"Most of the time I didn't," I said. "Anyway, he didn't used to be like that, not to me, anyway."

The night was cold and grey as though snow might still come. We started down one of the riding paths and he didn't feel like talking any more than I did so that my anxieties began to unravel somewhat but then suddenly something, maybe the sound of the brook, maybe a twig catching in my skirt, reminded me and I stopped dead in my tracks.

"What is it?" Max asked.

"I just remembered," I said. "I don't even know where the land ends any more. I don't even know where I can walk. My God, everything's changed."

"I didn't understand what that was all about," Max said.

I explained it to him. He was silent for a moment. Then he said, "Well, there's nothing to stop us from going there now. There may not be for a long time."

"But it feels different already," I said.

"It's better than going back in."

"But we could go someplace else. I could show you the cottage."

He agreed and we walked back around the house and down to the cottage. I opened the door and turned on the lights; it was only a little warmer than the outside.

"This will be Josh and Lily's," I said. "So they won't have to stay in the house when they come."

"I guess you'll like *that*," he said.

"I don't know, I guess so. Actually I sort of had the idea that I could stay back here when the baby came. Not all the time, I mean, I wouldn't give up my room, but it would be someplace to go." I thought about adjusting the thermostat so the heat would go on but then it seemed unlikely we would be there long enough for it to get warm, anyway. We went into the big room that is the only actual room on the ground floor, with the kitchen at one end of it. We turned on a light and sat down on the sofa, huddling together for warmth.

"Did you ever think of getting out all together?"

"Leaving Yiytzo, you mean? No, of course not." It seemed funny that he should even ask it. "Why should I?" But I did have a reason now. No. Ridiculous. "Where would I go?"

He smiled. "You can come to California with me."

"California!" My first thought was that he must be crazy. Then I thought, I'm the silly one, he's joking, I didn't realize it and he's joking. But it wasn't really a joke, either. He was asking in seriousness but with the knowledge that I would rather die than accept. "Why would I go to California?"

"Just to see what it's like. I bet you've never even seen the ocean."

"I wouldn't have to go to California to see the ocean."

"That's true. But it's warm in L.A. right now."

"This is silly," I said. "Why are we even talking like this?"

"I don't know," he said. "I think about L.A. in this weather. About just taking off."

"You haven't sold the house, have you?" I asked anxiously.

He shook his head. "It probably won't sell now until around April. People like to move after the school year. Anyway, I'm not in any hurry, it's not as though it costs me so much to keep it up. And it's comfortable. As a matter of fact I've gotten kind of attached to it, much more than I used to be. I guess from doing all that work on it. In a way I'd just as leave hold onto it."

"I wish you would, Max," I said. "I'd love it if you'd hold onto the house and come back to it and visit me."

"It's complicated," he said slowly. "If I really lived in L.A. I couldn't hold on to the house unless I rented it. I mean, even if I could afford it, it's no good for a house to stay empty like that most of the year. But then if I rented it, I couldn't come back whenever I wanted to."

I nodded.

"So in a way it'd be much easier to live here and just take off every once in a while. There's no mortgage left on the house, except for the improvements I just made, so it'd hardly cost me anything to live there. On the other hand, I sure don't need all that space, and I don't know if I feel like it, really . . . except there's one way I'd stay. If you'd marry me and we lived there."

My mind went completely blank. No, that's not what I mean. We became blanks, Max and I, but the room existed around us. What he was saying was so ridiculous to me that I had no choice but to make us both cease to exist for a while. When he started refilling the space next to me I just stared at him.

He laughed.

Still I stared.

He took my hands, which were stiff with the cold. He held them between his warm hands.

"Do you want me to make a fire in here?" he asked.

I shrugged helplessly.

"I'm sorry I upset you," he said. "I guess I took you by surprise."

I nodded.

"I should've realized," he said. "I've been thinking about asking you for a while and I sort of took it for granted that it at least occurred to you."

I shook my head.

"I suppose that's part of the reason I took to you," he said. "Most unmarried girls, you feel as if they're out for your scalp."

"I don't want to get married," I said. "I mean, I never even thought about getting married. I don't want to leave Yiytzo. I've never even thought about leaving Yiytzo."

"I'm not asking you to answer me now," he said.

I'd thought I had.

"Just so you know. I can wait. I don't have to decide what I'm going to do for a while."

I nodded. I was shivering. My hands were still in his.

"Do you want me to make a fire?" he asked again.

"It must be almost morning," I said. "Maybe we should go back to the house."

He kissed my hands and released them. I kissed his cheek, which was rough and warm, and then we put our arms around each other, holding tightly, kissing, and I was flooded with pleasurable feelings and suddenly for the first time it seemed strange to me that I hadn't missed these feelings in all the years since Vincent had held me like this in the forest for until now he was the only one who ever had, and for the first time now I wondered how I could have gotten along without being held and fondled and kissed, and I thought of the substitutes I'd made for myself, of the cats petted and birds tended and rugs hooked and blankets crocheted and straw nests made for myself in the meadow, and none of those things seemed adequate now. Then, suddenly uneasy at the thought that I had acquired some new dependency, I stood up and turned off the light and we closed up the cottage and went back to the house.

Only Josh and Lily and Myrna were still downstairs. Lily glared at me, which was exhilarating. I said goodnight to Max and he left. Then I said goodnight to the others and went upstairs.

"Beth?" Mimi called as I went past her door. "Is that you?"

"Yes," I said. More or less, Mimi.

"Okay," she said. "As long as you're back. Goodnight."

The next morning Josh had disappeared with Mimi's car. He left a note saying the car would be at the station, and a separate note for Lily saying he'd felt the walls closing in on him again and he'd see her sometime. Mimi said he was ashamed for the way he'd acted but I didn't know and I didn't care if that was the case.

The fear of death. New to me. What character defect had left me unafraid before? I would wake up and find I was sleeping with my head at the foot of the bed and not understand why until I realized I was trying to deceive the angel of death. Mimi too was afraid. Restless and afraid. I couldn't really see why she was afraid and she couldn't understand why I was afraid.

"Are you awake, Beth?"

"Yes."

"Do you feel like talking?" Laughing apologetically. "I'm so restless. When I try to turn over in my sleep I wake up."

"Come in if you want to."

"Okay . . . Why are you sleeping that way?"

"I don't know." I sat up. She waddled in and sat down in the rocker. Her nightgown had no sleeves. I shivered.

"Aren't you cold?" I asked. "It's freezing in here."

"I'm suffocating," she said.

I pulled the quilt up around me.

"My room is impossible," she said. "All the windows are open and I can't breathe. Barney's been sleeping in the little room, it's so cold, but . . . I had this crazy dream. The room was sealed up and I was flying through space in it. It wasn't so terrifying or anything except . . . the being sealed up." She stood up and began moving around the room in her comical laborious way. "Everything seems so ominous, I don't know why. I don't know what's wrong with me."

"It's being pregnant," I said. "It'll go away when the baby is born."

"That doesn't make sense." She sat down again. "A baby in the village strangled on a Venetian blind cord. There were three children in the family, all of them slept in that same crib with that same Venetian blind near it, only this one got tangled in it."

"Where did you see that?" I asked. "It wasn't in the *Weekly*."

"A woman told me while I was waiting for my meat in Tony's," she said. "Someone I didn't even know. She just started talking to me, then she told me about this baby. People talk to you more when you're pregnant. People you don't know, I mean. It's funny."

What was funny really was that she was dwelling on such things. People have often talked to Mimi, sensing that they would find sympathy without understanding, which is what they want. But if their stories were morbid she barely heard them, much less dwelled on them later.

"I met Carol Wallace on the street," Mimi said, "and we went into the fountain and had a soda together. She was all upset. Her friend's five-year-old girl had her tonsils out and wouldn't stop talking and something ruptured and she died. Did you ever hear anything so horrible?"

"It doesn't sound right," I said. "Why didn't they put her to sleep?"

"I don't know," Mimi said. "I didn't ask. It was too horrible."

"Carol Wallace always has stories like that," I said. "Whenever she drops in here it's because she's got something like that to tell."

"I don't know," Mimi said. "I never thought about them before."

"It's freezing in here," I said, wrapping myself more tightly in the quilt. "I don't know how you can stand it."

"Beth," she said, "do you realize that I'm almost thirty-six years old?"

"Yes," I said. "Of course I realize."

"I mean, do you realize you're not supposed to have babies at this age? First babies, at least? Do you realize that a much higher percentage of women who have first babies past the age of thirty have something wrong with them? With the babies, I mean?"

"Who told you that?" I asked.

"I don't know," she said. "It doesn't matter. It's true. I checked it and it's true. I don't know what I'll do if there's something wrong with the baby." She sounded as if she was crying a little but I couldn't see her face in the darkness.

"I don't think you should worry," I said uncertainly.

"I can't help it," she said. "I've been thinking about it all the time lately. It's driving me crazy."

"Did you tell Barney?"

A long sigh in the darkness. Then in a very low voice with a bitterness that I had never heard until that night, "I told Barney. Barney said if it's a real freak maybe we'll make our money back."

I smiled and thanked God for the darkness.

"What do you think it feels like to die?" I asked—and realized only when it was out that Mimi would think my question related to what she'd been talking about.

"Oh my God, Beth! Why are you asking me that? I don't want it to die, no matter what it's like!"

"No," I said. "That's not what I meant. I wasn't even thinking about the baby."

"What were you thinking about?"

"About dying," I said. "About how it feels. I suppose it feels something like when you catch yourself falling asleep and you stop yourself, only you can't stop yourself."

"I don't think you should think about those things," Mimi said. "I don't see any point to it."

"I never thought about them before," I said. "I don't know why I'm doing it now. I *feel* like doing it now. I feel like figuring it out."

"What is there to figure out? It's not as though you can do anything."

"Well that's not exactly true," I pointed out. "I mean, it's true that you can't defeat death but it's not true that you can't disarm it."

"I don't know what you're talking about," she complained. "Anyway, I'm starving. Do you want to go down to the kitchen with me and get something to eat?"

"I'm talking about going more than halfway to meet it when it doesn't know you're coming. Jumping instead of falling."

"Beth," she said, "do you want me to call Dr. Angstrom for you to talk to?"

It was a vulgar question. She'd never used my illness against me before.

"I'm not talking about madness, Mimi," I said. "I'm talking about suicide."

"Well don't!" she snapped at me, throwing me off with her vehemence. She went to the door. "There's no *reason* for you to talk about it. I feel as if you're *threatening* me when you talk about it."

"That's silly," I said. "It was just what was on my mind."

"Well get it off," she said. "Come on, let's go downstairs. I'll make you some tea."

I wrapped the quilt more closely around myself and followed her down. The living room was dark but the kitchen light was on. Barney was sitting in there, a glass and a bottle of whiskey on the table in front of him. He stared fixedly at the bottle. Mimi got some cheese from the refrigerator and began eating it before she even put up the water to boil. I sat down opposite Barney.

"'m'I in the way?" he asked.

"Don't be silly," Mimi said.

"I wanna be silly." Drunkenly, childishly defiant.

"Then go away," Mimi said, more upset than his words warranted. "We're talking about all kinds of things, important things; if you're going to be silly then go away."

"I don't wanna go away," he said the childish thing now obviously deliberate. "I was here first. Beshides . . ." I couldn't tell if he was deliberately making his s's sound like sh's or if he was really that drunk.

"Beshides . . . you set off a very tender memory, trying to chase me out like that. My most distinct memory . . . from my whole childhood . . . is getting chased out of the kitchen so my mother could talk to her friends . . . talk to my sister . . . talk."

"I'm sorry," Mimi said after a moment. "You're welcome to stay, you know that, but we want to talk."

"What choo talking about?" he asked me.

"Mimi or me?" I asked. "We were talking about two different things."

He laughed. Poured a drink. "Both."

"Mimi was talking about babies and I was talking about death." Or was it the other way around?

"What a way to put it," Mimi complained.

"What about them?" Barney asked me.

"I don't know. I suppose we were both talking about things we're afraid of. Mimi's afraid there'll be something wrong with her baby and I'm afraid of dying. Suddenly, I mean. I'm not afraid of suicide, there's nothing frightening about suicide." A contradiction more apparent than real.

"That's a crazy thing to say," Mimi called out from the pantry, where she was getting cookies. "How can you be scared of one and not the other?"

"It's being sneaked up on that I don't like," I told her. "I'm not scared to seek it out. To sort of walk into it."

"Scientifically unsound," Barney said. "You'll have to think of something more effective."

"That's *not* very funny," Mimi said, dumping three boxes of cookies on the table. She was furious.

"Are you sure?" Barney asked.

"I'm sure you're being disgusting," she said.

"You're right," he told her, draining his glass. "I'm disgusting. I don't blame you for being disgusted with me because I'm disgusting. I don't know how you could have married me." He looked up at her in a sly, drunkenly canny way. "How could you have married me?" She wheeled away from him to get the tea kettle. "I know!" Suddenly he brightened. "You just walked into it!"

Mimi poured tea, put milk and sugar in her own and began cramming Fig Newtons into her mouth. There were tears in her eyes but I hadn't noticed them until she began eating, so that I briefly had the uncanny sensation of watching a machine which consumed cookies and produced tears.

"Now this shuicide thing," Barney began. Mimi lifted her arm as though to strike him but instead knocked over her teacup so that the hot tea spilled all over the table and into her lap. "Why would you commit shuicide?" Barney went on, ignoring her and the tea.

"To avoid death."

"Or to avoid babies."

"I don't have to do that to avoid the baby."

"What else can you do?" He leaned on the table, quite deliberately resting one elbow in the center of the spilled tea, blocking Mimi's attempts to mop it up. "I mean," he said conspiratorially, "I'd like to know because we're in this thing together, kid."

"Don't you ever let up on me, Barney?" Mimi cried. "You used to tease me but then it was just sometimes and I didn't mind but now you never stop and it's so vicious."

"It's compulshive," Barney said. "Like having a baby when you're pregnant. Having jokes because you're malignant."

Her tears renewed themselves.

"I can get married," I said, as much because her crying frightened me as because I felt like talking about it.

"What are you talking about?" she screamed through her tears, startling and upsetting me.

Barney just looked at me thoughtfully.

"I'm just talking about things I can do," I told her.

"Why?" she asked, still screaming although not as loudly. "Why do you have to do *anything?*"

"I mean if I don't want to stay here," I said. Surprised that after my brief moment of upset I was becoming more and more calm. "You know I don't like babies."

"Oh, my God!" she wailed. "Are we going to go through that again?"

"Not again," Barney said. "Still."

"Nobody says you have to like the baby," she said. "You can ignore it. You can do anything you want. Pretend it's not here. I mean you don't have to *do* anything. All this talk doesn't make sense, you don't just get *married*, just like that."

"Why not?" I asked.

"Well because you know perfectly well you don't just get married, Beth, it's not this abstract thing, there has to be someone who asks you, and you have to be someone who . . ."

Were you ever that stupid, Mimi, except in a dream?

"Max asked me," I said.

She looked at me blankly. As I had looked at Max. Tears disappeared. Hours passed. Six imaginary boxes of Mallomars disappeared into Mimi. Did any of it happen, Mimi? Did you really, after all those hours passed by, say to me, "Max? But Max isn't really a person, he's just someone who drops by."

And did Barney and I stare at you, astounded, after all those years you astonished us both, and then did we both burst into laughter, and then did you blush deeply, realizing or at least partly realizing the absurdity of what you'd said, and did you then, your voice trembling, say . . .

"I know why you're laughing, Beth, but you know what I meant."

Thus in some way signifying the end of an era. You had never before seen the difference between your intentions and your effect. All sorts of possibilities opened up, most of them only to be closed again during the next few minutes.

I nodded.

"What did she mean?" Barney asked.

"She meant she didn't know I cared about anyone outside."

"Do you?"

"I think so. I think I'd better."

Barney laughed but Mimi said, "My God, Beth, do you know what that sounds like? It sounds so cold and calculating, as if you don't even care if you love him."

"It's not that I don't care," I said. "It just isn't the only thing to think about."

"Well it ought to be," she said indignantly. "There's nothing else that really matters but loving somebody."

"That's not what you told Vincent," I said, "when he told you he might marry Myrna."

"That was different."

"Why?"

"Because she had no stake in it," Barney suggested.

"I hate you," she shouted at him. "I hate you, I hate you, I hate you."

"Very good," he said, pouring another drink. "Nurse it along."

"I don't understand you," she said. "I don't understand either of you. I can understand how you feel about the baby. No, that's not true, I can't . . . I can partly understand how you feel, about things changing, but you're making me feel like a leper colony. People have babies all the time, it's part of life, why is everybody running away from me?"

"I'm not running away from you, Mimi," I said.

"From the baby, it's the same thing. Almost the same thing. It's not right for you to run away like this, Beth." Giving the marriage fantasy a certain currency. "I just feel as if it's not right. Not for me but for you, for your sake. You ought to at least talk to the doctor before you do something like this, you're not really going to do it, are you, Beth? Did he really ask?"

I nodded.

"Will you talk to Dr. Angstrom?"

"I'm nearly thirty years old, Mimi," I said.

"So what?" she asked. "What does your age have to do with it? What if you get married and have a baby yourself?"

"Oh, but I won't," I said quickly, feeling a surge of panic in spite of myself. "I'll never have a baby."

"But how can you get married not meaning to have a baby?"

"Plenty of people don't have babies."

"But they don't get married not meaning to have them, it just happens that way. Barney and I never *meant* not to have a baby . . ."

"Speak for yourself," Barney said.

"What about *him?*" Mimi asked.

"Max?"

She refused to say his name. "What about him? Does he know you don't want to have babies?"

"I'm sure he does. He wouldn't have asked me to marry him if I wanted to have babies because then I would have been a different person."

"I can't cope with your logic, Beth," she said. "I can't believe all this is really happening."

Silence.

"I think," she said, "I think you should tell him and see what he says."

"All right." I smiled to reassure her. "If you want me to. I'll ask him if he knew when he asked me to marry him that I didn't like babies and if he wants to reconsider." Thinking how funny it was that she was acting as if I were going to do it. I'd never said I would get married nor did I intend to get married.

Pause. Everything was still bothering her but one of the apparent reasons had been removed.

"When did he ask you to marry him?"

"Christmas."

"You see, Mimi?" Barney said. "You were right. You shouldn't have let them out of the house."

"You haven't known him very long," Mimi said to me.

"Since last summer."

"But you hardly . . . do you know him, Beth? I mean, is there something to know? He seems like such a boy, not at all interesting, do you know? One dimensional, sort of. He's very pretty, of course."

"It's not like you to be so critical," I pointed out.

"I don't mean to be critical," Mimi said to me. "I just—something about him bothers me, I don't know what it is, but ever since he started visiting . . ."

"Maybe that's it," Barney said.

"Maybe what's what?" Mimi asked.

"Maybe it's that he started visiting."

"You're not being funny," she said without looking at him.

"I don't think he means to be," I said.

She looked at me suspiciously. "The two of you," she said. "The two of you are against me."

"That's not true." That was true.

"I feel as if it is. I'm only trying to understand. . . . I mean, how did he ask you to marry him? What did he say?"

I chose to receive the question seriously. "He said that he didn't really want to sell the house, he'd rather live there with me."

"That's not the same as getting married."

"Oh, Mimi, he meant getting married. He *said* getting married. Please."

"Anyway, that's a very strange way to ask somebody to get married, as though the house were the whole thing."

"But it's a part of it, obviously. If I have to leave this house then I have to go to another one."

"You keep saying you *have* to leave this house, you keep acting as if you're being forced out of it."

"But I feel that way, Mimi. However well you mean toward me." This was the thing she wouldn't face. She was still always trying to reserve the right to determine the results of her actions. Does the first frost ever beg not to be blamed for killing the flowers?

"Feeling it isn't the same as if it were true."

"Why not?"

"Because—" But of course there was no answer. "Oh . . ." She waddled around the kitchen, looking a little ridiculous, her mind searching for something she hadn't used yet. Moments like that were useful to me, Mimi, serving as they did to make me see that it was only as a symbol that you couldn't be replaced. Suddenly she realized it'd been there all along, the thing she wanted, and she whirled on me.

"Beth, how much does he know about you?"

"As much as he needs to know, I imagine."

"What does that mean?"

"I mean if he only knows a part of me then that's the part he'll deal with."

Failure to be willing to comprehend. Distractedness. Then, quietly, "Beth, I want to know if you've told him your history."

"He knows all about us," I pointed out. "Apparently everyone in town knows about us."

"Have you told him about being in and out of the hospital?"

"She means did you show him your aberrations?" Barney put in.

"I don't remember if it ever came up."

"I don't see how you could not remember something like that."

"It doesn't seem very important to me. Certainly in the terms that you're talking about it. The last time was fourteen years ago, what does it have to do with knowing me?"

"I think he should know what he might have to cope with."

"Why?" I asked. "You didn't cope with it. Sending someone to a hospital isn't a way of coping with their madness, it's a way of not coping with it." Which was surely true although I'd never thought of it that way before. "That's why I don't see why you think I have to tell him. It wouldn't tell him anything about me that he probably doesn't know already, it only tells him how you dealt with me when I was a certain way."

She stared at me wildly. "You're turning everything against me. You're trying to make me feel guilty. You never told me before that you held it against me, sending you to the hospital."

"I didn't. I never even thought about it before. I'm only saying it was what *you* did so it tells Max about you, not about me."

"Mimi was sixteen years old the first time, Beth," Barney said. "The doctor said you should go and Josh had to consent, she had nothing to do with it." Suddenly he sounded completely sober.

"She apologized to me," I said. "Why did she apologize?"

"It had nothing to do with your going," she said heatedly. "My God, you remember these things for years and then you turn them against me! It had nothing to do with your going."

"What did it have to do with?" Barney asked.

"You just sit there and butt in when you feel like it," she said to him bitterly. "It doesn't matter. I don't want to talk about it, I only wanted to know if this boy you're talking about marrying . . . this little thing you might do to get away from here . . . if he can take care of you."

"If he can't," I said, "I suppose he can send me back here or to the hospital."

"You never used to be spiteful, Beth. Even when you . . . you weren't always easy to take care of, but you were never spiteful."

This was true. Perhaps, like Josh, I had been restrained by my idea of her idea of me. No, it was more than that. I had lacked the impulse to voice my meaner thoughts.

"Why did you send me to the hospital?"

"You wouldn't get out of bed, Beth!" she said, her voice wavering. "How old were you, eleven, twelve? You wouldn't eat and you wouldn't talk and you wouldn't even get out of bed to go to the bathroom, you just lay there and looked at me and even then I talked Mrs. Cushman out of calling the doctor for a day because I kept thinking you'd come back to yourself."

"Then why did you apologize?"

"Because I thought maybe I caused your breakdown, that's why!" she shouted at me. "Does that satisfy you? It was a crazy idea of mine, it had nothing to do with your *going*, it had to do with why you were sick in the first place. I thought you were getting even with me for something I'd done but it was a crazy idea because you didn't even know about it, it was crazy to think for a minute that you knew about it, you didn't know anything about it, you were just having a breakdown, that's all!"

Barney whistled in the silence. "If you live long enough . . ." he murmured.

I was terribly curious. I could remember only up to the day before the day when I decided not to get out of bed. What could have importance of what I remembered? Darkness. Looking for Mimi. Where was she? She came home late. Went to high school. Had boyfriends. If I woke up and found her bed empty I couldn't go back to sleep.

"What was it?" I asked.

"It doesn't matter," she said. "It had absolutely nothing to do with you. Nothing."

There was a gang of boys from the village who hung around a lot during that period. Rather rough boys. I stayed away when they were visiting because I was upset by the way they talked to her. Their manner was at once brutal and condescending and I was upset at her putting up with it. It made her seem someone less than she'd always seemed to be.

"Then why did you feel guilty?" I asked.

"I don't know," she said, "I shouldn't have. Sometimes when two things happen together you think they have something to do with each other even if there's no reason to think so."

One of the boys had been the one she was with during the riots the following year; another was the one who'd told her she was lucky he hadn't seen her during them. I couldn't remember seeing them around after the riots—of course Mimi was in college by the following year.

"Anyway," Mimi said, "I don't know how we got on to all this."

"Max," Barney said. "Remember Max?"

"Max," Mimi repeated. As though she didn't quite.

"You know Maxsh," Barney said provocatively, "Beth's boyfriend. The kid who's been hanging around here."

"He's thirty-eight years old," I said.

"It doesn't seem possible," Mimi said.

"A darling boy," Barney said. Genuinely drunk, he could turn on or off the drunken speech.

Pause.

"I'm the one who ought to leave here," Mimi said. "You two get along fine, you should stay here, both of you. You'd probably be happier if I weren't here anyway."

"That isn't so, Mimi," I said. "Feeling that way about the baby isn't the same as feeling that way about you."

"I think it is," she said. "I think if you loved me you'd love my baby."

"Not really," I said. "Only if I loved you without needing you."

A long silence. Then Mimi, in the saddest softest voice I'd ever heard, said, "But what if it's just the opposite?"

And when I could find nothing to say—because reassurances of love seem to me worse than meaningless—Mimi left the kitchen and went upstairs. Barney and I looked at each other guiltily. We looked away, doubly guilty at relieving our guilt by sharing it.

"I haven't been in the hospital for nearly fourteen years," I said.

He nodded.

The year after they were married. Once that year and once the year before and twice in the four years before that. Mimi always took me back as soon as I asked to go. She let them send me but then she took me back. Would she take me back now? Now that she would have a baby to take care of that cried in the night and wanted things in its own time?

"Do you have an opinion about my marrying Max?"

"No opinions. Only reactions."

"Do you like him?"

"What's not to like? He's a prince. A pauper's Prince Myshkin."

"About my marrying him . . . all these reactions you have . . . where does the burden lie?"

"On me," he said. "The burden lies on me."

"That's not very helpful."

"What do you want from me?" he asked. "I don't want you to get married. You know damn well I don't want you to get married. Asking me if you should get married is like asking some broken-down old shoe husband if you should divorce him for someone better. I may know some good reasons for you to do it but that doesn't say I have to like it. You and your sister . . . between you you make up something resembling a complete woman. The qualities you lack . . . the qualities that because you lack them it wouldn't be possible for me to be married just to you, the resilience and so on . . . Mimi does have. Which is why I can be married *only* to her, if necessary. Even if some of the pleasantest parts of my married life will go if you leave. The qualities that make me love you are qualities I can live without. The softness. The reticence. The complex hypocrisy. The deep conviction that in the long run nothing of real importance goes on outside the boundaries of your own skin. The sensual reservoirs that attitude implies but that I'm too much a coward to try to find. Mimi has a deep conviction that nothing has any real pleasure or importance except insofar as other people react to it . . . a kind of philosophical whoredom. Anyway, I can survive without your presence. I maybe couldn't survive without my fantasies but that doesn't matter because your presence isn't required for my fantasies, either of the day or night variety. So . . . what have I told you that you didn't know?"

Nothing. That my anxieties were for myself and therefore didn't bother you. That my vices were reflections of yours and served to soothe you. That I did nothing that required one to be grateful to me. That you loved me and I loved you because you were Mimi's husband. Could I love Max if he were my own?

"What I meant was whether you had any reaction in terms of how it would affect *me*."

He laughed. "No, I don't have any opinion on how it'll affect you, Elizabeth. For all I know it won't affect you at all. I'm not sure how much you're affected by outside realities. I mean there are obvious things, Mimi's having the baby, and the house business, but those hardly qualify as exterior."

"I make believe everything is still ours," I said, "except that I can't take walks outside without remembering and then it's spoiled." How long could I make believe when the bulldozers came in? "Sometimes I think I should force myself to do it even if I don't want to."

"I wouldn't," Barney said. "You can't be that sure of the results. Maybe you'll have a breakdown."

I was surprised and hurt. "You're threatening me. Is it because you don't want me to go?"

"What difference does it make? It's a possibility, you must've thought of it."

"I don't think I thought of it the way you did. Not as something that would happen to me. I thought of it as one of the ways of escaping if I wanted to. Going down into myself. That was silly, I suppose, it never used to happen because I willed it to. The times when it's occurred to me that it might be convenient, say when Lily's around, it's never happened, at least while she's there, but anyway . . . it was stupid to think of it that way. It's more frightening to me, really, than death is."

"How about being married?" he asked. "Where does that fit on the fright scale?"

"Well," I said, "there are frightening possibilities." Thinking as I went along. "Max could turn out to be not the way he seems to be. Unwilling to let me be the way I am, which is all I really would ask. The idea of marriage . . . why should it frighten me? I'm not sure I've ever been frightened of marriage, I just didn't think of it in relation to me. Nobody ever asked me and I never in a million years would have gone out to look for a husband. But here's Max. What does it mean to go and live with him? It means leaving this house and of course that's what's frightening to me. I'm not sure I'll be able to do it even if I decide to. Part of me can never be removed from here and I'm not sure I could tear the rest of me away from that part. But assuming for the moment that I can do it . . . that I can leave Yiytzo . . . go to Max's . . . the really frightening things aren't in Max's house. They're beyond it. There's nothing inside to be scared of . . . I'll take my own bed and dresser and clothes . . . but . . . my life there wouldn't be so different . . . the things I do here I can do there."

If I wanted to do them. That was the thing I was unsure of. Would the flowers at Max's house respond to me as did the flowers at Yiytzo? More than that, would I *want* to tend the flowers at Max's house? A very long time passed. Barney stared at me and stared at me and stared at me. Making me conscious of how long I'd been talking. How did this baby of Mimi's turn me into a talker? I suppose by forcing me to seek understanding from other people. Barney shook his head as though to wake himself up.

"Does Max share your bucolic asexual vision of this marriage?" he asked.

I laughed. "Why do you say asexual? Just because I don't talk about sex with you?"

"This taking-your-own-bed bit. You sound as if you're carrying a portable shrine to your virginity."

"It's a huge bed, Barney, I've slept in it since I was seven years old and they made me give up my crib. It's very big and I've never slept anywhere else since then."

"You know what I mean."

"Why do you pick that to talk about, out of everything I said?"

"Because you didn't say anything else I can quarrel with."

"And you want to quarrel."

He nodded.

"Because you're angry with me."

He nodded again.

It was too simple to be interesting. I almost wanted to quarrel just to please him but I didn't have the interest. He seemed very distant from me at that moment. As though I'd gone already. As a matter of fact, it was frightening, how distant he seemed. Frightening because it suggested that I had no control over whether I would go. As though some sort of tearing or falling had begun already. I was someplace else. There wasn't even room for him where I was.

"I think I'd better go up," I said. I was frightened. My heart was beating very rapidly.

"Why bother? It's almost time to get up."

Hot and cold. Panic.

"I have to."

"What do you mean, you have to?" Irritably.

"I want to," I said, and dashed up to my room before he or anything else could stop me.

A letter from Vincent.

Dear Beth: Mimi told me you're thinking of marrying Max. I'd like to come and talk to you about this but I can't right now because Myrna was ill with the flu and Steven caught it and developed pneumonia. He's getting better but meanwhile it's difficult for me to get away.

I wish you'd wait a while. I'm not saying I have any right to ask you to wait but I'm asking anyway. I'm not sure why. For Mimi's sake if not for your own. She seems to feel that you're going for the wrong reasons and that this is almost a guarantee you'll be disappointed. She may be right. I have nothing against Max, he's a good kid although I'm not sure he has any better an idea than you do of what marriage involves. Anyway, as I say, I'd like very much for you to wait until I can talk to you before you do anything. What's more important, Mimi cares terribly that you should wait, and I think you owe her that much.

Love and see you soon,
Vincent

So much for Vincent's homework assignment from Mimi. I spent three days framing answers in my mind but never sent any of them.

Dear Vincent: You do see you have no right to stop me. How can you fail to see that she has no more right than you? Why should you think that because for thirty years she Mimi'd me and I Beth'd her she has a right now to stop me from doing what inner need compels me to do?

In my unmailed answers I always sounded more certain than I was that I was going to do it.

Max would call and Mimi would race me for the phone. If I picked it up downstairs I could hear a click on the upstairs phone. If he came by to take a walk with me she would be hovering tight-lipped near the front door when we got back.

"Max," she'd said to him the first time, "there are some things we think you should know about Beth."

"Fine," he said. "She can tell me while we're walking."

"Have you heard from Vincent?" Mimi asked me.

I nodded.

"What did he say?" she asked.

"He said what you asked him to say," I told her.

"Beth," she said a few days later, "could you just do one thing for me? Could you call Dr. Angstrom?"

"If it's for you," I said, "why don't *you* call?"

"That's not very funny."

We had entered a phase where Mimi was always telling me of the unfunniness of things I didn't think were funny in the first place.

"Anyway," I said, "you probably called him already. Didn't you?"

She nodded unwillingly.

"And what did he say?"

"He said you should call him."

"I think maybe he said that if I wanted to talk to him then I should call him."

"I don't really like glass walls," I said to Max. "They scare me, walls that aren't walls."

"What do you think," he asked after a few minutes, "of glass walls that have sliding doors, or some kind of louvred wooden doors in front of them that you can keep closed if you want to?"

"I think," I said, "that they're much better than plain glass walls."

"It was Max's grandmother's," I said to Mimi when I found her in my room examining the beaded bag Max had given me. "She only passed it on to his mother."

"She was a horrible woman, his mother," Mimi said, as vehemently as though she'd had some personal experience with that horribleness. "Vincent said she was the worst battleaxe he's ever known, he'll never forget her."

I smiled.

"Don't you think he must have been scarred, having a mother like that?"

"Mmm," I said.

"Are you being this way on purpose?" Mimi fretted. "I mean, I'm trying to have a conversation with you."

"Mimi," I said, "I'm going to marry Max or I'm not going to. What does conversation have to do with it?"

"Do you even *think* about things like birth control?" she asked Max suddenly, having finally forced herself to have him to dinner.

"Oh my God!" Barney moaned.

"What are you oh my godding about?" she asked him, furious. "Someone has to think about these things."

"Why you?" Max asked impassively.

She looked at him, tears springing to her eyes. She would have squirmed in her chair had there been room left between the arms for her to squirm.

"Because," she said, steadying her voice, "Beth doesn't want to have children."

"So?"

"May I suggest . . ." Barney drawled.

"No," she said. "Who are you to suggest? You stay in there in your little study, I never see you, you only want your bottle for company, and then you come out and say oh my God and suggest." She burst into tears. Barney was only bemused but Max was upset.

"Look," he said, "I'm sorry. I didn't mean . . . I didn't want to hurt your feelings, I just . . ."

"I didn't want to hurt yours, either," she sobbed. "I'm only trying to help."

"It is more blessed to be able to stand aside," Barney intoned, "than it is to need to help."

And with that Mimi let out a long wordless bloodcurdling scream that silenced us all.

Mimi ceased to move. She was always sitting in the rocker in the kitchen. When she had to get out of it, to go to the bathroom or whatever, it was as though she were a large inert object being moved across the floor by an invisible crane. She refused to go to any more Village Board meetings. Max went and told me they were still fighting, but neither of us mentioned it to her. She said if they were going to do it they were going to do it. It was like various things in life, if they were going to happen they were going to happen, you could only fight them for so long and then you got tired. I began having dreadful headaches. Long dull ones. As though my head were in a vise. Mimi turned the calendar to March.

"I can't believe it," she said. "Three weeks. I can't believe it's going to take so long and I can't believe it's so close. I can't believe the whole thing."

"What is there to believe?" I asked.

"I don't know," she said. "It's not that I'm scared. There's nothing to be scared of."

"Pain?"

"No, of course not," she said too quickly. "How much pain can I feel? At the beginning it doesn't hurt, there're only just these mild contractions, and then you get to the hospital and they have all kinds of stuff to keep it from hurting. Not anesthesia, I mean, I don't want to be put to sleep. I'm terrified of being put to sleep, I mean, not terrified but . . . I don't see any *need* for it. I wish I'd gone through with the exercises. That would've made it even easier. But they were too hard, I mean, with all this weight on me . . . my weight . . . I should've kept my weight down. He kept threatening me, telling me how terrible it was, telling me my blood pressure would go up but it never did, and then telling me how bad my delivery would be if I got too fat, I mean I was already a little overweight, but really fat, you know, like I did. Last week I asked him if it was true, what he'd said about the delivery, and he said not necessarily, you couldn't really be sure in advance. I couldn't tell if it was the truth or he was just saying it because it was too late, anyway."

"Doctors use whatever part of the truth they feel like using," I said.

"Oh, I don't know," she said. "I don't know if that's fair." She looked down at the bright orange sack of a dress she wore every day now. "Where's Max?" she asked, smoothing the orange cotton over her belly—a territory which now gave the appearance of beginning below her neck and ending at her legs. "I haven't seen him for a few days."

"I don't know," I said.

"Has he called you?"

"No. Why should he?"

"I don't know," she said. "Just to show he's thinking about you, I suppose."

"Maybe he isn't."

"But don't you want him to?"

"Not really," I said. "I mean certainly not all the time. If he was thinking about me at bad times maybe I'd get bad vibrations."

She frowned. "I never used to realize what a tease you are." She looked at the calendar. "There's nothing on the whole calendar for March except my due date. I wonder what else will happen in March."

"The crocuses will be up."

"You know that's not what I mean," she said. "If you get married . . . when will you get married?"

"I don't know," I said. "When I feel like it, I guess."

"Good Lord, Beth, you don't just get married when you feel like it. I mean, you have to arrange things."

"I imagine Max would arrange things."

"You have to have a blood test," she said. "He can't do that for you."

"I imagine it'll all be taken care of in its time, Mimi," I said.
She closed her eyes and rocked.

"I wish if she were going to do it she'd do it," I heard her say to Barney one evening the next week.
Barney said nothing.

A few days later Vincent arrived driving a rented white Jaguar as though ironically aware of his new status as Mimi's knight. I don't know if he'd given her notice but no one had given me any. I went up to the attic to hide because I felt unprepared to see him and found that Mimi had hidden there quite a few things for the baby. A cradle, some blankets, packages of infant clothing. I picked up a yellow sweater and unfolded it but when I saw the size, the crazy ridiculous tiny helpless size, I began trembling and I was terribly cold and then before I knew what was happening I'd urinated on the cold attic floor.
Oh my God, oh my God. I was so upset by my accident that I couldn't move, I just stood there clenching the sweater thinking, *I can't go down now, I can't go down like this, now I can never go down.* I sat down where I was, resting my head on the old sofa where Mimi had piled the clothing, wrapping the sweater around my hands for warmth. But I was still cold. I got up and went over to the closet wall where all the old clothes and the summer clothes hung and found an old coat of Mimi's with a fox collar and wrapped myself in it. I sat down near the sofa again but the smell of the urine nauseated me. I took off the wet pants and crumpled them up and hid them in the farthest corner of the attic, but my dress had gotten a little wet and I could still smell the smell. I put the fox collar in front of my nose and settled down again.

They found me. Mimi couldn't make it up to the attic any more, of course, but she sent up Vincent.
Vincent said, "Oh Christ, sure she's here."
I didn't look at him.
"Come on down, Beth," he said. "I came just to see you."
I went without looking at him. Letting him lead me. Still wrapped in the coat, still holding the sweater, keeping it beneath the coat so he wouldn't see it.
"I don't want you to come into my room," I said to him at the door.
"Okay," he said. "Will you come down?"
"No," I said. "I don't feel like coming down."
"Come on, Beth," he said wearily. "I didn't drive a thousand miles to get the runaround from you."

"Talk to Mimi," I said. "She's the one you drove the thousand miles for."

Being Vincent, he could not easily deny the truth. The best he could manage, and it took a while, was, "That's not entirely true."

"Yes it is. True enough. You're not worried about me. You came because Mimi's worried about me. You're much too involved with that woman and her boy to be worried about me."

"All right," he said after a moment. "It's true."

"What happened with them?" I asked. "How come you left them there? Because it was a business trip?"

"I'll answer your questions if you're interested in answers, but let's sit down and talk. There's no sense standing out here in the hallway."

"Vincent?" Mimi called. "Is everything all right?"

"Fine," Vincent called back. "We're just talking."

We went into my room and I locked the door behind us.

"The answer to your first question, what happened with them, is that nothing's exactly happened but things are very difficult. Myrna seems to be testing me, seeing how far she can go before I walk out. Sometimes I'm sure she wants to drive me out."

"I thought you were going to marry her," I said.

"I asked her. She doesn't want to."

I was surprised in spite of my determination not to let him get me caught up in his affairs. He smiled grimly.

"Why not?"

"She says I only want to do it because of Steven."

"Is it true?"

"I'm not sure. I don't think so. It's hard to be sure, they've always been together in my mind. Sometimes I know, when she's on one of her rampages, I know I'm only sticking around to protect him. Her temper is incredible. I don't know if you could tell. She has such a temper she makes me feel nearly placid. But on the other hand there's that very fact that makes it hard to tell. She does bring out these things in me that haven't come out before. I get along better with myself than I did before I knew her. You'd be surprised to see me out there. Very domestic. I've been *enjoying* doing stuff around the house. I don't do it to mollify her. And I work well there. Writing, reading, whatever. The interruptions only seem to make me more eager to get back to work. The difficulties I have with her, God knows they're tremendous but for some reason they're not the kind of difficulties that interfere with my work, that get way down inside me and eat away at me. Of course maybe they would if we got married. That's something it's impossible to tell in advance. Anyway, it looks as if we're not getting married so it doesn't matter."

Silence. Shadows between us. We had been a family without births, marriages and deaths. Somewhere . . . in Montreal, in Vincennes, in Minnesota, we had cousins, sons and daughters of Lily's three older brothers and Josh's younger brother and sister none of whom Josh and Lily ever saw, and these aunts and uncles and cousins had deaths and children and sent us announcements and Mimi sent presents and told them that if they were ever in the East they really should come and see us and every once in a while one of them did come to see what exactly these strange almost-family people were like, and then they went home to their Elks Clubs and their supermarkets and their Sunday schools.

"So," Vincent said. "That's what's been happening to me. Now you."

"Nothing's been happening, exactly," I said.

"Don't be evasive. This isn't the time for it."

"What is it time for?"

"Well . . . Mimi feels that what it's *not* time for is for you to rush into a marriage that may not be good for you."

"I'm hardly rushing, Vincent. I've known him since last summer and he asked me at Christmas and here it is March and I haven't done it so it's hardly rushing."

"You know what I mean, Beth. Rushing to avoid the baby."

"But if I'm going to avoid the baby I'll have to rush, won't I?"

"Why do you have to? That's what I don't see. It's not as though anyone's asking *you* to take care of it."

In a house with a baby the baby took something from everyone, not just from the people who took care of it.

"I don't see why I should have to explain it," I said. "Talking about it won't make me feel any more or less that way."

"Because of Mimi," he said after a while. "That's why you should explain it. You've made her feel guilty about getting pregnant, for Christ's sake, as if she perpetrated some kind of fucking *injustice* on you having a baby."

I nodded. He stared at me with his mouth open, as though I'd said something he hadn't known all along.

"You once told me," he finally said, "that you owed her your whole existence."

"Yes," I said. "And the quality of it. I mean, existence in itself has no particular value, not to me, anyway. It's the fact of her having given me a certain kind of existence. Actually, when I say I owe Mimi my existence it's only a kind of semantic trick, because if anything, having kept me alive by maintaining a certain set of circumstances, she owes it to me to maintain those same circumstances."

"You are," Vincent said slowly, "the most incredibly self-centered human being that I've ever . . ."

"Whatever I am," I said, feeling quite threatened and upset, "I've always been this way. I was this way all through the time when you loved me and hated Mimi. It's only your needs and your perspective that have changed. I was this way when we first met. I was this way in the days when you made love to me."

He was startled again. His eyes narrowed. "In all these years you never mentioned it," he said. "Anyway, we didn't exactly make love, not technically."

"Technically!" I said scornfully.

"I thought you'd forgotten."

"You wanted to think so," I said. "I don't forget anything."

"Why didn't you ever mention it before?"

"To whom? Mimi? Barney? The psychiatrists?"

"To me. You never . . . it was as though the whole thing, all those afternoons, as if they'd been some kind of dream."

"I suppose you felt guilty," I said. "You were much older than I was, I was a child."

"I felt guilty, all right," he muttered.

"You shouldn't have," I said. "You didn't hurt me. Nothing you did ever hurt me until you stopped caring for me."

"Why do you say I stopped caring for you?"

"Didn't you?"

"I don't know," he said. "This has been a crazy year for me."

"You became a sort of parent," I said. "It changed everything."

"Do you think so?" he asked intently.

"It changed the way you look at me and Mimi," I said. "Mimi's changed some but that's not it, that's not why you see her differently. It wouldn't make sense. Because she's not as good as she used to be but you see her as much better. You used to think her goodness was all false and now you think it's all true. You didn't accept her the way she was and now you don't accept me the way I am. Maybe it's a natural thing, to think that if her giving is a virtue, then my accepting must be a vice."

"I never knew you," he said after a long time. "I never knew you at all."

"You knew as much as you wanted to know," I said.

"What I want to know," he said absently, "is what the hell is making it all come out of you now? What's turned you into a talker?"

"Everything, I guess. Talking is a kind of self-defense."

He smiled. "You don't have to defend yourself against me, kid."

Mimi knocked at the door and Vincent opened it for her.

"What's happening?" she asked. "What are you two talking about all this time?"

I didn't answer.

"Beth is convincing me," Vincent said, "that she can take care of herself better than anyone knows."

"What do you mean?" Mimi asked, glancing at me uneasily.

"I mean," Vincent said, "I think you just have to let her make up her mind and she'll be all right."

"You're going to do it, then," Mimi said to me.

I shrugged.

"When?"

"If and when," I said calmly, "I am moved to do it."

Silence.

A silence.

Stillness.

Stillness hung over everything.

The house was swollen with stillness and silence.

We talked to each other beneath water which deadened the sound waves.

Even my dreams were locked in stillness so that I couldn't move when I slept. I dreamed I was strapped to the bed having shock treatment. I dreamed I'd gone into a secret tunnel under the house and grown so much that I couldn't get out of it. I dreamed I was in a coffin and they were hammering down the lid because I was so still that they couldn't see I was alive. I dreamed I was swathed in a thick plastic film that permitted neither breath nor movement. The dreams left me too exhausted to talk or move and I had to force myself to get out of bed for at least a while each day. Mimi told me the crocuses were all up but I was locked in the stillness of the house and never went out to see them.

Max came.

"I thought you should see her when she's like this," Mimi said to him, I think.

He nodded gravely.

"Are you all right?" he asked me.

"Yes," I said, "except that I'm all locked in so I can't do anything."

"Max," Mimi said, "make her let me call the doctor."

"Mimi thinks doctors are magic," I said. "They can't do anything. I don't need a doctor, I need a locksmith."

Max smiled.

"Is there something to be lost by waiting?" he asked Mimi.

"I don't know," she said. "There are drugs now that they didn't have in the old days when Beth used to . . ."

"I don't want any doctors," I said, "and I don't want any drugs."

Barney slept in the Morris chair. He was drunk most of the time now. Waiting. Swollen. Mimi the Queen of Swollen. Mrs. Cushman brought in tea. Only Mrs. Cushman didn't wait and swell. Mrs. Cushman had grown thin and nervous. I had a vision of large globules of fat disengaging themselves from Mrs. Cushman and attaching themselves to Mimi.

"I had an offer for the house," Max told me. "I turned it down."

Total irrelevance.

"I hope it won't turn out to be a mistake," Mimi said.

"Mmm," Max said.

"Were they willing to pay what you were asking?"

"Pretty nearly. It doesn't matter."

They drank tea. Mimi was upset because I didn't want any. They talked.

"Did you know there were some men working at the farm?" Max asked her. "Surveying?"

"No," she said nervously. "I really hadn't noticed."

Gurgle gurgle. Mimi was the world's worst liar.

Max came every day, or so it seemed.

"Max," Mimi said, twisting a handkerchief, "I want to ask you a favor. If I should happen to . . . you know, if I should go into labor at a time when Barney can't take me to the hospital, could I—"

"Sure," Max said. "Any time. I'd be happy to take you."

"Really?" Mimi asked. She seemed to find it hard to believe. "I mean, there are other people I could ask, and I know we hardly . . . but you're here so much, anyway, if I could . . ."

"No sweat," Max said. "If I'm not here just call me. Whenever it is."

She breathed a sigh of relief. "That'll be great. Just knowing I can count on someone."

In the corner Barney began singing, "Everybody needs somebody," and was ignored.

"Max," Mimi said hesitantly, "I want you to know . . . I realize I haven't been exactly hospitable to you. I mean, I haven't encouraged you, you know . . . but I hope you realize it has nothing to do with you, it's not that I have anything against *you*, it's only that I'm so accustomed to taking care of Beth . . . worrying about what's good for her, and so on."

"Sure," Max said. "I understand."

"Really?" Mimi said. "Because I mean I'd hate to think . . ."

"No kidding," Max said. "Please forget it."

"All right," Mimi said. "Then I will."

Silence.

Suffocation.

Sleep.

I fell out of the bed.

"My God, Beth," Mimi said, "I only tapped you, I didn't push you, I wasn't even sure you were asleep."

She was clutching her stomach, grimacing.

"I wanted to tell you I'm going to the hospital. I didn't want you to come out of bed and find me not here and be upset. Barney's taking me. Mrs. Cushman's in the living room. Okay?"

I didn't answer. Too angry because I was sure I'd been pushed.

"I'll talk to you later, Beth," Mimi said. "I'll call you as soon as I can."

I was so angry that at first I was paralyzed by my anger and couldn't even get up off the floor. Then I decided to go. I put out my hands to steady myself against each wall but they weren't as close as they seemed. I felt dizzy and tried to sit down on the bed but it was rocky so I got up again. Rockily made my way to the door. Couldn't get it open. Finally forced it open, stuck out my head, changed my mind, tried to get back into my room but somehow my body was leaning against the door in such a way that I couldn't get my head back in to close it. The door. The damn door. I was afraid to go out and I couldn't go back in. I could barely breathe. Finally I fell to the hallway floor, or was it the outside. It was cold and there were lights, maybe it was the hallway. No, it was cold. And wet. It was the outside. I fell down the steps and onto the ground. Lights were on.

"Beth?" Mrs. Cushman called. "Beth? Is that you? I'm putting up some tea."

I felt choked with mucus. I coughed but I couldn't get it up. I cried but no one heard me. I lay there. Mrs. Cushman closed the front door without seeing me. I ran up the path through the interior garden, tripping several times but not falling. The one time I did fall the ground seemed to spring up at me as I went down so that only my palms touched it and then I bounced up as though it were a mattress spring. The outside gardens. Brambles catching my nightgown. The interminable driveway. Sugar Hill Road. I stopped for a moment, appalled by the dark winding length of it, thinking for a flash of a second that maybe the people were right who wanted to straighten it out and put lights along the side but I knew even then that I was being ridiculous, it was only that I was there at the wrong time in the wrong clothes— almost no clothes, and no shoes, I was very cold although the cold wasn't actually hurting me yet. Still it was hard moving up the road and I began resenting the fact that I seemed to have no *choice* in the matter, that is, I was doing the work of the movement but I couldn't stop if I wanted to, I was being propelled and yet the propulsion wasn't making the trip any easier for me. The surroundings became the enemy. The road pushed me on. Pushed me and tricked me with its miserable curves. If only, I kept thinking, if only Max would come and get me out of here, if only . . . but I had to keep on and on and on and on and I was so in agony as not even to notice the different details of my feelings until I got to Max's house and knocked frantically on the door until he opened it and when he did I fell to the ground, at once blinded by the entrance light, shivering uncontrollably with the cold I hadn't really felt until I left it, crying with the pain of my bare, cold, bleeding feet.

He picked me up. He was absolutely silent; not even the smallest exclamation to set me off from him. He just picked me up and at the first touch of his hands I began to cry. He brought me up to his room and put me in his bed and covered me, then he got more blankets from someplace and piled those on me, too. The telephone rang and he picked it up and I heard him say that I was there and then there was a long pause and then he said, "Suppose we wait a while. I don't know if there's anything that *needs* to be done," and then there was another pause and he hung up. My eyes were blurred so that he was a shadow.

"Do you mind if I go downstairs?" he asked. "I want to make you something hot to drink."

I smiled and his shadow moved away from me.

I got warm. My feet hurt more from the cuts as they got warmer. My hands felt stiff and dry. I wrapped them around myself so they wouldn't rub too much against the sheets. The bottom of my nightgown got wrapped around my ankles but I didn't really mind. I slept. The phone awakened me. I could see a little more clearly. I saw Max get up from the chair where he was sitting and pick up the phone. Monosyllables. Assurances that at the moment he couldn't see any reason to call a doctor. Tomorrow we would be in touch. He hung up again.

"Do you have my drink?" I asked.

He smiled. "It's cold already. That was a few hours ago."

"I don't mind."

He sat on the edge of the bed, took the cup of tea and milk, held it for me to drink.

"Was that Mimi?" I asked.

He shook his head. "Barney."

"Barney?" I was puzzled because I didn't remember yet. "What does Barney want?"

"To tell us Mimi had her baby. A girl."

Erica for a girl. Mimi wasn't home at all, she was at the hospital. With Erica.

"I don't really care for that name," I said.

"What name?" he asked.

"Erica," I told him. "Do you like it?"

He shrugged. "I don't really care about it one way or the other."

"Me neither," I lied. "I don't really care about it either."

And so, faced with a crucial decision, I let myself be pushed into the apparently sane choice. But that choice is not binding on all levels of me at all times. What is a marriage, anyway? Only a transplant. Nobody expects a plant to flourish immediately after being moved, it will need time and care to become accustomed to its new situation. Nor will the form and color God has given it be altered by its new position. If I move some blue phlox next to a brilliant pink azalea I do so only because they will look glorious together for a few brief weeks in the spring, and not because I think either plant will thus acquire some spectacular characteristic that it never possessed.

I am still Elizabeth. I have been married to Max for a year. I haven't been able to go back to Yiytzo but I haven't been taken to a hospital, either. I have given ground but I am still Elizabeth. That is a triumph of sorts.